The Visitor

Catriona King

Praise for A Limited Justice:

"a fantastic achievement... There is a new star on the scene... Belfast needs its own detective - and in D.C.I. Marc Craig it now has one"
Andy Angel, Ebookwyrm Reviews

"this is what crime books should be like; realistic, believable and slightly unnerving"
Page Central Book-Shelf Reviews

Praise for The Grass Tattoo:

"An excellent read with good characters and absorbing story line..."
Amazon Reader

"With A Limited Justice, Cat King was the 'new kid on the block', now, with The Grass Tattoo she's proved she can stand shoulder to shoulder with the best."
Andy Angel, Ebookwyrm Reviews

Printed for Crooked Cat by Createspace

First Black Line Edition, Crooked Cat Publishing Ltd. 2013

Discover us online:
www.crookedcatpublishing.com

Join us on facebook:
www.facebook.com/crookedcatpublishing

For my mother.

About the Author

Catriona King trained as a Doctor, and as a police Forensic Medical examiner in London where she worked for many years. She worked closely with the Metropolitan Police on many occasions. In recent years, she has returned to live in Belfast.

She has written since childhood, fiction, fact and reporting.

'The Visitor' is her third novel. It follows Detective Chief Inspector Marc Craig and his team through the streets of Northern Ireland and beyond, in their hunt for a killer.

A fourth novel in the D.C.I. Craig series is nearing completion.

Acknowledgements

Thanks to my brothers for growing up amongst their energy and fun.

I would like to thank Crooked Cat publishing for being so unfailingly supportive and cheerful.

And I would like to thank all of the police officers that I have ever worked with, anywhere, for their unfailing professionalism, wit and compassion.

Catriona King
Belfast, March 2013

The D.C.I. Craig Series

A Limited Justice
The Grass Tattoo
The Visitor
The Waiting Room

The Visitor

Chapter One

Monday 8ᵗʰ April 2013. St Marys' Healthcare Trust Belfast.

The man stood by the window and watched the builders outside. They'd been modernising the hospital for months and progress was slow.

Dr Katy Stevens searched her notes for his daughter's maiden name then hesitated, uncertain of what it was. So she risked a generic 'Mr?' hopeful that he would take the hint and fill in the rest.

Her hint was ignored, and instead, "Who wants to know?" came back in a voice that was pure Belfast. It had a deep-smoked rasping quality, and the man who owned it turned quickly, as if to protect his back.

His creased face and single pierced ear topped a neck with tattoos the length of one side. His bare, tanned forearms carried more intricate markings; a supermarket barcode the clearest. So far, so Belfast. The real surprise was that despite doing nothing aggressive, threat emanated from his every pore. It filled the room with a tension that festered in the brief silence.

After a moment he noticed her stethoscope and smiled, without easing the chill.

"The nurse said you saw our Evie, Doc. Will she be all right? And what about the ba? That's my first grandchild you know."

His bonhomie should have relaxed her, but instead it had

the opposite effect. Katy stumbled clumsily over her words. "Yes, yes, she'll be fine…" She hesitated, before deciding that she couldn't do another blank 'Mr'.

"Mr Murray-Hill."

The man gave a hollow laugh. "Don't call me by that shite Murray's name. I'm Tommy Hill." His right hand shot out and shook hers sharply, dominance in its small grip. "She married him, not me. And I told her not to. He's a waste of space."

Agreeing or disagreeing seemed an equal risk.

***

4am.

The room was in darkness when Evie woke, hearing a noise out in the corridor. She squinted at the watch her husband Brian had bought her for Christmas. Smiling at the thought of him with their new baby in two days' time.

It was four o'clock in the morning and she was wide awake. Great. No-one had told her how boring hospitals were - her side-room felt like a prison. During the day there was company at least. But all you ever heard at night were bleeps going and babies crying. Or some poor woman screaming the place down. She was growing more grateful for Wednesday's Caesarean by the day. She didn't fancy a normal delivery one little bit.

She reached for the side-lamp and flicked it on, her eyes blinking as they adjusted to the glare. Then the door opened and she turned and smiled, glad of any company.

"I didn't expect anyone at this time. Is it for more tests?"

"Just an injection."

"Everyone here's so clever. You all do everything, don't you?"

Her visitor smiled, leaving the question unanswered. Evie held her arm out obediently, watching as the plunger emptied the syringe. She'd become used to the drugs and tests 24/7, and her Mum said it was rude to ask questions.

"That should take effect soon, Evie."

"Can't you stay and chat? I'm lonely here on my own."

"Perhaps tomorrow."

Evie smiled and reached for the remote, thoughtfully hitting the mute button. "Night-night then."

An old Bruce Willis film was on Freeview. It was better than nothing. But it really didn't matter, she wouldn't see anything soon.

Her brown eyes closed softly and her right hand fell gently to rest, palm-up on the starched cotton cover. The remote control slipped down towards the floor, caught quickly by her visitor, just in time to keep the silence.

They held her hand calmly, curling her fingers over. And then stayed for a moment longer, leaning over the bed. Until Evie's last breath left softly and they weren't needed any more.

The Visitor smiled sadly, and then slipped out, mixing easily in the corridors with shift-workers; disconnected and anonymous. Then they left the hospital, nodding kindly as the ailing and their relatives passed by.

It was sad but it was necessary, and Evie had been chosen very carefully. No one had listened, but her father would make sure they did.

Chapter Two

Tuesday. 8am.

Marc Craig pulled his apartment door closed behind him, yawning as he walked towards the car. The boot opened remotely and he dumped his sports-bag amongst the detritus. Then he closed it again quickly, with a mental note to tidy up, sometime.

He'd been in the office till midnight, reading every inch of the Warwick file. But it had been worth it. The trial started tomorrow, and the truth was that, after months of hard work, it came down to these few days in court to get justice for Laura Warwick. It was the only chance they would ever have.

The sports-bag was a triumph of optimism over reality. There wasn't a hope in hell he'd find time for the gym today, but it made him feel better to pretend. And you never knew; maybe no-one in Belfast would get murdered this week.

He climbed into the car rubbing his dark eyes, and turned the engine over sharply, heading down through Stranmillis towards the lively University Road. It was full of students already. Some liberated from exams, others whose tired young faces showed that they were still trapped. Optimistic banners outside the Student's Union were advertising parties, pass or fail.

The radio weather girl was burbling on, telling everyone to expect a day of sunny drizzle. And she was right; the roads were slick with warm rain. But even so, the traffic past Botanic Gardens wasn't as bad as usual. Its plants were flourishing in the damp spring sunshine, and a queue of eager tourists stood outside the main gate, eager to explore. A young man at the back was holding his girlfriend's hand, blind to everything but her. Craig remembered being him once. He smiled, thinking of Julia's visit next weekend and then shut the thought down quickly, before it seduced him.

He drove in the same lane for ten minutes, too busy with thoughts of the next day's trial to concentrate on anything more complex than a straight line. The defence barrister, Doyle, was a tricky bastard. They'd need their best 'game-faces' on to deal with him. He'd tripped the police up before.

He'd just reached the Gasworks' business park on the lengthy Ormeau Road, when the car phone rang angrily, pulling him from his thoughts.

"Yes, Nicky. What can I do for you?" He laughed at his P.A.'s regular morning call, five minutes from the office.

"Honestly, sir. It's important today. Dr Winter rang and he needs an urgent meeting. You have Chief Superintendent Harrison at nine-thirty, so are you OK with eleven? He said you might want Inspector Cullen with you."

"Did he give you a clue what it's about?"

"Yes..." She winced, already regretting her next words.

"Sorry, but…There was a suspicious death at St Marys. About four hours ago."

St Marys' Healthcare Trust. *Damn.* Craig hated hospital cases. They were heart-breaking media fests. And he only hated one thing more than defence barristers. Journalists. He gave a heavy sigh.

"OK. Tell John I'll be there at eleven. And ask Annette and Liam to make themselves available please. Thanks."

The phone clicked off softly and he pulled hard left round Victoria Street corner, where the House of Fraser announced its presence in letters twenty-feet high. He sped towards Belfast's Dockland sprawl, thinking quickly. It wasn't like John to be urgent about anything. He was usually too calm, in his 'old-school' doctor way. This had to be important.

Within five minutes Craig was driving down Pilot Street, into Dockland's Coordinated Crime Unit. That was the great thing about a small city, getting anywhere was quick. London's gridlock had put years on him.

He held up his badge for the elderly gate officer and parked his aging black Audi in the first available gap, ignoring the privilege of his named space. Assigned parking was top of his 'naff' list. He was just pleased to park anywhere without getting clamped, after London.

The lift to the squad was deathly slow, punctuated by people clambering in at every floor, greeting each other like lost relatives. When he finally disembarked on the tenth, he tripped over an eager looking sixteen-year-old, whose 'Sorry, sir' words and voice gave her away as a nearer-twenty probationer. That meant it was attachment time. *Excellent.* Probationers rotated through squads for experience, and they were eager, un-cynical helpers, free at the point of delivery.

He crossed the floor of the bluntly named Murder Squad, heading straight for his glass walled office. Nicky's dark head was bent over her desk outside.

"Morning again, Nicky. Could you get me Dr Winter please?"

Craig smiled warmly at her, but he was in his office and across to the window before she could nab him with any queries. He stared through the ten-foot wall of glass at the river below. It was at its best in the morning, with its fresh tonal mixture of seagulls and boat-horns. And it reflected the weather far better than any radio report.

"Dr Winter for you, sir."

He nodded his thanks and mimed coffee hopefully, knowing she'd already have the percolator on. "Hi John. What's this all about?"

"Can you get the crime scene investigators to St Marys to secure a scene, Marc? It's the Maternity, Paediatric and

8

Endocrine complex on Elmwood Avenue. The M.P.E."

"Definitely the Trust then?"

"Yes, unfortunately." John sighed. He hated hospital cases too. He took them as a personal insult.

"We didn't get called to a murder. When did it happen?"

"About four hours ago in Maternity."

"Oh, God. A Mum?"

"Yes. Unfortunately so."

Craig hesitated, dreading the answer to his next question.

"What happened to the baby?"

"A little girl - she's fine." Good news. The words seem to relax them both.

"Excellent. Go on."

"The mother was dead when they found her, so they did a Caesarean section at four-twenty this morning. You didn't get called because they labeled it natural death. But I've had a look, Marc, and there's nothing natural about it."

"You're sure?"

Craig knew how stupid the question was as soon as he asked. John was completely brilliant. Not brilliant in the Belfast, "God mate, you're brilliant" way. Although he was, and they'd been friends since school. But he was intellectually brilliant. At forty-three he had a world class reputation in his field, and was the youngest ever Director of Forensic Pathology for Northern Ireland.

"You know what St Marys is like, so expect the usual self-protective crap. I had to argue with the Sister just to get the room sealed off."

St Marys' shiny new Trust was one of the biggest in Belfast, and never out of the news. Some said that its size wasn't necessarily a good thing – monopolies. But the politicians at Stormont argued that it saved money - less duplication, economies of scale. Management bollocks. Whatever the reason, they'd certainly become impressed with themselves lately. Or maybe they always had been, just a bit quieter about it before.

"I'll send Liam and Annette over with a team. They'll call you to find out what you need. Give me some more details."

"The deceased's name is Mrs Evie Murray-Hill. She was on the Maternity Unit. Her Consultant Obstetrician was Nigel Murdock and her midwife was called Beth Walker. She found the body. Just ask Liam to secure everything he can find. Needles, drips, everything. And all the medicine cupboards and drug-trollies. Annette's nursing background will be a good help on this one."

Yes it would.

"OK. Thanks for the heads-up, John. I'll see you at eleven."

He let the phone fall quietly, closing the desk-to-door distance like the winger he'd been. Annette McElroy heard the door swing open, shrinking down into her cubicle. She knew what was coming next and that it meant more work. But she was still excited. Excited by more work. There was something seriously wrong with her.

Craig stood in front of her desk, smiling at the top of her head. She stubbornly refused to look at him, willing him to disappear. But she knew that he wouldn't, not until he had what he wanted. They'd played this little game before.

"Annette, Liam, a word in my office, please."

Craig's deep voice was firm, but his soft, mixed accent eased the brisk words. Annette glanced up at his tired smile, knowing that he worked harder than any of them. She felt instantly guilty, but decided to have a brief huff anyway.

"I suppose this means I won't get my paperwork done today?"

He smiled ruefully and nodded and she gave in, following him into his office. They were sitting at his desk when Liam came lumbering in.

Liam Cullen's extreme height and blue-white pallor would have looked more at home on a basketball court. In Norway. It was certainly the only place that he could have gone undercover. When he opened his mouth, his words boomed out in a mangled Belfast/Crossgar accent. The Loyd Grossman of the force.

"Grab a seat, Liam."

He declined just as Craig knew he would, propping himself against the back wall with his neck bent. He lived with a permanent headache, complaining that the world was designed for pygmies. But John said he enjoyed the martyrdom.

"Right..." Craig hesitated for a moment, and then started.

"There's been a suspicious death at St Marys Trust, so I need you both over there now. Secure the scene, leave the C.S.I.s to do their thing, and then meet me at the lab at eleven. We'll go back after we've met with John. The deceased's name is Mrs Evie Murray-Hill, and..." He braced himself for Annette's reaction. "She was on the Maternity Unit."

Annette didn't disappoint them, giving a loud gasp. Craig nodded, answering her silent query.

"The Mum died. But thankfully the baby survived. John will tell us more later. But it's very emotional over there, so be sensitive please." He paused, looking pointedly at Liam. He wasn't known for his tact.

"Seal off what you can, without interfering with the ward-running. You both know the drill. Liam, ask for some uniformed assistance. Jack Harris at High Street can help with that. Start taking the statements - I'll need a list later. But wait until I get there for the main interviews please. And if anyone insists on seeing me or wants a solicitor, I'll take them personally. Nicky can set up a Rota."

Liam winked at Nicky through the open door. "You know the Docs will insist on seeing you, boss. Especially the lay-deez."

Craig nodded resignedly. He knew Liam was right about the doctors, if not about the female ones. Position meant everything to Northern Ireland's middle classes. Even interrogation had a social status.

"The deceased's surgeon was Nigel Murdock, and her midwife was called Beth Walker."

Annette's eyes rolled at the mention of Murdock's name.

"Anything you'd like to share with us, Cutty?" Liam's loud bass boomed at her. For all its volume it had a curiously soft quality, enhanced by his affectionate country language.

"All I'm going to say is that Murdock deserves his reputation for arrogance. Ask Dr Winter."

"Thanks Annette, I will. It might be relevant."

"Or it might just be part of a surgeon's job requirement."

Liam laughed at his own joke and Craig half-smiled, raising a warning eyebrow.

"You may be right Liam, but don't say that at the Trust. Annette, keep him right for God's sake. And remember. Don't speak to the media. Hospital cases are P.R. dynamite."

Annette nodded. Her nursing background might come in useful on this one. Public relations weren't Liam's forte. He longed for the 'good old days' when he could say anything he liked. He got a lot of flak for it and he took it well, unless it came from 'arrestees'. Then all the coffee-house bonhomie was seen for the politically correct bullshit that he really thought it was. And "What part of, 'we cops-you scrotes' do they not understand?" rumbled from his desk.

But his local knowledge couldn't be bought, after twenty-odd years policing during 'The Troubles'. While Craig had been at Uni and The Met, and Annette was nursing in Maghera. Plus, he made everyone laugh, even when they knew they definitely shouldn't.

"Liam, do you have a try-out next week?"

"Aye, for the football team."

Nicky popped her head around the corner and Liam was suddenly bashful. "What's that for?"

Annette was surprised she didn't know the World Police and Fire Games were coming in August. Then she realised she was feigning ignorance just to see Liam blush, confirming their office flirtation. Craig caught Liam's colour and gave them a wry look.

"OK, that'll do. Right, before we go. Is everyone up to speed for Warwick tomorrow?"

"As long as Doyle doesn't do his usual, and try to chuck the confession out."

"Which he will, you can bet on it. He'll say we obtained it under duress."

"But Ewing confessed in front of his solicitor, sir."

"That's never stopped a barrister trying before, Annette. Don't worry, just stick to the facts and we'll be fine."

"Aye. That the bastard killed her 'cos she wouldn't do what she was told."

"I'd bring back the death penalty for this one, and happily push the button myself."

"Between us we'd have the prison's cleared out, Cutty."

Craig smiled, interrupting. "When did we move to Texas?"

Annette laughed.

"Look, God knows we're all angry about Ewing, but stick to the point in court. I'm not handing Doyle an acquittal because someone loses their temper." They nodded at him, agreeing.

"But Dr Winter would just love Texas, sir. Just think of all those serial killers." John's obsession with American crime shows was legendary.

Craig smiled and stood up, ready to leave. "Right, I'm off to see D.C.S. Harrison. I'll meet you at the lab at eleven. By the way Liam, John says the ward Sister is a bit difficult, so bear that in mind please. Nicky, can you set me up an appointment with the Trust's Chief Executive today? Don't take no for an answer. And ask their press person to join us at the end. Thanks."

Then he left the floor quickly, disappearing into the lift.

Annette wandered back to her desk and slumped down in

her chair, looking mournfully at the pile of unfinished files. She'd needed today to polish them for the prosecution service. And to type up her 14 font crib-cards for the trial. Doyle was a cocky bugger who'd teased her before for squinting at her notes. He'd even offered her his glasses once, and she wasn't letting that little party-trick happen again. There was nothing else for it. She'd have to do them tonight.

Pete wouldn't be happy. The kids were staying at friends and she knew that he had a romantic interlude planned. She was dragged out of her thoughts rudely, by Liam booming in her ear.

"What're you doing, still sitting on your backside? Come on girl..."

Annette jumped and the whole squad laughed. So she grabbed her handbag and swung it at him, rewarding their hummed Cagney and Lacey theme tune with a bow. The place became more like school every day.

Chapter Three

D.C.S. Terry Harrison was one of five superintendents at Dockland's C.C.U. He ruled the Drugs and Murder Squads from his twelfth-floor office, keeping an iron fist on every case with his name on it. He wasn't a bad boss, as long as things went well. But he was a political animal, and they didn't call him 'Teflon Terry' for nothing.

Craig had earned a reputation in The Met. So when the Chief Constable heard, in 2008, that he was coming back, he'd pursued him for superintendent. Craig had railed hard against the promotion. The superintendents he knew in London were buried in budgets and community-policing meetings. Always accounting for the five things wrong, instead of the ninety-five right. Some of them never saw a crime scene. Paper-pushers and mouthpieces. He couldn't think of anything worse.

But he'd wanted to come home. His parents were getting older and London had lost some of its charm. Plus, John wanted his best friend back. And spent hours pointing out the benefits of 21st Century Belfast, like a tour-guide on speed.

Craig knew that he couldn't dodge rank forever, so they'd finally struck the only deal that he could accept. He'd come back in 2008 as a D.C.I. and make superintendent in a few years. Providing he could still get on the street doing the job, and keep his team. The clincher had been getting Nicky as his P.A. She'd been Harrison's for years and he never let Craig forget that she was his gift. He still borrowed her occasionally for meetings, just to prove it.

He'd done it once too often lately and Craig had finally been persuaded. Having Harrison as a boss was beginning to wear, so he'd agreed to take rank in July. Then Harrison would leave Docklands- he knew what was coming and he wasn't a happy man.

Harrison was sitting at his standard-issue veneer desk, writing, when Craig knocked. His slicked-back hair always made Craig think of an RAF officer from a World War Two movie. Christopher Plummer. It was probably exactly what he wanted. Image was everything. After a long wait while he kept writing, he finally beckoned Craig in.

"Come in Craig, and tell me about the Warwick case tomorrow. Reassure me we're on top of it."

Craig sat down in the indicated chair and was suddenly surprised - it was a good six inches lower than the last time he'd visited! For a split-second he considered standing again to balance things up. Then he decided that he couldn't be bothered and relaxed down even further, making Harrison lean forward to make eye contact.

"We'll be OK, sir. We have all the statements and witnesses in, and we have Ewing's confession. We've definitely tied the murder weapon to Laura Warwick's wounds. And, although the forensics putting it in Ewing's hands are weak, the close circuit TV pictures are useful. They were poor quality but the lab cleaned them up. And the witnesses are excellent."

He paused thoughtfully.

"Unfortunately his barrister is Roger Doyle - he's a real Rottweiler. I've been up against him before. He'll try to get the confession thrown out, but we're solid there. Ewing confessed with his solicitor present."

"I know Doyle. I encountered him a few times as an Inspector. He's a bugger, so keep it tight. And I don't need to remind you the media and politicians are all over this one. We need a good result."

No pressure at all then.

"We'll do our best."

Craig paused for a moment, considering whether to brief Harrison on the case that wasn't a case yet. Then he decided. "While I'm here, I need to tell you about a case we caught this morning, sir. It came in from Dr Winter's office."

Harrison sat up sharply. John was shit-hot and everyone wanted to be on his right side. Particularly operators like Harrison. Craig briefed him quickly, and when he'd finished Harrison shook his head in disgust.

"People aren't even safe in hospital now. That's a bad business. But it's early days yet, so just keep me up to speed. And handle the media carefully. You know what they're like on hospital cases. And with a young mum as well. They'll be screaming negligence. Watch them -especially that bugger Mercer at The Chronicle."

Craig nodded. Ray Mercer was a new low in the species 'tabloid scum'. "I may need to come back to you on that side of things."

Harrison puffed himself up importantly, convinced of his own indispensability and eager for any opportunity to show it in public. "Good. You concentrate on catching the bugger and I'll deal with the press."

That suited Craig fine, the farther away he was from journalists the better. He'd been trotted out for one too many photo-shoots, using his Italian half to show how 'European' the force was.

All of a sudden, Harrison's expression morphed into what he thought was an engaging smile. It flattened his nose and showed his teeth, making him look like a Bull Shark.

Craig recognised the signs immediately. He wanted something.

"Now, let me ask you, Marc. How is your lovely mother?"

His use of the word 'lovely' made Craig's hackles rise instantly. But not half as much as if he'd used it about his younger sister, Lucia. Harrison had a reputation for

17

womanising, preferably with women twenty years his junior. And Craig's retribution would be swift if he ever tried it with her.

"She's absolutely fine." His tone was cool but Harrison didn't register the change in temperature. Instead he leaned back confidently, steeple-ing his fingers.

"Good, good. I was just wondering... How do you think she'd feel about playing at the Police Benevolent ball? And, maybe at the ceremony for the new Assistant Chief Constable?"

Craig smiled to himself. So that was what he wanted. He was tempted to mess him about, but he knew there was no point playing hard-to-get. His mother, Mirella, was a concert pianist, and she loved to play for charity, even more since she'd stopped touring.

She lived with his father Tom, a retired physics lecturer, in Holywood, six miles outside Belfast. Their marriage was a great one, their domestic bliss only marred by his father's newly diagnosed angina. But he wouldn't let it stop him doing anything, despite all their begging.

Craig knew his mother would want to play at both events, so he nodded at Harrison. "She'll cook the food too, given half a chance. I'll ask her to give you a call. Now I'd better head off to the lab."

Just as he said it his mobile rang - Liam. Harrison nodded him out and he strolled into the twelfth floor's carpeted reception, under the dry gaze of Susan Butler, Harrison's regal P.A.

"What do you have for me, Liam?" Liam's voice was as subdued as Craig had ever heard it. The case was getting to him. He had two children himself, the younger only three months old.

"They delivered her at four-twenty, boss. She was only twenty-six, so no-one expected problems. She was scheduled for Caesarean tomorrow. They checked her about midnight and she was grand. But when the midwife went back after four, she found her dead. And no one saw a thing, as-per-bloody-usual." Craig nodded to himself. Good witnesses were rare. Most people walked through life in a daze.

"They took her to theatre and delivered the baby safely. But that just was sheer luck. Doc Winter was on call and he started the post-mortem about seven. I just spoke to him and he's not a happy man."

"I know. We talked earlier."

"Aye. But here, there's an extra complication. Her father is Tommy Hill. Evie Murray-Hill was the daughter."

"Tommy Hill, the Maze release case?"

"Aye, that's the one."

Tommy Hill was well known to the police, for his exploits during the Troubles. He'd served ten of a twenty-year stretch for shooting four people on their way home from a wedding. He'd climbed calmly onto their mini-bus, killing three men and the driver as they tried to escape through the windows, and past him to the door.

It had earned him 'urban hero' status amongst his paramilitary pals. And twenty years in prison. But he'd been granted release in '98 under the Good Friday Agreement, despite widespread disapproval. Since then he'd apparently been a good little boy, working in youth-clubs, teaching young kids the error of his ways. Except that the Drugs Squad knew very different.

"He's going ballistic up here. Threatening the staff with all sorts of hell."

"Bugger." Craig let out a low whistle, and a prim-looking woman by the lift glared over. He held a hand up in apology.

"OK. What's the chance he'll do something stupid?"

"Two hundred percent, I'd say. He'd to be dragged out of theatre last night by security. He punched Nigel Murdock, the surgeon. Happy Days."

Craig smiled to himself. "Liam…"

"Aye right, not diplomatic. Sorry. Anyway, he's calling the doctors bastards and threatening the midwives. Can't you hear him?" Hill's yells grew louder as Liam held out the phone.

"OK. Look, I know he's a criminal, but it's a real loss for him. So handle him carefully. But he can't go around threatening people, so ask uniform to take him to High Street to cool off. Don't charge him, just invite him firmly. I'll see him there later. And get the doctor to check him- he's had a shock."

Liam shrugged. His sympathy didn't extend to criminals, no matter what the circumstance. He acquiesced, grudgingly. "We'll get him there now."

"Fine. The ward-staff need to make themselves available for interview. And pull any close circuit footage Maternity has. Have the C.S.I.s arrived yet?"

"They're here now."

"What about Evie's husband?"

"Young lad called Brian Murray."

Murray-Hill. They'd hyphenated their names. Craig pictured the confusion ten generations on.

"He's a real mess, apparently. Fell to bits last night, so Evie's mother took him home with her. He doesn't have anyone else."

Craig raked his hair despairingly. It happened every time. One person was murdered and the whole family died.

"OK. I'll see you both at the lab. Quick as you can please. I'm heading over there now."

He re-entered the squad just as he ended the call, and walked over to Nicky's desk.

"Nicky, I'm off to see John. Did you set-up that meeting with the Chief Executive?"

"No, sir. He's not free until after four. He's stuck in meetings all day and his secretary has refused to free-up his diary. She's a real piece of work."

"Keep trying please - I need to see him today. But leave

that just now. Would you mind checking whoever's in court on Warwick tomorrow? Make sure they're prepared and call me with any problems. And I'll need a statement pack at about five. Thanks. I'll give you a call after I've seen John."

He turned to leave and she called him back. "Sir."

"Yes?"

"Come here a wee minute."

Craig walked back to her desk, bemused. Nicky stood up and patted his hair down, as if he was her little boy. Then she handed him a takeaway cup full of hot coffee. He blushed, touched.

"Thanks Mum. I'll be on the mobile if you need me."

Chapter Four

When Craig reached the lab, John was hunched over his desk, reading a folder. Craig poured himself a coffee and took a sip, letting it wash down before he spoke.

"This is a bad one, John."

"Even more than you know. Let's wait till the others arrive before we start. There's a lot to go cover."

At that moment, Liam and Annette pushed through the double PVC doors, looking flustered. Liam started talking immediately. "Here, your man on the gate is a bit much isn't he, Doc? He nearly strip-searched me."

Annette's eyes widened. "God forbid! Liam's exaggerating as usual, but he was pretty unpleasant."

John laughed. "Yes, sorry about that. He's new. I should have warned you, they've decided they don't like visitors these days. They prefer us in splendid isolation."

The newly built Northern Ireland Pathology Labs were set in a Science Park on the Saintfield Road, two miles from Belfast's city centre. They shared the park with valuable research facilities, whose high security and alarms were a condition of the huge grants they received. Stormont had signed them up to it. Now they had to make it work.

Just then Liam noticed his surroundings, and his mouth dropped open in surprise. The lab looked like a brothel! It was a cavernous space, with steel instruments and tables like most dissection rooms, but that was where the comparisons ended.

John had always hated 'NHS green'; he thought it was the colour of public toilets. So when Stormont had given him a naive young manager 'to keep an eye on him', he'd brought her to the lab on her first day and swept his hand around dramatically.

"Now...tell me Mary. What do you see?" Given that there'd been a dead body on the table, she'd been speechless for the five seconds he'd allowed her to answer.

"I'll tell you what you see...it's cold and lonely. Don't you think the dead feel bad enough, without the place looking like a public lavatory? Does it have to be quite so stark around here?"

She didn't stand a chance. So after completing forms in triplicate, the 'NHS green' walls were now a soft, dark-rose colour. And alongside the laminated health and safety notices hung Manet prints and countryside scenes. There were plants in John's office, the blinds had been replaced by draped curtains, and music played softly throughout the floor. The whole impression was one of incongruously inviting warmth.

"I'd forgotten that you haven't been here for a while. They did it while I was away." John had just returned from a three-month research post in America. "How do you like it?"

Liam just kept staring, until Annette shot him a warning look.

"I hadn't noticed it either, John. But you've surpassed yourself. It's like the Folies Bergere."

Winter laughed. "That's what I was aiming for. Relatives don't see this area and we have to work here all day, so I thought I'd make it home. It gives the medical students something to talk about. Apparently they think I'm eccentric."

Craig glanced at his friend's blue shoes. "I wonder why."

Liam tentatively touched the red-pink wall.

"Careful Liam, it's still wet. It took several pints of blood to get that colour right."

He jumped back and then realised he was being wound up. "Aye...dead-on Doc. Very witty." The lab echoed with laughter and then John brought them back to more serious business.

"Everyone grab a drink and a seat and let's make a start." He turned on his laptop, and lifted two slim post-mortem files from his desk drawer.

"You're aware of what happened this morning. I'll cover that first, but there's a lot more to tell you. I've had concerns since my return last week, but nothing concrete until now." Craig's eyebrow rose questioningly.

"Mrs Murray-Hill first. Why do I believe this is more than just a medical incident? That would be the natural assumption, because of the location and circumstances of death. And I expect that's exactly what the killer would have liked us to believe."

He clicked open a file while he talked. "I'd have been happy to be proved wrong. But that's a lost hope, given the little gem that came through at eight this morning. This is why I called you, Marc."

He turned the slim screen towards them. It was logged onto the Pathology Lab Intranet.

"What is it?"

"A preliminary blood test. We need more detail, but basically her blood shows high but non-lethal levels of Pethidine and Insulin. We know she was on the Insulin because she was given it by a Dr Katy Stevens, the consultant who diagnosed her diabetes."

"But?"

"But she wasn't prescribed Pethidine, not at any stage. Not on the ward or during the operation. I've already checked with the pharmacy. It's nowhere in her charts or notes, but it is in her blood."

"Which means she was given it by someone else. Whoever killed her?"

"Exactly. Pethidine's a controlled drug and very hard to obtain legally."

"You said it was a non-lethal dose."

"Yes. Bear with me and I'll explain. It's early days, but this

24

raises some major questions. Especially in light of the others."

"Others?"

"I'll get to that in a moment, Marc. But you need to proceed as if this is a murder now." He paused. "Possibly three murders."

"What!"

John opened the two thin files. Each one contained a single sheet of post-mortem paper.

"You know that I took over as Director last year from Dr Alan Davis?" They all nodded. "Well, he came back to cover me when I was in the States. And when I returned last week, Stormont asked me to review his cases. This is all hush-hush, so please keep it confidential."

Annette stared hard at Liam, until he buckled. "God, why does everyone always look at me like that?"

"Experience."

"Apparently they'd had concerns about his work for some time, hence his early retirement at fifty. But from what I've seen now, I'm amazed they allowed him to keep practicing at all. And I'm furious they didn't discuss their concerns with me before they let him step in as my locum. The P.M. reports since January were the worst that I've ever read."

He pointed to the files. "All of them were thin, but not as thin as these two. So I needed to find out why." He paused. "They're post-mortems on two other mothers who've died at the Maternity Unit since January."

"Died of what?"

"I'll answer that in a second, but let me give you some background. Statistically, Northern Ireland should have no more than one or two deaths per year across *all* of its Maternity Units. But we're already looking at nearly twice that number in three months, just from one Unit. If this was a trend we'd be looking at almost a hundred per year across the province.

There are also very strong similarities between these two

cases and Evie Murray-Hill's. All the mothers died, all had Caesarean sections, and all the babies survived."

"But Dr Winter, maternity's a high-risk specialty. I worked there and I remember there was a lot of litigation.."

"That's a fair point, Annette, but these women weren't particularly high-risk. And the relatives didn't litigate or complain any more than expected. There were just tears and the usual enquiries made at the time. Bear with me and you'll see that there are more similarities." Craig could see where John was heading.

"Both P.M.s were summarised as 'natural death', which makes me very nervous. They were completely unexpected and yet Davis called them both natural. The first lady was a forty-three-year-old. Mrs Deborah McCance, a multip from the Demesne Estate in north Belfast. Her death occurred in January. It was her fifth baby, all perfectly normal. But this time she needed a Caesarean. The operation went well and she had a healthy baby girl."

"What's a multip, John?"

"A multiple times Mum." Craig nodded. At least that made sense, most medical terminology didn't seem to.

"Mrs McCance was well after the operation, apart from a bit of diabetes, which settled on Insulin. Her only other medication was some Pethidine for pain. Everything was normal, and she was due to go home on day five post-op. Then on day three she just didn't wake up. The P.M. revealed nothing to explain it."

"What about the tox-screen?"

"Just Pethidine and Insulin as expected, high levels but nothing lethal. The last time she was seen alive was 2am. But she was in a side room and wasn't found until eight the next morning. Her estimated time of death was 3am. "

"Who was the consultant?"

Winter rolled his eyes. "The dreadful Nigel Murdock, again." Craig glanced up sharply.

"That's the second time I've heard that today. Why so dreadful?"

"Because he's a total ass, Marc. He's the sort of surgeon who caused the old joke. 'What's the difference between God and a surgeon? 'God doesn't think he's a surgeon!' "

Liam laughed loudly. "Here, I'll have to remember that one, it's not bad."

"He delivered our Jordan when he was a junior, sir. And he thought he walked on water even then. He must be shocking now he's a consultant."

"It's even worse than that, Marc. You might possibly forgive some arrogance if he was a good surgeon, but his statistics are dreadful. But every time someone tried to start an investigation, he did the old-boys thing with Robert Moore, the old Chief Exec. And any complaints were hushed up. Until the next time."

John shook his head resignedly. He knew the medical hierarchy too well to be surprised at the ranks closing. He lifted the other file.

"The second death occurred in mid-February. A thirty-year-old called Linda Bryson, from Holywood. She was one of Murdock's private patients and was due for a normal delivery with her first baby. But she died during labour and the baby was delivered by emergency Caesarean after she died. Just as Evie's baby was. She was in a side-room as well."

"Privacy for the killer?"

"Possibly, but there are a lot of side-rooms on new units. Most wards are built that way now. Anyway, again it's Mr Murdock. And worryingly, the midwife was also the same on both cases. Beth Walker. And, here's a bit of hospital grapevine stuff for you. There's real animosity between those two, much more than the odd midwife/surgeon disagreement. Some nasty stuff apparently."

"They were Evie's team as well, boss."

"How many consultants work on Maternity, Annette?"

"Eight. And a similar number of midwives. But they aren't paired - they're allocated by the mothers post-code. Except the private patient. She must have chosen Murdock herself?"

"God help her wit."

Craig nodded. Three deaths in three months. Same place, same consultant, and same midwife. What were the odds? He could see why John had called him.

"Moving on. Mrs Bryson was in the side-room for twenty-four-hours but the baby wasn't progressing, so a drip was put up to help." Craig glanced at him questioningly

"It's quite normal procedure and she was fine. Nurse Walker recorded that she was chatting to her husband when she left the room to check on another patient. Murdock was due to call in when she was out. Except Murdock said that when he arrived the room was empty, and Mrs Bryson was already dead.

Her husband came back just as she was being rushed to theatre. He'd been getting himself a coffee. So although Mrs Bryson wasn't scheduled to have one, we have another emergency Caesarean."

"What about the post-mortem?"

"The same, nothing abnormal recorded. A healthy Mum on a little Pethidine for the difficult labour. And her Insulin level was non-lethal."

"Why was she on Insulin?"

"Sorry, I should have said. She'd been diabetic since she was fourteen, so it was just her usual dose. Both drugs levels were high but in the normal range. "

"What was the baby, Dr Winter?"

"Glad you asked, Annette. It was another little girl." Annette gasped, and even Liam shuddered.

"OK, John. So we have three women dead in three months. Same location, same consultant and same midwife. Three female babies delivered alive by Caesarean-section, and all three mothers on high but non-lethal levels of Pethidine and

Insulin. Two of them in side rooms. But nothing abnormal reported on the first two P.Ms."

"Three in side-rooms, boss ...Evie was in one too, near the Unit door."

"That about sums it up, Marc. Plus, these P.M. reports are much too brief, so you can see why I'm uneasy. And we can be certain that Evie's death was suspicious, because of the totally un-prescribed Pethidine. So, given the similarities..."

Craig finished his sentence. "We're looking at the two earlier deaths being suspicious as well."

Winter nodded. "Yes. It would have been easy to give the first two women higher doses of drugs that were already prescribed for them. To subdue them, before they were killed, by whatever means. But Pethidine wasn't even prescribed for Evie. And drugs definitely weren't her cause of death."

Craig interrupted him urgently. "What was, John?"

"It's not obvious, so we're doing more tests. But I'd say that she knew her attacker. They managed to get close enough to inject her without any signs of being fought off. Perhaps someone working in health? Or impersonating a health worker? And I'm uncomfortable about the two earlier P.Ms. Davis' incompetence seems almost deliberate."

He took a deep breath. "There's one more thing, Marc."

Craig sipped at his coffee, making a mental list of queries. "What is it?"

"Evie had a deep cut on her right cheek. It happened around the time of death and it was made with a very sharp implement. The clinical staff said it was there before they resuscitated her, so it could have been deliberate."

A cut. An anomaly or a signature?

"What I don't understand is why they added Pethidine for Evie, Marc. It's such an obvious clue that it was murder. Very careless of them."

Craig shook his head. "Evie's Pethidine is window-dressing, John. Either they wanted us to know that she was murdered, or the killer is deliberately trying to confuse us. I don't think they were being careless or trying to confuse us. I think that they wanted us to know they'd murdered Evie. They deliberately gave her un-prescribed Pethidine, knowing that we would detect it.

The question is *why* do they want us to know? And why kill all three women? Something must link them. We need to find out if Davis was involved in the killings, or just covering them up. Let's get him in, Liam."

Liam reached for his mobile and John shook his head. "Davis can't be a suspect in Evie's case."

"Why not?"

"He died a week ago from a massive heart attack. It was totally unexpected. He was only fifty and kept himself fit."

"Here, that's a big coincidence, boss."

"I agree. Let's check it out. But it doesn't stop him being involved in the first two cases, if only to cover them up. OK, no-one needs told about the sensitivity of all this, so it's a press blackout, please. The C.S.I's are at the Unit now and we've sealed the scene, so all that's in hand. Liam, anything else that we need to know?"

"Nope. All under control as far as the scene goes. Uniform has started interviewing the junior players."

"Fine. I'll see the others myself tomorrow afternoon. We're in court on Warwick all morning. Give us a steer here, John. What things should we be looking for, on the ward and with the staff? Anything that we need to do now to protect people, and before we lose evidence? You and Annette know hospitals, we don't."

"Get Evie's ward and theatre notes, and drug charts. There'll be things on paper that aren't on the computer, and vice versa. Check the Rota for who was covering last night, even for an hour – the personnel department will have copies. You should try the junior doctor's lounge at lunchtime as well. Juniors often swop their on-call nights between them and that won't be written down anywhere.

If you concentrate on Evie, I'll see what I can find on the other two. It all started in the past three months so ask if any staff have changed since Christmas, including admin and managers. Although whoever's responsible could have been in post for a while before they started all of this of course. Or they might have moved to another ward and come back. But thankfully I haven't P.M'd any other deaths like this in the past year, although I'll check with the other pathologists. Make sure the C.S.I.s get all Evie's needles, dressings and giving-sets for me please Liam. I need to have a good look at them."

"What's a giving-set, Doc?"

"The drip lines, fluid bags and the needle that was in her arm. And any dressings and tubes as well. We need to know what she was eating and drinking too. In fact, anything that came into contact with her in any way."

"How's Pethidine given, John?"

"Injection in the muscles by the nurses, but it can be in the veins and that would normally be a doctor. If they were trying to subdue her quickly they'd have given it in the veins in a higher dose. Its maximum time to clear from the body is forty-eight hours, so go back at least two days on everything."

"What about the insulin?"

"Insulin's given by injection or added to the drip bag. It's lethal in high doses but much harder to detect. But remember...none of the blood levels were reported as lethal, and Evie's were definitely too low to have killed her. I don't believe we're looking at a drug death here Marc, so I really don't understand the Pethidine. The first two victims were already on both drugs, but Evie wasn't."

"If they're clever enough to kill in such a complex way, John, they're clever enough to know that the Pethidine would be spotted. Either they deliberately wanted to draw attention to her murder, or they added the Pethidine desperately, to complete a particular scenario. I really hope that it's the former, because if they did it desperately then that's bad news. It would indicate that they couldn't wait to find someone who was *already* on the Insulin/Pethidine mix and fitted exactly. Which means escalation. And that means they'll soon start looking for another victim. So far we have an average six week's gap between deaths, and I want it to stay that way."

"But why Evie, sir?"

"Exactly, Annette. Why Evie? First of all, they want us to know that they're murdering. But they could have shown us that by just *overdosing* any woman who was already on the Insulin/Pethidine drug combination. They can't be that uncommon, John?"

"Well, most women get a bit of Pethidine, and they must have quite a few diabetics on Insulin through the Unit very month. So yes. I'd say there'd be a few already on that combination each month."

"But they didn't wait for one of those women. They *deliberately* gave Evie Pethidine to complete the scenario. So Evie herself may be significant."

"But what purpose could her death possibly serve, Marc?"

"I don't know. We need to look hard at her life."

"No-one has a bad word to say about Evie so far, boss. We'll keep digging, but..."

"Yes, Liam?"

"Well, it's just a thought. But couldn't they have killed her because she's Tommy Hill's daughter? He caused a lot of deaths. There are bound to be people out there who want revenge."

Craig nodded. It was exactly what he'd been thinking.

"That's a real possibility, and one we need to rule out. OK, we'll talk about that at the briefing. Sorry John, go on."

"Liam, get the drug registers for the ward and pharmacy. Then there are High Street Pharmacies, thefts and possibly even internet purchases of Pethidine, if that's possible. There may even be some street Pethidine on the loose."

"I'll get Davy on it. But here, Tommy deals drugs, boss."

Annette whacked his arm hard. "For God's sake, Liam. He didn't kill his own daughter."

"No. Liam's right, Annette. We can't rule anything out. Check out Tommy with Andy White in Drugs. They'll have him on their radar."

"If someone does have access to these drugs, Marc, we have to keep this quiet. Otherwise people won't come to the hospital. You might need to close Maternity, and we may be looking at two exhumations."

Craig drained his cup quickly and stood, ready to leave.

"I'm meeting with the Trust's Chief Executive later and we'll handle it sensitively. But we have to make people aware, John. By the way, you keep saying 'he' when you talk about the killer. You seem sure that a man did this. Why? Was there any sexual contact? Or D.N.A.?"

"No...No obvious sexual contact. The swabs are clear, I checked that first thing. And the D.N.A. is a maze because of the resuscitation and operation. It's a good point. I don't know why I keep saying 'he'. Of course it could be a woman. One in six serial killers is female, and many of those operate in health settings. When I was in America..."

Craig stepped in quickly before his day became an episode of Criminal Minds. "Sorry, John, but we need to focus on Belfast today."

John smiled and shrugged. "It could be someone who hates mothers, Marc. Or a Munchausen's by proxy."

"Or someone who thinks they're saving them somehow? Like an angel of mercy killer? Aren't they usually women, Dr Winter?"

"That's true Annette. Or perhaps I say 'he' because I find it hard to imagine a woman doing this...with the babies..." His voice tailed off and he smiled. "Old fashioned of me, I know."

Annette smiled. Chivalry wasn't quite dead while John Winter was around.

"Of course, a lack of sexual contact doesn't rule out a sexual motivation, Marc. All the victims are female, as are the babies, so it could just be revenge against the female sex. The only way to completely rule out sexual motivation is if they kill a man. That would point to a more personal agenda. I'll do a profile for you."

John had just completed his psychological profiler training in Virginia, and had drunkenly profiled them all in the bar one night. His analyses had been far too close for comfort.

"How did the killer know that they were all having girls, sir? Deborah McCance had already given birth, but the other two hadn't."

Craig stared at Annette. She was right, how *did* they know?

"Well spotted, Annette. Any suggestions, John?"

Craig caught her triumphant look and Liam's quick annoyance. More rivalry.

"Well, I know for a fact that St Marys don't tell women the baby's sex before birth. It's Trust policy. All I can suggest is that they might've had private scans, and someone wrote the result in their notes? That would suggest the killer was someone with access to the ward notes."

"Or the original scans, sir."

"Or the I.T. system, Doc. The Sister said everything's on computer now."

"OK, we need to check-out all of those. Best case scenario, it's not in the hospital records. That way only the scanners and families would have known they were having girls. That would certainly narrow the suspect pool. Worst case scenario, it's in the notes and on the computer. One last thing, John, you mentioned inquiries on the first two deaths?"

"Yes, they were quite in-depth in fact. Nothing negligent was proven, but then there never is with Murdock. The inquests are real performances - they should sell tickets. He always calls his friends to testify at them. Alan Davis was one of them." He gazed down at the thin reports again, disgusted.

"But, much as it grieves me, Marc, I have to be fair to Murdock. What would be his motive for killing Evie? I can see negligence or sheer stupidity from him, but murder? And so obviously murder? What would be the point? He has a lot to lose. He has a real jet-set lifestyle going on up in Cultra. And he'd be insane to think he wouldn't get caught eventually. Although I suppose this could be 'eventually'."

"We have a lot of questions ahead of us before we can answer that one."

"That's your bit. I'll stick to my P.Ms."

He handed Craig a page with the case details, and then remembered something. "I've just realised I didn't offer you all one of my special coffees." He pointed to an enormous new coffee machine in the corner and they all laughed. John was a real gadget-man.

He smiled. "Mary got it for me." Poor Mary.

"Sorry, it'll have to wait until our next trip. By the way, did Liam tell you who Tommy Hill is?"

John smiled thinly. "Yes. Such nice people you meet. Good luck with him, I wouldn't swop jobs with you. At least my patients don't attack me. Although there was that episode of C.S.I when the body sat up on the bed..."

Craig groaned and said good-bye, talking as they walked to the lab's outer door. "Liam, find out when we can meet Nigel Murdock, please."

Liam walked on towards the exit, pulling his phone from his back pocket. Annette followed, removing her own, as Craig returned quickly to the lab. John was focussing on his laptop and peered up at him quizzically over his wire-rimmed glasses.

"Did you forget something?"

"Julia and I can make that party on the 20th. But she's asked if Natalie will be there. We haven't seen her since you went to the States."

"NO."

John almost spat the word out and his abruptness took Craig aback. He and Natalie had been close before he'd left for the U.S.

"No?"

A pained look crossed John's face and Craig knew that something serious had happened. "Is Natalie OK, John?"

"Fine, as far as I know. But…"

"What?"

John glared at him, pulling off his glasses. "Stop interrogating me, Marc. I'm not one of your bloody suspects." It was an over-the-top response, and completely out of character. "Just leave it, OK?"

His hurt look told Craig not to dig deeper.

"And…don't try to fix me up with anyone else. I'm far too busy with work to have a relationship."

It was said almost pleadingly and Craig nodded, concerned. Then he watched as his friend returned to the safety of his computer. He wondered what had happened – John had been happier with Natalie Ingrams than Craig had seen him in years.

Maybe they'd lost contact when he was in America or… maybe she'd met someone else. He thought of how easily it had happened to him in the past, and the damage that he'd suffered. He wouldn't wish it on his friend.

He stood for a moment longer, then nodded and left the lab. There was nothing he could do until John asked for his help.

Chapter Five

"We have 4pm tomorrow for Murdock, boss. His secretary wasn't best pleased. Says he'll have to come back from the golf course in the middle of 18 holes..."

"Remind me to be sympathetic when I meet him."

They were heading down the concrete slope towards the Path Lab's car-park. It wasn't raining any more, although it felt as if it should be. It usually rained for some part of the day in Belfast, regardless of the month. The downside of coastal living.

Their exit from the Science Park was barred by an overweight security guard wearing an armband branded S.P. Science Park or Security Person? Craig wondered how far political correctness had gone.

"That's the Nazi I told you about." Craig smiled, instantly picturing the man in uniform.

The guard shuffled ponderously towards the car, glaring at them as if they'd stolen something. After an exaggerated scan of Craig's badge, he shrugged in defeat, pressing the barrier release with an air of thwarted boredom. Liam drove left onto the Ormeau Road, heading down the busy artery into town.

"I gave the ward a call and the midwife can meet us now, sir. She's taking her lunch break at twelve."

"That's great Annette. Where exactly is the Maternity, Paediatric and Endocrine complex?"

"At the Lisburn Road end of Elmwood Avenue. The Dunmore Medical Centre site, near where the old Elmwood Hospital used to be."

"I remember that hospital; Lucia was born there. They were really friendly." Lucia was Craig's sister; younger by ten years.

They reminisced while Liam drove smoothly through the late morning traffic, moaning about Belfast's gridlock. Craig just smiled and remembered the M25.

"It was a great place to work. I was there for two years and loved it."

Craig turned, looking back at Annette over the passenger seat.

"Do you miss being a nurse, Annette?"

"No. Well, maybe sometimes. But it took its toll. You see a lot. You know?"

Craig nodded, but he could only imagine. They saw a lot in murder too, but it was a whole different type of 'a lot'.

"Can you call Davy and ask him to check the Home Office database, please. For similar cases across the UK. Ask him to liaise with the Irish police as well. He needs to search under solved and unsolved suspicious female deaths and murders. Cross reference with pregnancy, Caesarean, female offspring, Insulin and Pethidine. And ask him to look for scars or cuts on the right cheek as well. That might be something. If anything at all flags up, I need the paper files.

Ask Nicky to contact the Drs' and Nurses' organisations for anything on Murdock and Beth Walker. Just whatever she can get without a warrant, for now. But quietly please; I don't want the trust alerted just yet."

Annette sent the requests through on her smart phone, following up with a call before they reached the Unit.

"Nicky says Davy was already on it, as background on Evie."

Liam nodded. "Davy's good, right enough. Far better than that other analyst we had before - Penny something. She was as thick as a brick."

"I think that counts as intellectual prejudice, Liam. There's probably a course I can send you on for that."

"Aye, equal rights for bricks, ha, ha." Liam pulled smoothly into the complex's car park and grabbed a ticket, opening the barrier. Then he waved his hand grandly at the building, like a tour guide. "Ladies and Gentlemen, welcome to the M.P.E."

St Marys' M.P.E. complex was set back from the urban Elmwood Avenue. On the 'Golden Mile' in Belfast 9. It was known as BT9 to the rest of Belfast. Shorthand for Northern Irish prosperity.

The complex was modern with corridor art and soothing waterfalls, to make the atmosphere less clinical. It had cost a fortune, a point the unions never tired of mentioning. Still, 'Art for Wellness' had given it five stars, so that was all right then. Bargain.

The entrance was designed to look like a pair of hands held apart, and Annette laughed loudly as Liam wiggled through them. Craig tried to look disapproving and failed, laughing as well.

The lifts were all busy, so they asked the elderly lady on reception for directions to Maternity. Then they walked up the stairs towards the bright second floor.

A strong floral scent led them to the right, and two parallel glass corridors, both ending at the Maternity Unit's locked entrance. Several anxious looking men lurked outside the Unit's door, wearing invisible signs that said 'New Dad'. They leaned against the walls and slumped tiredly on the comfy chairs. A strip of carpet in the corner looked like a runway, for pacing.

A woman in a red uniform so pristine that it shouted 'Sister' was waiting ready by the door, informed that they were coming by downstairs. Well spotted Miss Marple in reception. They must have 'police' written all over them.

Sister Laurie Johns stood with her hands crossed at waist height, and a thoroughly disapproving expression on her thin face. She was a tense looking brunette of around forty, with a strangely triangular head; a shape not enhanced by her tightly pulled chignon. Her skin was over tanned and her small brown eyes reminded Annette of wizened raisins. She somehow doubted that she soothed her patients.

When the Sister spoke it was in an affected middle-class accent, and her greeting was as cold as she appeared. She showed them to a small office with few niceties, setting off to fetch Nurse Walker, with a look that told them exactly what she thought of her.

Two minutes later Beth Walker hurtled into the room. She looked in her late twenties but she must have been years older, and she was absolutely tiny. She wore blue scrubs and yellow Crocs, decorated with flowers and peace symbols. She resembled a slim Telly-Tubby and Craig liked her immediately.

Annette didn't know what she'd expected the midwife to look like, but it definitely wasn't this. Someone rosy cheeked and plump probably, remembering midwives she'd known during her training. But then that was in a rural hospital, and this *was* St Marys.

The young woman's hair was jet-black and straight. Shoulder length on one side and shaved short on the other, its ends tipped with a purple-blue that exactly matched her eyes. She had three silver studs set high on her visible ear and another one in her lip. And her inner wrist held a Zen symbol tattoo. The whole impression was youthful and lively. Just how lively became apparent in the force of her next words.

"I knew this was going to happen. I knew it. I told everyone. I knew it was only a matter of time after the others. But no-one listens. Especially not to me. Why do people have to bloody die, to make you lot pay attention?"

The words came screaming out of her in a strong Derry accent. Craig watched her quietly, letting her vent. Even Annette was six inches taller than her, so he nodded the others to sit or prop themselves against any free surface in the small, windowed office. Then he spoke in a soothing voice.

"Why don't you tell us about it, Ms Walker?"

"What's the point? No one listens. We've killed her. She's not the first and she won't be the last."

Liam was watching her intently and Craig caught his look, knowing that he was desperate to ask a question. He shook his head gently, motioning to let her story come out, as she talked on in a stream of consciousness.

She'd started working in the Unit five years before. Everyone else had been there forever, so they all knew each other, and she knew they thought she was an oddball.

"They all think I'm a whacko, but I don't care. I worked in Australia for years and I'm keen on natural child birth."

She and Nigel Murdock were at daggers drawn. "It's no secret, everybody knows. He hates me because I've said he does far too many Caesareans. But he does. They aren't necessary and he just does them for his own convenience. It's lazy medicine."

It was also no secret that she was gay, and that seemed to cause Murdock even more problems. He was used to his Hugh Grant charm easing his way around women. But he'd hit a brick wall with Beth, and he knew it. He'd made openly anti-gay remarks, but she hadn't reported him.

"It wouldn't have got me anywhere. He went to school with the old C.E.O, Moore."

Liam whistled softly. Health seemed far less P.C. than the police. He'd have been sacked for the things Murdock had said! He felt unexpectedly bad for her - the sensitivity training was obviously working.

Her voice wavered for a moment, and she seemed so near tears that Craig wanted to reach out a hand in comfort. But he had to stay detached. This was a murder investigation and she could be a suspect. She wouldn't be the first brilliant liar that he'd encountered.

The thought made him sad somehow, but she had known all three women. She'd also been on the ward last night and discovered Evie's body. He stood up politely, making ready to leave.

"That's all for now Ms Walker. Thank you for your time. Would you make yourself available for interview tomorrow afternoon, please?"

Her face dropped suddenly. "But what are you doing about it? You can't just leave it and waltz off. This place is getting away with murder. Or does there have to be another death before you eejits pay any attention?"

She yelled the last comment so loudly that Laurie Johns heard and she bombed down the ward towards them. Annette quickly grabbed Beth's elbow and wheeled her round, out of the office and off the ward for a coffee, anywhere.

"Phew...she's a wee fireball. What a temper, boss. Just as well she's only a munchkin." Craig smiled broadly. Liam's quaint terminology always lightened the mood.

Just as Laurie Johns entered the office Liam's mobile rang. He disappeared to answer it, not missing her disapproving glare.

"Well really, Mr Craig. These are pregnant women. They need peace and quiet."

"I know, and I'm sorry Sister. We're just leaving. But may I ask you one question?" He knew what her answer would be before he asked. "How do you find working with Mr Murdock?"

Her expression altered at a startling speed, into a teenage girl gazing at a poster of 'One Direction'.

"Oh, he's so gifted. Such a wonderful surgeon."

It told Craig all he needed to know about the ward's dynamics, and exactly where Beth Walker stood in the pecking order. He nodded to himself.

"Thank you for your help, Sister. Now, Ms Walker is distraught, so I think it would be best if she went home early. I'll ask one of the female officers to take her now."

"Well honestly, Mr Craig! That means I'll have to do her work."

He left her still-protesting in the office, without either the patience or the inclination to placate her.

The round uniformed shape of Sergeant Joe Rice was standing in the internal corridor, and Craig walked over to him, nodding hello. He nodded back distractedly, staring intently at a freshly stacked tea-trolley, salivating. Craig smiled, knowing that a cupcake would be heading for his stomach in a minute, followed by a mug of tea.

Joe dragged his eyes away from the plates, greeting Craig warmly in a singing Cork accent.

"Hello there, sir. Rum old business this …"

"You could say that." Craig nodded in the direction of the office. "How are you getting on with the Sister?"

Joe grinned, a thin wide smile that creased his round face into the shape of a rugby ball. When he spoke he elongated his vowels, in the character of his home county. "Ahh…Frosty the Snowman …. Well if I was a baby and saw her, I'd refuse to come out."

He laughed loudly at his own joke. It was a high wheeze of a laugh that was joined by a guffaw from Liam, returning from taking his call.

"Nice nickname, Joe. Wish I'd thought of it."

"Here Liam, could a W.P.C. not take over from me? This isn't a good place for a man."

"That'll be why the Dads are hiding in the hall." They laughed again, and then Craig turned back to business.

"Joe, ask a W.P.C. to take Ms Walker home please. Be subtle, but she's not to return before her interview. Can someone keep an eye on Nigel Murdock as well? And we'll need an officer posted here 24/7. You're right; female officers are probably best until we decide if we're closing the Unit."

"That's grand. I'll sort it out." He stared pointedly through the glass at Laurie Johns. "There's not a lot of compassion in that one, is there?" It didn't require any confirmation.

"How many extra people can you let us have, Joe?"

"Well, Jack says they're fairly quiet at the moment and I've two probationers. So that's about six, for a few days anyway. Plus, me for part of the time, if that helps?"

"That's brilliant, thanks. Tell Inspector Andrews I'll get the paperwork to him."

Joe lifted a handful of cakes and a mug of tea and wandered-off down the ward. Just then Liam's mobile beeped with a text.

Craig shot him a wry look. "That's not supposed to be on in here."

Liam glanced at it, and then knocked it off quickly, pushing a cupcake into his mouth. "Sorry, I forgot. We're needed boss. That was High Street texting. Tommy's going buck-daft down there. They want us to see him or let him go. The medical examiner sedated him, but it's not working."

"We'll head over there now. I just need to check something." Craig walked quickly down the ward into the windowless office that they'd been allocated. Joe was already there, leaning over the screen of an old-fashioned computer.

"Can you work that thing, Joe? I need to check something."

"Aye, the wee nurse showed me. It came in on the arc but I'll have a go. What are you looking for?"

"I need the notes for Evie Murray-Hill. And another lady, Linda Bryson – she was here in February." He read their dates of birth off the paper John had given him earlier, and after a moments' whirring noise their records came up. Craig scrolled through them quickly until he found what he needed. They'd both had private scans to find out the baby's sex, and it was on their hospital records, clear as day. Where anyone could have seen it.

"Is there anything to say where they had the scans, Joe?"

"Aye, there. The Private Surgery, wherever that is. Leave it with me and I'll have a dig around."

"Thanks."

Both women had known that they were having girls before delivery, and the information had been easily accessible on the computer. Unless the scan technician's identity gave them some clues, the suspect pool was back to anyone who worked in the hospital.

Craig re-joined Liam quickly. "Liam - you come with me. I need Annette to stay here with Joe's team. Ask her to help them with the interviews for the rest of the day. And get Beth Walker on my interview-list for tomorrow. Find the doctor who prescribed Evie's Insulin as well, please. I'll need to interview him."

"Her. Tut tut, boss, such sexism."

Craig smiled ruefully. "OK, her then. Put her on tomorrow's list please."

"There's another senior doctor, boss. Iain Lewes. But he seems happy enough to see me. I'll take the builders who've been working on-site as well. There's plenty to go round."

"Thanks. Now, we'd better get going, before Tommy tears High Street down round him."

As they headed downstairs Craig pulled out his mobile, and Liam pointed smugly to a 'No Phones' sign. He stubbornly dialled anyway - a stairwell seemed a safe bet not to get caught.

"Nicky. Annette's going to co-ordinate my interviews with you for tomorrow afternoon. Any word on the C.E.O. yet?"

"Sorry, I'm still chasing him, sir."

"OK. We're heading over to High Street now, but keep trying for that meeting. Meanwhile, can you arrange for me to meet Evie's mother this afternoon? Before the C.E.O. please."

"There's a step-father too, sir."

"Fine."

"He's a Reverend."

Craig let out a low whistle. "A far cry from our Tommy then..."

Chapter Six

1.30pm.

If Belfast had been human they'd have diagnosed it with a personality disorder years before. It ricocheted between the "what're you looking at?" aggression of a sulky teenage boy, and everyone's favourite mother offering you tea. The problem was you never knew which personality was behind which face.

Katy had lived away for so long that she felt English now. No, not English, a Londoner, and that was very different. Either way, coming back to Northern Ireland was confusing. What were the rules here in 2013?

She'd loved the anonymity of London and was scared of Belfast pushing her back into a mould. Which school did you go to? Who do you know? Tell us right now, so we can be comfortable with you. She fought hard against it, and not always politely. Meanwhile, she had to deal with her new job.

There was a standing joke in medicine that you could guess which branch people would go into just by looking at them. It was a game every final-year student played. The rugby boys went into surgery. The clever faster ones into Cardiac or Neuro. The sheer strength of the hookers making them perfect for Orthopaedics. The nerdy ones went for Psychiatry or the labs. And the mumsy girls married some macho surgeon and disappeared into the G.P. wilderness, leaving hubbie to play away happily in the hospital.

The smart money had been on her doing medicine, but no one had ever seen shy Katy going to London. Yet she had, for thirteen years. She'd been back in Belfast for four months now and checked in with some of her old class-mates. She'd even made a new friend, Natalie Ingrams, a young surgical consultant. They sometimes worked together in the M.P.E., far away from the politics of the main St Marys' site.

The trust's main hospital was like a small city off the M2. It was enormous and sprawling, with cafes, shops and intrigue that could rival Holby City's. There'd even been a bar once, near where she was standing now. But that had gone years before, a victim of political correctness. She remembered going there, sticking close to her friends. The surgeons used it as a hunting ground for each new batch of female students. She smiled, remembering her friend Maeve complaining. "It's like a fox hunt in here, and we're Basil Brush."

They'd had to close it eventually of course. Not P.C. The health service couldn't afford people 'practicing under the influence', and there'd been a lot of them at one time. She wondered if patients were really any safer now.

The Visitor watched her from a distance, wondering why she didn't see them standing there. But doctors were always too busy with the mundane to focus on what was important. Too busy enjoying themselves to care about patients. That would change soon, when the father made them listen.

A soft tap on Katy's back made her jump "God, Rowan, you scared me. What are you doing here? Is this your audit meeting as well?"

Rowan Jones' handsome strong-boned face smiled down at her. He answered her in a welsh accent that contrasted sweetly with the Belfast background chatter. "No, but everyone's been summoned to the two to three bit. I'm not sure why."

He'd started at the trust in November, two months before her. And he was really friendly. Although, as Natalie said, 'I bet he'd like to get a lot friendlier'. The way she'd twirled an imaginary moustache had made them both laugh.

They wandered down the long main corridor together. It

was fluorescent and wide, with wards on either side, like shops on a village high-street. There was so much traffic at times that it needed stop-lights. Scaffolding loomed above a small newsagents halfway down, and a pile of leaking sandbags leaned untidily against a door. The whole Trust was being refurbished, and there was dust flying everywhere, here and at the M.P.E. complex.

After five minutes banter they reached their destination. The lecture hall was an old, high-ceilinged theatre, with wooden tiers sweeping down towards the front. Katy sat where she always had as a student; second row from the back, at the right-hand end. Far enough back to be cool, but not in the back row with the rugby boys. She'd never done any work when she'd sat near them.

She ran her hand under the wooden seat, checking for her initials. They were still there! At least the developers hadn't stripped away that little bit of history. She'd carved them through tears after Adrian Hughes had dumped her. It had been a brief romantic trauma and he was fat and bald now. She'd allowed herself a small smile when she'd spotted him in the canteen last week. Schadenfreude.

A woman turned around from the next row and smiled a warm hello, holding out her hand to shake. Katy reciprocated, vaguely recognising her.

"Hi. I'm Mary Hinton, Radiology. You two are new, aren't you?"

Rowan leaned in, introducing them both. "Do you know what this meeting's about then?"

"The new Chief Exec called it about the building programme. Apparently it'll be going on until 2015. The building-work that is, not this meeting. Although I'm sure it'll feel like it."

They all laughed, but Katy groaned inwardly. The M.P.E.'s building work had already been going on for months. She'd been at St Arthurs in London during theirs, and spent years sneezing out concrete dust.

She noticed Iain Lewes, one of the paediatricians she worked with at the M.P.E., sitting near the front. She felt really sorry for him. He'd had a terrible time over the past few years. She started to text him to meet for lunch when the hall's lights dimmed. After a few seconds darkness accompanied by childish whoops, a white screen lit up at the front. It highlighted a tall, round man of about forty. He was standing behind a lectern tapping at a laptop, while a technician fussed around him with some wires and a mouse.

"That's the new Chief Exec. He was brought in from Manchester last year, after the last one was sacked. I wonder how long he'll last."

The man at the front held his hand up for silence and started to speak. "Good afternoon everyone, I'm Charles McAllister. Some of you will already know me from committee. My apologies to those of you who don't. I haven't managed to meet all our new Consultants yet, but I promise that I will."

Rowan whispered. "Deep joy, I can 'ardly wait." Katy elbowed him in the side and Mary smiled at him over her shoulder, for longer than Katy thought strictly necessary.

"I know you're all very busy, and this is time out from your work with patients. So we'll keep it brief and let you get on with your audit meeting." He turned the screen quickly to a schematic of the St Marys' site.

"In a minute I'll hand you over to Ted Greenwood, our Project Director for the building work. He'll take you through the next phase of the refurbishment, and then I'll tell you exactly what it will mean for you. As you'll know, the M.P.E. complex has already had a great deal of work done, and we complete things there on the 26th. That's when the work here really begins. So you'll soon see Ted and his team wandering around in their hard hats."

Someone groaned loudly and McAllister jokingly said, "I

heard that", earning him a quick laugh. Ted Greenwood stepped into the screen's light and Katy assessed him quickly, before the overheads dimmed again. He was a tall, good-looking man, with the arty look that trendy building types often had. He wore designer rimmed 'Clark Kent' glasses, and a blue shirt without a tie. She recognised the look as American-preppy, although she thought she might be alone in that. The sartorial interest of most Belfast consultants stopped at early 'James Herriot'.

Greenwood contemplated his audience warily, knowing that they were expecting to be bored. Then he shrugged slightly as if to say 'tough' and started to speak in a flat accent, with an inflection that Katy recognised as London.

The mix of 3-D artwork, computer animation, and physical models he brought out, surprised and engaged nearly everyone. And at the end, several of the men, including Rowan, went down to the front excitedly, for a closer look at where their new offices would be. Greenwood seemed indifferent to their interest, but McAllister was buoyed, answering every nerdy question gleefully.

"It's great to see everybody so enthused. Keep that going when Ted needs to meet you. We need your help refining the designs. After all, we can't un-build it when it's done!" He paused for effect and was rewarded by a single weak laugh from the cynical audience, signalling his cue to leave.

"Thank you for your attention. I'll hand you over to Dr Bain now for your audit meeting. That's just for the medical teams, I believe."

It was the signal for everyone else to bolt for the door, while George Bain, the Director of Medicine, stepped forward, to start the purgatory of the monthly audit. Rowan took the stairs two at a time and winked at Katy, as he and Mary escaped through the back door for coffee. She gazed longingly after them, thinking about slipping out in the dark, but too guilt-ridden to skive as usual.

Katy'd just resigned herself to 'death by statistics' when her pager vibrated. It was the M.P.E. She left swiftly through the back door to ring her young P.A.

"Shauna, you must be psychic! You've rescued me from hours of charts."

"When you hear why, you'll prefer to stay in your meeting. It's bad news I'm afraid."

"What's wrong?"

"It's that lady you saw yesterday. Mrs Murray-Hill. Katy, she's dead."

"NO! How? When did it happen? I saw her last night and she was fine - her operation's scheduled for tomorrow."

"It was very sudden. In the middle of the night. The police…" She hesitated, wondering how to say it. "I'm really sorry Katy, but the police need to speak to you. A D.C.I. Craig. They want to see you at High Street station tomorrow. I've booked you in at three. Is that OK?"

"The police? But why?" Her mind replayed every decision she'd taken on Evie's care. Then she remembered Tommy Hill's threatening presence and didn't wait for an answer. "Don't worry, three is fine. What about the baby?"

"The baby's fine. A healthy little girl. But it's so sad - she was only four years older than me."

"Yes, it is." Katy felt like weeping. Partly for herself.

"Katy, her father ..."

"Yes?" She felt a sudden fear, and droplets of cold sweat trickled down her back.

"Well it's just…he rang about an hour ago, yelling about getting all of us. Do you think he really meant it?"

Katy thought that he probably did, but she didn't want to frighten her secretary so she lied.

"No, no, I'm sure he didn't. He was just upset. Go home now Shauna and we'll talk tomorrow. Leave her notes for me before you go, please. And don't worry, it will be fine." She sounded far more optimistic than she felt.

***

Tommy Hill was leaning over the table when they entered High Street's interview room. His eyes were closed tight and Craig thought that he saw tears on his cheek, but the neon light overhead was throwing strange shapes. He didn't move. Not when they entered. Not when they scraped the hard chairs out and sat down opposite him. And not now, five minutes later. Craig matched his silence, word for absent word, until eventually he reached across and pressed the button on the tape machine.

"For the benefit of the tape, this is Tuesday the 9th of April 2013. Interview commencing at 2.30pm. Present is D.C.I. Marc Craig…"

"D.I. Liam Cullen."

"And…"

Hill sat in silence, ignoring his cue. After a few seconds Craig filled in the details for him.

"Mr Thomas Hill, of 17a, Holchester Road Belfast 14. Please acknowledge your presence for the tape, Mr Hill."

There was silence for another moment while Hill opened his red, shot eyes, and stared slowly across at Craig. Finally he croaked. "Aye, Tommy Hill" in his rasping baritone.

"Mr Hill has agreed to have an informal chat with us. No charges have been brought and he has waived his right to counsel or companion. Could you confirm that you're happy to have this meeting recorded, Mr Hill?"

"Aye. I've done nothin' wrong, so I don't need no solicitor. But let's be real clear. I want the bastard who killed our Evie found an' done for. An' if you lot don't find them quick, I fuckin' well will."

"OK, Mr Hill."

"Tommy."

"All right then, Tommy. We all want the same thing. To find out what happened to your daughter. And if a crime has been committed, to catch the person responsible, try and convict them. Agreed?"

"Aye, agreed. But it'd better happen sharpish or I'll go an' find them mysel'. Then they won't be worryin' about no trial."

Liam leaned across the table, booming. "Is that a threat?"

Hill turned to stare at him with a curious look, as if he'd just noticed him sitting there. "No threat. Trust me, I'll do it. No bother." He smiled maliciously, as if imagining the happy scene.

"Look Tommy, we know you're angry and you've every right to be. But if you go around threatening people, it won't go well for you. And no-one wants that, do they? Mr Murdock is already considering pressing charges against you for assault, so don't make matters any worse for yourself. Just let us do our job, and give us the information to help us do it." Craig's voice hardened. "Don't muddy the waters, Tommy, or get in our way. For Evie and your granddaughter's sake." He paused to let his words sink in, not holding out much hope of their impact. Hill didn't move.

"This is just an informal conversation, but we need to find out everything you know or noticed. So please give Inspector Cullen here a statement. And then go and see your granddaughter, Mr Hill, and get some rest. The D.I. will take you to the hospital and stay with you."

Craig nodded to Liam and rose to leave the room. Then he stopped at the door and turned, motioning Liam to switch off the tape.

He walked back to the table and considered Hill sadly, hesitating for a moment, before putting a hand on his shoulder. "I'm sorry this happened to your daughter, Tommy, genuinely sorry. We will get them." Then he was out of the room before the other man could see his face, the door closing hard behind him.

***

53

Templepatrick was so well kept that it reminded Craig of Trumpton, one of his favourite childhood TV programmes. It basked in the honour of 'Best Kept Small Town of 1991', a title commemorated by a small plaque at the village boundary. It was quiet and sedate, the only noise disturbing the peace the traffic heading for the International airport. As he drove in past the Mausoleum, Craig was sure that even the town's 'dearly-departed' would have passed away neatly. It just seemed like that sort of place.

Evie's mother and step-father lived in a manse attached to one of the town's many churches. He found it easily, set at the top of a long side road. Its driveway was short and pebbled, edging a neat lawn filled with flowers of lilac and blue. Two trees stood by the garden-fence, one a glowing copper beech and the other an elderly willow, nodding down sleepily. The whole place was lovely. Evie Hill had lived her short life far, far away from her father's violent world.

As the church bell struck three, Craig parked outside an imposing grey-brick house. A tall, tired-looking man came to the door to greet him, extending his hand warmly. "Mr Craig, thank you for coming all this way. I was sorry to have to ask you, I know how busy you must be. But Miriam is so distressed that I couldn't take her from the house."

Everything about the Reverend Geoffrey Kerr was gentle, grey and ageless. Craig guessed him at somewhere in his forties, but his hair was already snow white, matched by grey eyes set below dark grey brows. His neutral jumper and trousers completed the modest picture. Nothing about the man was showy.

They walked through the porch into a square tiled entrance-hall, with glass fanlights that dated it as Victorian. Geoffrey Kerr ushered him into a cosy study, already laid out with a tray of coffee and cake.

"Please help yourself, Mr Craig. The ladies of the parish keep us well supplied with pastries. I wonder if we might have a quiet word - before I fetch Miriam?"

"Of course. I don't have another appointment until late, so we have whatever time you need. May I ask you some questions as well?" Kerr nodded, deferring to Craig.

"How long had you known Evie, Reverend Kerr?"

"Miriam and I met through a church group when Evie was three." He added hastily. "Miriam was already divorced, of course." He hesitated for a moment, as if considering whether to say something, then he continued. "I don't know if you are aware, Mr Craig, but Evie's father has an unfortunate history. He...he was in prison for some time during The Troubles."

"Yes, Mr Hill is known to us. I met him earlier and he's taking this very badly. Totally understandable, of course."

"Of course, of course. Particularly as he was just getting to know Evie again. We never tried to stop him seeing her, but she was at school in Scotland when he was released. She only returned five years ago. Then she met Brian and married."

"How is Mr Murray? I understand he's staying with you."

"Yes, poor boy. He's upstairs. He was very distraught so our G.P. gave him something to help him sleep. We're the only family he has now." He stopped abruptly and paused, as if what he said next might shock. "May I be frank, Mr Craig?"

Craig nodded kindly, certain that this man's frankness couldn't possibly shock him.

"Brian's a kind young man, and Evie loved him of course. But he is... How can I put this? He's perhaps not as responsible a person as we would have wished for her. But you know young people, Mr Craig, 'the heart wants what the heart wants'. He's a harmless boy, but I do know that Mr Hill dislikes him."

"Why in particular?"

The Reverend glanced away, embarrassed. "We're not a bigoted family, Mr Craig, genuinely not. I hold and attend ecumenical services, at all the local places of Christian worship. And we work very well with the local Jewish and

Muslim residents. So the fact that Brian is not of our faith is of no issue to Miriam or me. Indeed, I co-officiated at the wedding. But...I think that Mr Hill may have had a rather different opinion of him, based on that single fact. "

"Thank you for being so honest. That's useful information."

Geoffrey Kerr continued talking, filling Craig in on Evie's life as a child. And since she'd returned to Belfast five years before, and married. Craig knew, from the way that he spoke, that he was looking at Evie's real father. This man had dried all the tears caused by Tommy Hill's past.

"May I ask you, Mr Craig...why *are* the police involved in Evie's death? Is it because of Mr Hill?"

"Reverend, there are things I need to cover that require both you and Mrs Kerr to be here. And Mr Murray if that's possible. So I'd prefer to answer that question when they join us." Craig hated that he would have to gauge their reactions to his questions as if they were suspects - but that was the job.

"Oh yes, quite, quite. You have a job to do. But Brian is quite impossible to rouse. Perhaps I could bring him to meet you tomorrow?"

Craig nodded. Given the other deaths, Brian Murray wasn't high on his list of suspects. Tomorrow would do.

The Reverend rose to get his wife, lingering for a moment by the piano against the wall. He ran his hand over its mahogany lid, as if he was re-living a memory. "Do you enjoy music, Mr Craig?"

"Yes. My mother is a pianist."

"How wonderful for you. Evie played nicely you know. This was her piano." His eyes clouded over. "I must lock it now...her mother...you understand." Craig understood only too well. He would do the same the day his mother died.

"There's something else you should be aware of Mr Craig. Brian is quite feckless - he would admit that himself. And he has no close living family. He spent a much of his youth in care. So Miriam and I intend to seek custody of the baby, we feel it will give her a better chance. Mr Hill may contest it of course, but we have Brian's assurance that he supports us."

Craig nodded. He'd half expected it. "I doubt Mr Hill would win a custody battle, Reverend Kerr, given the circumstances."

"I believe in giving everyone second chances, so we will engage him in the child's life, of course. But not custody, you'll understand our reservations on that. Also Mr Craig...Miriam is desperately shocked by what has happened. I hate to ask, but you will take care when you question her, won't you?"

Craig nodded. "As far as I can. But I must be honest, there may be difficult moments. There's a great deal that neither of you are aware of yet."

The other man stared questioningly at him, then nodded and left the room. Craig sat waiting for Evie's mother to come down, his coffee untouched. He was dreading the encounter.

Miriam Kerr entered the room slowly. Her face wore the confused look that Craig had seen on many people who'd lost someone they loved. She was a small woman with short, dark hair and enormous brown eyes, dressed simply in a green floral skirt and cardigan. She looked just like the picture he'd seen of Evie, or how Evie would have been in twenty years. Her eyes were completely dead.

She crossed her arms, hugging herself, and sat down, turned half-away from him. She gazed out of the window at the trees, rocking slightly in her seat. And after five minutes of silence, broken only by the faint sound of traffic, she started to speak, in the softest voice that Craig had ever heard.

"Ask me anything that you like, Inspector. If I can first ask you...why are you here? Surely the police don't investigate hospital deaths? It's a medical issue. But the Sister told me that your men have been interviewing her staff all morning. Why? Why is that Mr Craig?"

Her accent echoed her husband's soft Antrim lilt, no trace of her harder origins on Belfast's Springfield Road leaking through. Craig had the impression that the change wasn't deliberate. She had simply loved a different man and lived a different life for twenty years. This wasn't the woman who had married Tommy Hill. Not in any way.

She turned to him with a dull look, and continued speaking before he could answer her.

"I know that you're trying to picture me with Tommy. It's all right, I don't mind. I've seen lots of people with that look before. But I was very young then, and he was very different...before The Troubles. That's no excuse for his actions. There'll never be an excuse for what Tommy did. But he changed from the man I married. And now he has to grieve for Evie, just as he left other families' grieving. God pays debts without money, Mr Craig."

Geoffrey Kerr sat down on the arm of his wife's chair, more dominant now in her defence.

"Why *are* the Police involved in Evie's death, Mr Craig? Do you think that there was medical malpractice? Is that why? I heard that Mr Hill said as much to the ward staff last night – quite loudly I believe."

"Reverend and Mrs Kerr..." Craig hesitated, finding the next words almost impossible to say. He'd thought about enlisting Geoffrey Kerr's help, by telling him that it was a murder enquiry before he brought his wife downstairs. But he needed to tell them both together, to gauge their immediate reactions. It was a sad thought and very unlikely, but even they were suspects in Evie's death until proven not.

"My team has become involved at the request of Dr John Winter, the Director of Pathology for Northern Ireland. He feels...I'm very sorry...but he feels that there may be irregularities in your daughter's death." He paused to let the words sink in.

"I want to be completely honest with you. But I must also insist on your complete confidence regarding everything I say now. And that includes not discussing anything with Mr

Murray. We will speak to him separately. Tomorrow." He stopped speaking until they both nodded, then continued. "There are things about your daughter's death that we need to clarify."

Miriam Kerr found her voice. "You mean medical negligence?"

"Perhaps. Or perhaps something..." He paused. God, he hated this job sometimes. "Something worse."

"But what could be worse than that?"

The sudden dawning of the truth on relatives was one of the hardest things that Craig had to deal with. And something that they all steeled themselves for, working in murder. That suspended moment when they realised that not only had they lost the person that they loved, but that someone had deliberately taken them away. There was nothing that could prepare the families. Or prepare the police for the pain that their honesty would inflict.

The wail that forced its way from Miriam Kerr froze her husband completely for a second. Then he moved quickly to grab her, before she fell from her seat onto the floor.

"Oh God, he's saying that Evie was murdered. Stop him saying that, stop him, Geoff."

Her soft brown eyes turned pitifully towards her husband, and tears edged rapidly from them and streamed across her cheeks. Geoffrey Kerr's eyes filled quickly in return. Craig felt like joining them, but he had to stay professional. He helped them back into their seats, their unguarded reactions underlining their barely-questioned innocence. Then he hunkered in front of Miriam Kerr, taking her hand.

"I'm so sorry, Mrs Kerr. I'd like to say that we don't believe it's murder." There, the word was out now... "Or that we don't believe it's even a possibility. But sadly we do. You see...Evie may not have been the first."

Geoffrey Kerr regained his composure and helped his wife across to a small settee. Then he held her in his arms while she cried and Craig continued. He asked them all the difficult questions. About any possible enemies that Evie and Brian or their families might have. Their answers yielded nothing except bewilderment, just as he'd expected. Evie and her husband were just innocent youngsters starting a family.

Then he outlined what they knew already, emphasising that they wouldn't stop searching until they'd caught those responsible for Evie's death.

He stayed with them for hours, answering their questions until the afternoon light faded; long after the liaison officer had arrived. Finally he gave Geoffrey Kerr his private number, outlining his availability, and his sorrow for the hurt that he knew he'd added to. Craig's frustration grew as he headed for his car, crunching angrily past the willow, definitely weeping now. All they could do for victims was find the killers. Then make sure that the case was so well sealed, that no arrogant bastard of a defence barrister would ever get them off.

He sat in the car for ten minutes listening to his messages. Nicky had worked wonders as she always did. He called her back, just to let her husky voice wash over him therapeutically.

"I finally got hold of the Chief Executive, sir. He can see you at six at their management offices. I've e-mailed you the map. Did you manage any lunch?"

He suddenly realised that he'd forgotten to eat again, the manse's cakes still untouched. "Don't worry, I'll grab a sandwich on the way. That's brilliant work, Nicky. Will he have his P.R. guy there?"

"For the last ten minutes as requested - it's all arranged. And I'll put everything for Warwick on your desk before I leave. I went round everyone and they're ready."

"Great. I'm in court tomorrow morning and at High Street all afternoon, so my phone will be off for most of the day. Just leave me messages and I'll get them. And see what you and Davy can find out for Dr Winter on the other two cases, please. He'll give you all the details."

"Other two cases?" His silence answered her, and she knew better than to push.

"That's grand, sir. I'll speak to you tomorrow. And remember to give that C.E.O.'s secretary a dirty look for me."

Chapter Seven

The Chief Executive's offices were in an old training centre on Belfast's leafy Knock Road. Craig wondered why they were so far out of town. Sure, it was a picturesque setting, near Shandon Park's popular golf club, but driving to the St Marys' site must have taken him ages. Then he realised it was equidistant from the Trust's six hospitals and that the unions had probably pushed for the equality. 'All about the politics' as usual. All it would achieve was high petrol bills and wasted time. Welcome to the public sector.

He arrived ten minutes early so he parked up and flicked on a Duke Special C.D. He listened to 'Lucky Me' and picked half-heartedly at the tuna roll he'd bought in transit, way past hungry. He was perusing a piece of lettuce warily, deciding it was too long dead, when his phone rang and John's name flashed up. He answered it quickly, grateful for the company.

"Hi John - what can I do for you?"

"Are you hungry?" The man was a mind reader. "I should be finished in an hour, and I was thinking of giving that place, Ivory, a turn. I can't be bothered cooking."

Translation. 'I'm too lazy even to microwave'.

Craig glanced at his watch, considering. Thirty minutes with the Chief Exec then sixty back at the ranch reading tomorrow's statements. Yes. John had rescued him from the lettuce, so the least he could do was rescue him from a salmonella dinner.

"You're on. I'll meet you there about eight, OK?"

"See you there - I'll be three drinks ahead by then."

The call ended with abrupt familiarity, giving Craig the nudge that he finally needed. He left the car and pressed the Management Offices' intercom. It was answered sharply by a woman and the door opened remotely to admit him.

The office block was pretty comfortable by public sector standards, but it was definitely no Michelin Building. There were steel-railed stairwells and peeling-paint walls, but at least the lift worked.

A frosty P.A. showed him into an oak-panelled office with Chief Executive marked on the door. A middle-aged man was sitting behind a modern plywood desk. It seemed incongruous in the room's wood-lined grandeur. The overall impression was the inherited oddment décor of a first home. The C.E.O. stood up urgently to shake Craig's hand, while the woman grudgingly took orders for tea, her lack of charm echoing Nicky's earlier description.

Charles McAllister was tall and nearly as round as his wide chair could hold. He had a florid complexion that probably owed a lot to outdoor pursuits...or alcohol. Craig thought that his clear eyes ruled out the booze, and he'd already noticed the golf-bag leaning against the wall. Shandon Park was handy then. He revised his earlier thoughts about the unions.

McAllister spoke quickly in a strong Northern English accent that Craig immediately recognised as Manchester. Shades of the Gallagher brothers. It was deep and thick, and without the cool intonation he was used to, from London and the south-east.

"Well Mr Craig, what can I do to help you? I'm sorry we're not meeting under better circumstances. It's a very sad business - mothers and babies touch us all."

"Yes it is, Mr McAllister."

"Charles."

"Charles." Craig didn't offer his name in return and McAllister quickly spotted the distinction, immediately on-guard.

"Before I outline the situation, I'll need your assurance that our conversation doesn't leave this room."

"Of course, whatever you say. But what are we talking about? And why are the police even involved? Isn't this straightforward medical negligence?"

"I'm sorry, but we believe it may be more than that. We're at the early stages of the investigation, but we're treating Mrs Murray-Hill's death as suspicious." He paused, watching the man's face carefully as each snippet of information sank in. "And we believe it may not be the first."

McAllister's' politeness slipped rapidly and his round face flushed bright red. "What in God's name do you mean, man? You're not talking about murder?"

Craig sat quietly, leaving the abrupt words hanging. He was never rude, just selectively polite. Or totally silent. McAllister filled the quiet with scores of agitated words while Craig listened. People often had whole conversations with themselves in front of him.

"Now look, Chief Inspector, I know that Nigel Murdock's practice has been queried for being ropey, and he's sky-high on my list for early retirement. But murder?"

"Why do you mention Mr Murdock?"

"Well, he was her consultant, wasn't he? And they're responsible for the patients."

McAllister's slight emphasis on 'they' was unmistakable, and Craig could see the buck about to be passed. McAllister's voice dropped suddenly, almost to a whisper, as he searched around for invisible listeners. Craig had seen it before. At the first sign of the police everyone thought they were in a TV series.

"Now, let's be very frank, Inspector. When I was brought in last August, it was initially in an interim role, now permanent. I was parachuted in to deal with major concerns about the last Chief Exec, Robert Moore. One of Stormont's biggest worries was the death and sickness rates of patients, for some consultants in particular. And Murdock was very high on their list."

He inhaled before restarting, tapping the table for emphasis. Craig noticed a pale line on his finger where his wedding ring used to be. Divorced or having problems? He shrugged to himself. High earners paid penalties that had nothing to do with Her Majesty's Revenue.

"The medical training here is good, but there's been a lack of organisation in some places. And some people have really 'played themselves'. Swinging the lead and what have you. They got away with murder, if you'll excuse the pun."

His voice grew more determined and Craig could see the leader emerging. "But that's all over now, mark my words. I was an engineer before I went into management, and avoiding risk has always been high on my list. Our accountability's in line with the rest of the UK now. Any old boy's network sheltering ropey practice has long gone.

That was a big part of my remit when they brought me in, and Moore and Murdock seem to have had a little network all of their own. There were rumours they were too chummy with the old head pathologist Davis as well. Lots of sick jokes about 'burying their mistakes' - you know the sort of thing. Anyway, rest assured any irregularities on this case will be dealt with. We've a hot-to-trot new Medical Director and he won't stand for any crap. So if it's Murdock's negligence that you're on to, then we're already there."

He stopped talking and took a long breath, satisfied that he'd defended himself against Craig's anticipated assault. Craig considered him coolly.

"That's excellent, Mr McAllister. But, and without pre-empting the outcome of our enquiries, we also have major concerns about a number of other cases. They were brought to our attention by Dr John Winter. Do you know Dr Winter?"

"I know *of* him, new Director of Path. He has a reputation for a very low shit tolerance."

"Indeed he has - and he's right."

McAllister caught the look in Craig's eyes and pushed his chair back, as if to escape what he was hearing. He was about to enter every Chief Executive's worst nightmare and he knew it.

"Dr Winter has brought two other cases to our attention which show striking similarities to today's. So we have more than enough concern to launch an enquiry. I really hope that we'll have your support. Investigations in hospitals always cause public anxiety and that's the last thing we want. Will we have your full co-operation, Charles?"

Craig's voice had hardened incrementally as he spoke. Now he was staring coolly at McAllister, weighing him up. The C.E.O.'s face reddened in panic at the mention of more cases.

"Of course, of course. Absolutely. But tell me about the other cases you mention. When did they occur? Was it before I arrived?"

His voice rose hopefully and Craig saw the Kevlar vest coming out. McAllister's face said he was about to distance himself from any blame. Terry Harrison obviously wasn't the only one made of Teflon.

"Which wards were they on? Are any other consultants implicated?" Then he added, hopefully. "What were the dates? I was in England on and off until November."

Craig sighed inwardly at his self-protection. But he knew McAllister would be no use covering his ass, so he decided to cut him some slack. Without naming names, he laid out all the facts. Yes, the cases had all occurred since he'd arrived, since January in fact. And they were all on the Maternity Unit. No, the patients weren't under anyone but Nigel Murdock. And, although another consultant had given an opinion on Evie's diabetes, they hadn't consulted on the first two cases, so they were low on the suspect list at the moment. Although that could always change.

Craig casually slipped in a question about McAllister's own

66

whereabouts on Monday evening, making a mental note that he'd been at home with his wife. Not divorced yet then. They'd be interviewing them both on the alibi.

The rest of the meeting was spent formulating a plan to tie down the risks. Maternity would be closed immediately, with services diverted to Bangor. They might have to suspend some staff members in the future, but not just yet. For now, all maternity staff would be on leave, pending investigation.

Craig knew that the press would come knocking once they sniffed a story, so when the P.R. manager joined them, they hammered out a press release to Ralph Jameson at The Telegram. He was the most responsible journalist Craig knew. Well, he could be trusted not to terrify people at least. The last thing they needed was 'Police Penalise Pregnant Women.' as tomorrow's headline. Craig sighed, knowing that no matter what they did, Ray Mercer at The Chronicle would write it anyway. The alliteration was already making his teeth hurt.

At 6.40 he finally stood up to leave. "Right, I'll run this past the superintendent before we give it to Jameson. We'll secure the Unit tonight with uniforms, and the staff can just deal with any emergencies that come in. Leave the statement with me. And no-one here speaks to the press please. I'm the S.I.O. so all queries come through me."

"What does S.I.O. stand for? The Board will want all the details." McAllister sighed heavily, exhausted by just thinking about the questions heading his way.

"Sorry, we use too many acronyms. Senior Investigating Officer."

"Yes - we have lots of those as well. Unfortunately everyone in the public sector suffers from A.R.S.E."

"What!" Craig stared incredulously at the professional man in front of him. He couldn't have heard him correctly.

"A.R.S.E.: Acronym Rich Service Environments. We work in them."

Craig laughed, making a note to tell Liam. He would love

it. Or maybe not - his language was bad enough already.

They shook hands, and Craig left for the rush-hour drive back to Belfast. And another hour's work before he met John.

***

The mousey-haired bouncer nodded Katy into Ten Square's bar with a smile. It was a bright spring evening outside, but the warm walls and wooden floors gave the bar a cosy autumn feel. She felt soothed immediately. The wine-bar was heaving with suited workers from the nearby banks and offices, and she couldn't see Natalie anywhere. Until a small hand waved frantically through the crooked elbow of a man at the bar.

Natalie's smiling face and dark hair popped into view and Katy laughed. It didn't matter that she was only five-foot tall, she always managed to get served somehow. Katy would have been standing there for hours. Natalie indicated a small table, where her coat was already draped across the chair. "I thought I'd get the drinks in. White wine spritzer OK?"

A small bottle appeared for Katy with the straw already in the neck. Natalie hefted a larger bottle of Sauvignon Blanc onto the table, falling heavily into her seat.

"God I'm wrecked. What a day. Owens was being a real get. He had me in theatre holding-up a leg for three hours! I thought my arm would fall off. But I wouldn't give him the satisfaction of admitting it."

She grinned and waited for Katy to laugh as she always did, but was greeted with complete silence. Katy was staring at the table, lost in thought. After a minute she realised Natalie had stopped speaking, and smiled apologetically.

"I'm sorry Nat, but I've had a shocking day. I warned you I wouldn't be much fun tonight."

"What happened?"

Natalie stared in horrified sympathy as Katy told her, springing immediately to her friend's defence.

"It's not your fault that she died, Katy, I'm sure it was something completely unrelated. Do you want me to come to the station with you tomorrow? I'm not scared of the police." Her fiery voice took on a wistful tone. "I know lots of people who work with them..."

Katy missed the nuance, deep in her own misery.

"Would you, Nat? That would be brilliant. To be honest I'm terrified. I've never been interviewed by the police, apart from giving expert testimony."

Natalie gave her a hug and nodded. Although she was a year younger, and tiny, she wasn't afraid of anyone. She called a spade a JCB and didn't care what people thought.

"Don't you worry, I'll ask Rowan to cover my theatre list and go with you. I won't let them bully you. I'll punch them in the knees if they even try!"

Katy managed a weak laugh but their drinks went untouched, as the horrors of medical negligence haunted both their thoughts. Finally they gave up on the wine, retreating to Katy's flat with a rented romantic comedy. It was Natalie's choice, although she wept all the way through it.

Katy didn't see the screen at all.

Chapter Eight

The Visitor was growing tired of the charade. It was a challenge to hide in plain sight. But in a few days the father would seek vengeance for Evie, and the guilty would be exposed. Then the police would arrest them all. Just a few more days until it was finally over.

Wednesday. 12pm.

"God, that was rough. But at least the Judge let the knife stay in."

Craig was running a finger under his collar like a strangling man. He finally gave up, ripping off his tie and opening his top button. Annette rarely saw him rattled, but murderers getting off topped his list of mood-altering events.

"They haven't won yet, sir. The trial's just started."

"But did you see Mrs Warwick's face when they tried to throw the knife out? I wish she wouldn't come to court, Annette. It's killing her hearing the details."

"I tried to stop her, but she wouldn't listen. Look sir, you know they'll try every trick in the book to acquit. But we have it tight enough. You'll see."

"Aye boss, sure the whole justice system sucks and we all know it. It's always on the side of the scrotes. In the good old days her Da would've just got a gun and done the job himself." Craig knew that he should say something disapproving, but he didn't have the energy or the inclination.

Just then Liam tensed. Roger Doyle and his black-suited

posse of barristers had walked up behind Craig before he could warn him. Doyle was pontificating loudly to his juniors and his affected drawl made Liam want to deck him.

"Well...round one to us, don't you think? Given that the prosecution's evidence is circumstantial, I think our client should walk free very soon. Justice must be done, you know."

Craig knew that he was meant to hear and he glared at Doyle in disgust. He wondered, as he often did, what kind of man defended the ones he knew were guilty. But discussion outside the court-room was forbidden. And Doyle would just trot out the 'every man deserves a defence' crap that they'd heard so many times before, usually from ambitious barristers out to make a name for themselves.

John said he'd like to devise a version of the movie SAW, just for defence barristers...

Craig's silence spoke volumes, so Doyle shrugged and indicated his juniors with a sweep of his hand. "We're off to the Harbour View for lunch, after a very successful morning."

Annette caught Liam's angry look and quickly stood between the three men.

"We have a meeting, Mr Doyle." Then she grabbed Craig and Liam by the elbows and wheeled them towards the patrol car, before testosterone got the better of them.

"What meeting?"

"Be quiet, Liam." She turned to Craig. "Let's go to The James for lunch, sir. We have interviews all afternoon."

It was a statement not a question. At times like these Annette went into 'mum-mode', with damage limitation her main aim.

"I just need to speak to the Warwicks, Annette."

"No you don't sir, not today. With respect, they won't want to hear it."

Craig nodded. She was right. "OK. Lunch is on me then."

"Aye, that'll do, boss. We can comfort-eat. Well, that's what Danni calls it when she's shovelling-in the chocolate."

Annette raised her eyes in sympathy with Liam's long suffering wife and climbed into the car.

The patrol car dropped them by the boarded-up Rotterdam Bar in Pilot Street. They wandered past the once-famous venue onto the reclaimed land of Barrow Square, then over the tram lines in Princes Dock Street, towards The James.

Liam grabbed a small table inside, arguing it was too breezy to sit out, despite the sun. "I'm not getting dirt in my chips, even for you two." Just at that moment, a seagull swooped low enough to make his point and they conceded.

They relaxed to the sound of Anthony Toner's 'Sailortown' as the bar's older occupants gazed out the window, remembering the thriving area before the developers had come.

"Annette, give Nicky a call and invite her to join us please. She can divert the phones to my mobile for an hour."

Liam lit up immediately. "Excellent idea." He had a real soft spot for Nicky. They were both happily married and neither would have taken it further, but their innocent office flirting amused everyone. Nicky was as sharp as a whip and handled Liam's banter brilliantly.

Craig's mobile rang and he coloured, recognising the caller. Liam smiled to himself. Craig had been dating D.I. Julia McNulty lately. And although he didn't say how it was going and they'd never ask, at least it took him away from work occasionally.

Craig waited until it cut to answerphone and then turned the phone to silent. He wouldn't call her back at work. Julia would understand - work took priority for both of them.

The welcome sight of food coming towards the table interrupted his thoughts, just as Annette came back in. "Sorry, sir, Nicky had to take Jonny to view a school. She can't make lunch."

Liam's face dropped.

"There, there Liam, you'll see her later."

"Ach, away on with you…she's just good craic." But his red flush gave him away. "Anyway, what do mean view a school?"

"You've all this ahead of you with Erin and Rory. Jonny's doing his transfer test before he moves to secondary school."

"Thank God, I've eight more years before that."

They ate in silence for a moment until Annette broke it. "I meant to tell you something, sir…it's about Nigel Murdock."

"What about him?"

"Well…I was chatting to my friend Jo last night. She's a Sister I trained with, and she works in Obstetrics now. Anyway, I happened to mention Murdock, just by-the-by."

"Annette…behave yourself. We have nothing on him yet."

"No honestly, I didn't give anything away. It was just medical gossip. If you think the police force is small then the health service here is even smaller. Everyone knows everyone."

Craig shot her a slight frown, but he was curious. "Go on."

"Anyway, it seems that old Nigel gets up to all sorts of stuff, but no one's been able to touch him for years. He's been reported by patients loads of times. But his best mate from Windsor College, Robert Moore, was the C.E.O. His other mate was Alan Davis, Dr Winter's predecessor, so he was flameproof. Now Moore's been sacked and this new guy McAllister has been brought in from Manchester to shake things up. So they're all hoping that Murdock finally gets his."

Craig nodded slowly. It tallied with what he already knew. Annette leaned forward, dropping her voice.

"There's more, sir, and this *is* gossip. But Jo's a reliable source. Apparently Murdock and his wife, she's one of the Burton family, her grandfather made a fortune out of the ships. Anyway, apparently they belong to a racy little sailing crowd up in Cultra. There are rumours about their wild house parties. Car keys being chucked into the fruit bowl and white powder up the nose."

'Coke and Key Parties'. Craig had dealt with them in London.

"Jees, you're joking, Annette! They're swopping their women? What do you think I'd get for swopping Danni?"

"A thick ear, if I tell her."

Liam smiled sheepishly. "Ach now, you know I wouldn't change her for the world. But tell me more about this wife-swopping. I have to get my thrills at arm's length these days."

"Well...apparently Murdock's crowd are known locally as the White Waves."

A confused look crossed Liam's face.

"You know. Because of the boats."

"And the Cocaine, I imagine, Annette."

"Oh aye. I see now."

Craig picked at his food thoughtfully. "It's just gossip, but the drugs aspect is interesting."

He thought for a moment. "We can't dig deeper on the drugs without getting warrants, but it's useful background. Follow it through carefully, Annette, and do a bit more digging on any complaints made against Murdock. But without contacting the Trust just yet please. Nicky and Davy are looking at the professional side, so work with them on it.

Look at Murdock being under the influence of anything at work; legal or illegal. But quietly, please. The last thing we need is a harassment charge, and he sounds just the sort. I'll have another word with John and see what he knows on the drugs score."

Craig stopped. "Liam, did Joe check McAllister's alibi?"

"Aye, his wife confirmed he was home all night. But Joe said that she was wild shifty, wouldn't look him in the eye at all. And wives *have* told wee lies for hubbies in the past, so I'll dig a bit deeper there."

"OK, go ahead. Just be aware that the marriage many be ropey." He told them about McAllister's ring and his suspicions. "His appointment to St Marys was before the murders started, so he's not off my hook just yet. See what else you can get when you interview him, unless he insists on me."

"Aye OK. Here, I've found out about the Private Surgery, the place they had their baby scans. It's in the private patient's wing of the M.P.E., up near the paediatric wards. The private wing has a contract with the Trust. I had a word with them and the scans were done by two different female doctors, both juniors at St Marys. I've put them both up for interview. But to be fair, anyone could have accessed the notes on the computer and known the babies were girls."

Craig nodded. It was a dead end, he was sure of it.

"The man we need to talk to in the Drugs Squad is Karl Rimmins, boss. He knows all about Tommy's little operations. He's one of Andy White's team."

"Right, I'll nip down and see Andy later."

Annette interjected sheepishly. "Sir, I asked Jo about Beth Walker as well." Craig raised an eyebrow at her.

"No, honestly - she really didn't know why I was asking. Anyway, it seems that Beth's well-liked by everyone, especially by her patients. But she gets a hard time from some of the higher-ups for her lifestyle. You saw the purple hair - well apparently it was green last year. And she's very open about being lesbian. She hangs out at Sarajevo a lot - that's a gay club in town. But there's a steady girlfriend on the scene. She works in a bank. Shall I dig there a bit as well?"

"Yes...but softly Annette. Remember we have nothing firm on either Murdock or Walker yet. You're interviewing Brian Murray this afternoon aren't you?"

"Yes."

"OK. I know I don't need to tell you, but be careful with him. The Kerrs said he was in a real state yesterday. The G.P. had to be called."

"Will do, sir"

"What'll I do, boss?"

"See if Karl Rimmins has anything on Murdock and Tommy Hill. And don't you worry Liam. You'll be busy enough, trying to stop us telling Danni what you said about swopping her!"

***

"Close that bloody door, McCrae. I don't want that nosy cow next door listenin' in. She spends her days doin' nothin' but hangin' over her hedge. An' her brother's a bloody Peeler."

Rory McCrae banged the front door shut and scanned the small, cold living-room. Its décor was sparse and beige, unchanged since the 80's when Tommy went inside. It seriously needed a woman's touch. Or a decorator's.

A draught was sifting through the dirty net curtains and Hill was sitting on the room's only chair, an old stuffed recliner. His cracked leather car-coat was pulled tightly round him. "Away into the kitchen an' grab a chair, McCrae. An' put the kettle on while you're at it."

McCrae returned a minute later gripping a hard-backed foldaway, with its tied cushion falling off. He turned it around so that his arms rested on the back. Only his inner thighs rested on the seat, their full muscles spilling over the edge. He was as large and wide as Hill was wiry, but his bulk didn't give him any sort of edge. Tommy ruled by history and legend. People still stared when he walked down the street.

"I was wild sarry to hear about your Evie, Tommy – she was a real queen. How's the babby? Wee girl I heard."

He stared deferentially at the floor, focusing there while Tommy swallowed. Neither man said anything for a few minutes, until finally Hill broke the silence. He spoke so quietly that the other man strained to hear him.

"I need you to do some stuff for me, McCrae. The Pigs ar saying it's suspicious."

"Suspicious! God aye, Tommy, no worries. I'm with you. What kin I do to help? Whatever it takes. Do you know what happened? Is it one of them doctors not doing their job? Or...do...do they think its murder then?"

Hill sat forward so violently that his face nearly hit the other man's.

"What do you fuckin' mean, murder? Why wud anyone murder our Evie? She was brilliant. Ar you trying to say this is someone gettin' at me, that it's *my* fault she's bin killed?"

Saliva gathered at the edge of Hill's mouth, and his eyes burned into Rory McCrae's face. McCrae reared back in fear, nearly falling off his chair.

"Fuck no, Tommy. That's not what I meant. Honest to God Tommy, it wasn't. It was just...when you said the Peelers was gittin' involved. Sarry Tommy, sarry. God I'm sarry. Evie was a lovely wee girl. No affence meant Tom. Fuck no."

A hostile stillness fell over the room, until eventually McCrae scraped his chair back, standing up as if to leave.

"Where the fuck do you think you're goin'?"

The snarl in Hill's words made McCrae sit down again rapidly. Tommy sat forward sharply and clasped his hands. Whiteness spread up from his knuckles throwing his forearm tattoo into focus. His voice was low and cracking.

"The Pigs is on the bloody slow track as usual. An' I'm not waitin' for them to drop the ball like they alays do. I'm sortin' this out mysel', an' I need you and the lads to help."

"Tommy, you know me, Gerdy and Coyler will be there. Whatever you need, just you say the word."

Hill stared down at the worn carpet. "If someone delibertly did for my Evie, then they're fuckin' well dead. They just haven't stopped breathin' yet. But they will, as soon as I know their name. I don't give a shite if they throw me in Maghaberry. It'll be worth it to put a bullet in their fuckin' hed."

He glared at the younger man, saliva covering his thin lips. His hoarse voice was harder than Rory McCrae had ever heard it. "This is goin' the whole length this time McCrae. I mean it."

McCrae smiled. This was just like the good old days. "Now

77

yer talkin, boss"

"It had to be someone who was with her last night. Gotta be. I saw al' three of them docs 'n nurses in an' out of her room al' evenin'. No-one else was there but her Ma. An' she'd rather die than hurt our Evie. That wee shite Murray was there too. The first time the wee fucker had been there al' week. He'll need to be knocked off soon."

McCrae smiled, hopeful of getting the job.

"One of them killed her but I don't know which one yet. So I want them *all* fallyed. I need enuf men to tail the three of them, so git your lads together. Meet me tomara night at eight. Up at the centre, near the Windsor playing fields. I'll get the info you need for then. I'm fallyin' that stuck- up prick Murdock myself. I need you lot to tail Murray, the lezzie nurse, an' the blonde Doc 'til I say so."

"I'll have the blonde."

Hill stared coldly at him.

"You put your dick away, McCrae. No-one gits touched except the fucker who killed our Evie. Do you hear me? An' no-one touches the weemen, unless they did it. Then you can do whatever you want with them, *after* I've killed them. For now, just watch them an' report back to me. And keep away from the Pigs. They don't git told nothin' that they don't need to know."

McCrae laughed nervously. "Aye, Tommy. Treat the Peelers like mushrooms, keep them in the dark an' feed them crap, ha ha. I'll get the lads and see you here tomara night."

"Not' here, for fucks sake. Wise up and listen. At the centre, near Windsor fields..."

"Sarry, sarry. The centre, that's right." McCrae stood up and headed for the door.

"Where the fuck do you think you're goin'?

Hill's rasping voice spat menace and the bigger man froze, waiting for permission to move.

"Get in there now an' make my fuckin' tea."

Chapter Nine

The Visitor found it hard to focus on this temporary life, when the real pull was towards exposing the guilty. But it was necessary. Food had to be eaten and bills had to be paid, and the job gave access. And without that of course, there would be nothing.

One of the guilty ones walked onto the Unit, preening. Walking the corridors as if they were hers. Straight-backed, head in an arrogant child's pose. Spoilt and self-indulgent like her type always were. Talking down to some faceless companion.

Soon Tommy Hill would expose the truth for the whole world to see. And then there would finally be justice.

***

"Hi Nicky, could you get everyone in the briefing room at four, please. I'll be finished at High Street by then. I need Joe Rice from uniform and Karl Rimmins from Drugs there as well. Also, could you give John a call, and see if he can send us through a quick update. Thanks. I'm switching my phone off now. If you need me urgently contact High Street, otherwise I'll be back before four."

Craig shut his phone off quickly and walked down Belfast's High Street into the station. He was resigned to an afternoon in a dimly lit room, and intent on begging a coffee from the duty sergeant, Jack Harris.

It was a short walk to the city centre's cafes and he could

always go for one there, but it was better to stay in the station and chat. Relationships built over the years were worth a fortune, as Liam often proved. As well as being great craic.

He never tired of Jack's stories. He'd been the sergeant at High Street throughout The Troubles and there was little that he hadn't seen. He was one of the most laid-back men Craig had ever met. And one of the most astute.

Craig pulled open the heavy street door and noticed two people sitting on the bench in reception. A slim woman sat several feet away from a well-fed, expensive looking man. Sleek was the word that best described him. He looked just like a surgeon. Not that Craig had anything against doctors. It was John who was hard on his own. But his air of unquestioned authority was easily identifiable.

If he was Nigel Murdock he could wait until after coffee. He was too early anyway. And Craig wanted him off-balance, in the way that only prolonged waiting could achieve.

The woman sat with her head down, but there was no missing how pretty she was. Fine-featured and blonde, with a light tan. She was hard to miss in the drab surroundings of the station. It was like seeing a flower growing through tarmac.

Craig pressed the desk buzzer and stepped back from the outward opening door. His foot knocked over the woman's handbag, and a sheaf of papers fell out onto the floor. He bent to retrieve them, his face flushed with embarrassment.

"I'm sorry. That was clumsy of me."

He held the papers out towards her, looking down at her still-bowed head. Without looking up she said softly. "Please just leave them on the seat. Thank you." And continued reading her book, as if it contained the most fascinating words ever written.

Craig felt like a sixteen-year-old boy, knocked-back by the prettiest girl in school. He left the papers and turned back quickly towards the door, trying to regain his composure. Jack Harris was already standing there, amply filling the doorway.

"Hello there, sir. Come on in."

Craig entered gratefully, walking quickly through to the staff room. He wondered if Jack had seen everything and carefully timed his rescue. If he had noticed the episode he was far too discrete to comment, and Craig morphed back to his forty-something self over coffee.

They chatted comfortably for ten minutes, about the weather and the latest Northern Ireland match. Craig's father had held a season-ticket since George Best had played for them and David Healy had renewed his zeal.

Jack followed every game so Craig just relaxed and listened. Letting a five minute commentary on the last match at Windsor Park flow pleasantly over him.

A few minutes later the door was knocked quietly. The desk constable, Sandi, a dark-eyed girl about twenty, entered, looking strained. She spoke anxiously, hardly pausing for breath.

"Sorry sir, but that man in reception's really not happy. He says he'd been waiting thirty minutes. I pointed out that he was early; his appointment isn't for five minutes yet. But then he phoned his solicitor, and now he says he's not seeing anyone until she arrives. That could be another twenty minutes. She's coming round from Victoria Street. Morris and Harden's Solicitors, sir. Sorry, sir."

"Sandi, take a breath love. And don't keep apologising. Wait till you've done something wrong first. And I'll tell you when that is, never you worry."

"Yes sir. Sorry sir."

"Is Dr Stevens here? The three o'clock."

"Yes sir, in reception now."

"Does *she* want a brief?"

"No sir. At least she hasn't said, sir. Should I ask her?"

"Don't you bother your head asking her. Just show her into the interview room and tell her that D.C.I. Craig will be through in a minute. And give whoever's out there a cup of tea."

He shook his head kindly, like Craig imagined he'd done when his kids were small. Sandi flushed to the tip of her chin and turned to put the kettle on. Craig moved to help her get out the mugs. He was being kind but he also had an ulterior motive. He wanted to ask her something, without Jack overhearing.

"Sandi, is Dr Stevens the lady who was in reception when I came through?"

"Yes, sir."

Craig's stomach dropped like turbulence at thirty thousand feet and he mentally gave himself 'The Lecture'. Get a grip man, *you're* in charge, remember that. Nope, it wasn't working. He was even more embarrassed by his assumption that Dr Stevens would be male. Lucia would have a field day with that one.

Jack didn't need to hear the exchange to know exactly what was being said. He gazed at them over his glasses, smiling at Craig's discomfort. He was a grown man, but only three years older than his boy Euan, so Jack felt he had parental rights.

"These doctors are getting bonnier every day, aren't they now..?"

Craig smiled at him. "Something you'd like to say, Jack?"

"No, no...Just an observation, sir. But I think you've finished making that tea, don't you? Off you go now, mustn't keep a lady waiting."

Chapter Ten

2.40pm.

Katy was sitting in the interview room still reading her book, when Craig came in. She didn't look up when he entered, despite him willing her to. She felt even more nervous than she'd expected to, and it wasn't helped by Natalie being delayed. She just prayed that she was outside when they finished.

Craig pulled-up a chair and sat across the table at a slight angle. Facing her straight-on felt wrong somehow - too confrontational.

"Dr Stevens, I'm D.C.I. Craig. Thank you for coming in. It would be helpful if you could answer some questions. Anything you can tell us about your involvement with Mrs Murray-Hill would be useful."

Katy glanced up from her book without making eye contact. Then she held her hand out to be shaken, in what seemed like an oddly formal gesture. Her hand trembled slightly when Craig took it and he realised that she was nervous too. The knowledge rescued him from a repeat of his adolescent backslide.

When her words eventually came, they were so soft that they were almost a whisper. Craig asked her to repeat them.

"I said I hate this! I feel like a criminal."

"We just need your help, Dr Stevens."

At the sound of her name she gazed at him across the table. Her eyes were large and petrol blue, set wide apart in a heart-shaped face. Everything about her seemed fragile, set in such stark surroundings. He felt almost protective of her, until he saw the flash of anger in her gaze.

"For God's sake, don't you think I wish I *could* help you? But not half as much as I wish I could have helped that poor girl. She's dead, it's too late and we killed her. One of us, all of us, it doesn't matter. It's our fault."

She stopped abruptly, her eyes dropping back to the table. Then after a moment's pause she spoke again, her voice heavy with emotion. "She's dead and her child's alone."

Craig realised that she was edging towards tears and rose hurriedly to open the door, sensing the danger of them being alone. Then he lifted the phone to call Sandi in.

"I think it would be better if you had some support, Dr Stevens. Police interviews can be upsetting. Would you like a glass of water?" She nodded quickly.

"Constable Masters, could you cover the desk and join us please. And bring a glass of water? Thanks." Sandi appeared quickly, and took the seat beside Katy on his nod.

"Dr Stevens, I know how upsetting this must be and I'd like to minimise that. So how would it be if we taped this interview, to avoid future repetition?" She nodded silently.

"Good." He pressed the recorder.

"For the benefit of the tape, it is Wednesday the 10th of April 2013 at two-forty pm. This interview is being held at High Street station. Present for the tape is..."

"Dr Katherine Stevens, 69a St John's Harbour, Belfast."

"W.P.C. Sandra Masters."

"And D.C.I. Craig. Now Dr Stevens, in your own words, please tell me about all your encounters with Mrs Murray– Hill."

Katy recounted the process that had brought her to see and treat Evie. The meetings with her and Tommy Hill. And the tests, results and treatment prescribed. Then she brought out the papers that had fallen from her handbag earlier. They were copies of Evie's tests and charts. Craig had already seen them but he took them again politely, thanking her as she handed them across.

"Thank you for that. That brings us to the day before Mrs Murray-Hill's death – Monday the 8th of April. Could you tell me about your movements that day please? And particularly about any meetings you had with or about her."

Katy relaxed slightly and as her voice grew clearer and stronger, Craig could see the professional asserting herself. "I called to see her several times on Monday, because she was due for her Caesarean soon. It should have been today at three, in fact. About now." She paused, re-starting after a sip of water.

"I wanted to keep an eye on her tests and be there to assess the baby with the paediatricians if necessary. She was absolutely fine. Except…she can't have been fine, can she? Or she wouldn't be dead." Her voice rose slightly in volume then she fell silent again. Craig waited, smiling slightly at her in encouragement.

Katy had an incongruous thought that he was very handsome. He had slight sideburns and she'd always liked those on men. Then she felt guilty about such a frivolous thought when a woman was dead, and re-started, more professionally.

"I last saw her at nine on Monday night. I know that was the time because I was recording her blood sugars on a chart. We did other tests as well, and they were all fine. The results are there."

She pointed at the paper in front of him, then realised that it was rude to point, pulling her hand back quickly. Her fingers were long and slim, with clear oval nails. And he noticed that she wore no rings.

"She hadn't been diabetic for long and it was very mild. It would probably have disappeared after the birth, until perhaps her next pregnancy." She realised what she'd said, and her voice faded away painfully. Craig could see sadness written on her face and something occurred to him.

"When did you become a consultant, Dr Stevens?"

She glared at him defensively and her voice hardened. "Why? How is that any of your business?" Then she realised how she sounded. "I'm sorry. I don't mean to be rude. It's just ..."

Craig knew from John that it was a long path to becoming a medical consultant. Her sex couldn't have made it any easier. She'd probably spent every day proving herself to dickheads like Murdock. Sandi gave her a sympathetic look that said she understood completely.

"I was made consultant in December. This is my first consultant post and my first job in Belfast in thirteen years. I went to London immediately after graduation, so I'm still settling back." Craig nodded, remembering how displaced he'd felt when he'd returned home five years before.

"Shall we continue with the events of the 8th of April, Dr Stevens?"

She nodded tiredly, restarting. "I saw Evie at nine pm and stayed with her for about twenty minutes. I was examining her at first, and then, well just chatting really. She was so excited about the baby. She told me that her husband Brian had been down earlier with her Mother."

"Did you ever meet either of them?"

"No. I saw her mother once. She was at the end of the ward chatting to Beth. That's the midwife. The only person I'd actually met and spoken to was her father, Mr Hill."

"How did you know the woman you saw was her mother?"

She smiled slightly. "Well, I didn't for sure, but I think it was. Evie was very like her." Craig nodded. He'd noticed the resemblance at the Manse.

"How did you find Mr Hill when you met him?"

She smiled ruefully and Craig noticed her teeth. They were white and pretty. How could anyone have pretty teeth?

"Honestly? I thought he was scary. He was concerned

about Evie of course, but... Well it just seemed that everything about him carried some sort of threat. I'm not sure how exactly, but that's the feeling I got. He was polite enough, just scary."

Craig nodded coolly, not giving anything away. He recognised her description from every career criminal he'd met. Years of violence and greed ingrained in every pore.

"Please continue."

"When I left Evie, I noticed Beth at the other end of the ward. So I waved at her. We've known each other for years."

It occurred to Craig that she might be gay and he pushed the thought away. None of his business if she was.

"She seemed busy, so I left, intending to check on Evie the next day. I was going to my office to do some letters. I had to stay around the M.P.E. because we were covering admissions that night. Anyway, I was on my way there when I noticed Mr Hill standing outside the ward, smoking. He was in the patio garden between the glass corridors, so I went to have a word with him. He was devoted to Evie so I just wanted to assure him everything was fine.

We chatted for about five minutes, or should I say he interrogated me again. But he seemed happier when I left. I had the impression that the baby meant almost as much to him as to Evie somehow. Anyway, just as I left I saw Mr Murdock approaching. He was on the parallel corridor, so we didn't actually cross paths. Then I went to my office to work."

"Where is your office?"

"In the old part of the hospital, at the back. It used to be the Dunmore Medical Centre."

Craig nodded, remembering it from his youth. It had been a student health centre.

"All the consultants' offices are there now - in the Admin Suite."

"Did anyone see you there?"

She bristled immediately. "Yes actually, they did, Chief

Inspector. Tell me something Mr Craig, am I a suspect in something here? Apart from obviously missing something that could have saved my patient's life?"

She leaned forward angrily and he noticed how blue her eyes were, pushing the thought away quickly. "Don't you think I feel bad enough without having to give you alibis?"

Craig considered her calmly. She was an interesting combination of gentleness and force. The only other woman he'd encountered that in was Julia. It was an attractive and dangerous mix. He sat back in his chair, distancing himself.

"I understand that this is difficult Dr Stevens, but it *is* routine. We've already asked all your colleagues. So please just answer the question."

His voice had become firmer, as if that somehow compensated for his whole body's inclination to give her a free-pass. She sat back defiantly for a moment, hating him. As she stared him out he realised that she looked like someone he knew. His ex-fiancée Camille! The only woman who'd ever broken his heart. It made her even more dangerous and he moved his chair back slightly. When she finally spoke she ground the words out.

"Iain was there."

"Iain?"

"Yes, Dr Iain Lewes. He's a paediatrician. He checks out all the new babies." Then she smiled, distracted for a moment. "Evie's baby's beautiful, I saw her this morning. Have you seen her?" She immediately felt foolish, realising that he was unlikely to be interested.

"No, I haven't seen her, but I've been told she's lovely." His voice softened and Katy smiled, liking him a bit more.

"I first knew Evie was dead yesterday afternoon. I was intending to go and check her at five after my meeting at St Marys, when my P.A. phoned to tell me. I wasn't called to either Evie or the baby on Monday night. I wasn't even aware that she had been born." She looked sad, remembering. "Evie was declared dead in theatre, by Mr Murdock. I think it was at four-twenty, but you'll have those notes already." She hesitated for a moment.

"Mr Hill rang my office yesterday and shouted at my secretary. But that's totally understandable, it was just grief talking."

Craig didn't want to frighten her, so he parked the comment for later action. Maybe it was just Tommy's grief talking, but he wouldn't put a bet on it. The room fell silent for a moment, and only the tape's slight buzz was audible. Eventually Craig broke the quiet. "Thank you, Dr Stevens, that's nearly everything now. I'm sorry if this has been stressful. I only have one question left."

She gazed up at him and he could see that her eyes were wet.

"Why do you keep saying it's your or the other staff's fault that Evie is dead? Surely you did your best to help her?"

She shook her head slowly, weariness settling on her slim shoulders. "When someone comes into hospital, they trust us. If not to make them better, then at least not to make them worse. So if someone, especially someone so young and fit, dies, then it has to be our fault. You must see that?

If we'd done our jobs better she would be alive now. But she's dead, so someone failed her. I don't believe in medical accidents, Mr Craig, it's always someone's fault. Beth will tell you the same. I know she will."

Craig regarded her carefully, his eyes searching her slim face. It was tempting to be cynical. So many people were liars, and some people lied like it was their hobby. But he'd never managed it completely, because he knew there were good people. He just got to meet more of the bad. Finally he nodded and pressed off the tape, watching as she relaxed. "Thank you for coming in, Dr Stevens. I hope we won't have to bother you again. But please, if Mr Hill gets in touch with you, or you have any questions, don't hesitate to call us." He produced a card from his pocket.

"This is the squad number and you can access me 24/7. We give this information to everyone we interview."

Sandi turned her head away quickly, but not before he caught the start of her smile. Craig shot her a pleading look. Thankfully Katy missed the exchange.

"Thank you Chief Inspector, but I don't think he'll bother me again. He was just lashing out. But it's reassuring, thank you."

He didn't put out his hand to shake, knowing it was just his excuse to touch her again.

"Sandi, could you show Dr Stevens out please. And ask Sergeant Harris if he's free for a moment."

When they emerged Natalie was sitting in reception, noticeably ignoring Nigel Murdock. She fixed Sandi with a chastising glare and cosseted Katy like a mother. Then they left the station as if it was on fire. Sandi watched them head across the road to The Merchant Hotel, perhaps for a drink. She wished she was going too, instead of having six more hours to work.

Jack popped his head around the door of the interview room.

"Jack, I need Tommy Hill watched. Do you know who's on for the Demesne Estate these days?"

"Reggie Boyd's team."

"Ask them to keep an eye out, will you? They can link back with Liam. Dr Stevens's putting Tommy's threats down to shock and grief and that's definitely the trigger. But you and I know him of old."

"We do indeed. Leave that with me, sir." He paused and smiled at Craig. "Nice wee thing, isn't she?" Craig treated the question as rhetorical, and Jack smiled wisely.

"Is Murdock's brief here yet?"

"Not yet. And he's got steam coming out of his ears."

"All the more reason to have another coffee and let him

stew. Anyway, we need to choose the Fantasy League for the FIFA Cup."

As they walked into the back office Craig pulled a tenner from his pocket. He turned to Sandi.

"I don't suppose I could persuade you to nip out for some donuts, Sandi? I need to check in with Nicky."

She smiled, admonishing him gently. "Now, sir, you know that's not in my job description."

"Quite right too, Sandi. That's you told off, sir."

Craig smiled an apology. It wasn't sexism. He'd often done the donut run when he was a constable. But things were different nowadays. He was just about to put the note away when Jack snatched it from his hand and opened the reception door.

"However, I have no such principles and I'm starving. Sandi, you watch the desk and I'll nip out. They do Krispy Kremes three doors down." He patted his stomach and grinned, heading off while Craig made his call.

"Hi Nicky – do you need me for anything?" He listened for a few seconds, as she outlined a query from the records department.

"That's fine, it can wait. I'm back at four. Could you call Liam and ask him to check out a Dr Iain Lewes, please. He's a paediatrician at the Trust. Ask him to verify his movements on Monday night. I need to know if he was in the consultant's offices after nine on Monday night. And, if he saw Dr Katy Stevens there. He's her alibi." He listened for a moment longer, then said. "Fine, bye." clicking his phone shut just in time for a glazed ring.

When it finally happened, the interview with Nigel Murdock went exactly where Craig had expected. Nowhere. His glamorous solicitor made him to answer 'no comment' to so many questions, that virtually all they got was his name and that he'd been Evie's consultant.

He was willing to confirm that she'd been well when he'd

91

called in at nine on Monday evening. And that he hadn't expected to be called back that night at all. Her Caesarean wasn't due, and anyway the registrar would have been carrying it out when it was! The last piece of information was stated as if she'd somehow inconvenienced him by dying. Craig was starting to loathe the man.

"Can you tell me what happened at four-twenty on Tuesday morning, Mr Murdock?" Murdock glanced at his solicitor and she nodded. Then he turned back to Craig with a sneering smile. He had a very ugly expression. Each feature taken separately might have worked, but put together, he resembled an arrogant ex-boxer. One who'd taken too many punches. Craig recognised old rugby injuries in his upper lip scarring, and sincerely hoped that they'd hurt him. A lot.

"Waaall..." He drawled the word loudly in a Cultra accent. No question about it, this man was the product of too much in-breeding. "Of course...she was dead before we got to theatre. Just being oxygenated so that I could get the child out. Which I did, through the usual Pfannenstiel incision. I saved its life of course."

There was no emotion apparent in the man except pride at his own expertise. Craig compared his coldness to Katy Stevens' groundless guilt, and wanted him out of the station fast, before he hit him. He wrapped up the interview quickly, pressing the tape recorder off far too hard. There was nothing to be gained from sitting opposite this 'no commenting' slug, except a headache.

"Thank you for coming in Mr Murdock. That's all for now, we'll be in touch. The W.P.C. will show you out." He rang through for Sandi and left the room so quickly that even the jaded solicitor seemed surprised. Then he walked straight past Jack, through the side-door and into the parking lot, sucking hard at the fresh air.

Jack followed him out and stood beside him, shaking his head. "Some people make you want to bring back the stocks."

Craig laughed out loud despite his anger. "They had stocks outside the Rotterdam Bar until the nineties. Could we re-instate them for obnoxious bastards? What do you think, Jack? A memo to headquarters might do it."

"I'm sure they get worse suggestions than that."

Craig stood for a moment, relaxing. Then he stood up straight, mentally deleting the last half-hour, and Nigel Murdock. "Right, here we go. Last interview and then back to the ranch. Has Beth Walker arrived yet?"

"Aye.... she has that. And a bit worse for wear too. I'll send Sandi in. With two extra strong coffees this time..."

***

Liam yawned and stretched, gazing around the small ward room they'd been allocated for interviews. It was windowless and airless and he was fighting hard not to fall asleep. He had print-outs of Davy's background checks in front of him. Most people had been relegated to the 'innocent' pile, but one still sat there, read and re-read. Charles McAllister's.

It read like an example of the perfect life. Good school, good university, health service management scheme and on up through the ranks. Hardly a post lasting longer than two years before promotion to the next rung. He was only forty-five and this was his third Chief Exec's post, each time running bigger trusts. Until now he ran St Marys. One of the largest in the UK.

What was even more interesting was that he'd done it without the traditional executive's stay-at-home wife. With 2.4 kids trotted out for photo opportunities, to gaze up at him adoringly. In real life, Mrs McAllister was a partner at Feeney's Accountants. And there were no photo-ops and no kids; whether by fate or design. Then there was her avoiding Joe's eyes when she gave McAllister his alibi.

No, something was wrong here. It was all too perfect, and

Liam didn't like 'perfect'.

He got a sudden ache in his shoulder and nodded to himself. He always got it when there was something not quite right. And there was something very 'not right' about Charles McAllister. He was up to his eyes in something. But what?

He yawned again and then lifted the phone to the squad, catching Davy at his desk. "Davy son, I need a wee word…"

Chapter Eleven

Beth Walker was definitely the worse for wear. She looked nothing like the bouncy little thing Craig had met the day before. Her eyes were swollen from obvious crying and he could smell alcohol on her breath. A lot of alcohol. The scent rose from her like perfume, despite her minty attempts to hide it. She was dressed in a scruffy t-shirt and torn skinny jeans, with a pixie hat perched precariously on her head. She waved a vague apology for her dishevelled look, chewing gum sheepishly.

"Sorry, but I just couldn't cope last night. I went home and got drunk. No crime there officer... is there?" She giggled. When Craig didn't laugh back her eyes widened and she pulled herself upright, suddenly realising that the interview might be recorded.

"Hang on. What's happening? I agreed to have a chat to tell you what I knew, not to be interrogated. Do I need a solicitor?"

Craig leaned back in his chair trying to look serious, but fighting the urge to laugh. If Beth had looked like a Telly-Tubby yesterday she resembled a drunken elf now.

"I don't know Ms Walker. *Do* you need a solicitor?" She scowled at him and her lip ring dug in. It looked painful. "We haven't actually asked you anything yet."

"Yes, but she doesn't look very friendly..." She indicated Sandi with a small finger. "And I don't like the look of that tape-recorder. Did you do this with the others? Is this 'cos I'm gay? Although I certainly don't feel very gay today."

She giggled again and Craig regarded her despairingly. They might need to leave it until she wasn't fifty percent proof.

"It's just an informal chat, Ms Walker. We're offering to tape everyone so we don't have to repeat the questions. But we can leave the tape off if you wish? Or hold the interview tomorrow when you're feeling better...rested? If you'd like someone here with you, then that's fine. We can wait until you get a solicitor."

"Am I being accused of something?"

"No. Not at all. We're just piecing together what happened on Monday evening. You were the deceased's midwife and you were on duty."

She relaxed instantly and shrugged. "Oh well. I know I'm drunk, but as the Nuns used to say, 'In Vino Veritas'. I think that means when you booze you tell the truth. Or something like that. I don't have anything to hide and I want to help Evie. Sorry for being defensive. I'm just a bit pissed-off that no one listened to me before. I've been telling people this was going to happen since February. Even earlier - since Deborah McCance died.

And now, here we are again. A few months later and another death. How many women have to die before people do something? If they'd listened to me back then, maybe this wouldn't be happening. Sorry. I know that's nasty of me and I don't mean that it's your fault personally. But, well, you know what I mean."

"Yes, I know. Don't worry, we're not that easily offended."

"OK. How can I help you then, 'Spector?"

She nodded to switch on the tape and confirmed her name and address.

"Right Ms Walker, could you please outline your movements on Monday night, from the moment you came on duty."

"Well, I came on at eight for the night shift, and Evie was one of two patients I had on the labour ward. I was keeping an eye on the post-natal ward as well. That's where the mums go when they've had their babies. It's just through there." She pointed to the floor map that Craig had spread out on the table.

"Is that normal practice?"

"Aye. Yes, totally. If you're a midwife with mums due to deliver, then you get post-natal to cover. Post-natal's nearly always quiet. You work with another midwife and she takes the emergencies. And anything else that comes up.

Anyway, Evie was fine. All her observations were perfect. She had a drip up, with her Insulin being injected twice a day. She'd had some at lunchtime, and wasn't due again until midnight. So we just chatted away for fifteen minutes. About baby names mostly. She was still choosing, but she liked Ella... she knew it was a wee girl."

She stopped speaking abruptly, and a small stream of tears started down her cheeks, freed by tiredness and alcohol. It was a minute before she could talk again. Craig stayed silent. Alcohol was lowering her inhibitions and she wouldn't thank him for pointing it out. Plus it could prove useful for getting at the truth. In Vino Veritas indeed.

She sniffed loudly and re-started. "She wasn't in any distress. She was really happy, honestly. That was about nine on Monday night. She said that her mum, step-dad and husband had been up earlier. Her father, Mr Hill, had been around all afternoon. He was often outside on the patio smoking. Anyway, then Katy Stevens arrived to check on her. She was Evie's physician."

Craig interjected. "Could you tell me why she needed a physician?"

"It's Trust practice for pregnancy diabetes now. Every woman must have oversight by an endocrine physician – that's Katy Stevens. She's lovely. I've known her for years."

"How long was Dr Stevens with Evie?"

"About fifteen minutes. Then she left the room to chat to

Mr Hill, outside in the patio garden. I could see them through the glass." She pointed to the garden on the map. "Then Mr Hill came back in to sit with Evie, and I went to see another patient."

"Was Dr Stevens alone with Evie?"

"Yes of course. Why?"

Craig didn't answer but she hardly seemed to notice, rambling on.

"Five minutes later I noticed Murdock going into the room so I stayed away. I really can't stand the man. Mr Hill must've felt the same 'cos he left the room immediately. He went outside again, probably for another smoke. He always smells of cigarettes - it made Evie a bit queasy. Anyway, then Murdock left and I headed back in, just to check that she didn't need anything. But she was grand. She wasn't even nervous about her operation. It wasn't due until today anyway."

Craig feigned puzzlement. "Why was she having a Caesarean?"

Beth's expression set hard. "My question exactly! Because Nigel Murdock's a selfish, lazy shite, that's why! That's part of the reason I'm not very popular with him. He Caesareans practically all of his health service patients, between nine and five. It's a major operation but he still puts women through it. Because it's more convenient for him than being called in at three in the morning, for an 'inconvenient' natural birth. We've had loads of rows about it." She snorted in disgust. "Conveyor-belt medicine."

He nodded her on.

"Anyway, I was in and out all evening. And I was just walking down the corridor to check on Evie at about three-thirty, when I got an urgent call to post-natal. One of the mothers had picked up the baby bath with baby in it, and her scar burst open."

Sandi winced...babies could definitely wait.

"Anyway, all hell broke loose while she was calmed down. And the registrar was called to take her back to theatre. We had to get that all sorted, so what should have taken me fifteen minutes actually took me about forty-five. But I knew that Evie was fine. Katy and Murdock had checked on her earlier, and her Dad was always around. I knew he'd fetch me if there were any problems."

She stopped dead and was silent for at least a minute. When she started again her voice was slow and halting. Craig leaned forward encouragingly. "What happened then, Ms Walker?"

Beth took a tearful breath. "I walked down the corridor towards Evie's room. She was in the side-room nearest the Unit entrance. But you know that already."

She pointed to the floor plan again. "Just there. But as I approached, somewhere, on some level, I registered that it was just too quiet. You know how you can tell that a room's empty even before you go in? Well I just sensed that there was no life in there. When I walked in, Evie was lying halfway out of the bed with her arm nearly touching the floor. She was completely pale and..." She stopped abruptly.

"And what, Ms Walker?"

She stood up and leaned across the table, shouting at him with the freedom of drink.

"She was dead! I knew she was dead. Is that what you want?" She turned around and shouted at the tape recorder. "Did you get that, tape? Are you happy now?"

Sandi stood, ready to restrain her if she lashed out, but Craig shook his head. Then Beth sat down again abruptly, and slumped, like a deflated balloon. The interview room fell silent, except for the sound of her crying, until finally Craig spoke softly.

"How did you know that she was dead?"

She swallowed hard, not looking at him. "Experience, some sort of sixth sense. I knew she'd gone before I even touched her. And her father was nowhere to be seen. She died alone. Twenty-six and pregnant and she died alone." She paused for a few seconds, collecting herself.

"I felt for a pulse but there was none. So I hit the crash button and resuscitated her until the team arrived. As soon as they came in I put a monitor on the baby. Its wee heart was still beating, so Evie can't have been dead for long. We had to get her to theatre quickly, for the baby to have any chance. The registrar was with the other lady, so I crash-called Murdock. Then I got her into theatre one, for an emergency Caesarean."

"The records say that the crash team got there within three minutes, Ms Walker - is that correct?" Then Craig startled; had they interviewed all of them? He made a mental note to check.

"I think so. I remember there was an anaesthetist, the on-call doctor and nurses. Evie already had lines up, so they rushed her into theatre two. It's only down the corridor. The whole Unit's laid out in a cross-shape. Look, there." She pointed to the map again.

"Then Mr Hill suddenly appeared. He'd fallen asleep on a chair outside. Evie was being wheeled into theatre and he grabbed her hand and refused to let go. There was no time to argue, so we just threw a gown over him. No one said it, but we all knew she'd already gone. All I remember then was Murdock arriving and him saying 'here's the baby'. Then the paediatrician took her to check her over. Murdock called time of death on Evie, and that was it - there was a big bang, and instruments fell all over the floor. Mr Hill had punched Murdock when he said that Evie was dead. He was swinging for everyone, yelling he was going to kill us all. I didn't pay much attention to be honest, I felt so sorry for him. And truthfully, I was really pleased that he'd punched Murdock – the man's a pig."

Craig knew exactly what she meant.

"After I checked the baby, I went to see if Mr Hill was OK. But he just said he was going to kill me. Murdock had disappeared with his bloody nose, and then the security men arrived. Murdock called them. I was really pissed-off about that. We didn't need them. We could have calmed Mr Hill down ourselves. The poor man didn't need manhandling when his daughter had just died."

She gasped for breath and wiped her face with her ragged sleeve. Sandi gently put a tissue in her hand. Craig leaned forward and smiled at her kindly.

"You saved the baby by your quick actions. Dr Stevens says she's beautiful,"

Beth blew her nose loudly. "But why has it happened again? Evie was such a nice wee girl and so excited about the baby. Who would do this? What sort of animals are they? I'm going home to Derry the first chance I get. Nice people don't behave this way."

"We don't know who yet. But I promise you we'll find out."

"I can't keep working here, or anywhere as a midwife now. That's three of my patients dead in less than six months."

It was a stark truth. And although Craig recognised that her guilt had nothing to do with being a murderer, he had to be certain. He made a note to question her about the two earlier deaths. But not today - she was exhausted.

"D.S McElroy will contact you to take your statement about the other two cases. But I think that's enough for today. You should go home and rest. And if you don't mind me saying so, please don't drink anything more, you'll only feel worse. Believe me, I know. Thank you for coming in, Ms Walker."

Beth sniffed again and nodded, shuffling out of the room in an erratic line. She'd managed to cycle down but Jack had a taxi waiting to take her home. Otherwise he'd have to book her for being 'drunk in charge of a bicycle'. And that wouldn't look good on her C.V.

Craig walked out to the back office, raking his dark hair. "Well I know we've got to keep an open mind, Jack. But if either of those women are murderers then there's no hope for the health service."

"True. But you'll be checking them both out just the same."

Chapter Twelve

"Liam, it's Davy. I've got that information for you on McAllister. You w...were totally right! But how did you even know to look? It didn't come up on any of the first level checks."

Liam nodded to himself. He knew it. McAllister was lying.

"Experience has to count for something lad. Print that out for me, would you? And just keep this to yourself for the minute. I want to do some more digging."

***

3.55pm.

The briefing room had three boards set up at the front. Liam had anticipated Craig's approach well. One of them was covered with information on Evie and her father. Liam indicated the others. "I thought we'd be looking at the McCance and Bryson cases too, boss."

Craig nodded, hanging up the flip chart he was carrying, on a free tripod. Then he leaned against the front desk and looked at the wall clock. Three-fifty-five. Nearly time to start.

People filtered in slowly and Liam stretched his long legs out across the doorway, playfully making new entrants hop over them.

"Where are Nicky and Davy, Annette? Could you get them down please? They'll need to be in all the briefings. Liam, do we have a probationer attached to us?"

"Aye, a wee lad called Martin, up from Fermanagh for a few weeks. He started this morning."

"Get him here as well then. Plus, Joe Rice is coming, and possibly Karl Rimmins from Drugs."

"Joe's definitely coming - he's upstairs now. But I didn't see Karl."

Craig handed round coffees as everyone trickled in, calling them to order at five past.

"OK. Hello everyone. Do you all know each other? And welcome Martin, glad to have you with us. We'll have a chat at some point this week, but I'd like to move on for now."

Martin nodded, surprised at being addressed so amiably by a D.C.I. He was a freckled lad of about twenty with a broad open face and the high colour of the healthy. He wore a brand new suit and a tie with a knot so small that it looked like a tourniquet. Craig remembered his own early attempts and smiled at him.

"Right. Liam's going to update us on what's been happening since yesterday."

"Aye. Now, the M.P.E., that's the slang for the Maternity, Paediatric and Endocrine part of St Marys' Healthcare Trust. It's on Elmwood Avenue, near the junction with the Lisburn Road. Where the old Dunmore Medical Centre used to be."

Craig leaned forward and Liam paused to let him speak.

"Sorry Liam. But before we get to specifics, I need to tell you that this case has top priority. Both Dr Winter and I believe this to be, not one murder, but possibly three so far that we know of. Most likely by the same killer."

Joe and Martin were shocked and immediately started asking questions. Craig held up a hand, quieting the room.

"Let Liam outline things first please, then we can deal with any questions. But we have to catch this one quickly, before they kill someone else. There's possible evidence of escalation. Joe, is Karl coming?"

"Sorry sir, but he's in Court until Friday. I'll get what I can from him."

"Thanks. I'm nipping up to see Andy later as well."

Liam ran quickly through everything they knew about the first two cases, and then paused for a question from Annette.

"Did these women have anything in common outside the hospital, sir? Did they know each other, or did they all know anyone at the hospital?"

"All good questions, with no answers. We've a lot of the preliminary interviews covered but we're not deep into the detail yet. Joe, Davy and Martin, could you work with Liam and Annette to get deeper background on the victims and ward staff please? Nigel, Murdock and Beth Walker in particular. Include all the issues Annette's just asked about. Davy, can you start looking for sources of Pethidine? Liam can give you John's list on that."

Davy Walsh was the squad's handsome twenty-five-year-old analyst. He was brilliant with technology and shy with people, an impression added to by his dark Emo fashion and mild stammer on 's' and 'w'. When he'd joined the squad the year before he would hardly speak to Craig. But his confidence had grown now, enough to present at meetings and banter Liam ruthlessly. It had also gained him his first steady girlfriend, Maggie Clarke, a talented journalist. Unfortunately, she worked for The Belfast Chronicle, the local tabloid rag.

Davy worked at the speed of light for a salary half of what he was worth, and Craig hoped that he would never leave them. But the public sector never paid analysts enough to hold them long.

Davy started speaking confidently. "The retail pharmacies and G.P.s aren't a problem. I can contact the professional and retail bodies easily. But the s...street drugs could be an issue."

"Yes. It'll be nearly impossible to access the supply. But try D.C.I. White on that, Davy. He'll know the local dealers, if anyone does."

"Aye, ask D.C.I. White, hey."

Liam imitated Andy White's Dungiven accent with astounding accuracy. Never missing out his tendency to say 'hey' after every other word. Craig laughed and then stared him down, in case he was working up to one of his bantering sessions. Fun as they were they were too busy for one right now. Liam stared back at him, feigning hurt.

"OK, thanks Davy. On the victims. We need to know everything about them and whether they knew each other? Did they have anything in common? Look at their causes of death and what information that gives us about our killer? We'll get more from John on that soon, but we can start building a picture now.

Why were they killed? Unknown as yet. But Evie is our best chance to get leads, so let's look at her closely first. Evie is Tommy Hill's daughter, so we need to look at his enemies as well as any that she might have had personally. In particular, look at the families of the men he killed in the 1980s. And Joe - ask Karl what enemies Tommy might have made from his drugs racket."

Joe nodded sleepily, eyeing the plate of biscuits sitting beside Craig on the desk. Craig caught the look and handed the plate around, not skipping a beat.

"When were these women killed? We know the answer to that. And so far the killings have been six to eight weeks apart. We also know where they were killed. In the Maternity Unit at the M.P.E., in side-rooms near the Unit's front door. How were they killed? Liam has covered the use of drugs and Caesareans, but *why* was that method used? It's very unusual. And in Evie's case Dr Winter doesn't think that was her final cause of death. We don't know what was yet. The answers to all these questions should tell us who killed them." He turned back to Liam. "Carry on please."

Nicky was sitting beside Liam and Craig watched as she busied herself, minuting the meeting in her own quirky shorthand. Her crossed leg was swinging rhythmically, moving her sequined high heels back and forth in a flashing arc at the edge of his vision. They were matched by sequins on her swan patterned jumper and black leggings. It was a conservative outfit by Nicky's standards. Craig smiled to himself. She always brightened up the squad.

She worked quickly and quietly, somehow managing not to recoil in horror at the things she heard. As Liam's deep voice outlined the trauma that Evie had suffered, the only sign of Nicky's emotions was in her change of speed as she wrote. Slower at sad information, faster when they broke off to banter and chat.

Craig wondered how she coped with everything she heard. She was a secretary, not a police officer. But she gave nothing away. Only glancing up occasionally during the fifteen minutes it took Liam to cover Monday night's events. And summarise Tommy Hill's history, known habits and associates.

"Since he came out of the Maze in '98, Tommy says he's been the model citizen. Helping at the youth-club. Gardening, golfing..."

"And grass." Joe's sing-song voice broke through Liam's bass and Craig nodded him on.

"Tell us what you know, Joe."

"Well, as you all know, Tommy's well known to the Drugs Squad. They have him under surveillance on and off. And they figure that his community work is a front for dealing."

"Dealing what?"

"Pretty much everything below Heroin, sir. But I'm sure he'd know where to get his hands on that as well."

"That could be important, Joe. Drugs were part of the murder, although we're not sure that they're the cause of death. We're still waiting for Dr Winter on that. But if Tommy has access to hard drugs, follow it up with Karl, please."

Annette leaned back in her chair and stared at Craig. "But why would he kill his own daughter, sir? Or the other women? And aren't drug murders normally a woman's game?"

"You're right Annette. What motive would Tommy have to kill them? On first look he's got no motive to kill Evie, but we need to trace any connections there might be between Tommy and the first two women. Female serial killers are still rare, despite the Jessica Adams case."

Craig was referring to a case that they'd encountered the year before, where a young women had killed three people and then herself.

"Studies show women tend to murder men they're emotionally close to." He glanced over at Liam. "Usually their husbands." The men gave a dry laugh and Annette and Nicky nodded in agreement, looking pointedly at Liam. "I don't know how Danni didn't do it years ago."

Craig laughed and continued. "It's also usually for material gain. But you're right Annette; women's preferred methods of killing are poisoning or drugs. They also often kill in healthcare settings."

"Hence the Angel of Mercy label from the press, s...sir. Or they've got Munchausen's by proxy."

Craig nodded at Davy, agreeing. "Does everyone know what that means?" Martin stared blankly at him. "OK, briefly it means someone who seeks attention, and gets it by injuring someone else and then saving them. Typically it's a carer."

"Like the Beverly Allitt case."

"Exactly. OK, moving on and keeping an open mind. If our killer *is* a woman, then Beth Walker has to be our top suspect. But it's still much more likely to be a man. And this one looks like an organised offender; a Double-O. I was going to come to this later but we might as well cover it now."

Craig nodded his thanks to Liam, and then turned over the cover of the flip chart he'd brought. The first sheet was covered in bullet points headed 'Serial Killers'.

"I'll run through a few general points and cover the typical Double-O profile. Then let's see what fits our killer."

Martin sat forward eagerly and Annette noticed his face

reddening as his tie tightened, threatening to cut of his oxygen supply. She reached over and tapped him on the shoulder, signalling it was OK to take it off. He smiled gratefully at her as his colour returned to normal. Davy watched the interchange with a quick flash of jealousy - he was the baby around here. Craig was still talking, completely missing the exchange.

"I'm not getting into 'Criminal Minds' depth on method or signatures today, just the general points. Other than to say you all know the modus operandi is the killer's particular way of doing things. They're the things they see as necessary to committing and getting away with the crime.

And the signature is an act that usually has nothing to do with getting away with the crime, but is important to the killer in some personal way. Such as religious symbolism, leaving tarot cards etc. There's often a psychological basis for the signature, something in their past that they feel compelled to show. M.O.s can change but signatures rarely do. They can evolve, but basically signatures are consistent and true to the killer. They're the killer's compulsion."

Martin's eyes widened in excitement - a serial killer on his first day! None of his class would believe it. Liam caught the look and shook his head. The things that thrilled kids nowadays...

"OK, we know that every murder is committed because somebody wants something, even if it's just the buzz. A serial killer is someone who murders three or more people over more than thirty days, with a 'cooling off' period between each. The motivation is based on psychological or sexual gratification, or both.

Most serial killers are in their twenties to forties and, sorry guys, but almost all are male. That's why Jessica Adams was so unusual. The murders are often connected to some significant event in the killer's past. So whoever killed Evie may have something personal going on, that may link to a past event in his life."

Nicky stopped to listen, fascinated. Craig might have said that it wasn't 'Criminal Minds' but it seemed pretty close to her. He leaned against the desk and continued.

"Most kill close to home or work. They stick to familiar places - it's their comfort zone. Killers who use a ruse to trap their victims typically possess good social skills and are known as organised. Whereas those who use a blitz-style attack are less comfortable with conversation - they're disorganised killers. As I've said, I think we're dealing with an organised offender here.

This is someone who walked confidently into Evie's room and managed to put drugs in her arm, without any signs of her fighting them off. Perhaps someone working in health or impersonating a health worker.

An organised offender plans their killings carefully. They're often of average or higher intelligence. Well educated, stable, employed, and have good social relationships. Even though they're driven by their fantasies, they maintain enough control to live a normal life. This is someone that you could have a normal conversation with, and who probably chatted comfortably to Evie. She wasn't scared of this person.

They prepare well and tend to use control measures such as drugs or restraints. And they're likely to have a dumpsite already selected. Or, as in this case, they leave the victims where they die. So I agree with Annette, I don't think this is Tommy. It's far too sophisticated for him. But we have to investigate every possibility to rule it out."

Martin was sitting with his mouth open, stunned by what he was hearing. Liam leaned over and tipped it shut, making everyone smile.

"In terms of the killer's signature. In Evie's case, we have very careful staging with the use of Insulin and Pethidine as in the earlier two cases. But we also have a clean laceration on Evie's right cheek. This wasn't an accidental cut, it was a clean cut made at the time of death which John can't find any cause for. So just bear in mind that it might have significance. Either to the killer, or to someone in their past."

"No-one I interviewed had a scar on their right cheek, boss."

"Nor me, sir."

Craig nodded, listening. But the laceration was still significant, he could feel it.

"Unfortunately we don't know if the earlier victims were similarly marked, but bear it in mind. I don't want to get bogged down in this profile, but we'll leave it up and refer back to it. It's a useful framework, but we can't let it blind us. OK, comments or questions anyone?"

There was a few minutes silence while people milled around the flip chart, staring at it as if it could magically yield a name.

"Doc Winter would love this, boss. It's like an American cop show."

"Thankfully America gets more serials than we do, Liam. But there's nothing random about this scenario. The killer has a reason for wanting us to know that Evie was murdered. But there's been no contact or taunting, so they don't want us to catch them. We need to think hard. Why did they want us to know? And what are they trying to draw our attention to?"

Craig allowed a few minutes murmured discussion before he called the room back to order, updating them on his High Street interviews. Then Annette fed back about Brian Murray.

"He's a lovely wee boy, and there's nothing suspicious at all there. He cried about Evie all the way through the interview. I wanted to take him home by the end of it. He's definitely heart-broken, sir, but he seemed a bit scared as well. He wouldn't say why, but I had the impression that he's wary of Tommy. All he would say was that Tommy really doesn't like him. Maybe it's just the usual protective Dad-daughter stuff?"

"The Kerrs told me that as well, Annette. But they said it was something to do with religion. Liam, have a word with

111

Tommy and warn him off Murray. And chat to Reggie Boyd at the Demesne - he can keep an eye on things up there."

"Will do."

Craig suddenly noticed the time. Four-fifty. Time to wind up.

"OK. Joe, can you dig deeper into Hill's relationship with Evie? Talk to her mother and step-dad again. He's a vicar and he seemed saintly enough, but there's no love lost between him and Tommy. He might tell you something useful. And Brian Murray - again can you dig there and see if anyone hates him enough to kill Evie. Annette, meet with Beth Walker again and get more detail on the first two deaths. Liam, is that it from your side?"

"There are a few more things, boss. One of the builders, a spark called Michael Randle, is a wee hard man. Lots of 'front' in the interview, you know the type. So I'm following up to see if he's got any form. And that Dr Lewes is a strange one too. He was wild nervous in the interview, although happy enough to tell us he'd been in and out of the ward. He'd been looking after a baby who's Mum was still there."

"Let me guess. She had a Caesarean?"

"Yep. Another one of Murdock's. Anyway, Lewes got very twitchy when questions came up about his private life. Even simple ones like. Married? Yes or no. Children? Etc. And he was the only Doc who didn't ask to be interviewed by you."

"Right. Nicky, put Dr Lewes down on my interview list. If he wants to know why he's being re-interviewed, fudge it with 'questions we forgot to ask'. It could be something or nothing."

Nicky nodded and smiled at him, without breaking her shorthand stride.

"That's all we have so far, boss. I've met the two scanning doctors and there's nothing there. They did the scans, told the Mum's the baby's sex and put it on the computer – end of. We've seen all the building project people, and the ward interviews have given us nothing so far. But we've only done half of them. It takes a hell of a lot of people to deliver babies nowadays. Gone are the days when you had them in a field and went back to work."

Annette snorted. "I'd like to see you try it! They'd have to knock you out for the whole nine months."

Craig smiled, knowing Liam had only said it to get a reaction. It had worked. He nodded him on.

"It's mostly the resuscitation and theatre teams left to see. You'll have a few more doctors from there as well."

Craig sighed. "I'll look forward to it. OK, sort out the scheduling with Nicky when you know the final numbers." He scanned the room quickly for any other comments, but there were none.

"OK, summarising. Our killer targets women who are patients of Nigel Murdock and Beth Walker, but so far only those pregnant with girls. They use Insulin, Pethidine, and skilfully engineer their victims into having Caesarean sections. Even when they weren't originally scheduled. All of that implies close knowledge of the Maternity Unit. Remember, organised killers kill close to home or work, so the Trust is most likely their base in some way. Probably for work.

They want us to know that they're killing, for whatever reason. Attention, a cry for help? We don't know yet. But there's a reason that these particular women were killed. It wasn't random. When we find that reason, we'll find their killer. And we have to do it before they kill again. One last question, Liam. Was there anything on Maternity's close circuit TV for any of the earlier cases? Or Evie's?"

"There's no Unit CCTV on any of them, boss - nothing. There's only one camera at the Maternity Unit, and that's above the door looking out. There are going to be eight new ones, but they're not going up until sometime next week. There've always been cameras in the corridor, but apparently nothing seemed abnormal at the times of the first two deaths.

But then, they wouldn't have been looking for a killer. I'll get hold of the tapes and have another check."

"If they still exist."

Liam nodded ruefully. Far too many places reused their tapes.

"CCTV becomes standard inside Maternity this year, and even then, only in some areas. The strange thing is we don't have *any* camera views for the time Evie was killed. Not even the corridor or door ones. Randle said it was because of the building work inside the Unit. They're all on the same circuit, so they had them switched-off to connect up the new internal cameras. Makes sense I suppose. Safer for the electricians."

Everyone nodded except Craig. "But if the new cameras aren't being positioned until next week, why switch off the door and corridor cameras until then? Why do it until it's absolutely necessary for the electricians' safety? Dig a bit deeper there please, Liam. That's too much of a coincidence. Martin, can you help Liam with that?

Davy, do a check with the Australian police for the years that Beth Walker worked out there. Give her a call and get the exact dates. And check her out with the Australian Nursing Council as well. And I need deep background on Iain Lewes before I see him too. John's coming back to me later with anything more that he needs answered, so we've a lot of basic digging still to do."

Craig leaned back on the desk, folding his arms, and Annette noticed a sudden flash of silver at his wrist. She peered more closely. A new pair of cufflinks was glinting against his shirt. A present from Julia McNulty? If they were she was glad. He'd been single the whole time she'd worked there. It was about time he had someone to look after him.

"OK, we have what we have, so let's get on with it. We'll be briefing every day at four unless you hear otherwise. Thanks everyone."

They filtered out and Craig waited behind as the room

cleared, deciding whether to call it a day or to visit Andy White. Andy won and he took the stairs to the drugs squad quickly, in search of a bit of craic.

When he entered, Andy was standing behind his desk as usual, and Craig wondered if he ever sat down. Also as usual he had on a sky-blue shirt that exactly matched his eyes. He wore one every day, on his wife's orders. Craig didn't know how he coped with the lack of variety. He must have loved her very much.

"Hi Marc. What's happening, hey?" Craig stifled a laugh, thinking of Liam's earlier mimicry. They sounded exactly alike.

"Here to pick your brains, Andy."

White was grinning and Craig knew he wanted to be asked why.

"OK. Why the grin?"

"It's a great day, hey. We've found a cannabis farm up near Stormont. That'll wreck the Assembly's parties."

They laughed at the thought of the politicians passing a joint around the chamber, and generated a few one-liners. Then Craig got to his visit's purpose. "How much do you know about Tommy Hill?"

"Karl Rimmins is your man for the detail, but I know Hill's been bringing coke over from Scotland for sure. Too many ferry trips for my liking. We got close to making something stick to him last year, and then one of his crew gave himself up instead."

Craig nodded. People followed Tommy blindly and then he sacrificed them to save his own neck. It often happened when the heat got close to a gang leader.

"Liam had dealings with Hill a few years back, and he doesn't have much good to say about him either. I know he's a thug, but can you think of anyone who *really* hates him?"

"What! You mean more than the families of the men he killed on that bus? Or the parents of the Demesne junkies? I could write you a list, hey. But what's he done now?"

"It's not what he's done - it's what's been done to him."

He filled him in on Evie's murder and Andy's next 'hey' was preceded by the words 'poetic justice'.

Craig began to think that he was the only one left with any sympathy for Tommy Hill.

Chapter Thirteen

Thursday.

The ward interviews had taken forever. But by Thursday, almost every member of the nursing, ward and portering staff had been covered. Only Sister Johns remained, and Liam planned to interview her next. He was surprised she hadn't insisted on seeing Craig. Maybe Murdock had squashed that notion with feedback from his interview.

The interviews hadn't yielded much. As usual, no-one had seen anything. They all walked around in their sleep. But Liam was too long in the tooth to get worked up at the blinkers most people wore through life. He was guilty of it himself when he wasn't working.

As predicted, everyone but the most junior doctors had insisted on Craig taking their interviews. So his morning had been booked solid again with medical staff. They'd been nice enough about it, but explained that their insurance companies had insisted on Craig and solicitors for everyone. Liam chuckled to himself and hoped they liked the décor at High Street. It was hardly the Ulster Clinic.

He'd sent Martin off to the lab with the last lot of equipment for examination, and his own morning had been spent examining the CCTV for all three cases. It was very thin. There was virtually nothing on any of them. The Trust was on an economy drive and re-used all its tapes. They'd been lucky to get one corridor view from the security archive. Liam was pragmatic about it - it was three months ago after all.

He was lost in thought when Martin appeared behind him, catching him unawares. He jumped, and was ready to launch into a lecture about 'not sneaking up on people' when he noticed that Martin had brought two coffees. Liam welcomed him like a man after a month's drought. He was developing nearly as bad a caffeine habit as Craig.

"You're a star, son." He took a deep slurp at his Americano and sighed, satisfied. "You even remembered the sugar - you'll go far. Grab a pew for a minute while I finish this tape. Have you seen Annette around?"

"Aye, she was down the corridor earlier, calming that Sister down about something. She's a brittle one isn't she?" They both nodded, with an empathic look that said women were a foreign country. Eventually Liam potted his cup in the bin, like a man who'd played one too many games of snooker. Then he stood up and stretched broadly.

"Right lad. Finish checking those other tapes for me, then go and find that Greenwood fella and ask him for the schematics for the whole M.P.E. complex. Particularly the area around Maternity. Get one that shows the electrics if you can." That would keep the young cub busy.

"What should I be looking for on these, sir?"

"Well now, let's see...that'd be anyone who looks like a murderer."

Martin blushed, throwing his freckles into bright relief. Liam patted him on the arm, relenting.

"Just go through them and mark anything you think we should have a second look at. But mind and get those copies of the floor plans before you come back for the briefing. I want to get them enlarged."

Joe's team had finished their last interview, and when Liam entered their allocated office, he was on the landline, nodding. "That's great. See if Meg can copy the files for me, the D.C.I. will want them. OK, OK, that's grand. I'll see you then."

"Was that Karl?"

"Aye, he's got some stuff for us on Tommy. He's in court again today, but he'll be at the briefing tomorrow."

"Grand. Look, it's twelve o'clock now, Joe, so why don't you go and get some lunch. Can you nip back afterwards and check on Martin? I'm interviewing Frosty the snow-woman after lunch, so we'll meet you back at the ranch at three-thirty."

"Good luck with that."

Just then Annette wandered into the office.

"Here, speak of the Devil and she shall appear."

"Oh, that's lovely talk. I'll just leave again then, will I?"

"No, I've a better idea, Cutty. Joe's heading on, so I'll buy you lunch and you can update me. Then we can do the Sister's interview together." Joe stood up to go.

"I'm away now Liam. I'm nipping out for a burger. I've tried hospital food before, and I'm surprised there aren't more deaths. See you at the squad." He waved goodbye and left the Unit through the front security door, as Annette scanned the ward nervously.

"Liam, I've just had the strangest feeling walking through the foyer. As if someone was watching me. Have you seen anyone strange hanging about?"

"No, Cutty. But hospitals are busy old places so they'd be hard to spot. Did you have a good search around?"

"Yes. Nigel Murdock was standing near the lifts with a crowd of men. I recognised some of them. The Chief Executive and your Dr Lewes, and there were two other men as well. But I couldn't see any of them watching me. It was just weird. It really made my skin crawl." She shuddered, shaking the unease off her like snow. "It was probably nothing. I expect we're all just tired."

"Aye...we're all that, right enough."

"Anyway. The reason I'm here was to say, have you noticed that the Unit door only allows admission through the intercom or a swipe card? I've had to buzz the office to get in every time. But you can get out very easily. It's all changed since I nursed. You used to be able to wander in and out of every ward then."

"What's your point?"

"Well, that means that whoever was in here on Monday night was buzzed in by someone on the Unit. Or they had a swipe card. Have you checked the CCTV yet?"

"Not Monday night's yet. We already know there was nothing for the time that Evie was killed. But I've just had a thought. Give me a minute to phone Martin."

"You lazy thing, Liam Cullen! Go and see him. He's just down the corridor. Anyway, you're not supposed to be using mobiles in here."

"Oh aye, forgot again. I'll nip down. Wait here."

Annette could hear his booming voice all the way down the ward. It was so loud sometimes that it hurt her ears.

"And can you pay particular attention to any shots of people entering the Unit on Monday night, Martin? Buzzed-in people and swipe card entrants. Pull any records they keep on the swipe-card activity. The computer people at the Trust should keep them. Grand, grand, good lad."

Annette peeped into the post-natal ward while she waited. It held all the new mothers, some needing special care. The women were holding their tiny offspring with varying levels of confidence, and she smiled, remembering. A young mum by the door was gazing at her baby as if she was surprised it was there at all. Its shock of black hair was pointing in different directions and it completely ignored her stares. Its eyes screwed-up in sleep and its curly mouth moved softly.

Annette didn't even notice Liam coming back to stand beside her.

"God, Cutty. That's my life at the moment with Rory."

"I remember being that shocked when Amy was born. I used to hold her at arm's length, like a china teapot."

"Me too. That's when Danni would even let me touch Erin,

120

she was so protective. She's the same now with Rory, except when she wants a nappy changed." His nose screwed up in distaste. "Here, what sort of a dad do you think the boss would make?"

"Great. And they'd be the best dressed babies in town."

They walked off the Unit laughing loudly, until Annette remembered her training and quietened Liam down a bit. Then they followed the signs to the first floor canteen, tailing the crowd wandering in to brave the health service cooking.

Katy and Natalie were near the top of the lunch queue, standing with Iain Lewes. They were chatting when Katy noticed Liam, spotting his police look immediately. She tapped Natalie on the shoulder.

"Natalie, look. I bet that's one of the policemen."

"Oh, is he your one?"

Natalie turned and immediately recognised Annette, from a Christmas party she'd gone to with John. She felt a sudden pang, remembering the great time they'd had.

Katy flushed. "He wasn't *my* one. He just interviewed me, that's all. His name's Craig. And no, that isn't him. The woman must be police as well."

At the mention of Craig's name a hurt look flickered over Natalie's face. "I know Craig, he's nice. I...I dated a friend of his. Until last week."

Katy was surprised. Natalie hadn't mentioned that she was seeing anyone, but then they hadn't known each other long. The emotion in her voice stopped Katy asking for more details.

Natalie lifted her tray determinedly. "Well, I'm going to say hello. They must feel awkward not knowing anyone." She hesitated for a moment, uncertain what to say to them. Then she shrugged and marched off.

"Don't you dare, Natalie. You know you're just being nosy."

But she was already halfway down the queue, heading for Liam and Annette. They were at the hot food counter having chips shovelled out by a glum Victoria Wood caricature.

"You should try the cheesecake - it's almost edible." She stood grinning up at them, eye-to-eye with Liam's chest. Then she extended her hand warmly to Annette, smiling at her confusion.

"We met at a party, at Christmas. I...I was with John Winter."

Her voice broke slightly as she said his name, but she pushed her smile firmly back into place. "My friend Katy was interrogated by your boss yesterday."

Annette put her hand out to shake. "I remember now. Natalie isn't it? Dr Winter is…"

Natalie nodded and quickly interrupted, afraid that Annette might reveal something about John's life now that would hurt her. "Hey, your boss scared the life out of Katy yesterday. But then she's easily scared. I'm not."

Liam gazed down at the chirpy five-footer, amused by her directness. Most people stayed as far away from the police as they could. "I just bet you aren't. Will you join us?"

"Sure. I'll get us a table."

She grabbed a free table, calling across to the others, and Katy glared at her murderously. The queue was slow but eventually Katy paid and sat down beside her, soon joined by Liam and Annette.

Natalie beckoned to Iain Lewes, pulling out a chair for him. But he gave his pager an intense stare that implied urgency and indispensability. The doctor's universal cover. Then he abandoned his tray and left hastily.

Liam noticed his move and nudged Annette, whispering. "Well now, wasn't he in a hurry...?"

"Don't be so suspicious, Liam. He's probably just busy." She made a mental note to get to Lewes first, before Liam scared the life out of him.

Once Katy got past her embarrassment it was a fun lunch, and the case wasn't discussed at all. After thirty minutes of banter, Natalie was bleeped away and they all filtered off. Liam and Annette headed back to the ward with Liam smiling wryly.

"That Dr Stevens is someone new to slag the boss about. He forgot to mention she was pretty, didn't he? I'll save it up for the right time. He's got a bit boring since he paired up with McNulty."

"She had great shoes too, although God knows how she walks in them. And just think of the lovely designer babies they'd make..."

***

John Winter examined the rubber connector closely. It had linked the clear drip-line to the needle inserted into Evie's arm. He lifted his glasses and rubbed his green eyes hard, then he heightened the microscope's resolution and scrutinised it again. There was no doubt about it, Des had been absolutely right. There was a significant needle track running through the rubber. An electron microscope photo showing it would follow from the Materials Lab soon.

He lifted the phone to forensics. "Des, would you mind coming up for a moment please? And bring the needles, I need to check something."

Two minutes later the bearded figure of Des Marsham, Head of Forensic Science, ambled in. He carried a sterile box in one hand and his lunch in the other. He handed the box to John and sat down heavily beside him, biting into a sandwich.

John removed three different needles from the box and tried them each in turn, inserting them gently into the rubber without damaging the track. Both the orange and blue needles were too small. But a standard 'green' needle slipped in, fitting the hole exactly. They were available in every ward.

"Des, how do you fancy a quick road-trip to Docklands? About three-thirty?"

"Sounds great, it'd be brilliant to escape lab-rat-ness for an hour. I'll do a one page summary of my findings and ask Marcie to make copies of the drug charts and notes as well."

"Right, I'll meet you downstairs then, with the photo."

There was never any question that Evie had been murdered, she had Pethidine in her system that should never have been there. But now John knew how it had been introduced. Giving several types of medication through the same line was usually done with a three-way switch, and Evie'd had one fitted. Yet the drugs had been injected through the rubber connector instead. Injecting drugs that way was called 'piggy-backing'. But it had mostly gone out of vogue in the '80s, except in dire emergencies.

That meant that if the killer was medical they were unlikely to be recently trained. Anyone under forty would just have given the drug through the switch.

So either the killer was clinically trained but over forty, or they weren't clinically trained at all. It wouldn't narrow their suspect pool much. It didn't rule-out any of the older ward staff in fact. But finding out who did it was Marc's job, not theirs.

John was taking extra care on Evie's post-mortem because two others hinged on it, so he wasn't finished just yet. And he still had to go over the other P.M.s. Still, at least this information might help the murder squad a bit. And he wanted to present it at the briefing and answer any questions himself.

But the biggest question of all still had to be answered. What was Evie Murray-Hill's cause of death?

***

Liam and Annette wandered back to the ward-room, resigned to their fates. "Here we go, Cutty. Only one more interview before we head home. Sister Laurie Johns, God help us."

"I saw her wandering down the corridor as we went to lunch. I'll see if I can find her. She's too power-mad to be away from her empire for long. You go down and see Martin - I can tell you're desperate to check if he's found anything."

Liam laughed out loud. "God! I can't fool Danni at home and I can't fool you at work. It's like having two wives."

"You wish. Five minutes, and don't be any longer."

He wandered down the short corridor and reached the room, where Martin was still sitting in the dark. "Martin lad, what've you got for me? Anything?"

"Well sir, we've no camera views at all outside the door. Or in the Maternity corridor." He saw Liam's face fall and added quickly. "So I walked down and had a look, and there's a cross-corridor. Anyone turning right from it, at either of two points, could only be heading down the glass corridors towards Maternity. They don't lead anywhere else. It was designed that way especially, to isolate Maternity for the women and baby's safety. Paediatrics is exactly the same on the opposite side of the building. So the tapes from the cross-corridor could be worth viewing."

"Well done son. Top of the class."

"I'll get the tapes and mark any sections showing people entering or leaving the corridors. The interviews say there was a lot of coming and going from Maternity on Monday night, especially from 9pm till 6am. With the tapes we should be able to confirm some alibis."

"Can you check for any trace of the cards swiped then as well?"

"Will do. I'll call I.T. now, sir."

"And did you manage to get the floor plans yet?"

Martin was about to say 'what did your last slave die of?' but he thought better of it. He bit his tongue and fixed his smile firmly in place - Liam would be writing his assessment.

"I collected them twenty minutes ago. That's partly what

put me onto the cross-corridor. That project manager Ted Greenwood's a real geek. Totally dead-pan. When I told him what I wanted, he just leaned back over his chair and handed me a roll of plans. No chat, nor nothing!"

"It takes all sorts lad. You'll soon find that out. And if boring equalled bad we'd be locking up half of Northern Ireland. Right, I'll see you later."

He left the room, and then stuck his head quickly back round the door.

"Have a break and get a sandwich before you get stuck into that. And...you're doing great work son." Then he disappeared again quickly, leaving a beaming probationer. Annette's people skills were definitely rubbing off.

***

The Visitor leaned coolly against the wall, watching as the female police walked back onto the Unit. People milled around her, rushing to their lunches. But how could food matter when there was important work to do?

They had such power and such access, and yet none of them had dealt with the deaths. It was disgusting. But now the father would take the steps needed. The guilty had to be exposed. And they all had to pay for the pain they'd caused.

Chapter Fourteen

As Craig walked onto the squad at 3.40, Liam and Annette were discussing their interview with Laurie Johns.

"God, she was dire! Everything was Beth's fault, and Murdock walks on water. And she couldn't wait to tell us that Beth had been seen at Sarajevo wearing PVC. As if PVC's a crime!"

Joe popped his head over a cubicle wall hopefully. "PVC?"

"Nah, forget it Joe. You're not her type. You've got too many bits."

He screwed up his face, confused, until Martin leaned forward and said quietly. "Sarajevo's a gay bar, sir."

"What? Are you telling me that gay men have fewer bits than us?" Annette and Nicky laughed simultaneously and Liam helped him out.

"God Joe, keep up. There are gay women as well. She's a lesbian, so all men have too many bits. Get it?"

"Oh...I see. Ah now, you know, I'm pretty sophisticated when all's said and done. Live and let live, that's me."

Craig's deep voice joined the conversation.

"Glad to hear it Joe, otherwise you would be on that equal rights course next week with Martin. Right, we've a briefing in twenty minutes so get as much together as you can. Grab a coffee and I'll see you downstairs at four. Martin, could you go down to the front desk and sign-in Doctors Winter and Marsham please? Then bring them down to the briefing room."

"Let's make a start. We've a lot to get through. You all know Dr Winter, the Director of Forensic Pathology, and Dr Marsham, Head of Forensic Science. That's C.S.I. for the Wii generation amongst us. Welcome, both of you. I see Nicky's got you coffee."

"Aye, hello again, Doc."

John nodded and then took off his suit jacket, revealing a pair of red braces that exactly matched his shoes. Then Davy appeared, displaying his newest ear piercing, and Craig laughed as Martin gawped at the fashion show.

"OK. Before we start, most of you will know that it was Dr Winter's eagle-eye that first brought us this case. He also alerted us to the possible irregularities in two older cases. So without him we might never have realised this is potentially, and I still say potentially, murder number three. And this might have gone unchecked for much longer." John gave a mock bow.

"OK, everyone please give an update on your interviews. Then we'll take Joe about the Drug Squad info. And Liam and Martin on the preliminary CCTV, swipe cards and floor plan information. Then I'll summarise. But before all of that - perhaps our guests would like to tell us what they've found?"

Nicky distributed the summaries that John and Des had brought with them, and they outlined their findings in tandem. They steered suspicion towards either a clinical person over forty, or someone completely non-clinical, but with easy access to drugs and needles. They'd brought a sample giving-set, a green needle and the electron microscope photograph. Des confirmed that traces of Pethidine had been found along the needle track in the rubber connector. While a summary of the drug charts and notes tied everything together.

"The post-mortem's not finished yet and we'll be collecting

more swabs for D.N.A. from Evie's body." John twisted his face in disgust. "I also found out an hour ago that unfortunately, or very suspiciously I believe, the first two victims were cremated. So we have to get everything we possibly can from Evie."

"Cremated? That's convenient, Doc."

"Too convenient, Liam. If Alan Davis wasn't already dead I'd kill him myself."

"But he couldn't have had them cremated, John. Surely that's the family's decision?"

"Two doctors have to sign cremation forms, Marc, He's the first signatory on both, so he could easily have encouraged or pressured the families to do it. But I'll be looking into that."

Martin raised his hand politely and Annette smiled like she was his Mum.

"Yes Martin?"

"Can I ask...why is D.N.A. worth taking, Dr Winter? Won't it just be a mess of trace evidence? After all, the crash team worked on her, and she was in theatre as well."

"A very good question." Martin beamed. "But there are still some areas of the body where we shouldn't find foreign D.N.A., even in those circumstances. Whatever we do find, we'll eliminate anyone involved in the resusc and operation of course."

"God! Does that mean we need to get D.N.A. from everyone on staff, Doc?" Liam looked exhausted even thinking of it.

"Let's not jump ahead of ourselves, Liam. We need to find something worth comparison first."

The meeting continued for over an hour, until eventually, Craig saw everyone flagging and summed up.

"OK. Here's what we know for sure. Over the past three months there have been three deaths of healthy youngish women on the Maternity Unit. They all occurred either before or soon after they gave birth to baby girls. All had Pethidine and Insulin in their blood in high but non-lethal quantities, and all had Caesareans, either before or after death. The UK and Irish police have come back with no similar cases. But we might have a vague hit now in Australia - during the period that Beth Walker was there. Davy's chasing that up.

All three patients had the same male surgeon, Nigel Murdock, and the same female midwife, Beth Walker. The surgeons and midwives don't work in set pairs, and there are sixty-four possible combinations in the Unit. So the fact that they were paired during all three deaths is much more than coincidence. We also have knowledge of a very difficult relationship between Walker and Murdock."

Annette interjected. "And she was openly against Murdock doing so many Caesareans, sir."

He nodded, continuing. "Ms Walker lives an openly gay lifestyle, as is her right. But this has led to public disapproval by both Nigel Murdock and Sister Laurie Johns. It's safe to say that Sister Johns is a great fan of Mr Murdock and not a fan of Ms Walker at all. The deaths all occurred on the same ward in side rooms. Different ones, but all on the corridor nearest the Unit's front door. And the Unit is a locked one, with access only possible by buzzed admission or swipe-card. The last death shows Pethidine was deliberately introduced by a non-standard route called-'piggy -backing'. It's a method rarely used since the '80s. So probably done by a non-clinical person with drug and needle access, or by an older clinical member of staff. The drug seems to have been given as part of a set scenario, the significance of which is so far known only to the killer. Evie also had a laceration to her right cheek that was made deliberately. We don't know if that was also present on the two earlier victims.

None of the interviews yielded anything except unbelievable arrogance, or declarations of guilt about the fact that Evie died. And there's a lot of finger-pointing going on. No-one saw anything that points to a stranger attack. We were just lucky that it was a closed Unit. On an open adult ward strangers would have gone un-noticed."

Annette nodded and stared at John meaningfully. They both remembered when anyone could walk into wards off the street, relying on the busy staff to notice. Craig kept going, the length of his summary showing the complexity of the case.

"Liam, Annette and Joe's team have accounted for all the staff and builders present that evening. We caught a break with the relatives of other patients. They were few and far between from six pm on Monday until Tuesday morning. That saved us quite a bit of leg work."

He paused to draw breath and Liam filled the gap. "Boss - you still have Iain Lewes to see again, and we've got some cleaners to interview. Otherwise we're done."

Liam updated them on the episode with Lewes in the canteen, watching Craig closely when Katy was mentioned. He didn't even blink. He was good. Annette noticed John's discomfort when Liam said Natalie's name, and she shot him a 'shut-up' look that he completely missed.

"Lewes seemed pretty shifty, boss."

Annette interjected quickly. "Can I do Dr Lewes' re-interview with you, sir?"

"Here - do you fancy him then, Cutty?" Annette rolled her eyes. They *were* back at school.

"Don't be stupid, Liam. But the way he left the canteen so quickly made me think that he might be shy. Our Amy's shy and she acts just like that. Eating with her in public is a complete nightmare. Anyway, I asked around and everybody says that he's very nice, but he's become a bit reclusive since his wife passed away last summer. She got breast cancer and died...at thirty-three. And they lost a baby the year before."

Liam looked sheepish and immediately thought of Dannii. "Oh... That's why he didn't say much about family when I was interviewing him. Sorry."

"What was the baby Annette?"

"What?"

Craig's voice took on an urgent tone. "Which sex was the baby?"

"Oh. It was a little boy, sir. A miscarriage at twenty weeks."

He nodded. It was a long shot, but Lewes wasn't off the suspect list just yet. Annette saw where he was heading and continued tentatively.

"We don't want to give him a heart attack in the re-interview, sir. So I wondered if I could help. As a nurse maybe? No offence."

"None taken, Annette. I'd be glad of your company. But we do still need to talk to him. He's the only doctor who hasn't insisted on me doing it, so that's a mark in his favour as far as I'm concerned. But he *was* on the ward on Monday night, so he had access. Nicky, could you contact him for re-interview at High Street tomorrow morning, please."

Nicky smiled smugly. "Already done."

"Thanks. Let's continue. There's no CCTV inside the Unit, although it's now universal Trust practice. Please confirm that with the Chief Exec. Liam. We've released a brief 'holding' press statement, closed the Unit and redirected all maternity patients to Bangor. I've agreed press handling with the C.E.O. and signed that off with Superintendent Harrison. There's absolutely no delegation on dealing with the media, so find me on everything please, Nicky." She nodded quickly, knowing from his tone that there would be trouble if it didn't happen.

"All ward staff are on temporary leave. But the M.P.E. has the biggest Maternity Unit in Northern Ireland, so inconvenience for the public is a significant factor. That means time is a pressure. The press will harass the life out of the D.C.S. until the Unit re-opens, and he'll roll it down to us. So we need to solve this quickly. Right. Next steps. Liam?"

"Chase up the CCTV absence. Why wasn't it working if it should have been? Get the swipe-card data and locate anyone who went in and out on Monday night, swiped or otherwise."

Craig smiled at his anticipation and nodded Annette to do the same.

"I'll take Martin, Davy and anyone Joe can spare, sir. And dig deeper into the backgrounds of the three dead women. We need any connections at all to each other, the hospital, its staff and Tommy Hill. If they exist. We also need to find out more about Beth Walker, Iain Lewes and Nigel Murdock. And I'll have a good look at Sister Johns as well."

"Good. You all know what you're doing then. Has anyone met with the '80s' families yet? Joe?"

Everyone turned to look at Joe Rice - he was slumped back in his chair with his eyes closed! When he heard the sudden silence he jerked himself upright. Then he gave them all a challenging look that said he hadn't been asleep, just listening intently. His next words showed that it was the truth.

"I contacted the victims' living relatives, sir. Out of eight parents, five are dead and three are in their seventies. There are five surviving siblings, all in their forties. But only two are still living here and we're interviewing them tomorrow."

"That's brilliant Joe. Try to gauge any vengeful feelings. You know what to look for." Martin leaned forward eagerly.

"Sir?"

"Yes, Martin."

"All the babies were girls, sir. Should we add that into the record search details?"

He was right. They'd used it for the police checks, but nearly overlooked it for the records.

"Thanks for the reminder. Davy's already been using it his database searches. OK. When you're checking for records, can everyone focus on past maternal deaths with surviving female children please. Well done Martin. OK Joe, the Drugs Squad link. Take that further and find out more about Tommy's little operation. How big is it? Who are his rivals? Who has he annoyed? And does anyone want to hurt him badly enough that they would use his daughter to do it?

Ditto with the two earlier deaths. Were the women or their families connected with anything that could provide a motive for murdering them or Evie? Look for any links they had with Tommy, however tenuous. Go back as far back as the 80s' murders. And get Reggie Boyd's team to give you daily updates - they're keeping an eye on Tommy locally on the Demesne. Tommy's been pretty clear that he would happily do our job for us. He's impatient, and remember, he believes in capital punishment without trial."

Craig paused and rubbed his eyes tiredly. Nicky glanced at him sympathetically, realising the pressure he was under. She'd brew him some of her best coffee when they got back upstairs.

"OK, Martin. Go back to the Trust and liaise with the medical records office, the C.E.O. has assured their complete co-operation. Find out if there were any other deaths before January on that Unit. Women giving birth, any and all deaths where the female baby survived. Caesareans in particular.

Go back twenty years if there are records, our killer could be a surviving child, or a sibling whose mother died on the ward. They would be adults now and capable of killing. Check Murdock's cases particularly. Bring the data summary directly to me, and copy it to Dr Winter please. If you've any queries, check with Liam and Annette. And there *has* to be a data file for the swipe-cards somewhere in the hospital system. Go straight to the C.E.O.'s office if the I.T. staff aren't cooperating with you."

"Hospitals are obsessive about information now, sir. They horde everything in case there's a negligence case." Annette nodded in agreement.

"Davy, chase that hit on Beth Walker in Australia - it's probably nothing but we need it cleared. OK, I have my last interviews tomorrow morning, and then I'm in court on Warwick all afternoon. Let's have the briefing tomorrow at twelve please. I want to make as much progress on this as we can before the weekend. John, Des, anything more you would like to say before we close?"

Des shook his head but John spoke, his mellifluous baritone echoing around the hard-walled room.

"I've started to go back over the three known deaths. Looking at the notes and P.M.s, and any inquests where they happened. Also any reports to the General Medical or Nursing Councils, defence unions, insurance claims etc. I'll do the same for any other similar deaths that Martin can find, although I hope that there aren't any. We know that Evie didn't die from her drug levels, but we're waiting for the stomach content analysis to rule out other forms of poisoning. There's one other idea I want to check out, so I haven't quite finished the P.M. But I should have a definitive cause of death for you by tomorrow, Marc. Then there's the D.N.A. to check of course."

"We've quite a bit of the G.M.C. and medical defence stuff already, Dr Winter. I'll get it over to you."

"Thanks Nicky, that's helpful. Just one question - can anyone tell me how old Dr Lewes is? Doctors usually marry people they meet during training, so he's probably in his thirties like his wife. But that's young for a consultant."

"I've got that one, Doc. He's forty–three." Older than John had expected.

"Right, then that means he *would* have learned to 'piggy-back' medication, Marc. As he's a paediatrician, he'll be up-to-date with injecting techniques, so it's unlikely that he'd ever do it. But it's not impossible that he could have made a slip and 'piggy-backed' if he was under pressure."

Craig nodded. Pressure. Like when he was killing someone.

"OK, that's great everyone. Look, it's been hard week and it's nearly six now. Anyone who doesn't have to rush home, let's head over to The James for a quick one."

"Aye, that'll do, boss. Danni can simmer for an hour. It's never good for women to get passion as soon as they demand

135

it."

Joe laughed so loudly that he spat out his coffee. Nicky rolled her eyes and Davy stifled a laugh. Liam used the natural break to push his luck.

"Here, Doc, like I was saying, we met that doctor you brought to the Christmas party. Natalie something..."

Craig couldn't work out whether John didn't hear Liam, or he was actually ignoring him. Either way he was out of the door before any of them could ask.

Chapter Fifteen

Thursday. 8pm.

Sharp echoes traced Tommy's steps around the draughty hall, until he reached a side window and stood completely still. He peered through the dirt and cracks at the '70s housing estate outside. The graffiti on the walls had all changed. It had said 'Fuck the Pigs' when he was a lad, now it was 'Banksy is a Wanker'. But even the hopeful fairy-lights winding around a balcony opposite couldn't make the grey concrete sprawl look any more inviting.

It was one of the last of the architect's mistakes that had once covered every city in the U.K. They were knocking them all down now, to build red-brick starter homes clustered in streets. The planners were finally realising that streets were communities, just like the ones they'd destroyed forty years before. Pity he hadn't shot a few architects if he was going to do time anyway.

He'd grown up off the Springfield Road, playing in the streets outside, with his mother ever watchful at the window. His Da did piece-work at the Docks, out at five o'clock every morning to be 'schooled' for the boats. They were always broke, but it was a hell of a better childhood than hanging off a balcony twenty floors up. Mind you...he'd still turned out to be a bollocks, so the kids here had no hope.

Hill didn't turn when the door opened, the heavy thump of a bag already identifying Gerdy. Instead he just threw, "what kept you?" and, "where's McCrae and Coyler?" coldly over his shoulder.

"Comin' now boss, they're just lockin' the car up. Don't want to get it nicked. There's all sorts of scum about nowadays."

Tommy ignored him and walked towards the stage at the front of the hall. He sat down heavily, propping his feet up on an old Formica table. Then he dumped a wad of papers on top of it, and waited to be joined by the rest of his little gang. Gone were the days when his name could've mustered twenty men at an hour's notice, but his best man, Robbo, had gone to Maghaberry after last year's drugs bust. There was nothing else for it. He'd just have to make do with these Muppets now.

Rory McCrae and Ralph Coyle dandered casually into the hall, scanning its dark corners - old threats and learned behaviour. Hill lit a cigarette and jerked his fist at them, beckoning them down.

"Hurry up an' come here. I've info for you. I want you al' out there workin' on Saturday night."

"Aye right boss, keep yer hair on." They all laughed at the old joke. Tommy had shaved his head years back.

"Very funny, like I niver heard that one before. Now shut up!"

His shout echoed around the hall and the men fell immediately silent, watching as he pulled the papers into three neat piles. He placed one in front of each of them. They were names and addresses, and as soon as he'd lifted his, Gerdy started moaning.

"Fuck! Why do I hav to fally Murray? Can't I hav a girl?"

"For fuck's sake Gerdy, you whine worse than any woman I've ever had. You're gettin' Murray 'cos you're the strongest, an' he's a big bastard."

"Oh, aye. Right..."

"Coyler, you take the blonde Doc – 'cos you're not ruled by your dick like McCrae. McCrae, you get the lezzy nurse."

"Thanks a bucket load, Tommy. And what'll you be doin'

all this time?"

Hill snarled and leaned forward ominously, his voice rising in volume.

"An' how's that any of your fuckin' business? Who the hell do you think you are, questionin' me?"

The three men stiffened immediately. The legend of Tommy Hill was still enough to subdue them.

McCrae's bravado evaporated rapidly. "Sarry. I didn't mean nothin' by it, Tommy, you know that. Sarry."

Hill stared him out until McCrae dropped his gaze, then he leaned back and lit a fresh cigarette. He held the silence through three long drags before he spoke.

"What I'll be doin' is takin' down the boss man. That stuck-up shite Murdock. He's all mine. Now - have you all got the stuff?"

Gerdy leaned forward eagerly. "Aye. Lots of roofies an' rope. An' I've got a Colt, Coyler's got a Taser, and McCrae's a Stanley knife."

Tommy lunged towards him and all three men leaned back in reflex.

"What the fuck do you think you'll be doin' with those? You're not Dirty Harry for fuck's sake! You're only fallyin' and reportin', till I say to lift them. The only one that'll die is the guilty fucker...An' where the hell did you get a Taser from anyway, Coyle?"

"I bought it off a guy in the Elm one night. He wis a real nice guy too. Bought me a pint. He had a fair load o' them."

"Jesus H. Christ! Luk, watch my lips." Hill spoke with exaggerated slowness. "Yous-are-just-fuckin'-fallyin-them. An' when I tell you, you'll bring them here for me to talk to. WHEN I tell you."

"Oh aye...aye. 'Course Tommy. That's what we're goin' to do. Just fally an' bring em here. 'Course, aye. Dead-on Tommy."

Hill squinted at him, checking his sincerity before

continuing.

"You'll start on Saturday night. That's when they'll be out of the hospital for sure. Murdock will be in Belfast doing his stuck-up private patients, an' the others'll be off home. Their stuff's in your notes there. An' remember, no one gets hurt till I say so. An' you'd better get ready till sleep in your cars. Ring me every three hours after six on Saturday night, till I give you the word to lift them. An' mind me well - I want regalar reports from all of you."

He waved his hand dismissively. "Now, piss off. I've important things to do." Then he banged his fist down hard on the table to signal that the meeting was adjourned.

Hill rose and strolled slowly out of the hall, not looking back. No-one spoke until they heard his car revving.

"Fuck, I widn't like to be the one who did for his Evie. There'll be no day in court before they die."

"He'll cut their balls off."

Gerdy and Coyler speculated wildly on the fate of Evie's killer, while McCrae stood up to go. He was bored by the lack of entertainment now that Tommy had left. He feared his boss, but he always enjoyed the fireworks he created.

"Cheers lads, I'll catch you later. I'm away to the Elm for a pint an' some pussy. I've a real wee goer waitin' for me the night. Happy Days."

Chapter Sixteen

Craig's Friday morning interview list had four doctor's names on it, including Iain Lewes. He saw the others quickly, certain that they wouldn't need to be seen again. None of them had the sang-froid required for murder. He was waiting the five minutes it would take for Annette to reach High Street, when his mobile suddenly vibrated.

"Hi Liam, what's the news?"

Liam's voice boomed through the ear-piece, so Craig put it on speaker and set it on the desk.

"Martin's doing the cross-corridor stuff, and it's all a bit tasty, boss. The M.P.E.'s cameras were due to for set-up and testing three weeks ago. CCTV's already working 24/7 in most wards, basically anywhere where there are children. You remember that case where a woman stole a baby in London? Well, CCTV's recommended for kids protection now."

"So why wasn't it set-up on Maternity? You'd think that would have been one of the first areas."

"Why indeed. Well, like we knew, the building works are winding up and moving over to St Marys soon. And the last cameras are being fitted in the complex next week, including in Maternity. The Maternity corridor connections had been shut down to protect the sparks. Far too early in my opinion. But what's really interesting is the lack of swipe-card data for Monday night. There's none. Somehow *that* circuit mysteriously got broken as well."

"Yet it was working fine on Tuesday morning when we arrived on the Unit. This is too convenient, Liam"

"Way too convenient. The cross-corridor pics should help, so I'm on a dig there. And I've another meeting with the project lead at eleven. He's the guy Martin got the floor plans from – Ted Greenwood. I did his interview yesterday and he's had a real charisma bypass."

Craig laughed. It wasn't a crime, although maybe it should be. "OK. Follow that up and get back to me. I've got Dr Lewes to interview before the briefing, so I'll catch you back at the squad at twelve."

"Oh aye, one last thing. I've Martin doing the cleaners' interviews, so I'll update you on those at twelve as well."

"Don't work the boy too hard, Liam."

"Ah, sure he loves it. " He smiled smugly. "He keeps calling me sir as well. Bye."

Craig smiled and the phone clicked off. He called out through the door. "Sandi, any chance of two coffees and whatever Dr Lewes wants? And is Annette here yet?"

At that moment Annette rushed in, short of breath. "Sorry, sir, it took me longer than I'd thought. I had to bypass Custom House Square or get run over by skateboarders. There's some practice session going on. I've no idea how they don't kill themselves on those things."

"Lucia can skateboard you know. She learned during the summer she nannied in Florida, if you ever fancy it?"

"Ha, thanks, but I'll give that one a miss. Dr Lewes is sitting in reception and he looks terrified. No solicitor though. The mark of an innocent man?"

"Or one who thinks he's flameproof. OK Annette, I'd like you to lead on this please."

She smiled, knowing he was saying he trusted her judgment. "Thanks, sir. Step in as you need to."

Sandi came in with the drinks and greeted Annette warmly. They knew each other well from the Association of Women Police.

"Thanks Sandi. Could you bring in Dr Lewes, please?"

Iain Lewes came into the room like a hanged man. He gazed longingly at Sandi's disappearing back, as if he could cling onto her and escape. Then he sat down in worried silence, everything about his body language flat and confused. Craig motioned to Annette, and she pressed the button on the tape machine gently.

"For the benefit of the tape, this is Friday the 12th April 2013, interview commencing at 10.40 am. Present are..."

"D.C.I. Marc Craig,"

"D.S. Annette McElroy."

There was complete silence, until Annette spoke again. "Dr Lewes, could you identify yourself for the tape, please."

Iain Lewes startled as if he'd been woken from his sleep, and realised that he had a part to play. He was a thin, handsome man, well over six feet tall. With dark blonde hair and skin so pale that it looked as if he never pulled back the curtains. His expression was completely dead, as if he was defeated by life. Annette recognised the signs - she'd seen it before in patients with depression. She immediately wondered if he was on medication, thinking that he probably should be.

In that moment she became a nurse again, and glanced at Craig for approval. He nodded imperceptibly and she stood, moving across to sit beside Lewes. He jumped at her sudden proximity and then smiled tiredly at her, recognising the kindness. It was just a small smile, but it was enough to start with. Annette nodded encouragingly and he finally spoke.

"Dr Iain Lewes, 25b, Osborne Quay. BT9 7BU." His voice surprised her. It was a soft, beautiful baritone, like a Radio 4 newsreader's.

"Dr Lewes has agreed to have an informal chat with us. No charges have been brought and he has waived his right to counsel or companion. Could you please confirm that for the tape Dr Lewes? And that you're happy to have this meeting recorded?"

Lewes nodded. "Yes, that's fine...fine."

There was silence for another minute while Annette considered her first question. It couldn't be intimidating, or there mightn't be a second one without a solicitor. But she needn't have worried. Iain Lewes started talking spontaneously, and he didn't stop for ten minutes. He answered every personal and professional question that they asked him. Only hesitating once, when they asked about his wife and child.

He'd graduated from medical school in '92 and had gone to London to train, returning to Northern Ireland as a young consultant. He'd worked at St Mary's for eight years now. He'd met his wife there, and lost her there. Yes, he knew how to 'piggy-back' drugs, but it wasn't a technique they used often nowadays. He seemed genuinely confused at being asked about it. And yes, he knew Mr Murdock, but he didn't like him much.

He knew that he was clinically depressed - he'd already diagnosed himself. But he explained that doctors rarely admitted it, and even more rarely got treatment. There'd been a stigma attached to it when he'd trained. Medicine was a macho world where doctors were supposed to be perfect, and being ill was a prerogative awarded only to the public. They recognised what he said - policing was the same.

Annette asked every difficult question that needed to be asked. She framed them sensitively, but this was a murder investigation and Iain Lewes could still be a liar. Finally Craig was satisfied that Lewes wasn't their man, and the interview ended. Then he stood up and shook hands with the doctor, giving him back some of the status that a police presence always took away.

"Thank you for agreeing to a second interview, Dr Lewes. I know you're a busy man. Sergeant McElroy will show you out." Then he left the room diplomatically, leaving Annette to make Iain Lewes understand that doctors get sick too. And hopefully to get some help.

He stood outside the station in the warm April sunshine

and phoned Nicky. "Hi Nicky, can you get on to the D.C.S.' office and see if he has ten minutes to meet?"

"Actually, sir, he's asked if you could go up as soon as you get in. Something about wanting an update." Craig rubbed his temple and resigned himself to a grilling. Then he headed back to Docklands, leaving Annette still talking, with Jack keeping a watchful eye.

***

Terry Harrison had his sleeves rolled up when Craig arrived in his office. His hair was slicked back so hard that Craig swore he could see comb marks on his scalp. There was an angry glint in his eyes and Craig knew the signs. He wanted a quick result.

"Good morning, sir, you wanted to see me?"

"Sit, D.C.I. Craig. And tell me where you are with all this."

'Sit'. It was like a dog-training session. Well, if Harrison couldn't be bothered with the niceties then Craig was in the mood to play hard to get.

"The Warwick case, sir?"

Harrison lunged ominously across his desk. "No! The Trust one, of course! I'm having a hell of a time keeping the tabloids at bay. We need to issue a statement today and I want your input. Here's what I've drafted." He thrust a sheet of A4 rudely across the desk, and Craig scanned it deliberately slowly, just to annoy him.

Eventually he spoke. "Well, yes. That about sums it up. We've had a suspicious death. We've closed the Unit and diverted services, and there *is* no immediate danger to the public. That's really all we can say, until we get further with the enquiry." Harrison talked on without acknowledging what he'd said. He was a rude bastard and Craig hoped that he'd never become the same.

"Then there's the problem of Thomas Hill. The deceased's

name hasn't been released, but you know these reporters, they'll get it somehow. And then Hill's face will be all over the papers and bang goes our low-key investigation. We need a quick result on this, Craig."

We always did, sir, and not just for the sake of your career.

"We've got the Assistant Chief Constable interviews at the moment. And those talentless hacks will take great pleasure in putting Hill's photograph beside pictures of the successful candidate. Calling it a failure of policing, or some other rubbish. I need your assurance that another week won't pass without an arrest."

Harrison glared at him over clasped hands, his elbows propped on the table. He looked like he was praying, except Craig doubted he could even spell the word unless promotion was involved.

"I'll do my best, sir. We've got everyone working flat out - those that aren't at court on Warwick. And I've authorised overtime. Let me give you more detail of where we are."

He brought him up-to-date quickly, so that by the time that he'd finished Harrison was a lot calmer, and he was 'Marc' again. Not that he gave a toss about that.

"That's much more reassuring Marc. OK. Have a good weekend but I'd like to see you first thing Monday morning. Meanwhile I'll give this to The Telegram and The Chronicle and see if that calms them down."

Craig's thoughts as he walked down to the briefing room fell far short of charitable. 'Have a good weekend but come and see me on Monday with answers, Craig'. The two were incompatible. Julia was coming to stay for the weekend, now he'd hardly get to see her. He bet the same wouldn't be true of Harrison and his mistress.

***

By twelve the briefing room was full of the murder team,

plus Karl Rimmins from Drugs and Reggie Boyd from uniform covering the Demesne. Liam came hurtling in and beckoned Craig urgently to one side, showing him a plastic evidence bag. Craig nodded to get it to the lab and turned to start the meeting.

"Right. You'll be pleased to know that this is going to be quick. There's a lot to cover so I'll go round everyone first for updates. Let's start with Liam. The CCTV footage first please, Liam."

"Well, Martin was right." He scanned the room. "Where is Martin, by the way?"

"I haven't seen him, but don't probationers have to go to lectures?"

He shrugged and continued. "OK, Ted Greenwood's a real computer geek. Same as I told you earlier boss. The last CCTV cameras are being fitted this week and they had to switch off the system so the electricians didn't get a shock. He got defensive when I asked why they had to be off for so long. Just said scheduling was a difficult thing to organise, and better safe than sorry for the sparks. Aye, and oh yes, how would I like to try organising a new hospital build? He was stroppy enough with it too.

Anyway, no-one knows why the door swipe-system was off on Monday but Martin got all the available swipe-card data for last week. It shows Greenwood and his team in and out of the Unit all last week, all over the weekend, and this week every day and evening. So it's fair odds that they were in and out last Monday as well. He says they'll be around the Maternity Unit until next Friday, the 19th. And they'll leave the M.P.E. completely on the 26th. I've checked that with McAllister and it ties in with the Trust's building schedule." He stopped to draw breath and Nicky pushed a cup of tea towards him. He gulped down a mouthful gratefully and restarted.

"Aye, well. The swipe-card traces show Beth Walker, Katy

Stevens, Murdock and Laurie Johns swiping in and out from Sunday until the system 'failed' at Monday lunchtime. The interviews confirm Tommy Hill, Brian Murray and the Kerrs were buzzed in at various times on Monday daytime. The Kerrs and Murray weren't there after six on Monday so that rules them out on timing alone. We've confirmed their alibis."

Craig leaned forward, interrupting. "Where were they, Liam?"

"The Kerrs were seen at church on Monday evening, and Murray was in the Botanic Inn with two of his mates, wetting the baby's head in advance. Everyone else freely admits they were in the Unit on Monday evening, in the hours before Evie died. Dr Lewes swiped himself in and out all weekend, and Beth Walker remembers buzzing Dr Stevens in on Monday night. She also said that she found the door wedged open at one point, but no-one has owned up to that."

"What time was that?"

"About two o'clock on Tuesday morning - two hours before Evie died. She thought it was one of the night cleaners. They'd been mopping the corridor floors. But remember, any one of the others could have hidden on the ward all day if they'd wanted to. There are plenty of empty side-rooms. So I'm not sure how far any of this gets us.

But, as of now, the only people known to be on the ward after nine on Monday night, in the seven hours before Evie's death, were Katy Stevens, Nigel Murdock, Beth Walker and Iain Lewes. Tommy Hill was in and out all day and night. Everyone else has been interviewed and eliminated."

He paused for breath, taking another drink, and just then Martin rushed in, flushed and waving an apology.

"But, as I've said, anyone could have hidden there all day. Or got in when the cleaners propped the door open. Anyway, the cameras will be up and running by next week – that's why Greenwood's lot have been working so hard. They've to be ready to start over at St Marys on the 29th and they've still to finish the other wards and outpatient clinics at the M.P.E. before they leave on the 26th. So, like I said, they need to finish in Maternity by the 19th."

He pointed to a back-lit board with the schematics of the M.P.E. enlarged, just as Annette entered. She sat quietly to one side, raising a hand in apology.

"The floor plans here show the location of the cables, and where all the future camera points will be. There'll be a camera outside the main door, and eight inside the Unit. Two on each of the four corridors. Their exact positions haven't been decided yet. When they're up-and-running they'll be on a continuous loop, with the records stored digitally in future. Too late for Evie unfortunately."

Martin moved to sit beside Craig and whispered something in his ear. Craig interrupted Liam's flow. "Sorry Liam. Martin has just said he was looking at the cross-corridor tapes, and surprise, surprise, they're showing nothing but static from nine am Monday until nine am Tuesday. So we can't see who went down the parallel corridors towards Maternity in that time. So now we have no CCTV or swipe-card data at all for the relevant time window. This is definitely the killer covering their tracks. We have a killer with detailed electrical knowledge, and access."

"That could be an electrician, builders, most anaesthetists...the list is endless, sir."

Craig raked his hair in frustration. "You're right, Annette. We'll have to dig deeper into people's backgrounds. In particular we need to re-interview Greenwood and Randle. OK, Liam, let's move on."

"Aye well, the rest of the time I've been helping Annette look into everyone's backgrounds. There's nothing startling on most of the doctors. The only excitement is Beth's lifestyle, but even that's fairly tame. She's had the same girlfriend for six years, Janey Holmes. They met in Australia. Anyway, they go out clubbing a lot and there might be some Ecstasy being used, but nothing else." His face widened into a grin.

"But we've just had a breakthrough with one of the night cleaners." He consulted his notes. "A Mrs Lily Irvine from the Tullycarnet estate. Nice wee woman. Martin interviewed her." He nodded Martin on.

Martin sat forward, his face flushed with excitement, and Craig smiled. He remembered feeling that excited on his first case.

"She was on a few days holiday at her daughters in Glasgow, sir, so we only caught up with her today. She was cleaning on the ward from midnight on Monday through to eight on Tuesday morning, and she remembers Evie very well. She was very sad about what happened, especially as she had to clean-up the room after the resuscitation.

She didn't see anything during the resusc 'cos she was cleaning in post-natal when it all happened. But, when she was cleaning Evie's room later, she found a piece of paper on the floor in a corner. It must have got thrown there during the resuscitation. She stuck it in her overall pocket, to dump in the bin later."

Liam interrupted. "Bit of luck. She forgot all about it until she put on her overall today, boss. She gave it to Martin immediately. So we've sent it off to the lab."

"Martin - would you like to tell everyone what the note said?"

Martin beamed gratefully at Craig. "It was typed - just five words. It said 'I'm sorry, but it's necessary.' That's all it said, nothing else. It doesn't look like hospital paper, just a white A4 printer sheet. Do you think it's significant, sir?"

"Definitely. So well done. The lab will tell us more, but this could be a break. It's not something that you would see written randomly, so let's hope it's from our killer. And it's an educated sentence construction, so think back to the Double-O profile. We could have an educated killer. Right, let's keep going. The note's of interest, but we can't base a case on it."

Annette raised her pen politely to interrupt and Craig mentally contrasted it with Liam's bulldozer style of interjection. "Annette?"

"Yes, sir. Just on the note. They wanted it found, didn't they? They must have wanted it found?"

"I'm sure that they did." Craig nodded her on.

"Well also, remember that I mentioned Mr Murdock's slightly fast lifestyle? His sailing crowd is known to use coke. And they swop their wives around."

Joe's eyes nearly popped out.

"Here Joe. If you're shocked at that, you need to get out more, man."

"Anyway, there's information that Murdock socialises heavily with that crowd. After Deborah McCance's death in January, there was a query about whether he was entirely sober when she died. He'd been on the ward about thirty minutes before she was found, and one of the junior nurses noticed a strong smell of alcohol from him. If he smelled of alcohol, that might mean he was also on coke. And he was supposed to be on call that whole week.

But it was all hushed up as usual. There was nothing on the second death to suggest anything irregular in his behaviour, but Martin is still trying to get the last twenty years' records out of the Trust archives. They had everything on hard copy files but they were scanned to disc, and now some of the discs have corrupted. So we've had to send for all the original paper files again."

"How many deaths were there on the Unit in that time?"

"Very few until 2006, sir – just what you'd expect from Dr Winter's statistics. It went up in 2006, about the time that Murdock became a consultant there. But still not up to three deaths a year."

"When did Beth Walker join the Unit?"

"2008."

"OK. Martin, just focus on the cases since 2008 initially.

They were both working on the Unit then. But I'm not ignoring that we could be being fed a false trail, so do a quick scan of the Unit's cases for twenty years. And all Murdock's clinical practice as far back as you can."

A panicked look flew across Martin's face.

"Yes, I know he's been a doctor for nearly thirty years. But for the years before 2008 just look for anything reported for P.M., or to the Coroner, the General Medical Council and medical insurers. That should cover it. Even Murdock can't have that many of those in his career. Nicky and Davy have probably got most of it for you already."

Nicky nodded at Martin comfortingly.

"And I want to see the paper files ASAP, Annette. Go to the archive and pull them manually if you have to. Don't they do random alcohol and drugs tests on healthcare staff? The military and airlines have been doing them for years."

"No, not randomly, sir. They closed the hospital bars a few years back though."

"You used to have bars in hospitals, Cutty? Happy Days! Can we have one, boss?"

Craig laughed. He remembered one of his RAF friends telling him about the 'bottle to throttle' rule. The minimum time between drinking and flying a plane. It made sense that the rule should apply to anyone handling lives, but it obviously didn't.

"Joe, what's the story on Tommy Hill and the '80s' families?"

"There are only two people from the families who are local, young and fit enough to kill. I interviewed them and they both have sound alibis. They actually seemed sad that Evie had been killed, and made it clear that if they were going to kill anyone it would've been Tommy himself. As far as Tommy's behaviour nowadays is concerned..." He pointed towards the group's two new members. A skinny lad of about twenty-five, with a spiky, gelled hairstyle, and a tall older man.

"This is D.C. Karl Rimmins from the Drugs Squad, and Sergeant Reggie Boyd from uniform up at the Demesne, Tommy's stamping ground."

"Thanks for coming along. What can you tell us?"

Karl spoke first. He had a dark and dangerous look that would blend in well at clubs and drug haunts. Craig wondered if it was his own style or an undercover one. When he spoke his voice was slow, with a surprisingly polite accent, although Craig was sure he could switch it to Belfast slang at a moment's notice. It was almost a job requirement.

"Several of your people are known to us, sir. Beth Walker, Nigel Murdock and Tommy Hill."

Liam whistled. "Dear-oh. It's junkies anonymous up at the M.P.E."

"Walker and Murdock are just users, but Tommy's definitely dealing. Walker's been seen by the undercover teams at Sarajevo, on Ecstasy for sure. But it looks as if she's only taking it herself.

Murdock's little crowd are known as the White Waves locally. There's so much coke up their noses when they go sailing that I'm surprised no-one's fallen over board. But, again, they're just users, so less interesting to us than the dealers." He smiled at Craig with a glint in his eye. "Although we can bust them both if you want us to?"

Craig laughed, imagining Murdock being arrested at the yacht club. "Thanks, but not at the moment Karl. Although if we find out it's affected their patients in any way, you can have them both with my blessing. What about Tommy?"

"Yes, he's dealing everything he can get his hands on. Crack, coke, hash, skunk, Mephedrone, roofies; the lot. About all we don't have him on are the heavy opiates. Smack...sorry, that's Heroin.

"What about Pethidine?"

"It's not common on the street, but some users will take it if they can't get their hands on Heroin. But there's no sign of

Tommy actually dealing it. That's not to say that he couldn't get his hands on it if he wanted some. But I understand that it was his daughter that was killed?"

"Amongst others."

"Then, with respect, sir, why would he kill her? And I know Tommy's made a few enemies around the Demesne because of the drugs, but they're mostly rival dealers rather than users. And no-one springs to mind as the sort to kill his daughter to get back at him. Unfortunately there are more than enough addicts up there to keep all the dealers in business."

"What about an addict's family?"

"It's possible, but Reggie could tell you more on that than me."

Reggie Boyd was a fiftyish country man who was nearly as tall as Liam. But where Liam could give a fog horn a run for its money, Reggie was so quietly spoken that people strained to hear him. His lilting Donegal accent and quaint language made everything he said sound like an episode of Jackanory. Craig could almost picture the big storybook in his hand as he spoke.

"Well now, ladies and sirs, our Tommy's been out and about since he was released from the Maze in '98. He was a good wee boy for about two years, finding his feet again I suppose. And a lot of his playmates were up in Maghaberry for various bits of naughtiness. But since they've re-grouped he's been up to all manner of evil.

We know that his youth-club work is a front for a load of scams. Drugs, DVDs, counterfeit goods, petrol-stretching. You name it, Tommy will flog it. He's a real wee Demesne Del-boy. But everyone knows how much he loved Evie. He thought the sun rose and set on that girl. He missed a lot of her growing-up - she was only a year old when he went inside. So he'd been trying to make up for lost time recently.

The word is that his ex-wife is very saintly, and was being as good as gold. Supporting Evie getting to know her daddy and all that, 'aul lag that he is. I hear she's a good-living Christian woman who believes that Tommy will improve with forgiveness."

A derisive snort went around the room.

"Aye well...my feelings exactly. But there you go, it takes all sorts. Anyway, Tommy's been running around buck-daft for the past few days. Gathering up his crew and telling anyone who'll listen that he's got no faith in us. He calls us 'Pigs', which is lovely of course. And he says that he'll find her killer before we do - 'for sure'.

We've had words with him a few times already this week. But, to be fair, unless he actually steps out of line, there's not much we can do to stop him talking the big fight. I actually feel sorry for the wee villain. He really loved Evie. And I don't think there's any chance of him having killed her."

Craig nodded. Tommy wasn't one of his suspects but he still needed to be watched - for what he would do to anyone who actually was. Reggie was still talking and his soothing tones were calming the whole room. Craig couldn't imagine anyone staying agitated for long when he was around.

"Evie was a lovely wee girl. I met her a couple of times - bonny and polite as they came. Of course that'll be the mother's influence. Tommy didn't go to the right kind of finishing school." He broke off for a well-earned laugh, led by Liam. "But, well sir, it's a huge loss to him. Of course, we'll keep a close eye on him and report back."

Craig nodded. "Thanks Reggie, and everyone, for the updates." He brought them up to speed on the D.C.S. meeting and the likely weekend press coverage. Finishing with his last few doctors' interviews, and pretty much ruling-out Iain Lewes. Liam shrugged, disagreeing.

"OK, thanks everyone – keep on the background research today. I want to know of any connections between these women, anything at all please. I'm authorizing weekend over-time if it's needed. We need to find out who this is very quickly. And I'm available 24/7 - you all have my number."

He glanced at Nicky for confirmation.

"Yes. And switchboard has it too, sir."

"OK everyone, just do what you can and we'll meet on Monday morning at eight."

They all started to leave and Nicky walked past, smiling at him.

"You need a break. Have you had any lunch? I can get you something from the canteen."

"Thanks Nicky, a sandwich would be great – whatever there is except prawn. I'm in court again at two, and then I'm going home at five for a quiet night in." Then he startled, remembering. "Oh hell! No I'm not. I've just remembered I promised I'd go to my folks. And then on to the Cathedral Quarter with some of Lucia's friends. They're heading for some place called 'Job's Haven'. I don't know what it is, but it sounds like hell."

Martin overheard and chipped in. "It's a club, sir, in the basement of a restaurant. It's great - really dark. I might see you there. A crowd from my year is going tonight."

Oh God. Craig's heart sank, that meant it was a kid's place. There was no way he was going now.

"It's one of Lucia's friend's birthdays. Probably their eighteenth, judging by how young they all look. I'm not going to a kid's club - I'll look like a dirty old man!"

Nicky wagged a finger at him, and Martin stared open-mouthed at someone chastising a D.C.I.

"They won't be that young! Lucia's only ten years younger than you - you're just too serious these days. And don't you dare cancel your sister. I'd kill our Ron if he ever cancelled me. A good night out with a bunch of giggly women will do you a power of good. And you never know, you might even dance." She stifled a laugh at the thought of it.

"Now listen, Mrs Morris - just because you think I'm boring! When I lived in London I was last out of the Ministry of Sound at 7 am, and then on to breakfast with the traders at Smithfield market. Now, I wonder what I did with my tight jeans..."

Nicky laughed. "Stick to the leather jacket, sir. I don't think anyone could cope with those..."

***

The court room was only half full and John knew that Craig would be relieved. He hated an audience. It was Friday afternoon, and even those people who'd been ghoulish enough to spectate earlier in the week, obviously preferred to start their weekend in some happier place. John wasn't testifying, just here to support Mike Augustus, one of his team. But he knew that Craig would be sitting outside on an unforgiving bench, waiting to be called.

He was. Sitting with him was Augustus, and Laura Warwick's best friend. All of them due to give testimony about the hell that Laura Warwick had lived and died in.

All of a sudden the court's side door opened, and a swarm of black-gowned barristers entered, like a murder of crows. The court stood and an elderly Judge appeared at the front, beckoning them all to sit, as the barristers took up their opposing positions.

Amanda Graham, the prosecutor, smiled out at Craig just before the door closed. She was all right - he'd known her since Uni. He just hoped that she was tough enough to cope with Roger Doyle. Annette and Nicky had given him the 'stay calm' lecture just before he'd left the squad. But they needn't have worried. He'd stay calm. He had to. Letting Doyle rile him wouldn't help the Warwicks, or the conviction that they'd worked for months to achieve. He wouldn't let anyone goad him into blowing it now.

The witnesses stood up and sat down, entering and exiting in turn to give their evidence, while Craig sat waiting on the bench outside like a team reserve. Finally he heard his name being called, cutting through his thoughts. Lucia said it was

157

called the 'Cocktail Party Effect'. Where you always heard your name being said, regardless of other distractions. Just like at a party. Some party.

Craig stood up and entered the court, taking his indicated seat on the front row. The courtroom was modern and bright, with pale wooden benches and a high bright ceiling. But the gravitas that hung over it made it feel like a tomb.

Roger Doyle was sitting in front of him, so close that Craig could have hit him. And he would have done if he'd had less self-control. John sat in the front row, listening intently. He nodded at Craig reassuringly then shot Doyle a look that said 'pompous wanker'. Craig hoped that the jury agreed.

The defendant, Kenny Ewing, was sitting in his accused position, staring into space. He was a tall, muscular man with swarthy skin and coarse black hair, and hands that looked like slabs of ham at the ends of his arms. Even without a knife, any of the blows he'd landed on Laura Warwick would have killed her easily.

He had the dull look of a man whose mind had left him long before, aided and abetted by his 'little helpers'. First skunk, then Ecstasy, and finally Heroin. By the time he'd met the Warwick's lovely daughter, all thought and conscience had already left him. Replaced by need and addiction, and every selfish human urge.

Craig could see Laura's parents sitting across the atrium, ashen and tired, with their heads down. Saying nothing to each other, afraid to break the silence. He glanced again and her mother was gazing straight at him now, with a desperate look that said, "Help us...help Laura."

He thought of how his parents would feel if Lucia was the victim, and it made him despise Doyle even more than Kenny Ewing. Which one should you hate more? The wild animal? Or the person who sets them free to kill again?

Craig heard his name called and walked to the witness box. He was sworn in taking a seat, and Amanda Graham took her position close in front of him. She questioned him well on the evidence, so that it came out focusing the jury on the certainties. The signed confession, the witness statements, and the enhanced, clear images shown on the CCTV. He could see the jurors nodding, gazing at Ewing's dull stare and lack of emotion, and then back at him as he described their findings. He hoped they would look past his professional front and see how much the case moved him.

He stopped for a drink of water, swallowing hard, and the Judge smiled encouragingly at him, knowing that even the most senior officers found his world daunting. Craig appreciated the smile, but it wasn't that he found the place or proceedings too much. It was fear. The fear that giving Doyle any small gap to widen, would lead to the Warwicks never receiving justice. And that was all anyone could give them now.

After twenty minutes Amanda Graham nodded and sat and Roger Doyle stood up. He leaned over to his sycophantic junior to whisper something, with a sarcastic smile. And then, with a swish of his gown, he walked over and stood directly in front of Craig.

"Good afternoon, Detective Chief Inspector Craig. I am, as you know, Roger Doyle, Queen's Counsel. I am now going to ask you some questions. Most particularly regarding the *lack* of forensic evidence linking the alleged weapon to the defendant, Mr Kenneth Ewing. Please answer them succinctly."

Cheeky bastard - telling him how to give evidence.

"Now..." Doyle paused for so long that Craig thought he was waiting for a drum roll. He looked like some grotesque pantomime villain in his black cloak. All that was missing was a handlebar moustache.

"On the evening in question, the 20th December 2012, my client does not deny that he was at his home, at 28 Morris Heights Belfast 4. A home that he shared with Ms Laura

Warwick, and had done so happily for five years."

Happily? Not judging by the number of old fractures she had.

"Nor does he deny that he returned home that evening, as confirmed by the extremely poor quality CCTV photographs." He paused and stared at the jury, emphasising his next words. "Photographs so kindly 'cleaned-up' by your police laboratories." Craig could see annoyance on some of the jurors' faces. He hoped that it was directed at Doyle, not the evidence.

"He also does not deny that Ms Warwick received a fatal injury from a knife, shown and entered into evidence as Exhibit 15. No-one denies any of this. It was confirmed by your Forensic laboratory and by the post-mortem evidence given earlier by Dr Augustus."

Wait for it...here it comes... the 'however'...

"However...my client maintains that he was, in fact, merely sitting in the kitchen of the home he shared with Ms Laura Warwick. When she came into that kitchen behaving hysterically. That she was holding a knife. A knife with which she had in fact already been cutting herself in self-harm that evening, before he arrived home. Just as she had cut herself many times before. Facts which have been amply confirmed by her medical records.

Mr Ewing further asserts that he attempted to stop her from harming herself, by removing the knife from her. And that, after a struggle where she tried to stab him, he defended himself by pushing her away." He paused again, contorting his face into a facsimile of sorrow and lowering his voice to suit. "She then fell upon the knife, sadly killing herself."

Craig was starting to wonder if it was a question or a soliloquy. Get on with it.

"Can you therefore tell the court, D.C.I. Craig, why your statement, that he was holding the knife, should be believed, when there is no forensic evidence to support that assertion in any way? Mr Ewing's prints are not on the handle of the knife, nor indeed are they on the blade of the knife. In fact, there was nothing to show them on the knife at all! But Ms Warwick's prints were on both the knife handle and blade. Please answer the question, Mr Craig."

Oh, he was going to answer the question all right. Craig stood up.

"There is no need to stand, Mr Craig."

Craig ignored Doyle's protest and turned to the Judge. "I would prefer to, if the court has no objection. It helps me to think."

Doyle's objections became louder but the Judge nodded for him to go ahead. Craig thought he saw a smile in his eyes. John's smile was much more obvious.

"As Mr Ewing entered their home, he was pictured on the estate's CCTV weaving from side to side, in a manner consistent with alcohol intoxication. This was later confirmed by a blood test. High levels of opiates were also found. In his urine. It was a very cold evening - in fact it had been snowing earlier in the day. And in the CCTV it can clearly be seen that Mr Ewing was wearing a jacket, scarf and gloves. All of which he was seen still wearing exactly three minutes later when he re-emerged from his home.

When he re-emerged, his scarf was knotted in an identical way to when he entered. This was confirmed by laboratory measurement of the CCTV footage. Therefore it is highly unlikely that he had in fact removed his scarf in the house. And likely therefore that he had also not removed other items of clothing, including his gloves, during his brief three minutes indoors." Each time he said three minutes, Craig made eye contact with a juror.

"The neighbours heard Mr Ewing enter his house and they heard him shouting almost immediately. The timing of this was later confirmed as the exact time that he entered. They then heard several loud bangs. These were consistent with noises that they had heard in the past. During the frequent domestic violence that Laura Warwick endured during their relationship. Violence that is confirmed by the medical records, from her frequent attendances at St Marys' Trust. And by the many complaints made to the police, by Ms Warwick and neighbours between 2010 and 2012. Unfortunately Ms Warwick later withdrew her complaints."

"Your Honour, I must object. These allegations were never prosecuted or proven. This is highly prejudicial to my client."

"Objection over-ruled, Mr Doyle. D.C.I. Craig clearly stated that Ms Warwick had withdrawn these earlier charges. Continue, D.C.I. Craig."

"Thank you, your Honour. Furthermore, on the tape we can see Mr Ewing shouting as he enters the house. Two independent lip-reading experts and our lip-reading software have since confirmed, that he was in fact repeatedly saying. 'I'm going to kill you, bitch'."

Doyle tried to interrupt again. But Craig drove on with his monologue, ignoring every attempt at objection or questioning. It was his turn now. The court was completely silent and the jurors remained still, listening intently. John leaned forward, urging Craig on and Amanda Graham smiled down at her notes, not daring to make eye contact in case it broke the spell.

"If Ms Warwick had been holding the knife when he approached her, as Mr Doyle would have us believe. Then he could not have got close enough to her to have inflicted all of the other fresh blunt injuries that were found on her body. She would surely have used the knife to defend herself, and stop him before she received them. Additionally, he would have displayed some signs of defensive wounds, which he did not.

Equally, had she been holding the knife by the handle as one normally does, and had he attempted to remove it from her, then he would have received cuts, either to his bare hands or to his gloves, from grasping the blade. Neither of these was found. The absence of his fingerprints on the knife handle can easily be explained by his wearing gloves." Craig paused and took a sip of water and John knew he was about to start summing up. He restarted more forcefully.

"Mr Ewing freely confessed to the killing, in the presence of the duty solicitor. He admitted that he walked into his home that evening fully intending to kill Ms Warwick, falsely believing that she was having a relationship with another man. You heard other witnesses testifying that he had said as much earlier that evening, in the Reverie Bar. He also admitted on tape that he walked into their kitchen and hit her with his fists several times. He accurately described those fresh injuries and their positions. He admitted that he then, without removing his gloves, lifted the knife from the kitchen drawer and stabbed her several times with it. First, superficially on her face and arms, as she attempted to defend herself, effectively mimicking the injuries of self-harm. And then the deeper, fatal abdominal wound described earlier by Dr Augustus. She lay on the floor bleeding to death while he watched her. He did not call an ambulance. Instead he casually left their home, again captured on CCTV, having taken a total of three minutes to kill Laura Warwick. Mr Ewing's signed confession gives us the only version of events which is entirely consistent with the post-mortem findings and forensic evidence that you have already heard."

As he described the signed confession, Craig turned and made eye contact with the jury, underlining in graphic detail each of the wounds received by Laura Warwick. He couldn't let himself look at her parents as he spoke, in case their hopeful pain distracted him. He only had one chance to make the jury hear the truth.

Doyle hadn't managed to divert or stall him. And Craig really hoped that any questions he asked now, attempting to discredit the evidence, were going to fall on deaf ears. Finally he sat down in the witness box, exhausted, catching the Judge's

163

quick acknowledgement of a job well done.

Doyle blustered on for another thirty minutes, trying to find gaps in his testimony. Re-asking each question with different angles and cadences. But Craig had done his case serious damage and he knew it. And as Craig stepped out of the witness box, he finally allowed himself to look at Laura Warwick's parents, hopeful that it would be enough.

Chapter Seventeen

Friday Evening.

The answer phone was flashing 'one' as Craig walked through the living-room, pulling open a cold beer. He knew who it was without listening - everyone but his Mother called his mobile, but she hated them. He rang her back, the phone in his right hand, holding his beer with his left.

"Buon giorno Mum, what do you want? I promise I'll be there in half an hour."

"Now Marco, don't ask your Mama what she want. You know she only ever want what best for you."

He laughed as the long running banter between himself and his vivacious mother ramped up.

"I'll tell you what I want. I want you please to pick up some oregano for me on way. And no be long. You have not see your sister in weeks."

He rubbed the cool bottle over his forehead. She was right, as usual. "How is Luce?"

"Lucia is fine...except for mad old boyfriend. He is stalking her!"

"What? Which one? Can't Richard sort him out?" Richard was Lucia's long-term boyfriend. A concert pianist who was away on tour.

"Ah, you see now...if you came 'ome more you would know these things. We see more of you when you live in London." They both laughed.

"OK. This is me, Mum. Leaving right now." He thought of

all the paper work that he should be doing, burying the thought quickly under her excitement.

"Excellente. We 'ave Penne al' Arrabiata."

"That's great, but go easy on the garlic please. I'm on-call all weekend, and I have to work with non-Italians remember. Have some pity on them!"

He ended the call and turned his back determinedly on the mountain of paperwork in the corner, throwing his suit jacket deftly over it. It would wait until tomorrow. Julia wasn't arriving until lunchtime, so he could make headway on it in the morning. He pulled off his tie and grabbed a worn leather jacket, and a box of chocolates he'd bought in France the month before. Then he pulled the front door hard behind him, relaxing already.

The block's communal hall light flickered on, just long enough to brighten his four flights to the car park, and he held the door open for one of his homecoming neighbours as he left. She was carrying a pile of books. He wasn't the only one working at the weekend then. Strangely it didn't make him feel any better.

As he drove the six miles to Holywood deliberately slowly, he could feel himself starting to relax. Flicking-on the CD player to what he thought was 'Snow Patrol's 'I'm Ready' he was surprised at the song that crooned out instead. Annette... She'd been changing the stations again.

Instead of the CD or his usual Radio One it was an overly sentimental ballad. It seemed familiar and for a moment he tried to place it, then he suddenly did and fell down the rabbit hole back to 1992. It was 'I will always love you', a song he really hated. The original by Dolly Parton was bad enough, but he'd wanted to hang himself every time Whitney Houston's version had come on. And it had come on in every bar and restaurant in London between '92 and '94.

It reminded him of his long-term ex, Camille. But not in a bad way anymore. They'd made their peace in London before

Christmas and moved on. He'd been seeing Julia McNulty for four months now and it was going well. Although she worked at headquarters in Limavady, and the travelling distance was wearing them both down. Limavady was Terry Harrison's part-time base, soon to be permanent. So Julia would soon have the joy of his company full-time.

Craig pulled into the driveway of the 1940s house he'd grown up in and sat in the car for a moment, his forehead resting tiredly against the cool steering-wheel. He thought of Julia's cherubic face and smiled, wishing that she could have come up tonight. But it was a long drive after a tiring week.

Just then, the light went on in the porch, as Murphy his elderly Labrador ran out, recognising the car. He knew that his mother would be next and he didn't want her to see his fatigue - she worried enough about her children.

Lifting the chocolates quickly he headed through the open porch-door, holding them high above Murphy's barking mouth. Then he turned into his mother's old-fashioned kitchen, its rustic atmosphere a world away from the violence he worked with.

It was warm and brightly-lit, with weathered wooden floors and overhead beams. Dean Martin sang soulfully in the background. The décor exactly mimicked her family's house outside Rome. Craig thought of the courtroom he'd been in that afternoon - how could six miles create two such different worlds? It was a silly question when two miles took you from the Shankill Road to the Falls in Belfast. And from Blair's Islington to the day-light drug dealing of Hackney.

Mirella Craig was standing at her Aga stirring a pot. Craig hugged her warmly, wrapping his arms around her increasingly ample waist. "Marco pet – it so good to see you," burst out in her hybrid Belfast-Italian accent. She greeted him so enthusiastically that anyone would have thought she hadn't just seen him a week ago.

"Have some bread and wine. Your father he gone for Lucia

and her friends. Her car is broken again. Please have look at it - your father is hopeless with practical things. How that man ever run a laboratory?"

She didn't pause for breath once, and the musical way she said lab-or-at-or-y clearly revealed English as her second language. When they were kids John had deliberately asked her to say long words, just to enjoy the melody of her accent.

"OK, Mum, I promise. I'll take a look over the weekend. Here are some of those chocolates you like. I forgot to give them to you last week."

"Oh Bella, Bella. Thank you, thank you." She kissed him quickly on both cheeks, excited and happy. If he'd given her a cup of tea she'd have been just as excited. Anything from her children was gold to Mirella. Then she launched into her next tirade and he laughed - his mother could talk for Ireland *and* Italy.

***

The Visitor watched the young man return to his car. They'd exchanged greetings and commented on the evenings getting brighter, then the package had been signed for and he'd left. The Visitor closed the door and walked back into the empty storeroom. Everywhere felt empty nowadays, but there would be peace soon, once the father made his move.

The boxes were opened, and their contents scrutinised. Each item stroked lovingly, never to be used. But Evie had been the last time they'd needed to kill. Soon the father would act and that would suffice. Should suffice.

A wave of regret rose at the thought that they would view justice at arm's length, as a mere spectator. But that was how it was, and as long as the father played his part, that was how it would stay.

***

Tommy shivered in the cold living-room. He made up his mind to fix the draughts soon, once he'd fixed the people who had killed Evie. He flicked on the electric fire and sat down, pulling his leather jacket round him. His thoughts went straight to Evie. He could almost feel her long hair tickling his cheek, the way it had done when she'd hugged him. She'd hugged him a lot in the last two years, her strangeness with him finally wearing off. He closed his eyes tight, picturing her face - soft and round, with huge dark eyes like her mother. Regret overwhelmed him at the way that he'd hurt them both. Miriam had loved him since they were kids, and he'd taken that love and ripped it in two, leaving her alone with their baby daughter. Tears pricked at his eyes as he thought of Evie's little girl, left now, just as he'd left her. He was going to kill whoever had done this. They'd destroyed his family.

As Tommy sat shivering and thinking, feeling sad about his life, he didn't spare one thought for the four families he'd left feeling the same.

***

"And please move Lucia from that place she live – it really not safe."

Mirella was setting out the plates for dinner, still talking. She'd hardly paused for breath since Craig had arrived twenty minutes before. He laughed to himself. His mother should have been a politician instead of a pianist; the opposition wouldn't have stood a chance.

His sister Lucia lived in an area of Belfast that was politely called 'distressed', although she told everyone it was 'up and coming'. His mother's response had been scathing. "It may be up and coming, but it still too low for you."

Lucia had ignored the jibe. The Georgian house she'd bought would have cost a fortune anywhere but an historical trouble spot. She was stubborn and independent and Craig could remember her being the same when she was three.

A car pulled into the driveway and a dark-blonde head appeared at the kitchen window, smiling. Lucia ran into the kitchen and hugged him. Then "Hi Marco, great to see you. What's for dinner Mum, I'm starving. Dad tried, but he said he can't fix the car, so will you fix it?" flew out in one breath.

Craig smiled down at her fondly. He was always surprised at how pretty she was, and how determined. She would march to ban the war, save the whale and even the disenfranchised ducks if they needed it. He admired her for it, but he dreaded every march - Tactical Support ribbed him about her for days afterwards.

They all knew her. She was too noisy to miss. And, as they never failed to tell him, 'we don't fancy you half as much, sir'. Craig hoped she never dated a policeman, he'd find it hard not to interfere. But she'd date who she wanted to, regardless of what he thought – as the parade of Goths and Rockers over the years had proved. At least Richard played the piano - his mum would forgive him anything for that.

Lucia threw a bread-stick across the table at him interrupting his thoughts, and they sat down at the scarred wooden trestle, lapsing into in-jokes. His father entered the room, much more sedately. He looked paler than Craig had ever seen him. They needed a trip to Italy.

"Hi Dad, how are you? Do you fancy a Northern Ireland match soon?"

"Ah, hello son. That would be grand. But...I'm a bit tired at the moment. Maybe in a few weeks."

His voice was quiet and he eased himself gingerly into a chair, loosening the tie that he always wore, even though he was retired. Craig could barely hear his words against the background music and asked him to repeat himself. When he spoke again, Tom Craig's voice was frail, a shadow of its normal cheerful tone. "How's work going, son?"

Mirella spun round and frowned at him. "No, no, Tom.

NOT the work talks this evening, he need a rest. Look at him, he's exhausted. He needs to eat and drink, and forget about dead people."

The words flew from her mouth in a sharp staccato, until she realised what she'd said and smiled sheepishly. "For few hours...please." Her pleading made Lucia play an imaginary violin, until Mirella threw a dishcloth at her.

Craig said nothing, just watched intensely as his father sat silent in the chair, not joining in the fun. It wasn't like him. Suddenly Murphy's cheerful barking stopped and he sat down beside the chair, whimpering. Craig's father sat back ashen-faced and silent, closing his eyes.

"Dad? Are you all right?"

Tom Craig didn't answer the anxious words, just waved his hand weakly towards his chest. Craig moved quickly to his side, recognising the signs. "Are you having chest pain?" Mirella turned instantly from her cooking and rushed across the kitchen, a look of fear on her face. His father nodded and Craig pulled out his mobile, dialling 999 and nodding Lucia to calm their mother down.

"Hello, emergency? I think my father's having a heart attack. The address is 300, My Lady's Mile, Holywood... Yes, yes. OK."

Craig dropped the phone and whipped into the bathroom, searching for his father's nitrate spray. It wasn't there! He ran back to the kitchen and his father indicated his jacket. Craig searched it urgently, finding the spray and squirting it twice under his tongue. His colour heightened slightly and his breathing slowed to normal, just as the ambulance arrived to take him to St Marys'.

All thoughts of food were forgotten as they readied their mother for the trip. Then they followed the sirens signalling Tom Craig's journey, into the world where his son had just spent his week.

Chapter Eighteen

2am.

Saturday morning started earlier than planned for Craig. He sipped a vending machine coffee, and stared exhausted through the window of the cardiac unit. Where the man he loved most in the world lay attached to machines blinking his vital rhythms. Tom Craig opened his eyes slowly, sensing his son's gaze. He beckoned him in with a single weak finger.

Craig cast a look back at the waiting room, where Lucia sat with her arm around their mother, and smiled at them both reassuringly. Then he pushed open the door and entered his father's room.

Tom Craig went to remove his oxygen mask and Craig stilled his thin hand with his own. He sat down, holding his father's hand in his, and started to speak reassuringly.

"You're OK, Dad."

His father opened his mouth to talk and Craig shook his head, restarting.

"The doctor said it was severe angina, not a heart attack." His father nodded, looking suddenly old. Craig stared at him, wondering when he'd aged. He'd always seemed so invincible.

"It was a godsend, Dad. A warning of what will happen if you don't get treatment." Craig gazed directly into his eyes to make sure that he was taking him seriously. "They say that the arteries in your heart might be narrowed. They want to check tomorrow by injecting dye."

Tom Craig nodded, understanding. "If they are, then

they're going to widen them. It's called angioplasty - they do it all the time. You'll be home in a few days."

His father gave a small smile and Craig knew that the scientist in him was admiring the medical advance.

Craig stood up. "I'll explain to Mum and then bring her in for a minute. Then I'll take her and Lucia home. I'll come back in an hour. They're putting up a bed in here for me."

His father shook his head weakly and Craig smiled, nodding his own in return. Then he brought in his mother and made the arrangements, temporarily becoming head of the family.

***

Julia brushed her hair hard then threw the brush on the floor, sinking her face into her hands and starting to cry. Oh God, why was life so hard? Was it this hard for everyone?

She didn't know how she was going to say it to him. How she would even start.

'I love you, Marc, but...' or, 'Marco, I've never felt like this about anyone, but we have to stop seeing each other'. Or 'Why can't you see this isn't working? Why are you so blind and stupid?'

The tears ran down her pink cheeks and she stared at herself in the mirror. Watching her own pain in some numb mime show. She'd rehearsed the words again and again and she still didn't know if she had the courage to say them.

Eventually she climbed into bed, exhausted. Dreading her trip to Belfast the next day, when it should have been a journey full of excitement. Would she really have the courage to say it? All she knew was that she had to.

***

Tommy drove off the Lisburn Road into Owenville Park,

173

slowing his pace to a crawl. He squinted at the house numbers, but it was too dark to see. It didn't matter, he knew what he was looking for. After five minutes driving he glimpsed Murdock's car on the forecourt of a house. The tip-off on his Belfast pad had been right.

He parked across the street, and then strolled past the house several times, casing it as he'd done so many others. Suddenly he glimpsed Murdock through the window. He was still awake.

Tommy snarled as the surgeon poured himself a whisky. He might be operating. If he'd been drunk when Evie had died, then he'd make him pay double.

***

By Saturday lunchtime, the diagnosis was confirmed and Tom Craig's angioplasty was over. It would normally have waited until Monday, but the tests had showed that every coronary artery was blocked. Immediate treatment was essential. It was either angioplasty or open heart surgery and angioplasty won. He was expected to make a full recovery and Craig knew that he was a very lucky man.

Tom Craig lay flat, smiling up at his son with all the curiosity of a true scientist. The consultant had shown him his X-rays, with dye outlining blocks in the three tubes that kept his heart beating. The information had fascinated him, and made Mirella cry in the corner. She was fussing around now, forcing water on him through a bent straw, while Lucia flicked though a pile of CDs, settling on some Mozart to calm her mother down.

Tom batted his wife's hand away with far more strength than he'd had the night before, and lifted off his oxygen mask. He smiled up at Craig, who was pacing the room. "Thanks Marc. Your quick actions saved my life." Craig shook his head silently, not wanting to think about the night before, and not trusting his voice to be unemotional.

Lucia grinned at him cheekily. "Yes, thanks Marco. I knew you'd come in useful someday." She smiled at her father, knowing exactly what he was thinking. "Now go back to work. Your pacing is doing my head in and you've got murders to solve."

She gave him a hug and smiled up at him, saying quietly. "I can take it from here. I'll call you with regular updates."

His mother smiled as well, then she tried to feed their father something pink from a cup. He raised his eyes to heaven in a look that said, "Take me with you, son." Then he smiled, waving Craig back to work.

***

Craig had thought about cancelling Julia's visit, but her anxious voice said something was up - he needed to see her. He got home at twelve o'clock, after the night and Saturday morning from hell. And after a full pot of coffee he speed-read his way through his mountain of notes and ordered his thoughts.

One quick call to John later and they'd finalised the profile of Evie's killer. Twenties to forties and male. Working in the Trust, well-educated and with a detailed knowledge of and access to, electrics. The well-educated part nearly ruled out Michael Randle, but only nearly. The pool of suspects was definitely shrinking.

He was just tidying-up when the entryphone buzzed and he pressed to answer it. John. His curiosity was immediately piqued. He'd just spoken to him an hour before and John always phoned rather than drop in. Then Craig remembered - he'd been going to visit his father when they'd talked. Something must be wrong with his Dad!

He buzzed him up urgently and pulled open the front door, meeting him out on the stairs "What's wrong? Lucia didn't ring me."

John stared at his anxious friend, instantly joining the dots. "God no, Marc! Your Dad's fine. I've just left him chatting away."

Relief flooded Craig's face and John turned to leave again. "I'm sorry, it was thoughtless of me to come."

Craig smiled at him, ignoring his protests. "Don't be stupid. It was my mistake. Come in."

He waved him into the flat and turned the percolator to high, re-heating the ever-ready coffee. As he was putting out the mugs John walked to the window, gazing through it miserably. Craig knew he needed to talk.

He quickly sent Julia a text asking her not to come until three. Then they sat down with a coffee, and he waited for John to speak.

He sat staring at his feet for almost ten minutes, sipping at the slowly cooling drink. Craig let him think, running through the things that could be bothering his friend. Top of the list was Natalie Ingrams.

He was right. When John finally spoke, it was in a whisper. As if admitting, even to his best friend, that there were things that he couldn't deal with, was somehow a failure. He was used to having the answers, not asking for them.

He spoke haltingly at first and each time he stalled Craig urged him on, reminding him he'd listened to him after Camille. He'd put up with his moods for years, now he would return the favour.

When John finally got the words out they made little sense. On one hand praising Natalie's virtues, on the other saying that he couldn't be with her, but couldn't explain exactly why.

"It all crystallised when I was in America."

"What crystallised?"

He shook his head, as if not understanding things himself. After ten minutes of broken, faltering words, he fell into a long silence and Craig interjected.

"It's hard missing someone. Not only if they've left you, but sometimes even when they still love you. Like Natalie does."

John glanced up from his cup hopefully, urging Craig to continue.

"Missing someone means you've got feelings for them. And that makes you vulnerable. You saw that with me after Camille."

John stared hard at the ground, and Craig knew he was on the right track. Might as well be hung for the whole sheep.

"You can spend your life alone, and never get close to anyone. That way you'll avoid all the pain that relationships can bring."

John stared pathetically at him and Craig's voice softened. "But you'll also never know the happiness."

The look in John's eyes said that he'd missed Natalie desperately in America, and it had made him feel unsafe. John's world was science. Logic and answers. Love was far too uncontrolled for him to cope with. That was why he'd ended their relationship when he'd returned. He'd probably thought it would make him happier, but it hadn't.

"Let me ask you something, John. Did you really think that you would stop missing Natalie just because you dumped her?"

Confusion flashed across Winter's face, followed by realisation. He nodded. "I suppose...yes...I did."

Craig shook his head. "It doesn't work like that. To use an analogy you're familiar with, falling in love is like being dead. And you can't be a little bit dead. Once you fall in love, it doesn't disappear just because you stop seeing the person. All you do by ending the relationship is leave yourself with all of the feelings, but none of the fun."

"I thought...if I didn't see her, then..."

"Then she could never hurt you?"

John nodded, looking down at the floor.

"Well, missing her will fade eventually, except when you're

reminded in some way." Craig remembered how long he'd missed Camille. Then he shook himself back to the present. "Then you'll get on with your life alone. Or maybe you'll meet someone else, and have emotions for them that aren't so strong. Feelings that you can control. But tell me something...Do you really want to feel less, John? Do you want to be with someone you don't love, or be on your own? You can do that if you want to. Or do you want to be with someone you really love? And take all the risks of being hurt that come with that?"

John shook his head. "I...I don't know, Marc. I really don't. What should I do?"

"No one can tell you that. But you're a scientist, so look at it logically. Life with Natalie, loving her, with all that brings. Or life without her feeling like this?"

John didn't answer, and a minute later he stood and left without a word, wandering slowly down to the car-park.

Craig watched him drive away and shook his head, hoping he would make the right choice. He would understand whatever he chose.

He'd leapt into love wholeheartedly with Camille and suffered five years of pain when she'd left, building a wall around himself that no one else could climb. Now he was taking the risk again with Julia. Was he the wise one, or was John?

***

7pm.

The Visitor watched from a distance, focussing on the exit from Owenville Park onto the Lisburn Road. It was a warm Saturday evening and Belfast's bars and restaurants had grabbed desperately at the weather, setting their tables out on the pavement, adorned with giant umbrellas more fitted to a sandy beach. This was BT9's answer to St Tropez, except the only St Tropez around here came in a bottle. The Visitor smiled wryly, amused by their own cold wit.

Young girls draped themselves against the railings, like pretty jewellery glittering to catch the eyes of passers-by. Men ostentatiously placed their car-keys on the table, ensuring that their high-end symbols were right side up, advertising their worth. It was entertaining enough street-theatre, and of course it was always fun to watch the watchers. Sitting in their cars, trying to blend-in with the locals, but so obviously far from home.

The father was in Owenville now, watching Murdock. But why hadn't he made people listen yet? Why hadn't he exposed them all? The Visitor had tried hard to be patient, to wait and see, to trust in the father's anger. Now that patience was running out. The father *must* act tonight.

***

Katy struggled through the block door buried under shopping bags, and half-fell into the communal foyer. She hit the lift button and slumped in, lying back against its mirrored wall. It was badly-lit and worn, like in a '70s Fonda movie, except without the 'Musak'. She reached her apartment and dropped her bags in the hall, pushing off her high heels and relaxing. Fingering her mother's heels as a toddler had left her with a love of them, and all they implied about a woman. But ten hours walking in them was enough.

She stood by the window, squidging the cool carpet between her toes. Across the river were the yellow steel cranes of Harland and Wolff. They *were* Belfast. Strong, dirty, aggressive. And modern and arty. The planners had finally realised what 'every man' already knew, Belfast already had its monument to urban renewal. Who needed a Hirst on the wall, when a glance out the window gave you Samson and Goliath?

The early evening sky was dimming, reddening the river. The closer sights faded as the faraway view grew, dominated by Stormont, Belfast's very own 'White House'. The graffiti artists had been at work on the wall opposite, with SICKO spray-painted eight feet high. Michael Moore had reached the Lagan. The brick canvas might be gone soon, a new development taking its place. Then the artists would have to find a new screen.

She fingered her waves, freed from her work chignon, and wondered what Craig would think of them. Then she shook the idea away quickly - he probably had a wife and children.

After a minute's more dreaming she yawned and poured herself a glass of wine. Shopping the week's stress out had definitely helped, but the thought of an evening spent in a noisy bar held no appeal. So she grabbed her mobile, cajoling Natalie into a quiet evening with a DVD. It didn't matter what it was; the wine would wash over it anyway.

***

Tommy sat in his battered Saab, parked opposite Murdock's house in Owenville Park. He'd done his homework. Murdock never went home to Cultra when his private patients were in labour, preferring to stay in his Belfast home. His wife was safely tucked-up in the suburbs, so Tommy wasn't surprised when a BMW pulled into the driveway and a slim brunette got out, carrying an overnight case. He doubted Mrs Murdock knew about her.

He lifted his camera and shot off a few frames. They might come in handy if blackmail was in order. Then he checked his watch. Seven-thirty. Murdock hadn't gone out and, now the brunette had arrived, it looked as if it would be a long wait before he did.

Tommy was in no hurry. He settled back in his seat, thinking of Evie and the baby. He pictured them together, happy, and sudden tears coursed down his face. They flowed unchecked for a moment, then he sniffed loudly, wiping them away with the back of his hand. He pushed all thoughts of Evie away and replaced them with ones of vengeance, returning to his sojourn. That was one good thing about doing time. It taught a man patience.

Ninety minutes later Murdock rushed out to his white Mercedes, driving it down Owenville Park to the Lisburn Road exit. Then he turned right, towards the M.P.E. Tommy followed at a safe distance, keeping his lights off until he got to the busy road. If Murdock was going to see a patient, he could get him in the car-park afterwards. It was all working out.

He completely missed the unmarked police-car watching him, and they both missed the other car parked across the road.

The Visitor turned the car key, ready to follow, and the caravan of watchers moved slowly, parading down the busy Lisburn Road. Past the glittering girls and their St Tropez-ed mothers. The over-priced boutiques and exclusive bars - catering for their customers' affluence in divorcee's heaven. Past the football-match overflow and the cheerful pubs, and down to the student end. With schools on the right and digs on the left, and the M.P.E. close by.

Murdock pulled into the consultant's car park and parked randomly, hurriedly lifting his briefcase from the boot. While Tommy settled down to wait again, relaxed. However long it took was fine with him, he had nowhere to rush off to. His phone rang abruptly, disturbing his rest.

"What do you want, Coyler? It's too early – I said to call me every three hours."

"Aye I know. But like, Tommy... it's this Doc. She's just been down to the gates an' collected a takeaway. She'll not be goin' nowhere the night. It's not worth me bein' here, I swear. Two hours, an' al' she's done is close the bloody curtains."

Tommy roared at him. "Don't you tell me what's worth it an' what's not, you wee shite! Just you remember who you're talkin' to." Coyler stared at the receiver nervously, glad that Tommy was a safe distance away.

"No affence meant Tommy, honest to God. But it's a waste o' time. Maybe I cud go help McCrae an' Gerdy instead?"

Tommy thought for a moment, cheeked by the suggestion. But he knew Coyler was right - it *was* a waste. And he might be seen. He could tail her tomorrow. I suppose...

He was going to agree but he made Coyler wait for his answer anyway. Tommy believed in the Reginald Perrin School of Management. 'Five, six, seven, eight, always pays to make them wait...' Finally he broke the silence, with a grudging. "A'right then". He hated anyone but himself having a good idea.

"Leave Gerdy – he'll sort Murray out by himsel'. You go an' find McCrae an' help him with the lezzy nurse. But mind you an' call me back every three hours like I said. An' just fally her. *I'll* tell you when to bring her to me. Now piss off, I'm on important work here wi' Murdock."

He slapped the phone shut angrily. He didn't like his plans going wrong, or other people making suggestions. He'd just sat back again and was nodding off, when his driver's window was rapped abruptly, jerking him out of his doze. He turned his head, ready with a mouthful of abuse, to be greeted by the smile of a plump young police officer. He motioned for Tommy to wind down the window.

"Good evening, Mr Hill. Now...I wonder if you could answer me one little question."

"What do you want, for fucks sake? I was half asleep."

"Well now, here's the thing. Exactly why were you sitting outside Mr Murdock's Owenville Park home twenty minutes ago? And just why are you sitting here now?"

"I don't know what you mean. Where's Owenville?"

"Now, now – don't be telling porkies, Mr Hill. We were

keeping an eye out anyway, but BT9 residents notice cars more than five years old, unless they're vintage. We had a wee call from a concerned neighbour and followed you here. You're not very good at this subterfuge lark, are you?"

"It's not against the law to sit in a public place, is it?"

"No...No, indeed it's not. That is, not unless you're keeping an eye on someone that you've recently assaulted and threatened. And very publicly as well. So let's just go to the station and have a wee chat." He gestured towards a second officer in the patrol car. "You come with me, and Alastair here will drive your car."

Tommy thought about arguing, but he knew the drill. The sooner he got it over with, the sooner he'd be back on the street to get Murdock. He shrugged and handed over his keys. There would be time for Nigel Murdock later. He was stuck in Belfast all weekend.

***

The Visitor watched them furiously in the darkness, rage gathering in his chest. The father was incompetent. He wouldn't expose the guilty, and he wouldn't make them listen. All he sought was his own small revenge. Disappointment welled up in the Visitor's throat and he roared wordlessly in the public place.

This couldn't happen, it couldn't be allowed. If they couldn't be exposed then they must all be punished. The father and police had had their chance, now he would do what was necessary. He smiled coldly and a frisson of excitement ran through him. It was his turn at last.

His hand drove deep into his pocket, his finger running along the smooth razored steel of a scalpel. Back and forth, back and forth, lingering at its wire-thin edge. He pressed down desperately until his own skin broke, and warm, sharp blood flowed in release. Then he sighed, savouring the thought of the other cuts to come. It would start soon. The pushing down, slicing through soft flesh to firm muscle, all yielding to the blade's sharp edge.

His excitement built and heat rose between his thighs. He let it grow - the time for restraint had gone. The father had had his chance and he had failed. Now there would be pleasure in the work and he welcomed it. He would have the pleasure of killing them all.

Chapter Nineteen

Craig and Julia were at Mumbai 27, one of Belfast's premier Indian restaurants. Craig was trying to have a life and make up for ignoring her all week, but he had too much on his mind and was failing badly. He knew that she had something to talk about and he was bad at deep discussions when he had a case on. His father's illness wasn't helping. Julia was stunning, bright and nice, but he was still relieved when his phone rang. The conversation had dried up after the Halim, and he welcomed any diversion.

Apologising with a smile, he went outside, staring down Talbot Street as he took the call. "D.C.I. Craig, Can I help you?"

"Sorry to bother you, sir, but it's Sergeant Maguire at Stranmillis Road station. I just thought you'd like to know we have a Tommy Hill here. We found him tailing a Mr Nigel Murdock and it flagged-up as your case. What would you like us to do with him?"

Craig sighed at the inevitability of it. "Thanks Sergeant, I'll come up now."

"As you like, sir. But I'm sure you shouldn't disturb your evening just for this. We can hold him a while until we get your cover officer."

"No, it's fine, Sergeant. It's a major case so I'll come. Give me twenty minutes."

The phone clicked off and Craig felt immediately guilty. He wanted to see Tommy before he did something stupid, but knew that the diversion served two purposes. He ignored his guilt quickly. If he was thinking about the case Julia would get no sense out of him tonight anyway. He'd drop her home and they could talk tomorrow.

***

Tommy waited patiently in the cell. He'd done it loads of times and it didn't take a fizz out of him now. When he was a young rip he'd have been sweating and smoking. But these days he just closed his eyes and dozed. Getting older had its pluses.

The cell door opened noisily and the saturnine custody sergeant walked in. "C'mon Mr Hill, let's go." He led him down a long corridor and then up two flights of stairs, then down another corridor. Until they finally reached a large interview room, where he did some more waiting.

Tommy wondered where they found the space for all the corridors. The station didn't look that big from the road, wedged-in between a wine-bar and a takeaway. He laughed to himself. It must be like the Tardis - a real police-box.

But he knew they'd moved him for a reason. Craig must be coming. Or that big ghost Cullen. Batman and Robin. Wallace and Gromit more like.

He gazed around him, bored. All interview rooms looked the same. They must've had the same crap painter too, judging by the drips they all had on the floor. He played with his lighter, clicking it against the top of the table in a rhythm, until he'd even managed to annoy himself.

Craig stood at his vantage point behind the mirror and watched him, hidden from view. Tommy already knew that someone was there, someone always was. Craig couldn't make up his mind whether to pity Hill or despise him. Pity him for Evie, or despise him for the drug dealing and the lives that he'd wrecked. He decided on a bit of both. Karma. What goes around, comes around, Tommy.

He hadn't actually touched Murdock, so all they could do was warn him off. Unless...until...a crime was committed. Real life policing wasn't like 'Minority Report'. You couldn't lock them up in advance because you knew what would happen. Pity. Then he realised he was thinking like Liam and shook himself hard.

After another minute watching Craig entered the room and sat across from the older man. He leaned back in his chair with his hands in his pockets and they stared at each other silently for a moment. Until Tommy blinked first, yawning noisily to cover it.

"Ach, just get the fuckin' lecture over with, would you. I've a home to go to the night, even if you like sleepin' here." He laughed loudly at his own wit. Craig didn't join in.

"Mr Hill, why were you following Mr Murdock? And please don't insult me by denying it. You were caught dead to rights."

Tommy pulled his mouth into a small twist, showing the same white teeth Craig remembered from Evie's picture at the Manse. He lit a cigarette and Craig let him take a single drag before he pointed out the no-smoking sign on the wall. Hill's only response was to blow a thin stream of smoke in his face. Craig shrugged, allowing the older man his small victory.

"I understand your grief Mr Hill. And I promise we're investigating the death of your daughter thoroughly. I have a full team working on it. But you know you were caught this evening. You also know that if a hair on Mr Murdock's head is harmed we will charge you. And if you obstruct this investigation in any way, then I'll find a reason to get you off the streets for longer than a few hours next time. That's a promise. Now, am I making myself clear?"

"Aye, aye, crystal. So I'll away home now. Unless you want me to call my brief?"

Craig shrugged indifferently and leaned back again, until Tommy capitulated.

"You've made your fuckin' point, Craig."

Craig slowly picked up the phone to the desk sergeant. "Sergeant Maguire, please escort Mr Hill off the premises… But hold his car, the tax disc expired two months ago." It might stop him following Murdock for a few hours at least.

Tommy rose abruptly and leaned threateningly across the table, his face six inches from Craig's. They locked eyes and neither man moved. The custody sergeant watched carefully from outside the door, ready to move the second that Tommy did. Then, just as suddenly, Hill sat down again, lounging back on his hard chair.

"You fuckin' Pigs. Y'awl think you're God. Well, fuck you. Do what you want, Craig. I'll have another motor here in twenty minutes."

"I don't doubt it Mr Hill. But you'd better make sure that it's clean this time, or it'll be joining this one in the pound."

***

10pm.

Coyler joined McCrae outside the nurse's home and they sat in the car, watching. Beth was staying there while her place was being re-wired. They saw the light go on in her ground floor room, exactly where Tommy had said she'd be. They had no idea how he'd found her, but he was good at the old research shit, right enough. That was why Tommy would always be 'Head Buck-Cat', and they'd always be following.

Ten minutes later Beth appeared, walking to a cab by the gate. She was dressed for clubbing, in tight jeggings and a black sequined top.

"Mind you Coyler - some of them lezzies is real cute."

"Just you mind what Tommy says, an' keep it in yer zip, McCrae. Let's follow that cab. Here, that's brilliant, I alays wanted to say that."

They drove off the M2 slip road towards town, and through the brightly-lit Saturday night streets. Finally the cab came to rest outside a restaurant called Made in Belfast, in the city's busy Cathedral Quarter. It was one of the 'in' places to go, and Janey, Beth's girlfriend, and some other friends, were meeting there for dinner. Beth had declined, in favour of a scented bath and her own thoughts. The week had been far too sad for small talk.

Janey was gazing through the restaurant window, and she came out immediately the cab arrived, one arm already in her jeans jacket. She had short brown hair and a slim pale prettiness, and they kissed briefly as she got in. Then the taxi drove off again towards Donegall Street. Where newspaper offices and funeral parlours, competed with nightclubs and nearby betting shops for anonymity. It would be a real challenge to look out of place there. The two men followed at a distance, trawling for somewhere to park.

"Look for somewhere close by, Coyler. To git her in the car easy."

"Tommy says we're just to watch her."

"Tommy says, Tommy says. I'm fuckin' sick of what Tommy says. Let's lift her an' have some fun. It's Saturday nite for fuck's sake!"

Coyler wasn't hard to persuade, and they searched for somewhere badly lit. It would be hard to get Beth into the car unnoticed if it was parked under a street lamp. Although, as McCrae said sarcastically. "Them club weirdoes will be so 'out of it', they won't even notice."

The music was thumping loudly through Sarajevo's open doors, and some of the waiting crowd were dancing, the warm night adding to their good mood. The queue's occupants hinted at a dress code of drag or high-end clubbing.

"Jesus Rory, we're gonna stick out somethin' wild in there. Its al' weemen."

"Na we won't, we're dead-on. Look at them lads at the

back."

He pointed to a group of men dressed as Clones, in matching black leather and chains. Others beside them sported tight t-shirts and tanned, shaved heads. He indicated Coyler's leather jacket and his own shaved pate, laughing. "We look just like them gay-boys. See."

"You speak for yerself, Gloria."

They dropped their wrists together, snorting as they drove around the corner. Then found a place high-up on a kerb, parking as far into the darkness as possible.

Coyler's attempts at mincing made McCrae's even worse, and by the time they reached the club they were hanging on to each other, laughing hard. The door-men smiled at them, 'young love', and waved them into the club's dark interior.

"Don't go wandrin' off on me, McCrae, ar I'll fuckin' well kill you. An' I'm not goin' anywhere near the bogs on me own."

McCrae laughed at him. "Don't be such a ganch, Coyler. Here, some of them lezzies is wild pretty. It's like bein' in McDanalds on a hunger strike. What a shockin' waste of weemen, when al' they need is a good man like me."

Beth was standing ten feet ahead of them now, handing Janey's jacket to the cloakroom drag queen. Then they headed into the bar, where Coyler recognised the music as '80's disco.

"At least I know some of this stuff, not like that thumping shite the kids listen to at the centre. One of them called it trance music. It was more like a bloody coma."

"Never you mind the music, just don't let them outta yer sight."

Beth was already at the bar, ordering, watching the bartender showing off like Tom Cruise in 'Cocktail'. Janey came up behind her, putting her arms around her waist. "Could you get me a beer please, babe?" Beth leaned back and kissed her cheek. "Sure, but go and mind the seats. We'll be standing for hours if we lose those."

"We're not sitting down all night! DJ Marius is on and he's brilliant. We're going to be boogieing, girl." She demonstrated her intentions by dancing her way back to their seats. Beth smiled fondly after her and then turned back to watch the bartender's show.

McCrae nodded Coyler to keep an eye on Janey while he slipped into place at the bar, two people down from Beth. Now that he knew which drinks were hers, the next bit was easy. He watched as Beth's cocktail was poured from the shaker, and placed beside the cold bottle of beer on the bar. While she reached into her bag for money, McCrae moved quickly. He deliberately knocked over the drink belonging to the girl beside her, so that it drenched both of their feet. Beth jumped back and turned to see what had caused the spill. Then she helped the girl, just as McCrae knew she would.

As she bent to fetch a hanky from her bag, he leaned over, dropping roofies into both of her drinks, slickly and unseen. Just as he'd done so many times before. Then he slipped away, unnoticed in the dark bar. Even if they'd used a drug dye, it was hard to see anything in this light. They were going to drink it all down, he was sure of it.

He swaggered over to where Coyler was leaning against the wall. "That's them al' done. Now, let's sit back an' watch the fireworks."

It didn't take long for the drugs to take effect. Within minutes, Janey was pulling at Beth's arm and dragging her onto the empty dance floor. They both weaved like they'd had a skin-full, and after five minutes frenzied dancing Beth staggered out towards the ladies, where Coyler was already waiting beside the door. McCrae followed, ready to lift her quickly off to the car. Just as Beth reached the toilets, she met a girl she knew and started spouting rubbish.

"Beth, I don't know what you're on, but it's a bit early to be talking crap isn't it? Is Janey out there?"

"Yes, yes, dancing – we're all dancing."

"OK, I'll catch you later." Coyler saw the girl look back at Beth concerned, and he hurried over as she passed McCrae.

"We'd better shift, McCrae. From the way she looked, she'll be draggin' the other one out here any minute." Just then Beth entered the ladies' toilets.

"For fuck's sake, Coyler. You shuda caught her before she got in."

They didn't have to worry. Beth was hardly in before she came out again, ricocheting off a wall. She swerved her way past Coyler, out through the fire door and into the stairwell for some air. Perfect.

They followed her quickly, and with one hand over her mouth and an arm under her knees, they grabbed her. McCrae started urgently down the stairwell, as fast as the steep stairs allowed without dropping her. Tommy wouldn't like the goods damaged.

"Tommy sed she wasn't to be hurt till he sezz so."

"Aye, aye. Just shut-the-fuck-up an' move. I've done this before you know."

The stairwell was deserted and they reached street level in under a minute. Then without warning, the fire door above them flew open, and a woman's high-pitched scream ripped through the air. "Beth, Beth. Leave her alone you bastards, leave her alone."

Janey flew down the stairs towards them, jumping on McCrae's back and clawing his face with her nails. "Fuck, you wee bitch. Fuck off."

His forearm crashed back, splitting Janey's lip, and her blood flooded his sleeve. Then he turned and kicked her legs out, fist raised to punch. Just then a sight he never wanted to see again greeted him. The fire door had re-opened as he'd thrown Janey off, and two men were jumping over the stair well. Both were big, and one of them was wearing full make-up and a dress!

"Fuck...drop her Coyler, an' leg it."

They dropped Beth hard onto the concrete floor and pushed through the fire-door, running fast, one of their pursuers hindered by the heels he wore. Disappearing quickly into the gloom, they slipped into a derelict shop, staying hidden in the darkness for over twenty minutes.

Their pursuers re-entered the club, returning quickly with the bouncers. The posse walked up and down Donegall Street searching every doorway and alley, until eventually the search felt fruitless. They gave up just as an ambulance appeared.

McCrae spotted the cover and they ran behind it to their parking space. Then he raked the car into reverse down Donegall Street. Screeching off towards Clifton Street, they hungrily lit cigarettes and sucked on them like oxygen.

"Oh shit...they'll call the Pigs. Tommy's gonna kill us...He'll fuckin' do for us both. You'd better ring him an' tell him what's happened, McCrae. This was your idea."

"Fuck! Are you mad? I'm not gonna tell him we got chased by a bloke in a dress! Fuck away off. You can tell him if you want to but I'm away to the Elm for a pint an' a woman. That's gonna give me nightmares for a year, that is. A bloke in a fuckin dress! I need a reel woman, right now. An' if you ever tell anyone what happened here the night, Coyler, I'll fuckin' kill you. Sure as shit I will."

Chapter Twenty

By one in the morning Gerdy's car was outside Stranmillis station, one officer studying its tax disc as another walked around it, scanning for faults. Tommy ignored them and sat in the passenger seat chain-smoking, until Craig nodded to let them go.

They pulled off at a scorch, heading for town, and Tommy quickly turned on his mobile. There were two messages. McCrae - they were tailing the nurse to the Sarajevo Club. What a picture, them two with the gay-boys. The second message was to ring Gerdy back, so he turned to his driver.

"An' what did you hav to say, Gerdy?"

"Tommy, that wee shite Murray's legged it."

"What do you mean legged it?"

"He took off on the Larne-Cairnryan ferry a couple af hours ago. Musta heard you was mad at him, an' knew what come next."

"Spineless wee shite, not even hangin' round for the funeral. An' what about his kid? Well he'd better stay away for good, or till I'm dead anyway, 'cos I'm gonna do for him."

He took a therapeutic drag on his cigarette and exhaled, dismissing Murray instantly. "Forgit him tonight."

Then his phone rang again - McCrae. Coyler had convinced Rory McCrae that they'd better tell Tommy about Beth, before the police did.

"What do you want, McCrae?"

Tommy listened in silence as the whole Sarajevo fiasco spewed out. His face got redder and redder until it was purple,

194

and spittle gathered on his chin. His phone hand shook violently and his left hand knotted into a fist, until he finally exploded.

"You fuckin' eejit, McCrae! Who told you to pick her up? What did I fuckin' tell you? Just watch her an' wait for my word. You stupid prick - fuck, fuck, fuck."

Tommy thought rapidly. "You two dickheads better hide out tonight, an' be at Windsor for twelve tomara. An' you'd better make your wills, 'cos I'm gonna fuckin' kill the pair of you."

He slammed the phone hard against the dashboard, until the froth at the side of his mouth finally seeped away and his breathing slowed. Then he turned to glare at Gerdy, who was staring straight ahead rigid with fear. Tommy was a killer and they all knew it.

"McCrae an' Coyler' was tailin' the lezzy an' they made a fuckin' bollocks of it. One fuckin' thing to do an' they can't even do that right. Now the Pigs will be after all of us. Fuck, fuck, fuck." His glare hardened and his low voice sank to a growl. "Did you know about this?"

"God, no - I was chasin' Murray like you told me. I knew nothin, nothin. Honest to God, Tommy."

"You'd better not have known, 'cos if I find out that you did..." He didn't need to finish the sentence. "Take me home an' leave me the car. I want you to fally the blonde tomara morning, so nick another one then. I'm tailin' Murdock again. It'll be our last chance to see if they're up to anythin', cos the Pigs will be pickin' us all up when the lezzy calls them."

He sucked angrily on his cigarette and swore under his breath. "McCrae doped her, so she'll be out for a few hours yet. I reckon we've most of tomara before they lift us, so we might as well be done for everythin'. That fucker Murdock's not getting' away scot-free. Meet us at Windsor at twelve. You can go back an' fally the Doc again afterwards."

His colour changed back to dark red as he thought again of

the mess. "I'm fuckin' gonna kill them both."

***

The Visitor waited, but by two in the morning Murdock still hadn't emerged from the hospital. Damn the father, damn all of them. It would have to wait, but only for tonight. He imagined the heady smell of sweat and fresh blood, and the heat rose in him again. With it the urge to cut grew stronger.

Tomorrow he would start. And if not Murdock, then another one of them would bleed. They would all bleed eventually.

***

Craig stayed at the station for a cup of coffee. He was still there at two, chatting with the night shift, when his mobile vibrated with a text. Who was texting him at this hour? Work always phoned him. It was probably a slow delivery from Lucia - it was always happening.

When he saw the name he was surprised. Julia. He was even more surprised by the content, when they'd only had dinner a few hours before. 'I need to see you urgently.' No smiley, her usual signature.

A myriad of thoughts flashed through his mind and none of them good. He abandoned his coffee and hurried to his car, for the five-minute journey to his riverside apartment. The light was on as he parked and he ran up the four flights of stairs, searching urgently for his keys. He dropped them noisily and winced, mindful that most people were already asleep, although not in the student streets he'd passed on his journey.

Before he could turn the lock his front door opened, and a small female hand shot out. It grabbed his jacket, pulling him firmly inside. Any fight or flight urges were tempered by the pair of full lips that locked softly onto his, and the long fine fingers stroking through his hair. Julia pulled back, looking at him intensely. Then keeping a firm hold of his hand, she drew him slowly towards the bedroom. Craig opened his mouth to say something, but was silenced with another kiss. The look in her eyes said that she was in no mood for discussion.

She led him into the softly lit bedroom, and with both hands pushed him down hard on his own large bed. Then she deftly removed his shirt and belt, and anything else that impeded her progress. Craig responded by flipping her over until he was looking down at her. Her hands moved slowly over his muscular chest, all the time her eyes saying 'yes'.

He vaguely noticed music pulsing in the background. It was her favourite singer, Gabrielle. A track he recognised from a few years back, urging sex on the dance floor. She had set the scene, this was what she wanted, and finally she broke her silence. Reassuring him that he wasn't to hesitate, that she'd been thinking about this since dinner. About his muscular arms, his tight tanned thighs. She needed this from him. This was her night.

All thoughts of work and worry and Tommy Hill and death instantly left him. All the tension of his father and court dissipated, and he lost himself in her smooth, soft skin as he took control. Leading and following, dominant and submissive, soft and hard and familiar. Until the sky lightened and they finally fell back together, into a deep, restful sleep.

Chapter Twenty-One

Sunday.

Daylight seeped through Katy's curtains, waking her. She groped for the clock, confused about the time. Nine am. Not as early as she thought, but bad enough on a Sunday. She could hear Natalie bashing about in the bathroom, in her version of 'being quiet'. She kept surgeons' hours, so this was probably a lie-in for her. But with the amount of red wine they'd drunk last night, Katy hadn't expected to see even her before lunch.

Her natural hostess kicked in and she dragged herself into a dressing gown. Opening the bedroom door just in time to see Natalie sneak down the hall, in what was probably her quietest tiptoe.

"Sorry Kate. Did I wake you? I have to go. I've work to do on my research paper. Owens wants to see it on Tuesday, so I need to get my skates on. Thanks for the Chinese. And keep me up to date with macho Craig and his merry men. Your life's far more exciting than mine nowadays."

Katy lied politely. "You didn't wake me. It's time I was up anyway. Do you have to go? If you fancy some breakfast we could go out for coffee and muffins." She was praying for a refusal. Sleep was much more attractive than any muffin.

"Nah - you go and get your beauty sleep."

"I need to buzz you out the gate. Are you sure you're sober enough to drive?"

"God yes – my body's very efficient, I had a misspent

youth. You're a hopeless drinker, by the way, Stevens. No stamina at all. I don't suppose you fancy lunch at Cutters Wharf about twelve? It looks like being a sunny day."

"Only if I can drink water."

"Wimp! OK, let me see how much headway I make with this paper and I'll call you." Then she laughed. "I sound just like a man. Sneaking out and saying I'll call you." They both smiled ruefully.

By the time Natalie reached her car, Katy was leaning sleepily out the window pointing the remote at the gate. It was a warm, hazy morning, and some excitable joggers were already running across the Albert Bridge, training for the May Marathon. Central Railway's sign was visible in the distance. Although sometimes broken letters meant that it was 'entral 'ailway' that people travelled on.

The usual row of cars was parked outside the apartments' gates. Sunday shoppers saving on parking fees - preferring five minutes' walk into town to a sixty pound ticket. She watched Natalie leave and then clambered back into bed headfirst, tossing up between breakfast and sleep. Sleep won.

***

The pink patterned duvet cover swirled violently in front of Beth's eyes and she knew that she was going to be sick. She'd barely reached the bathroom before she retched repeatedly, until there was only bile coming. What time was it? The only thing she could remember was a cab collecting her at the nurses' home, and then time evaporated. Kneeling over a toilet bowl wasn't helping with her recall.

She glanced down at her knees and realised she was still wearing what she'd gone out in. Shit! She'd missed work. Sister Johns would eat her alive. Then she threw up again, not finished yet. Resting back on her ankles, she suddenly remembered that she was on 'gardening leave'. The polite

NHS term for 'suspension, pending enquiries'. In this case, police enquiries.

Her head throbbed in vicious waves and the image of Evie hanging across the bed came back to her, with a force that put tears in her eyes. She buried her face in her hands as the week's events ran through her mind like an old movie. Could I have stopped her dying? I shouldn't have left her. I shouldn't have left her alone.

***

The slide focused and then blurred, and John twisted the microscope's dial angrily. Even science was letting him down now. He hadn't slept all night, going over Craig's words a hundred times in his head. He'd finally given up trying at five o'clock and driven to the lab, the only place in life where he felt one hundred percent safe. But he was too tired to work. He took off his glasses and rubbed his eyes, trying to make sense of things.

What if loving Natalie meant that he would always be a mess? Just more or less of one, depending on his emotions that day. He couldn't work like this. He couldn't live in this chaos. He needed to control his environment, not have it control him.

He slammed the slide down hard on the desk and it splintered into a prism. A thick shard of glass shaved off and pierced the palm of his hand, and he watched in numb fascination as his blood dripped onto the bench. Powerless to stem its flow, and more out of control than he'd been since he was a child.

***

Craig heard Julia tiptoeing around the kitchen and then the clink of mugs being set beside him. The soft sounds of Sunday filled the street outside, giving the time as late morning. He pressed his phone quickly. Eleven o'clock. He was shocked. He hadn't slept so well for weeks. Then he remembered what had happened the night before and guilt overwhelmed him.

Not guilt that they'd made love - they'd done that plenty of times before. But guilt that he'd ruined their dinner the night before, when this was their first weekend together in weeks. He needn't have worried.

Julia was holding a coffee towards him, with a soft smile that said she knew his thoughts. He opened his mouth to explain and she put a slim finger to his lips. "Shhh...Let me speak Marc. I have things to say." He nodded and she removed her finger, while he sat, mute and surprised by it all. Then she started speaking quickly, tripping over the words, desperate to get them out.

"Thank you for coming home when I texted. I meant to say all this at dinner, but...but your father was ill, and then you were called away so urgently." He felt a quick flash of guilt about his eagerness to leave the restaurant, and winced inwardly.

"I know you're on an important case, so I was going to wait until my next trip to say this. But then I couldn't sleep, and we've only got another day together."

She hesitated and glanced away, her voice breaking. "Marc...I'm sorry, but things aren't working for me long distance. Either...either something has to change, or...we need to stop seeing each other."

Every emotion available ran through him. Relief that she'd mentioned the distance when he'd been thinking about it all week. And then guilt at his relief. Gratitude that she'd tackled things head-on, but vague pique that she mightn't want him. And surprise at her complete self-control, last night and now.

She laughed weakly as the kaleidoscope of feelings crossed his face. "OK, let me just say this. You're great, Marc. Nice, kind, sexy...all the good stuff."

"But?"

"But you're also a workaholic. You're totally obsessed by your job, and I spend my days waiting for calls that never come. It's just as well that I know you're faithful or I might take it personally." Her voice softened and she smiled. "But I know I'm not competing with anyone but your victims, and I can't fault you for that."

The job. As usual. A detective's work got more attention than any woman did.

"I've been feeling this for weeks now, Marco. I love my job, but your work *really* comes first. It's a wall between you and the rest of the world at times. The real world. The one where people don't go around murdering each other and thinking of worse and worse ways to do it. And you're just like John, you love it. It's a game of cops and robbers for both of you."

He went to say something and her finger closed his lips again. All at once he saw how sad her eyes were, and how dangerously close to tears.

"No, don't stop me, please. The last thing I want is to stop seeing you, Marc, and I know how hard you work. But I can't cope with us only being together the odd day here and there."

Her voice broke and he could see that all her bravado was a front. Then she started again urgently, rushing through her words, as if stopping now would mean that they would never get said. "This distance and travel is killing me. I spend every day missing you. I need a real relationship now. I need to *see* you."

She stopped, spent, and stared mutely at the floor. After a minute of silence he reached over and turned her face gently towards him. He stared into her soft blue eyes, willing her to hear his thoughts. And in that split second he knew exactly what he wanted her to hear. 'I love you, Julia.' He felt it with a certainty that he hadn't felt for years. Too many years. Since Camille.

She was talking again, stumbling through the words in her

high clear voice. "It...maybe it means I'm selfish...I don't know...Is it selfish to want to be with you? Maybe...And I feel guilty for being demanding, because I know that you're helping people. Helping find their killers, and making people safe ...but..."

Suddenly she sobbed and the brightness in her eyes became tears that ran gently down her cheeks and across her freckled nose. She wiped them away with her fist, like a child, and he reached out urgently and took her in his arms, kissing her softly on the lips.

She tried to talk on but he covered her lips firmly. Unable to bear her sad asking, for something that he should have given her already. Something she should never have had to ask for. He was angry with himself for his thoughtlessness and blind obsession.

He kissed her for a long time. Long enough to still her crying, and her words. Then he pulled away slowly and gazed at her vulnerability, saying the words that she was desperate to hear. "I love you, Julia. I really love you. And I want us to be together."

Her tears flowed again as she laughed at him, astounded. Craig smiled at her, laughing at the fact that tears could mean so many different things. Then she climbed into bed beside him, kissing him softly, and they started to make plans for their future together.

**

The window was open onto the street and Katy pulled on her favourite shirt and jeans and sat beside it, shaking her long waves dry in the warm air. A single blue car was parked in the street below now and the joggers had completely disappeared. Gone for a muffin.

She left for Cutters Wharf at eleven-forty, already late, and pulled hurriedly out through the gate, missing the car start its engine to follow her. She was halfway to Stranmillis before she noticed that it was behind her. Maybe they were going to Cutters too? It was a popular venue. But she felt slightly edgy.

She found a space outside the bar, checking twice that she'd locked her doors, and scanned Lockview Road quickly just in case. There was no sign of the car and she laughed at her jitters. Paranoia. That's what came from mixing with the police all week.

Lunch was a quiet, tea-total affair. They were both tired from the night before's drinking and the MSG buzz from the takeaway. Finally even Natalie admitted that they weren't nineteen anymore. She headed back to her research, leaving Katy with the luxury of a free afternoon. She knew that she should do her letters, but it had been a bad week, so she rang her mother instead.

"Hi Mum. I was going to nip up for a cup of tea. How would that be?"

"Lovely, dear. Whatever time you like."

"Would you like anything brought in?"

"Just some milk."

"I'll be fifteen minutes. Pop the kettle on."

As she pulled off, heading up Stranmillis towards the Malone Road, Katy saw the blue car again. She wasn't paranoid - it was definitely following her. She noted the number as they drove through the traffic, hoping they wouldn't try anything in broad daylight. They stayed one car behind her the whole way to her mother's small bungalow opposite Musgrave Park. Her mother was standing at the door waving brightly as she pulled in.

"Hi Mum. I'll just run over to the garage and get the milk."

As she crossed the road, Katy noticed that the car had parked opposite, beside the Vet's surgery. Part of her was tempted to just knock its window, but common sense kicked in and she fished out Craig's business card instead. She paused before she phoned, reaching for her mirror. And then couldn't believe that she'd checked her make-up to call him!

He answered the call quickly, catching her unawares. "D.C.I. Craig."

"Oh, yes, sorry." There was a moment's silence.

"Why are you sorry, Madam? And may I ask who this is please?"

"It's Katy Stevens. We met the other day. You probably don't remember me. You meet lots of people. Anyway, you interrogated me."

Katy realised what she'd said and stopped - she was babbling. She noticed that he had a deep voice and a slight accent that she couldn't place. She hadn't noticed it before. She crossed the road quickly and walked back to the house as she talked.

Her mother appeared at the front door, carrying a heavy tray heaped with cake and biscuits. Katy moved forward to take it.

"Mum, let me carry that – it's too heavy for you."

Then she heard a laugh and realised that he was still on the phone. His laugh made her feel defensive and she could feel a huff developing in her own voice. "Oh, sorry, I forgot you were still there. It's probably nothing, so just forget it."

"No, please tell me what's happened, Dr Stevens." The authority in his voice said that he needed to know and she felt less foolish.

"You said to call if anything happened."

Just then Julia came into the bedroom and handed Craig an espresso. He smiled up at her and then shook himself back into professional mode. "Yes I did. Tell me exactly what's happened, Dr Stevens."

Katy moved down the path to stop her mother hearing. "There's a blue car and, well, I don't want to seem paranoid, but I'm pretty sure it's been following me for hours. It was outside my flat this morning, then at Cutters Wharf. Now it's at my Mum's. So I'm just a bit worried, for her mainly. I was just wondering if...maybe it's one of your people? I've got the registration number."

She read it out to him quickly, but Craig already knew that he hadn't arranged a tail. He also knew that Tommy wasn't going to give up. He made his voice as calming as possible.

"Let me check that and call you back. And I'll send a car to your Mother's, just to be sure. Could you give me the address please? This is nothing for you to worry about."

She felt instantly better, and then shook herself. She didn't need a man to protect her. She remembered the last time she'd relied on one of those. She ended the call quickly and turned, to see her mother smiling broadly. "New friend dear?"

Katy laughed at her mischievous face. "Now, don't start, Mum. I told you, I'm entering a convent."

"Yes pet, whatever you say. But before you do, have a piece of apple tart. I made it for your brother and there's far too much as usual."

They lapsed into thirty minutes of looking at photographs they'd both seen a thousand times before. And soon Katy had forgotten all about the car. A sudden, loud knock made her mother jump. They both froze, and then a voice came through the door.

"It's D.C.I. Craig."

She stood in the hall stunned, staring at his outline through the leaded glass. The last thing she'd expected was for him to come in person! She blushed suddenly, catching her scruffy reflection in the mirror. But she knew she had to answer him, so she leaned over reluctantly and turned the latch.

He was standing there grinning and she smiled back involuntarily, neither of them speaking a word. Until her mother appeared to see what was happening.

"Bring the gentleman in for some tea, Katy." Katy could have killed her.

Craig smiled down benignly at her mother. She was one of those sweet little ladies that Belfast produced so well. All powder and perfume and pink cardigans. He warmed to her instantly. Especially when he caught her twinkle as she smiled at her daughter.

Katy looked even prettier than she had on their last encounter. Softer and more approachable somehow, her hair a mess of fine blonde waves. But nothing compared to Julia's titian curls.

"Tea, Mr...? Katy, what's your friend's name?"

"It's D.C.I. Craig, Mum."

"It's Marc Craig, Mrs Stevens. Lovely to meet you."

Marc...

Katy's panicked look entreated him to be quiet in front of her mother. So they chatted for over an hour about everything and anything, other than the reason he was there. Finally he stood up to leave. "I'm sorry, but I must go. I've really enjoyed myself Mrs Stevens. Thank you."

"Not at all. Please come again. Katy will show you to the door. Won't you dear?"

The amused look in her mother's eyes said far too much for comfort, hinting at heavy teasing when he left. They stood at the door shyly, Katy aware that she kept staring at the ground. Craig broke the silence, keeping his voice low so that her mother wouldn't hear.

"I'm sorry, but one of Tommy Hill's crew was following you. We've picked him up now, so you won't be bothered again. But if you have any more trouble please call me. I'll have a car drive past your home and your Mother's this evening, just to be sure."

"I'm sorry to have bothered you, Mr Craig, but you should've just phoned rather than come all this way." Then she noticed his suit. "Oh, were you working anyway?"

"Until we get this case closed, every day's a work day. So don't worry, you didn't bother me at all. And I enjoyed the tea." He wasn't lying, he really had enjoyed himself. Mrs Stevens was like his own mum.

"I...my mother enjoyed it as well. Thank you again, Mr Craig."

Katy gazed into his dark eyes, losing track of her words. He was far too good-looking to be safe. She willed herself hard to dislike him, closing the door firmly as he climbed into his car. Then she walked back into the living-room, knowing exactly what came next. A suspicion confirmed instantly by her mother's impish smile.

Chapter Twenty-Two

Beth sat for hours on the bathroom floor, thinking and crying. Until the chilling room and the changing light made her realise she'd lost the whole day. Eventually she climbed up the sink, testing her nausea, until she was certain that it had passed. Then she guided herself slowly along the wall and back to the bedroom.

She reached across the bed and lifted her phone, flipping the screen open. Sunday 6pm. So where was Janey? She couldn't be at work on a Sunday. And why was *she* at home? She should be in her room at the nurses' hall.

The front door opened and Janey's familiar footsteps entered the living-room. Beth called her name and she ambled into the bedroom, looking tired, and with steristrips across her top lip. Beth stumbled across the room and held her face, examining the wound with professional eyes. Someone had made a neat job of it.

"What happened to you? Are you OK?" Janey sat on the bed, speaking very slowly.

"I can't remember, but Shirley said they took me to casualty. Damien brought you home. Apparently two men tried to kidnap you and hit me. But I honestly don't remember anything after the restaurant. Shirley and Damien chased them but they got away. God, my head feels really heavy. We must have been drugged."

"That would explain why I've been so sick. I feel like a truck hit me. We need a blood test quickly. Drugs can leave your system in hours." Beth flicked open her mobile. "I'm calling the police."

***

The Visitor had found it easy, far easier than he'd thought. A quiet venue, some chemical aids, and gravity. That was all it had taken. Now he had what he wanted, and he had the time and place to complete his work.

He kicked the body at his feet hard, checking that it didn't wake. The father had failed to expose them so he'd had to act. Now he had the first one, but it wouldn't be the last. Three more would pay before he was done.

***

Monday.

Craig organised his papers and walked into the briefing room, assuming his usual position as people filtered in. Everyone looked too tired for a Monday.

"Good morning everyone, grab a coffee and sit down please. We need to start quickly. There's a lot to get through."

He updated them on the weekend's events and just as he finished, Annette came rushing through the door, breathless.

"Sorry I'm late, sir. I've been taking a call about Beth Walker. We need to see her this morning. Two men tried to abduct her on Saturday night. Uniform attended but they've just flagged it through now, so I said I'd go over when we've finished."

"Here - that's the third one! Murdock and Stevens were tailed by Tommy's team as well, but they weren't touched."

"Maybe we just got to them before they could be."

"Or maybe Tommy thinks Beth killed Evie. We should have banged him up last week."

"There's no point beating ourselves up about it Liam. We

210

couldn't have anticipated this happening. Remember that Tommy's a grieving relative - we had no grounds to arrest him. And we didn't have the resources to tail them all. OK, let's finish the briefing quickly and then we'll sort that out. Background first. Liam, Annette, Martin – anything of interest? What's been happening with the background checks on Walker, Murdock and Johns?"

"Nothing criminal showing up, sir. Beth Walker, thirty-five, co-habiting in Eglantine Avenue, up near Queens. She has a slightly rakey lifestyle. Recreational drugs and the odd public fight with the girlfriend, Janey Holmes. She's a Kiwi and works at N.I.BANK. Beth's worked at the M.P.E. since 2008 and she's a good midwife by all accounts. She's well-liked by her colleagues, no complaints or actions against her, and she has a wall full of thank-you letters.

Sister Laurie Johns, forties, single, and living alone out near Drumbeg. No relatives except for an elderly mother. There's no love lost between her and her nurses or, it seems, many of her patients. But no official complaints or malpractice suits. In fact, she's viewed as very efficient by the management team. According to the other midwives, she's had her knife in Beth pretty much since she joined the Unit. Although no-one seems prepared to say why."

"Jealousy?"

"Maybe. But she's the boss, so why? I suppose she could resent the fact that Beth's so well liked. But I think there's more to it than that. I'll keep digging, sir. Anyway, apparently Johns had quite a thing with Murdock when they were juniors and she's been carrying a torch for him ever since. He still ignites it the odd time, rumour has it."

Liam laughed and was about to say something rude but Craig waved Annette on.

"Nigel Murdock, fifty-two-year-old consultant surgeon. He has two teenage children. A son and daughter, both at University in London. The family home is out at Cultra. He

211

married into big money - the Burton family."

Martin let out a low whistle. "They're richer than the Beckhams."

"But not as talented, son."

Annette ignored the exchange and went on. "He has an expensive lifestyle, and owns property in Northern Ireland and the Republic. As well as a place out in Florida. He took the M.P.E. post in 2006 - he was at St Joseph's Trust before that. Since he joined he's had complaints from patients about various things. They range from his rudeness, up to and including complaints about the three deaths we know of. And there are rumours of some earlier ones, sir."

She saw Craig's questioning look and answered it.

"As you know, we're looking into any deaths amongst Murdock's patients. They were all investigated internally and some went as far as coroner's inquest. But it's hard to get information when nothing negligent was proven, without ringing massive bells at the Trust. At each enquiry and inquest Murdock had support from his senior colleagues, namely..." She turned over her notes. "Dr Alan Davis - that's Dr Winter's predecessor. Sister Johns and Robert Moore, the old Chief Executive."

"Ring the Trust's bells as loudly as you like now, Annette. We've got as far as we can by being discrete."

"Right, I will. I've a lot of other information coming in today, but that's all I can add until then. But we know that Murdock and Johns both hate Beth, and I'll keep digging until someone tells me why. It's definitely more than a ward tiff."

"Great, Thanks Annette. Liam, you met with Ted Greenwood and Charles McAllister. What are the stories there?"

"Aye, well Greenwood's a typical project geek."

Martin piped up. "I said that."

"So you did, son. Aye, well. Greenwood was boring, but pleasant enough. He chatted a bit about the hospital but

212

mainly gave yes/no answers to everything. Although he seemed genuinely sad about Evie. He said that he and one of the sparks popped into her room to fit a cable and she was very nice. That checks out by the way.

I did a background check on him. Born here but lived in England for years. He's early forties but never married, although he has a girlfriend - she's a mature student. He trained as an architect and went into project management, but he had no links with St Marys until he started the job there last year. He was living in London when the original project manager had an accident - hit by falling masonry. So Greenwood stepped into the job a year ago."

Liam paused and pulled a tiny notebook from his pocket - it disappeared in his huge hand. He flicked slowly through its pages before continuing.

"By all accounts, he's good at running big projects. Worked on a shiny new shopping centre in Wembley. No criminal record and he does the territorial soldier thing at the weekends. So does the girlfriend. That's how they met. He even went on one of those jungle survival courses last year. You know the sort of thing - can I live by eating dung beetles for a month?"

"Like the Celebrity one?"

"Aye, but without the half-dressed women. Anyway, Greenwood looks clean boss, although I'm meeting the girlfriend tomorrow just to confirm things. I checked out his tradesmen as well. That stroppy spark Randle had a bit of form fifteen years back. For throwing stones at us poor Peelers. And a football knifing - superficial wounding. He got probation both times. But there's nothing on the other tradesmen. They're just the normal joiners, sparks and tilers."

"Was Randle fitting the CCTV in the Maternity Unit?"

"I'll check that. He may have been the one in Evie's room with Greenwood."

"Thanks Liam. Martin?"

"Just before you move on, boss. I've gone back over McAllister's background and something's definitely fishy there. So I'm getting him into High Street tomorrow too. I'll keep you up to date."

Craig shot him a questioning look but could see that he would rather wait before feeding back. He nodded, confident in Liam's judgement. "OK, let me know what you find out. Martin?"

"We've been pulling the records on any deaths for twenty years back, sir, and especially in the last five. But the Trust is going onto a linked computer network, and it's a complete fiasco. A licence to print money for the computer firms and running way over budget. Anyway, because of that, lots of the paper records are away being scanned. We've got a requisition in for the hard copies, but it could take a week, sir."

"We haven't got a week, Martin. Annette, contact the I.T. Director and get him to speed it up. I need those records today. Meanwhile, keep digging for any links between the dead women and the Trust, and with each other. Anything at all, OK?"

Craig turned to face a wall-mounted screen at the front of the room, and John Winter's image appeared from his lab. "Go ahead, John." He watched his friend's face for some sign of Saturday's emotional trauma, but he was cool and professional. John was far better at controlling his emotions than he'd ever been.

"Hello everyone. Well, there are a few new things that we're chasing. Ms Murray-Long had D.N.A. all over her that wasn't her own, which was to be expected because of the resusc and operation. There was little point looking at anything from her mouth down, but we found some isolated fluids on her forehead. It's a small patch and the diameter fits a mouth. Who leaves stains on a forehead? Suggestions anyone?"

Annette chipped in. "I kiss my kids on the forehead."

"Or Pete if he's on a go-slow, ha, ha." She clamped Liam's

mouth hard.

"Exactly what we thought Annette. It's a conciliatory or caring gesture. It's male D.N.A. but it's not in the system. We compared it to Tommy's and there's no match. There's no familial link with Evie at all, so we need to check it against Reverend Kerr's and Brian Murray's to rule them out. Can that be arranged, Marc?

"We'll chase it up."

"The point being, that if it's not them, then who else would be kissing Evie on the forehead? We may well be looking at the killer's D.N.A. The idea of them kissing their victim is definitely significant. Remorse? Or did he know her? Remorse fits better with the note that the cleaning lady found.

About the note. Well, it's basically an apology of sorts, although justifying what they've done by saying it's 'necessary'. We've drawn a blank on it Marc. Word-processed, bog-standard Arial font. Paper that could be bought anywhere, and no D.N.A. or prints. They must have worn gloves so that means that they're forensically aware, which nowadays could just mean that they watch C.S.I. Des is on it but it's doubtful that we'll get anything. There's just one thing. The sentence construction definitely implies a higher level education."

Liam let out a loud guffaw. "Great. An educated nutter!"

"But if the killer knows about forensics John, wasn't it careless to kiss her?"

"Well they might have been careless, but I doubt it somehow. It's more likely they believe they'll never get caught to compare the D.N.A. against. It probably also means they aren't in the system. This isn't a known criminal, Marc, so that would rule out Tommy's crew."

"What about the other two women?"

"There's nothing in their P.M.s, Trust notes or insurance reports that you don't already know. Murdock was suspected of drinking in the first case, but nothing went to the G.M.C. And both women were cremated so that's going to give us nothing. Also, none of their blood samples were kept. To be fair they wouldn't always be, but again it's an omission by Davis that needs to be investigated, along with the thinness of the files. I'm chasing up all of that. Marc, can you pop into the lab later please? I've an answer on Evie's cause of death, but I want to show you something first."

"OK, thanks - I'll see you then." The video link closed and Craig turned to summarise.

"All right. In view of the attempt to kidnap Beth Walker and the tailing of Murdock and Stevens, we must now consider these three to be at risk. We know that some of those tails were Tommy's crew and we'll be lifting them today, but we don't know what the killer might try next. Liam – can you organise protection for Dr Stevens and Nigel Murdock? And you'd better cover Sister Johns as well, just in case. Round the clock until I say otherwise. They won't like it, but insist. Annette - when you've finished taking Beth's statement, do the same for her. Joe, can you get uniform to round up any of Tommy's crew that we haven't already got in custody? Hold them all for questioning. And tell them to get solicitors - we may be bringing charges."

"Tommy as well, boss?"

"No, not just yet. He has a solid alibi for the time of Beth's attack - he was in Stranmillis Road station with me. We questioned him about tailing Murdock on Saturday night, but I've heard nothing from uniform on him since. So I have to assume that either he gave up, which I doubt, or they missed it.

We know who was tailing Dr Stevens on Sunday. It was Gerdy, Gerard Bonner. He's ours already, but he won't give Tommy up as ordering the tail. So just ask Reggie Boyd to keep an eye on Tommy locally for now, please. Tommy's definitely behind the tails, but unless one of his men confirms it we won't get anything to stick. But if we lift his crew he can't replace the tails - he only has a small team nowadays. So let's get them all in. It might just be enough to put the wind up them."

He lifted a folder from the desk and handed each of them a sheet of A4.

"OK. I want to look at the profile again quickly. We know they use drugs to subdue their victims, consistently Insulin and Pethidine. They appear to be part of some sort of 'scene' and symbolic in some way. On cause of death. John will give me Evie's final C.O.D. later today, but we have nothing concrete on the first two victims. However, the victimology is consistent - pregnant women having female babies. And they all had Caesareans, either planned or emergency. The victims don't appear to have anything in common other than that. They had different ages, backgrounds and their babies fell in different birth orders. The sex and survival of the babies is far too consistent to be accidental - and it's very tricky to manage if you're intent on killing the mothers at any costs. So, it all implies that the killer is extremely organised and accurate."

"Or psychic, boss." Craig smiled ruefully. He could so with a bit of psychic ability himself.

"The 'piggy-backing' on the intravenous drip implies skill and education, as does the sentence construction in the note. The note may be a part of the killer's 'signature'. We don't have notes from the first two cases, but they could have existed and been destroyed. The killer has easy access to their victims, so they either work in the M.P.E. or visit it frequently. And they know the layout of the Maternity Unit very well. They always target women in side rooms, probably for easy access and escape. They also know how to locate and disable electrical systems, so we have a killer with knowledge of electrics or electronics.

We have the same doctor and midwife team every time, Murdock and Walker. The odds on that are well beyond coincidence. I don't want us to get wedded to this profile but just bear it in mind. Especially that this is an educated killer, with electrical knowledge, access and knowledge of the Unit. And given the male D.N.A. now, almost certainly male."

He packed up, ready to go.

"OK, thanks everyone. Let's have a quick catch up at four o'clock. Nicky, could you get press liaison here for me about twelve?"

The room emptied quickly but Nicky waited behind, approaching him tentatively.

"How's your Dad, sir?"

Craig glanced at her quickly, wondering how she'd found out. She answered his querying look with a smile.

"Lucia phoned me earlier. She wanted me to know so that I could take care of you." She gave him a wry look. "Because you never take care of yourself."

Craig half-smiled, imagining just how cheekily Lucia had said it.

"Thanks for asking, Nicky, but I'm fine. Dad got good treatment and he'll be home within the week. We were actually lucky it happened. They picked things up before he had a full-blown heart attack." Then he grinned broadly at her. "And I had my tight jeans ready to wear at that nightclub too..."

**

"Beth, it's Sergeant McElroy. Can I come up?" Annette shouted loudly into the street-level entryphone, trying to be heard above the traffic in Eglantine Avenue. She hated entryphones - it always felt like she was talking to herself. Same with blue-tooth.

She scanned the wide street, a main thoroughfare between BT9's Lisburn and Malone Roads. It was only nine o'clock in the morning, and the traffic was already shocking. People were racing past like they were at Le Mans. She sincerely hoped there was a speed camera at the bottom. After a moment's silence the door opened remotely and a Foyle accent said. "Top floor."

Annette walked up three carpeted flights of stairs, until her ascent stopped abruptly, outside a cheerful yellow front door. Many of the Victorian houses in Eglantine had been converted into apartments, and their high ceilings and broad windows made them spacious and bright.

Beth opened the door cautiously, wearing her comfort clothes, and Annette was aware of someone moving in the kitchen behind her. Beth caught her enquiring look. "Janey took the day off work. She didn't want to leave me, after what happened."

Janey Holmes' spiky brown head popped out of the kitchen. She shot Annette a smile, the steristrips on her lip barely holding against the grin. "Coffee all right for everyone?"

"That would be lovely, thanks."

Beth led the way into a cosy living-room with Victorian charcoal sketches on the walls. They matched perfectly with the corniced ceiling and Annette openly admired her taste, making a note of the colour scheme for Pete's next bout of D.I.Y.

"This is lovely. Have you been here long? I didn't even know these flats existed."

"We've had it for four years. We were lucky - we got a bargain after the market dipped. Sorry about the cables - it's being re-wired. That's why we were staying at the nurse's home. We were supposed to be there for two more weeks, but they must have tailed me from there to Sarajevo, so I'd rather be here now."

Beth's dark purple hair emphasised the pallor of her skin, and the circles under her eyes definitely hadn't been there the week before. Annette got ready to tape the interview just as Janey came in with the tray.

"I know an officer took a statement from you both yesterday. And we've got your blood samples - that was quick thinking, well done. It'll be no comfort to you, but you weren't the only people targeted at the weekend. Although the others were more fortunate. They were followed but not touched. We're picking up the men responsible today."

Beth relaxed visibly when Annette said the men were being arrested, slumping against Janey in relief.

"When you're both ready, could you tell me again, exactly what happened?"

After a sip of hot coffee, Beth took a deep breath and started to talk.

***

Craig headed back to the squad after updating an unhappy Harrison, telling Nicky he'd be at the lab until twelve. Then he headed out of the building for some fresh air before leaving.

There were workmen all over Clarendon Quay, fitting moorings for some event. The place was buzzing in anticipation - even the seagulls seemed more excited than usual. He loved being near the water, there was always something happening. He'd even thought of a naval career once, before a trip to New Scotland Yard had hooked him on policing.

It was a bright day and the view in either direction was impressive. The river swept up past Samson and Goliath, towards the Albert Bridge. The other direction took it through the widening water of Belfast Lough and out to the Irish Sea.

He leaned heavily on the railings, listening to the soft sounds of boat-horns drifting in, as he stared down through the water. The slow moving waves had a hypnotic effect that helped him think, and he watched them undulating, hoping that they would give him some answers. But the sea never gave up its secrets.

***

By eleven o' clock Craig was walking into the lab, carrying donuts. John was leaning over his laptop, focusing intently on the screen.

"Sorry, are you busy John? I should have called ahead."

"No, it's just a boring conference paper. Anyway, I asked you to drop in. I've got something to show you."

"Evie's cause of death?"

"Yes. But we need to go down to the morgue for a minute."

On the way down Craig updated him on the weekend's events, volunteering. "I took Julia out on Saturday night - I've been neglecting her."

He paused, hoping that John would fill-in the gap with his own feelings, while John took it as a sign that his friend wanted to talk. He was grateful that Craig hadn't mentioned his breakdown on Saturday afternoon.

"How's it going with Julia, by the way?"

"Well, it wasn't really. We hardly got to see each other. She nearly dumped me yesterday."

John turned to look at him, shocked that Craig's love life was a shambles as well. "Why? I thought you were happy together."

Craig shook his head ruefully. "I'm too busy with work to be fair to any relationship. And the distance between here and Limavady isn't helping. We're both wrecked, trekking up and down the M2."

"I know what you mean, getting to St Marys to see Natalie is hard enough..." John's voice tailed off and he looked sad for a moment, then regrouped and turned back to Craig. He shook his head hard, as if it would erase Natalie's memory. "So what's the solution?" That was John, always logical. Everything had an answer.

Craig stared at the floor shyly and John saw the beginning of a blush. "Well...we chatted..."

"And? Cut to the chase, man!"

"She's going to request a transfer from Limavady. Then

we'll get a place together and see how it goes."

"My God!" John said it with the surprise that Craig still felt. He grinned at his friend and punched his arm cheerfully. "And a million women weep, ha ha. Good for you. When's the wedding?"

Craig's look of shock said 'slow down', and so did his next words. "We're nowhere near that yet! Let's just see how it goes." But John was on a roll and they walked into the mortuary to his incongruous whistles of 'Here comes the bride'.

Once there, the mood changed abruptly. This was a place where people who'd been loved or ignored slept in drawers. There wasn't much to laugh about.

John pulled Evie's trolley out gently and took a magnifying glass from his pocket, focusing it on the skin of her young throat. Craig gazed down at her sadly. What a bloody waste.

"What are we looking for, John?"

"The Pethidine and Insulin didn't kill her, and there was no ingested poison in the stomach analysis. Something else caused her death, and I've finally found it. It was strangulation. It wasn't obvious, or we'd have seen it on day one. The thing that confused me was the absence of external marks, or any internal damage to her hyoid bone and larynx. But then I realised. Of course! Simple occlusion of the Carotid arteries."

Craig gawped at him, marvelling at the 'of course'. He was sure that no one else would have come within a mile of the diagnosis.

"If the arteries are completely closed it produces loss of consciousness in less than fifteen seconds, followed by rapid death. And it doesn't leave a mark. The pressure needed to do it is about eleven pounds - indicating someone very strong. To avoid a struggle it's usually only used to kill children or women, or completely incapacitated men. Evie fitted the profile perfectly. Plus, she would have been almost comatose from the medication, so she wouldn't have fought back. That fits with the lack of the defensive injuries normally seen in strangulation attacks."

He gloved up to demonstrate, pointing at Evie's throat.

"Let's suppose that the killer used the palm of one hand to apply pressure across the front of her neck - here. That would avoid any of the external trauma that you'd expect to see from fingertips or nails. Also, the pressure is distributed evenly, so very often there are no internal neck injuries either. But you can see that my hand doesn't reach right across her neck - she was a sturdy young woman and she had a broad neck. So not only would the killer have had to be very strong, but they'd also need large and long hands. Hold your hand above her neck, Marc."

Craig complied. His hand reached - he was two inches taller than John.

"New research shows that hand size links with height. Large or long hands generally go with a taller man. So we're looking for a tall and very strong assailant here. She has some puncture haemorrhages in the eyes, which is a sign of strangulation. But they could also have been caused by vigorous resuscitation, and she definitely had that."

"How certain are you on this, John?"

"This is our answer, I'm sure of it. And I think that the D.N.A. on her forehead belongs to her killer. When you find him we can match it. Our murderer's a strong, tall man. Taller than me. And tell Annette that's not just chivalry. Even if the D.N.A. wasn't conclusive it would take an abnormally strong woman to kill this way."

"This is great, John. Brian Murray and Geoffrey Kerr are both tall and had a close relationship with her, so we'll chase their D.N.A. first. If they don't match we'll start wider sampling. I'll call you later."

He turned to leave but John's body language said that he hadn't finished. "Marc...this is a very unusual method of killing, so maybe that's a clue as well. I would look for men with combat training, if I were you."

Craig nodded. "That's exactly what I was thinking."

Chapter Twenty-Three

Monday. 2.30pm.

Annette caught Liam on his mobile. He was at home in the back garden, about to take a sip from a long cold beer. He'd booked the afternoon off weeks before to take Danni and Rory to the baby clinic, and they weren't long back.

It was a hot day, so he was playing at being 'King of the Barbeque' and Danni had her brother's kids coming over at four-thirty. So, as much as he liked Annette, he really wasn't pleased to hear from her. They'd worked so much over-time in the past week that everyone was getting frayed. The thought of a barbie and beers was the only thing cheering him up.

"Ayyye, Cutty. What can I do you for?" Annette heard the edge in his voice and knew that she was about to add to it.

"Murdock's disappeared."

Liam was focusing on the grill, absentmindedly turning a sausage, when what she'd said suddenly sank in. "What do you mean disappeared? He can't have! Maybe he's just pissed off on his boat somewhere?"

"Will you listen to me? He didn't come into work this morning and the protection detail has been trying to find him all day. His secretary called his wife an hour ago, and she phoned us. It turns out they'd been looking for him too. He had a full private clinic booked this morning and he just didn't turn up. They'd been leaving messages on his mobile for hours. It was only the fact that he'd no operations or deliveries scheduled that stopped them ringing the wife before now. The last time anyone saw him was on Maternity, last night about eight, when he delivered a private patient. He'd been in the M.P.E. most of the weekend so he stayed over at his place in Belfast."

"That'll be the place in Owenville, where Tommy was caught tailing him on Saturday. Has anyone checked there? The address is in the report."

"Joe's already checked. It's empty. The C.S.I.s are over there now."

Liam sobered up quickly. "Have you been in touch with the girlfriend? She was seen by the guys tailing Tommy on Saturday."

"Nope. Any idea who she is?"

"It shouldn't be hard to find out."

"That depends how discrete they were, Liam. And I can hardly ask the wife, can I? She's absolutely frantic – seems Murdock's the very devoted hubbie."

"Aye, right."

"Well, he does a good impression of one anyway. And she says it's not like him to miss patients' appointments...especially the private ones."

Liam whistled and stabbed the sausage hard, leaving the fork vertical.

"Did she actually say that? About the private patients?"

"Yep...and not a bit ashamed of it either. She sounds as stuck up as him."

"A match made in heaven." He paused, thinking for a minute. "Any signs of a fight at the house?"

"Joe says there's nothing to see. And Liam..."

"Aye?"

"Remember that Tommy's out there free as a bird. He's been loose since Saturday night, long before Murdock disappeared. He could have done anything to him."

Liam signed deeply, rubbing his eyes with his now-free hand. "Or... Murdock could be our killer, Cutty, and he's just staged his own disappearance."

"That's exactly what the chief said. You both have suspicious minds."

"And you still think too well of people - that'll come from being a nurse. You need to be a bit more suspicious. 'In God we trust, everyone else keep your hands where I can see them'"

She laughed despairingly. "That's shocking."

"Not half as shocking as me having to tell Danni I'm leaving. She's going to kill me." He paused, thinking for a moment. "OK, ask Joe to lift Tommy. You'd better phone the boss and see whether he wants to go to the house, or straight to interview him. And I'd better brace myself for Danni pouring this beer over me. I'll see you at Owenville in thirty..."

By the time they arrived at Owenville Park, the C.S.I.s were working in the lounge of the house, so they all gathered in the patio garden. Craig had already decided on his order. House, then Tommy. He was looking exhausted. Everyone was.

"Right. What have we got on Murdock? He was last seen in Maternity at eight last night. He was well when he left there and no-one's heard from him since. And there are no signs of a struggle here." Craig peered at his watch. "That makes a maximum of nineteen hours missing."

"Boss. If Murdock's the killer, couldn't he just have legged it?"

Craig nodded. "Already there, Liam."

Annette stared at them both, frowning.

"You don't agree, Annette?"

"It's not so much that, sir. It's more of a gut feeling. But, well, logically, why would Murdock have killed any of them? I'm not saying that he couldn't have...but why would he?"

"Well, I'm not sure killers always think logically Annette, but I know what you mean. I agree Murdock's a long shot, but we need to keep the possibility in mind." He updated them on John's findings.

"Evie's cause of death requires our killer to be a large strong

227

man - which Murdock is. And the kiss on her forehead had male D.N.A., so, if nothing else we need to eliminate him now. Liam, give John a call and see if there's any way that we can eliminate Murdock in his absence. Maybe we can use a source of D.N.A. that his wife could give us access to."

"I can think of one, sir."

"What?"

"He's a surgeon, so he'll have given blood for Hepatitis screening. We could be lucky there, if the lab stores the samples?"

"It's a good thought Annette, but we'd need permission anyway. Talk to his wife."

Joe Rice ambled out through the French doors. "Sir, Mr Murdock's car has been found at the M.P.E. It's not in his usual parking space, that's why it wasn't noticed before. He must've just parked it any-old-where last night. Apparently he was rushing because his patient went into early labour, so he must've just dumped it and run to the ward."

"I asked you to close the Unit, Liam."

"I did, but Murdock wouldn't move his private patients up to Bangor. 'Didn't want to inconvenience them'. The other consultants did, but he was stubborn, so he was still seeing them at the M.P.E. But their rooms are up in the private patients' wing, boss, that's the opposite end of the building to Maternity. The only time they'd be in the Maternity Unit was when they were delivering. And Murdock and their families would be with them the whole time. How the other half live, eh?"

"Doesn't he do Caesareans on everyone?"

"Not on his private patients, unless they request it. It's only forced on the poor NHS plebs. Anyway boss, there was nothing we could do to make him go to Bangor - I checked it with the Chief Exec. The private wing runs on a contract but it's not actually part of the Trust, so he couldn't close it down if he tried. Murdock wouldn't listen and it seemed safe enough for the patients. We kept a close eye, and they've all gone home now."

"It was safe for the patients, but maybe not so safe for Murdock. OK, what's done is done, there's no point worrying about it now. If someone wanted to get him they'd have got him wherever he was. Annette, can you go to the M.P.E. with Martin and interview everyone who saw Murdock last night. Take some C.S.I.'s down and go over his car, then get it towed to the compound when they've finished. Do we have anything on the girlfriend yet?"

"There's some stuff belonging to her in the house. But you're not going to like it, sir..."

"How much worse can it get? Go on."

"His girlfriend is a solicitor at Morris and Harden's. Her name's Ronni DeLacy. It seems they've been at it for at least two years."

The woman who'd been with Murdock at High Street.

Liam laughed. "Pheww, well now, there's all sorts of jokes in there. He'll be getting a discount on his fees anyway..."

"Yes, thanks for that thought Liam. Tell us in the pub when this is all over. OK Joe, get uniform to pick her up, just to assist us with enquiries into his disappearance. She might know something. But remember, she must have some feelings for him, so sensitively please."

"Aye well...there's a bright side, boss."

Craig squinted at Liam warily and then rose to the bait. "What's that then?"

"At least she won't refuse to talk because she's waiting for her solicitor..."

***

Ten minutes later Liam and Annette left in patrol cars and Craig moved to the French doors, calling Joe over.

"Joe, we need a sympathetic W.P.C. to take a statement

from Mrs Murdock, please. And make sure she doesn't even hint at the possibility of a mistress. That's the last thing she needs when her husband's disappeared."

"No problem, sir. It's already happening."

"Good man. We also need to sweep the obvious places for Murdock. Check out his work, homes, and sailing buddies. Is there anywhere special he escapes to when it all gets too much for him? Liam can help you on that. We're looking at a full-scale manhunt if he doesn't show in the next few hours, so let's deal with the basics now. I'm going to High Street to have another word with Tommy. He could have grabbed Murdock yesterday after we let him go. I wouldn't put anything past him. Gather everyone in the briefing room at four please Joe. And remember, some people are still in court on Warwick."

Joe disappeared into an area of better reception and made the calls, while Craig dialled Terry Harrison, updating him quickly.

"Right Craig, keep me up to speed. I've arranged a press briefing tomorrow at twelve, and I'd like you there please. I just hope that we aren't announcing another death by then."

Craig drove away from the house, looking around Owenville Park. It was a world of flowers and trees; its quietness whispering money. No one would ever know what was happening behind those elegant front doors.

**

By the time Craig arrived at the station Tommy had been picked up again and cautioned. But he wasn't talking. He was still pissed off about the Beth fiasco, and even angrier that his whole crew had been lifted, so he stonewalled Craig. His burly, crew-cutted solicitor was equally uncooperative.

"Either charge my client with something or release him, Detective Chief Inspector. You have nothing on him, and you know it. This is verging on the harassment of a grieving father."

"Please don't exaggerate, Mr Toner. You know we can hold your client for twenty-four hours, and we have more than sufficient grounds. Mr Hill assaulted and threatened Mr Murdock in front of witnesses on an open ward. He was caught following him on Saturday night, and he has plenty of motives to cause him harm. Plus, his known associates were caught tailing other members of the Maternity Unit's staff. Not to mention the failed abduction attempt on Ms Walker. So Mr Hill is going nowhere."

Tommy shrugged and lounged back in his chair.

"D.C. Karl Rimmins of the Drugs Squad is outside waiting for a word as well. So you'll be here for quite a while, Mr Hill. I suggest that you co-operate."

"Suggest what you like, Craig. I've all the time in the world. I've no-one to rush home to, now have I? I didn't touch that slime-ball Murdock, but good luck to whoever has done for him - I'll buy them a drink." He waved his arm at the room.

"All this is nothin' but you pissin' in the wind, an' you know it. You're just tryin' to show your boss what a busy wee boy you are. Now fuck away off an' get me a coffee."

He lifted a packet of cigarettes from his pocket and tapped one out. He was just reaching for his lighter when Craig tore them from his hand in one clean, hard movement, fighting the urge to rip him and them apart. His voice sounded cold, even to him. "I told you once before, Mr Hill. There's no smoking in here."

"Fuck you."

Craig handed the cigarettes to the constable and left the room quickly, before he did something he would regret. He could hear Hill's thuggish solicitor calming his client, immediately angry with himself for reacting to the obvious wind-up.

He stood in the corridor for a moment, rubbing his eyes

and knowing that Hill was right. They could hold him but they couldn't make him talk, their only hope was finding Murdock.

Karl wouldn't do much except rattle his cage a bit. The Drug Squad was working on a much bigger bust on the Demesne and they wouldn't blow it for a small fish like Tommy. But where the hell was Nigel Murdock?

***

9pm.

There was no way of knowing which day it was, but Murdock knew from the dark and cold that it was late evening. His hands and feet felt numb and he shivered violently through his light wool suit. The dust and blood in his mouth made a dry combination. Even swallowing his own saliva didn't help. So he spat it out in front of him, trying hard to turn his face out of the mix. His whole body felt like one giant hangover, without the joy of having earned it.

He tried to look up and then realised that his wrists and ankles were tied behind his back, limiting his movement. They were roped together in the mid-line - he was trussed like a beached turtle. The only movement possible was a laboured rocking motion, each arc thrusting his face further into broken gravel and dust.

Why was this happening to him? He tried to think of who hated him enough to do this. Probably too many; he was a pragmatist. He cleared his throat several times and tried to shout, the dry sound that emerged only half its usual volume.

"Is anyone here? Can you help me? Please, please help me." The words echoed back to him once for company, then there was silence.

There was something familiar above him, just out of his line of sight. He chased the image hard, but he couldn't place it. He didn't even know how he'd got here, wherever here was. There was just a dull memory of being hit...in his office. Yes, on Sunday night.

Was this still Sunday night? Hunger answered and told him it was unlikely. Monday then? Murdock speculated for a long time, until the deepening darkness told him that it was the wee small hours.

The darkness shifted suddenly, and a sixth sense made him realise he was no longer alone. Fear overwhelmed him, spreading through his mind and then onwards to his heart, speeding and strengthening its pulse. He struggled pitifully against his restraints, tightening them with every twist. Then something sharp pressed through the light cloth of his pinstripe, and a stinging pain seared through his left thigh, shocking him into high alert. He had a few second's thought that some bugger was ruining his expensive suit, and then it suddenly ceased to be important.

The rope's tension increased quickly, his back arching upwards as his legs fell, suddenly relaxed. The rocking it produced pushed his slumped head forward, into his own spit, and the gravel tore at his skin, new grazes streaking fast and bloody across his cheeks. He couldn't move, every sinew frozen, but he could feel everything that happened next.

The Visitor gazed down at Nigel Murdock, brimming with disgust. He was revolting, this...thing. His skin crawled, repulsed by the need to be in his presence. To have to touch him. This man with so much power and arrogance, who took risks with other people's lives. Not from any drive to help them, no, never that mitigation. Risks from his own avarice, his own egotistical needs.

He had to act. The father should have exposed them for the greater good, but instead he was driven by his own petty vengeance. And once again no one would understand.

The police were no better. They would only hunt for the woman's killer, missing her unimportance and letting the truly guilty walk free. He'd tried for months to make them see. Now, once again, it was left to him to seek justice. It was always left to him. And that meant being in the presence of this disgusting thing.

And yet, through the revulsion there was some small enjoyment. Some anticipation, now that the thing was helpless, this man's all too frequent view of others. Such power without compassion, it was almost sexual.

The Visitor's pulses throbbed and quickened with confusion at the thoughts. Punishing the guilty was a duty, but could it also be a source of joy? Yes, yes. So many months of expectation, so many foretastes, all gathering now in his throat. Spewing forward, until he roared at Nigel Murdock, roared at the sky, roared with righteousness.

The plan had been cool patience and restraint. Public justice through the father. But that hope had gone now, replaced by fevered need and a sharp surgical approach. Surgical justice, it seemed fitting. The scalpel was smooth, one metal sliver from handle to blade, a special gift to himself. Theatre gloves and speed without pleasure were still the plan, but indulgent lust welled up in him and flooded past it. There would be no gloves, no control, and no speed. Just pleasure and desire.

Heat spread through his groin and need overwhelmed him, allowing a frenzied personal gift to be taken urgently. The release of hot seeping blood was almost orgasmic. Ahhhh...there now...there now. Some faint control returned with the release, just as the thing's eyes opened, in time to watch his bare flesh yield to the blade. Cutting through the pale lax skin, the corpulent fat, then forcing, forcing, forcing down. Into the muscles, scything through, with all resistance gone.

Nigel Murdock stared up wretchedly into his killer's wild, cold eyes, recognising them, and their intent. He couldn't speak, his thick, drugged lips failing him. And for a moment he remembered other pairs of eyes, past eyes, looking up at him, pleading and begging when their loved ones died.

He'd been deaf to them then. He'd wielded power and walked away unfeeling. He couldn't feel their pain and he hadn't even tried. He didn't understand remorse. He'd tried to mimic his peers, but no feeling ever came for the vulnerable. But now *he* felt fear and hurt and pain. So much of it, but still only for himself...

The blood flowed out, warm, clear and metallic, over the man's large hands, etching out each joint and ridge and pore. He smiled at the colour, washing his hands in it, rubbing it in like cream. Inhaling the sharp scent and holding it up to the light like a prism. Until it washed away some of his own dull pain, and the life of the thing at his feet finally ceased its ebb and flow.

All gone. Punished guilt. Blissful peace now for a while. Sitting with the creature, smiling at the dead thing, pleased by the work. Time sliding gently past. Until the next one...

Chapter Twenty-Four

The Visitor's anger was still there. It was always there. No matter how just the kill, there was no peace from it. It would always be there, until the whole task was done.

***

Tuesday morning started far too early for everyone. Craig had called another eight o'clock briefing and everyone was groggy, except for him. He seemed to have found new energy from somewhere.

"Here boss, I'll have whatever you're on."

"No sleep and anger – still want it?"

Annette handed round the coffees. And everyone gave their drowsy updates between mouthfuls of Danish pastry, looking like a middle-aged 'Breakfast Club'.

Craig updated them on Evie's cause of death, alerting them to look for possible martial arts links. The spark with the record, Michael Randle, *was* the one who'd been in Evie's room with Greenwood. Liam was tasked to dig a bit deeper on his background. The C.S.I.s hadn't found anything out-of-place at either of Murdock's homes. And neither Murdock's wife nor girlfriend had heard from him since Sunday.

Both were being comforted. The wife totally ignorant of the girlfriend's existence, and the girlfriend defensive as hell. Craig understood. It couldn't be easy knowing what people were thinking about you, especially when you'd have to meet them all in court. But she obviously loved Murdock. 'I plead guilty to poor taste in men, M'Lord.'

The trawl of Murdock's usual haunts had produced nothing. The Irish police had checked his cottage in Wicklow, but it was empty. Just another part of his investment portfolio.

There was nothing new since the night before so Craig closed the meeting quickly. Everyone had plenty to do. Liam had McAllister and Greenwood's girlfriend scheduled for interview at High Street, and Craig had Harrison's press conference later. They all took one message away from the room. 'Find Nigel Murdock... fast'.

***

High Street station was scheduled for a quiet Tuesday. So when Liam arrived at nine o'clock, raring to go, it provided Jack Harris with a welcome diversion. And a chance for some sorely missed craic.

The station could be a bit boring at times. With it being beside the Passport Office people often confused the two, so some days they dealt with nothing but tourists, shouting questions in broken English. Jack had offered to sell street-maps as a side-line, but for some reason the Chief Constable had taken a dim view of that idea. So instead they offered rooms to the C.C.U. for interviews, and Craig's investigations provided them with some rare excitement.

Liam loped in and pressed the desk buzzer, deliberately ignoring the two people sitting on the bench. There'd be time enough for them in a minute and he didn't want to be too friendly. Especially to Charles McAllister. Liam was sure that he'd lied to them already. Jack opened the door cheerfully, grinning at his old classmate.

"Well, well, Inspector Cullen. You honour us with your presence, sir."

"Ach, away on with you." He glanced behind him towards the kitchen.

"Where's the tea then? I've a fair thirst on me, and it'll be a long morning."

"Come on, on, in."

Sandi had tea and biscuits already laid out and she headed back to her paperwork quickly. They'd be cracking on about the 'good old days' for ages, and the Antiques Roadshow bored her. She gave them ten minutes for banter and then interrupted.

"Sir - would you like Ms Murphy or Mr McAllister first? Mr McAllister's solicitor's just arrived."

"Solicitor. That's interesting - he didn't say he was bringing one."

Liam nodded to himself. He should have guessed that a C.E.O. wouldn't come near a police station without legal advice. It didn't matter. He'd dealt with bigger fish than McAllister. And he'd have to answer their questions, unless he wanted them digging even further into his life.

"In that case, Sandi, I'll take Ms Murphy first. Give me five more minutes to consult with my esteemed colleague here, and then take her through."

"Esteemed now, am I? Does that mean you'll finally give me that twenty quid you owe me?"

She left them to their craic, closing the door in case reception's occupants heard them laughing. It wouldn't do to ruin the police's image of gravitas entirely.

Moya Murphy was already in the interview room when Liam entered. She'd reversed the wooden chair and was leaning forward over its back, fiddling with the ends of her long brown hair. She glanced up indifferently as he sat down, looking like the picture of bohemian boredom, trapped by the fascist police state. Liam was certain he'd seen her at a few protest marches.

"Could you hurry this up? I've a lecture to give at eleven."

Liam stared at her, fascinated. It never ceased to amaze him how much some people disrespected authority. But then he'd been brought up on the 'fear of God' approach to child-rearing, and the sight of a uniform still made him defer. He wasn't sure whose view of the world was better.

"Thank you for coming in, Ms Murphy. I just have a few questions about your partner, Mr Greenwood. Background stuff mainly. But I'd also like you tell me anything you know about his whereabouts over the past week. Particularly last Monday evening. Do you mind if we tape this? It saves us having to repeat questions at a future date."

She shrugged. "I don't care, but why not ask Ted all this? He can tell you far better than me."

He smiled and realisation dawned on her. "Oh, I see. You want to check up on him, is that it?"

Liam didn't confirm it but she continued anyway.

"OK, well. I'm not sure I'll be much use to you - I've only known him for five months. We met at the territorials."

Liam stared at her, trying to picture her clambering around in the mud. She caught the look and laughed.

"I'm not *in* the territorials, I do their computer training. They teach all sorts of stuff, not just combat. Anyway, Ted doesn't take computer studies, he's already far better at it than me. No, we met at the Christmas party. To be honest, we'd both had a skin full, so we spent the night together and it just went from there."

He was impressed by her candour. She didn't act as if she had anything to hide, and she probably didn't.

"Can I ask how often you see Mr Greenwood?"

"Just once or twice a week, we don't live together. I study late most nights, I'm finishing my Masters."

Interesting. It was much more casual than Ted Greenwood had implied in his interview, but that could just be masculine pride. Liam had been guilty of it once or twice himself.

"Could you give me a quick rundown of his movements in the last week? Starting with the weekend before last, please. From Friday the 5th."

"Well, I know I saw him on the Friday night because we went to the pictures. That one with Robert Redford and Shia LeBeouf. God, what was it called? Oh yes 'The Company You Keep'. Anyway, he stayed over on Friday but I had to work on the Saturday and Sunday, so he didn't stay again until the Monday night."

"You're sure of that, Ms Murphy? He definitely stayed on the Monday night?"

"Yes, definitely. We watched that thing 'Scooters' on Monday night. That's how I know."

Liam's suspicion index ricocheted off the scale. Monday was the night that Evie had been killed and convenient alibis always made him suspicious. Actually, pretty much everything made him suspicious if he was being honest. But he had a hunch to back it up this time.

"Just excuse me a second." He reached for the desk phone and called Jack.

"Jack, could you just check what night a programme called 'Scooters' was on last week? Thanks. Right, he'll have that answer for us in a minute. Please go on Ms Murphy."

She frowned, annoyed by his doubts, but carried on. "Right, well, he stayed again on Thursday night. I'm sure of that because we went to dinner with some friends of mine. But I haven't seen him since then - we were both busy all weekend. I was working on a paper for yesterday, and Ted went to Dublin on Friday night, for one of his boring project conferences. He's not due back for a few more days."

Just then Jack entered and handed Liam a slip of paper. He read it and looked across at her calmly.

"Ms Murphy. Can I ask you again if you saw Mr Greenwood last Monday night?"

She seemed genuinely irritated. "I've already told you. We watched 'Scooters' and he stayed overnight. He was with me from about six o'clock Monday evening until eight on Tuesday morning."

"And you knew it was Monday night because...?"

"Because 'Scooters' was on the sodding TV!"

"What if I told you that they'd changed the programme scheduling? And that 'Scooters' was moved from its normal Monday night slot to Tuesday night last week?"

He placed the printout on the desk in front of her, watching her face carefully. Her mouth fell open and she appeared genuinely upset.

"Oh God, it must have been Tuesday night then! But Ted said it was Monday night that he stayed, because 'Scooters' had been on. He *told* me it was Monday."

The realisation that she'd provided a false alibi obviously shocked her, and Liam could see her growing upset and angry in turn.

"That bastard! He used me. I'm going to kill him. What a complete fucker."

Fucker indeed - but Liam had seen the trick used before. It didn't necessarily mean that Greenwood was their killer. He could simply have had no alibi and panicked, trying to generate one. But it certainly pushed him up the suspect list.

Moya Murphy answered all his remaining questions urgently, afraid that she was in trouble. Liam reassured her, confident that she'd been duped. He ended the interview by asking her not to contact Greenwood before they'd had a chance to interview him. And to ignore all his calls. She agreed without caveat, and Liam was pretty sure that their romance, such as it was, had just ended.

***

Craig took the lift to the Media Suite, where the invited press was gathering for the noon briefing. They circled the reception room like prowling lions, scavenging cups of coffee and the C.C.U.'s best biscuits from the table at the back. He spotted Davy's girlfriend, Maggie Clarke, amongst the crowd and nodded to her. She wandered over, smiling hello cheerfully.

Their relationship had been cool when they'd met on the Greer case in December, but she'd written it up responsibly and Craig respected that. Plus she made Davy happy, so he smiled warmly as she approached.

"Hello, D.C.I. Craig. Ready for this?" She smiled sympathetically at him, knowing that he hated briefings.

"Not so you'd notice. More a case of grin and bear it. Where's Mercer?"

She shook her head ruefully, acknowledging the shortcomings of Ray Mercer, The Chronicle's prize reporter. "He's on his way, unfortunately. I tried to persuade the editor that a woman would be better on a case like this. But..." She smiled up at him. "I'll write my piece sensitively, don't worry. It's far too sad to sensationalise."

Craig nodded and turned to escape from the room, feeling like a Christian in the Colosseum.

"Tell Davy I said Hi, and I'll be over tonight."

Craig caught her slight blush at the mention of Davy's name and smiled kindly. "Come up to the squad later and tell him yourself."

She grinned broadly as he turned again, heading for the corridor to wait for Harrison. He phoned Lucia quickly for an update on their father and then stared out the window, pointedly ignoring the hacks.

A few minutes later the familiar click of Nicky's high-heels signalled a friendly face. She walked towards him with the fully polished version of the D.C.S. and winked reassuringly. Then she dropped in beside him, as they entered the room to face the beasts.

***

Charles McAllister sat bolt upright, much too large for the

small interview-room chair. His width forced his young solicitor into the corner beside the tape machine. His posture conveyed authority and hid his thoughts, but his eyes said that he'd been caught out. Liam could read them easily, giving him the advantage from the off.

"Good morning Mr McAllister, and Mr ...?"

"Sayers." The young brief reached his hand across the table and Liam shook it politely, knowing there would be a business card next. There was.

"Right now gentlemen, I know we're all busy. So let's just get through this as quickly as possible. I'd like to tape the interview to avoid future repetition. If you have no objection?" McAllister glanced at the young man beside him and then nodded assent.

They cut through the preliminaries of age, address and marital status and covered the events leading up to Monday, the day before Evie's death. As they came to the events of that evening Liam's relaxed friendliness suddenly changed, into a cool formality that caught both McAllister and his solicitor off guard.

"Mr McAllister. Could you tell me exactly where you were on the evening of Monday the 8th of April, and in the early hours of Tuesday the 9th?"

Liam could see small beads of sweat settling on the C.E.O.'s top lip. When he spoke, his voice was defensive and strained, with an artificially high pitch.

"I've already answered that question. I was at home with my wife, which I believe she's already confirmed. "

Liam's voice deepened and chilled in counterpoint. "I'll ask you again, Mr McAllister. Where were you on the evening of Monday the 8th of April and the early hours of Tuesday the 9th?"

McAllister stared desperately at his brief and the young man leaned forward in his defence.

"My client has already answered that question, so can we

please move on?"

"No, I'm afraid we can't. Not until your client answers truthfully. Please instruct your client to answer the question accurately, Mr Sayers. But before he does so, he should know that we've already researched his background. And we have reason to believe that he wasn't entirely truthful in his earlier interview. We also believe that if we re-question his wife she will give us a different version of events. It's in your client's power to prevent us having to do that."

He stared intently at the two men. "Please answer the question, Mr McAllister."

Emotion ran across Charles McAllister's face like a bouncing roulette ball looking for the best place to stop. Finally his shoulders sloped, signalling defeat, and telling Liam that his next words would be the truth. All the fight had gone out of him.

McAllister leaned forward heavily on the table and shrugged. "All right. Ask me whatever you want."

"Where were you that Monday evening, Mr McAllister?"

McAllister's voice took on a flat, resigned tone. "I was at my A.A. meeting at Malone Town Hall. Monday is Alcoholics Anonymous, Tuesday is Gamblers Anonymous and Friday used to be Narcotics Anonymous. But I've had a bit of a relapse there recently."

Pheww... Liam could see why he wouldn't admit to that list before. He doubted he'd have got the big job with those on his C.V.

He hid his surprise professionally, and continued. "What time did the meeting end on Monday evening? And where were you between then and the early hours of Tuesday morning?"

"The A.A. meeting finished at ten, then three of us went to our usual Monday night card game. I was there until about four am. There are three other people who can verify that. They include a Bishop and an RAF Air Commodore." Liam knew he was supposed to be impressed, but he wasn't.

"You say you were there until *about* four am - can you be more accurate on that time?" McAllister stared down at the table in silence, until finally his solicitor moved to intervene. Then McAllister said something quietly, so quietly that Liam asked him to repeat it.

"I can't be more accurate."

As he said it he sat back and Liam could see that perspiration had soaked through his white shirt, making it transparent. "I can't b...because I was stoned." Liam could see why a quiet night in with the wife sounded like a better alibi.

"All I remember is waking up in my office on Tuesday morning at about seven. I showered, changed and started work." He hesitated before going on. "To be honest it isn't the first time." Adding defensively. "But it doesn't stop me doing my job, and I'm bloody good at it."

Liam couldn't have cared less what McAllister did in his spare time, he just wanted to find Evie's killer. But the man certainly had more than his share of demons.

He continued with more questions about McAllister's past. Why hadn't he said that he'd been married before? It was Davy finding that piece of information that had put Liam onto his lies in the first place. McAllister admitted that he'd been married but that his wife and baby had died in a car accident. He couldn't talk about them, but his addictions all stemmed from that time.

Liam felt slightly sorry for him, but Davy would be confirming everything before that sympathy grew. Especially the detail on the baby.

"Can I ask you Mr McAllister, which sex was your child?"

"A little girl...Molly." A baby girl.

Liam kept going relentlessly, until after an hour he wrapped it up, giving the C.E.O. fair warning that he was under scrutiny. He had a weak alibi and a hazy memory of the time that Evie was killed. Plus he'd lost his wife and daughter.

McAllister begged him not to disclose anything to the Trust, and reluctantly supplied the Bishop's name for his alibi. His Excellency would be thrilled. Then he shuffled out of the room in front of his young solicitor, who seemed stunned by his prestigious client's skeletons.

But Liam had heard a lot worse, and he could easily see how McAllister had got himself in such a hole. Grief. At least his vices only damaged himself. Although Davy would be checking on that as well.

**

The press conference was just as excruciating as Craig had expected. Awkward buggers asking awkward questions, with Harrison passing most of them onto him. Rank. He made up his mind not to do the same when he became a Superintendent.

Ray Mercer of The Chronicle had surpassed himself, bringing along sample headlines with so many exclamation marks they belonged in a comic. There was little difference between The Chronicle and one, as far as Craig was concerned.

There was nothing they could do to stop the hacks wandering off into 'speculation land'. They would do whatever they wanted, and the only way to stop them was to arrest someone and give them facts to write about - a point that Harrison made about five times afterwards.

Craig was walking slowly back to the squad when his mobile rang - Liam. He pressed the button impatiently, angry at Harrison, not him. "Yes Liam, what's up?"

"We've found Murdock, boss."

The tone of his voice told Craig everything he needed to know...*Shit.*

"I'm on my way. Tell me where."

***

Maggie walked tentatively through the glass doors into the squad and hovered uneasily beside Nicky's desk. She knew how much Nicky had disapproved of her and Davy getting together in December and she'd been wary of her ever since.

Nicky saw Maggie shifting from foot to foot out of the corner of her eye and smiled to herself. She actually liked her now. She was a good journalist. An endangered species, in her opinion. Plus she made Davy smile and took care of him. But it wouldn't do to let Maggie know she liked her, in case the day came when she hurt him. She needed to keep 'I told you so' in reserve.

She turned around from her computer and stared at Maggie questioningly, as if she couldn't possibly work out why she was here. The confusion on Maggie's face almost made her relent. Almost.

"Yes? Can I help you, Ms Clarke?"

The urge to turn and run swept over Maggie - cowardice was always the better part of valour in her opinion. Then she saw Davy's dark head across the room and affection washed away her doubts. When she spoke her voice was stronger than she'd expected.

"D.C.I. Craig said I could come and say hello to Davy."

As she said his name she lifted her finger and pointed at him, like a child. Then she caught her gesture and pulled her hand down again quickly.

Nicky made a mental note to have a word with Craig for undermining her armed truce. Then she gazed at Maggie with the chin down/eyes elevated angle that she'd seen people who wore glasses using. It always seemed grave and intelligent when they did it, but somehow the effect was lost without the props. Maggie knew exactly what Nicky was doing and thought she just looked like she had a sore neck. But she didn't dare smile.

After a moments consideration Nicky pressed a button on her phone and asked Davy to come to reception. He bounded over, his long hair flying like an Irish Setter. When he saw Maggie a wide smile lit up his face, almost making Nicky relent and smile too. But instead she looked sternly at the pair. "Thirty minutes Davy, and then back to work."

Davy gave her a deep bow and she arched her eyebrow at his cheek. "W...Whatever you say Nicky." Then he wandered off the squad in search of lunch, brazenly holding Maggie's hand.

***

By one o'clock Craig was pulling into a broad sea-gulled wasteland between the silver Titanic Belfast Centre and the river at Queen's Quay. A runway of flashing blue lights led the way to the crime scene. He dumped his car to one side, and forced his way swiftly through the police line. Liam was standing beside a derelict storage shed, and he left the constable he was chatting with to greet him.

"Who found him and when, Liam?"

"A rigger for some new funfair, at about eight this morning. Uniform didn't connect things until an hour ago. He had no I.D., so they named him through the number on his medical tag. Penicillin allergy. That'll not be bothering him anymore."

He caught Craig's disapproving frown. There was a time for dark humour and this wasn't it.

"Sorry, boss. Anyway, the rigger was putting some equipment up and he nipped into the shed for a quiet fag out of the rain. He literally stood on the body. It was spread-out just inside the door."

"They wanted him found. You're sure it's him?"

"Pretty sure. We need the formal I.D., but height, build and appendix scar match the description the wife gave. He was buck naked. Do you want to have a look at him? It's real biblical stuff."

"Go ahead."

Craig followed him into the echoing steel shed where the white-suited C.S.I.s were already busy.

"Don't worry lads, we're not going to mess up your scene. We'll stand over here. Could one of you just pull back the sheet and let the boss see his face?"

The thin sheet slipped back to uncover a man's grazed and blood-stained face. There were fine white particles spread all over his chin. Even from a distance, Craig recognised the man he'd interviewed the week before.

"Yes, there's no doubt it's Murdock. But get the usual I.D. please. Have you called John?"

"Yes. Hello Marc." A warm baritone turned them towards the lean figure of John Winter, already suited-up to approach the scene.

"Sorry to rush you, John, but we need a quick idea of how and when. Just a first impression."

"Right - let me see him then."

Putting on his glasses Winter headed over to their victim, walking on the C.S.I.'s metal pathway. He hunkered down for several minutes, studying Murdock's head, arms and torso closely. And finally his back and legs. Then he walked back to Craig, ready to give them a steer. John wasn't precious about educated guesses. He knew that giving one now might save another life.

"Well, this is interesting. Almost biblical."

"That's exactly the word Liam used. Why?"

"The whole scene, it feels deliberately barren. Right, well - he's been dead for several hours. The resolving Rigor indicates more than twelve. The Lividity is all on the front so he was on his stomach for at least the first six. There's no secondary Lividity on his heels or back at all, so he wasn't moved for at least six hours after death.

The primary surface wasn't firm enough to leave marks, so

249

no clues there I'm afraid. But this definitely isn't the murder site; there's nothing like enough blood. I'd say that he'd been dead for at least six hours when he was moved, possibly longer. Then he was brought here to be laid out on his back. This was a deliberate display - probably to humiliate him."

Craig rubbed his forehead as he listened, leaving a deep red mark. He nodded John on.

"He's heavily bruised all over, consistent with being handled roughly prior to death. The bruises are about one to two days old. And there are restraint marks above both wrists and ankles - deeper on the wrists, so his socks probably saved his ankles. He was a big man, so I should think he was drugged. He would have fought back otherwise, and there are no defensive wounds that I can see. Whatever they used to bind him was probably cut off soon after death - the Lividity indicates that." He paused and glanced back at the body, shaking his head. After a long pause he restarted, heavily.

"His face was superficially grazed before death, so that might give you some clues as to the surface he died on. Mainly small scratches, and there's what looks like a small piece of gravel embedded in his nose. The white powder on his chin could be Cocaine, or it could just be staged with something. I can't be sure until I get him back to the lab. There are bruises to the face and a contusion on the back of his skull - we'll probably find a depressed fracture there, consistent with a heavy blow. It was caused by something about the diameter of a two pound coin, maybe a hammer. But there's too much swelling to tell for sure without an X-ray. Des can tell this better than me, but those medical alert tags look platinum, and they're still there. So theft probably wasn't a feature."

A sudden look of disgust flashed across his face and Craig held his breath. He instantly knew what was coming next.

"What he does have is a transverse incision across his lower abdomen, right down to the abdominal cavity. It's an accurate Pfannenstiel - that's the incision used for Caesareans."

Yes! Craig mentally punched the air and Liam gasped loudly. That was a new one, even for him. John was the first to break the silence.

"It was done while he was alive, Marc. I'd say that he was bound, incised, left on his stomach to bleed out, and then stripped and arranged here later on his back. It's tempting to say that he bled to death, but I need to rule out other things first. This isn't the primary scene, there just isn't enough blood. This scene was purely about display. Maybe they knew the area would be busy with the funfair, so it wouldn't be long until he was found?"

"Which could mean that he wouldn't have been found at the primary site, John. Or at least that a quick audience wouldn't have been guaranteed there."

"Indeed. There's one other thing which is a bit strange. I think you'll find that Mr Murdock operated left-handed."

"Why do you say that, Doc?"

"They amputated his left hand above the wrist. While he was alive."

"God - this is really grim, John. It feels almost depraved."

"Yes, it does. And I think they took the hand as a trophy. The C.S.I.'s haven't found it. Anyway, there's obviously no doubt that this is murder. And there's no question in my mind that we'll find the Pethidine and Insulin mix in his blood as well. I'm sure this is linked with the deaths of our three women, Marc."

"I didn't like the man, but what a way to go. Someone must have really hated him. And they have to be insane. This isn't the work of anyone normal." He paused for a moment, thinking. "You and Liam both used the word 'Biblical' - presumably you mean the gruesomeness?"

"Not really, no. I meant wrath. Don't you feel that's what this was, rather than the usual robbery, rape or random? It's like one of those 'vengeance' scenarios from the Old Testament. I'm just waiting for Charlton Heston to appear."

251

He stared out at the Lagan, as if waiting for it to part.

"Aye, it is, boss. It's like one of those bible stories teachers used to scare the hell out of us with, when we were kids. Being struck by God's lightning-bolt if you were caught stealing a biscuit, and that sort of stuff. You know."

"God Liam, where did you go to school?" They all laughed, lightening the mood.

A sudden flash outside the shed caught Craig's eye. He turned sharply, expecting to see the C.S.I. photographer. Instead he was greeted by the sight of a young woman in jeans, clicking a camera straight at them. Journalist.

Liam had already seen her and he loped over quickly. He mentally replayed his 'dealing with the media' course to stop him ripping the camera from her hand, and boomed loudly in her face. "Which paper are you from?"

"The C...Chronicle." What a surprise. "Ray Mercer asked me to take some shots for him." She stammered and stared up at Liam in confusion. He was so much taller than her that she teetered backwards and he grabbed her to stop her fall.

At the mention of Mercer's name he shook his head, knowing that she'd been duped by an old hand. "That's because he knows better than to come near a crime-scene himself. You've been had, love. I'll need to take that memory card - you'll get a receipt for it. And tell Mr Mercer that if we see reports on this before we release an official statement, your editor will be speaking to us as well. You're compromising an on-going investigation."

She was about twenty years old and absolutely terrified - Mercer was a real shit. But Liam still took her details. Craig and John walked over to join them angrily. When Craig saw how frightened the girl was he replaced his anger with coolness.

"How did you find out about this scene, Madam?" The girl stared down at her muddy boots, suddenly ashamed.

"Mr Mercer pays for information. From the Police."

Police leaks - totally out of order, but hard to control. There'd been respect between the press and the police for a while, but Mercer was a law onto himself. He'd got someone around the force feeding him tidbits.

"Where is he?"

An involuntary flick of her eye indicated a slip road to the left of the shed, where Craig could see a solitary parked car. He called two uniforms over, indicating the occupant. He was in the mood to rattle Mercer's cage - mostly because he'd sent a youngster to do his job. Although the lunchtime press conference hadn't helped.

"Liam, ask uniform to take this lady home please. And bring Mr Mercer back to High Street for a word. I need to talk to Tommy again too. He didn't do this - it's too complex a kill for him. But he may have seen something when he was tailing Murdock. And he better talk to me this time or I will charge him with Murdock's murder."

"Made the call ten minutes ago, boss. He'll be calling his brief as we speak."

"Great. John - just give us anything you can please, as quickly as possible." John nodded, already removing his white-suit for Nigel Murdock's trip back to the lab.

"I'll need to speak to Harrison and Charles McAllister again, Liam. So if you get to High Street before me, go ahead and start. I'll see you there."

"Aye well, before you speak to McAllister, I'd better just update you." He gave Craig a quick summary of his morning's meetings.

"Well done. OK, I won't speak to him now then. Check his alibi, then notify him that Murdock's been found and watch his reaction. Don't give him any more detail than that. Greenwood and McAllister have to be high on our suspect list now, so let's get their D.N.A.s please. Give Mercer some grief and then let him go - I'll call his editor on my way back."

Liam's face lit up at the thought of giving Mercer and

Tommy Hill a hard time. This was his sort of day. Just as they reached the cordon a short man with a builder's tan and a cigarette in his mouth approached them.

"Here, when'll you lot be finished? We've a fairground to set up and it has to be ready for testin' tomara. None of them kids will come near us on Friday if you lot are here. An' the funfair pays us for the year."

Liam loomed over him, disdain flitting across his face. Then he said, as quietly as he ever could. "Well, here's the thing, mate. It'll take as long as it takes. And if you think the cops will put people off, a corpse will do it even quicker."

Instead of the shock he was aiming for, the rigger just shrugged and sucked on his cigarette, all sarcasm wasted on him. Not my problem mate.

***

Tommy was his usual charming self, no-commenting his way through every question. So after ten minutes Liam gave up, deciding to leave him to Craig. He'd have a go at Mercer instead.

Ray Mercer shifted on the hard interview-room chair, trying to get comfortable. He yawned loudly, knowing that someone was watching on the other side of the wall and drew his middle finger pointedly up his face.

He was thin, dark and angular, with a nose that his mother called Roman and others called hooked. He didn't mind what they called it. The severity of his look served him well, putting the fear of God into interviewees and editors alike.

He didn't care if people loved him as long as they paid him. And as long as he could write what he wanted 24/7. He was good at what he did and it wasn't a popularity contest. He tapped his finger pointedly against his watch mouthing 'time is money' to the wall. Following it with another middle finger in the air, and 'charge me or let me go.'

Liam stood on the other side of the mirror with his arms folded, watching. He hated journalists, except for Davy's wee lassie Maggie; she was all right. The concept that you had to ask them not to print things that could prejudice an investigation was completely beyond him. But most of them responded to a gentle warning and a raised eyebrow, scuttling off back to their offices to play nice. Not Mercer. He was the lowest form of scum and endowed with giant cojones. Even his best menace didn't work on him.

After five minutes watching Liam pushed open the interview-room door. He grabbed the chair nearest it, turning it around and leaning abruptly across its back. He was a good foot taller than Mercer and that, combined with his megaphone diplomacy, normally did the trick on everyone. He thought it was worth a try, not holding out much hope.

When he'd finished shouting, Mercer smirked, as if to say 'is that all you have?' And Liam could feel his fist curling under the desk. Five minutes alone with no witnesses was all he needed. Then Mercer would be writing cookery tips for beginners. But he knew it would never happen, so he bit his tongue and re-started the warning in his coldest, deepest tone.

"Mr Mercer. You know why you're here."

Mercer yawned open-mouthed and then sat staring at Liam in silence. After a moment he shrugged. "You want me to say that I'm a bad little journalist? OK then, I'm a bad little journalist. You want me to say that I buy information? OK, I buy information. You want me to tell you who I buy it from? There I draw the line."

He smirked so arrogantly that Liam wanted to reach over and smack him one. Then he restarted in a faux–noble tone that implied integrity. He probably thought integrity was a country in South America.

"A journalist never reveals his sources, Inspector, but there are plenty of them in the force. They don't pay you guys enough, so earning a bit on the side appeals to plenty of your colleagues. And I pay well." He smiled provocatively "You've a new baby, haven't you? Maybe you'd like to earn a bit more sometime?"

That was Liam's limit. Not the offer, but the mention of his family. How the hell did Mercer know about them? Before he could stop himself he was across the room, looming over Mercer with his fist clenched. The unflinching look on the hack's face dared him to cross the line.

At that moment the door opened and Craig walked in. He said nothing, just stared at the journalist as if he was something he'd stepped in. Liam glanced at Craig, then at Mercer, and backed off. He wasn't going to give him the satisfaction.

Mercer stared coolly at Craig. "You're my witness, D.C.I. Craig. That was police brutality."

Craig half-smiled. "I don't know what you're talking about, Mr Mercer. I just came in to say you're free to go."

"Come off it Craig! You saw it. I want you to charge him."

Craig shook his head gently. "It will be a cold day in hell before that ever happens. Now get out. And you're on a warning, Mr Mercer. If I see you at a crime scene you'll be lifted. I've already given your editor the message."

He shot Liam a warning look and then they left the room together, leaving Ray Mercer to find his own way out. On clear notice not to mess with the thin blue line.

***

4pm.

Craig walked into the briefing to find everyone already assembled, the buzz in the room telling him that they'd heard about the body.

"Right. You'll all have heard about today's events. We'll come back to those in a moment, but let's do a general update first. Annette, can you start us off please."

"OK, the death records. Since Mr Murdock joined the Unit in 2006 they've had a lot of complaints about too many Caesareans and his rudeness. But there was nothing much else. There are only two other deaths that could possibly fit our case. The first was in 2007. The lady was a known diabetic and she made a complaint about Murdock's bad manners weeks before she died. But Beth wasn't the midwife on her case. She wasn't even working in the Trust then."

"Did the patient have a Caesarean at any point? Before or after death?"

"No."

"Then let's rule her out for now."

Annette was about to ask something, but Craig gently motioned her on.

"The second case happened in March 2008. It was a young woman who had an emergency Caesarean. She bled to death on the operating table."

"What happened to the baby?"

"It survived, sir."

"Was Murdock the consultant?"

"Yes, and Beth was the midwife."

Craig sat forward urgently. "Was the baby a girl? And was the mother a known diabetic?"

"Yes, the baby was a little girl. But no sir, she wasn't a diabetic. Although there's a vague note referring to some Insulin two days before her death. The case-file is pretty vague overall, and the drug charts were being stored in the pharmacy for some reason."

"What was her name, Annette?"

"Melissa Pullman."

"Right. Annette and Martin - gather everything you can find on Ms Pullman. Get the drug charts and operation notes and start digging into her background. Anything you can find. Where she was born, parents, was she married, what did she do for a living? And the baby. Where is it now? And very importantly, who's the father? Get her post-mortem and ward notes, and any complaints against hospital staff. Anything and everything. Copy it all to Dr Winter and me urgently. And speak to the Trust Medical Director to see what help he can give you." He paused briefly. "But don't involve Charles McAllister please."

Annette shot Craig a questioning look, but he was pre-occupied, thinking. This was their link to the killer, he was sure of it.

The rest of the briefing was spent on the interviews with Tommy's men. Then Liam read out the report John had sent through, on the D.N.A. patch from Evie's forehead. "No match with Brian Murray. He's in Scotland, but he was happy to give a sample to the local cops. And no match on the Reverend Kerr either. We'll get it tested against Tommy's crew next - we already know that Tommy's in the clear."

"I don't think we'll get a hit from any of them, and it definitely wasn't Murdock. What's Murray doing in Scotland, Liam?"

"Basically, he's scared shitless of Tommy, boss. It seems Tommy never approved of Evie's choice of hubbie. And the word's out that he'd cheerfully do for Murray, now that she's dead."

"Ask him to come back please, Liam, the Kerrs are the only family he has. He needs their support, and his daughter needs him. Tell him Tommy's locked up at the moment and we'll warn him off. Right. Forget Tommy's crew for now, we need D.N.A.s from Greenwood, McAllister, Iain Lewes and Michael Randle for elimination." Liam smiled at the mention of Lewes name, the boss hadn't ruled him out completely then. Craig was still talking.

"We don't want the prosecution's well poisoned by cutting corners, so make sure you get a warrant for anyone who won't co-operate. I'm not handing them a mis-trial down the line on some technicality. Judge Standish is good for warrants, and he doesn't mind being contacted at home. He lives out in Moira. Davy, can you check if the D.N.A. matches anything on the databases, please?"

"Dr W...Winter's already checked, but the answer's no."

Craig rubbed his hand across his face. "OK. Liam, anything more on Michael Randle?"

"Well he's a violent wee bugger, even carries a knife to work. He's also had a bust for skunk. But he couldn't have killed Murdock, boss. I held him all weekend on possession of the knife. And I really can't see him for Evie. Surely our killer has to be brighter than Randle? He's a real 'equal rights for bricks' case."

"OK - but we could be looking at two people working together, and he had the skill and access to arrange electrical failures. Greenwood and McAllister have as well. McAllister let slip he was an engineer before he went into management. Check Randle's knife and all their D.N.A.s anyway, and get all their alibis from Sunday until today checked please."

"I can tell you where Moya Murphy says Greenwood's been since last Friday. In Dublin at some conference."

"Let's get him back, then."

Craig updated them on Murdock's gruesome demise, the detail of the abdominal incision shocking everyone. Annette understood now why only Melissa Pullman's case fitted. Craig grabbed a marker and started writing on the board.

"The Caesarean is a common theme. We don't know yet if Murdock was drugged or with what, but he's a big man. So unless he was subdued somehow, I'm certain he would have fought back, and there's no sign of defensive wounds. My money's on the Insulin/Pethidine cocktail being in his blood stream. Maybe Cocaine as well. Or maybe that was just window dressing to tell us something specific about him. It's unlikely the killer gave him a snort just to make him feel better, so the coke scattering is definitely significant. It's staging of some sort. And when we find it, the location of the primary scene will have importance as well."

"To Murdock, boss?"

"Or his killer. Murdock was bound, incised and left face-down to bleed out through his abdominal wound. He was clothed for part of the time they had him - the restraint marks show that his socks protected his ankles from the binding. He was probably stripped sometime after death but before Rigor was complete at twelve hours. He most likely bled to death, but John wants to rule out other methods. I doubt that Carotid occlusion will show up in Murdock, it's much too kind a way of killing. I think that's why our killer used it for Evie. The killer was cool enough to kill Murdock, and keep him somewhere for at least six hours for Lividity to set in. Then he moved him before full Rigor and displayed him naked on his back for maximum effect. Somewhere that he'd be found quickly. Indicating humiliation?"

Annette interjected hesitantly. "Violation maybe, sir?"

Craig nodded. Yes. Violation. That was it.

"Leaving him somewhere to bleed out, means that he was confident that Murdock *wouldn't* be accidentally found there. So we're looking for a primary scene with a lot of privacy. Somewhere that the killer knew he wouldn't be disturbed. Somewhere he has a degree of control of, and is very familiar with."

"Excuse me, sir."

Craig turned from the whiteboard and saw Martin leaning forward, eagerness written across his round young face. He'd learned not to raise his hand now.

"Yes, Martin?"

"Could Murdock's death be the killer copying what Murdock did to someone he loved? Did Murdock do this to a relative of the killer, sir?"

Craig nodded. "Yes. That's why the Melissa Pullman case could be so important. I know Beth has also been common to

260

all the cases, and that helped on timing as she's only been back here since 2008. But I've said it before - we can't get complacent on that. There could be deliberately false trails here, and Beth's presence in all of the cases could be one of them.

Perhaps Melissa Pullman was the pivot, and perhaps the killer's using Beth's presence deliberately, to point us to cases since 2008. They may want us focusing on more recent cases in the same way they wanted us to know that Evie was definitely murdered. Or, conversely, they could be deliberately pointing us away from an older case. If we think laterally, now that Mr Murdock has been murdered we can be sure he was one of the main pivots. So the worst case scenario is that, as he was a doctor for thirty years, a surviving child could be thirty now. Old enough to kill."

"But the cases that match were all female babies, boss, and the D.N.A. found was male."

"I agree that it's unlikely, Liam. The killer wanted us to know Evie had been murdered, so I think they're deliberately pointing us to the Murdock/Walker combination. And that means cases since 2008. But the D.N.A. stain could be a false trail."

Craig scanned their faces. Some were puzzled and some worried - his speculation was confusing them. He should keep it inside his head.

"Don't worry, I'm just being Devil's Advocate. The killer definitely wanted us to pay attention to Evie's murder and it's what that tells us that provides the focus for our case. That and Melissa Pullman. Beth was on both cases and so was Murdock. Our background searches didn't show any other matches to the method in Northern Ireland, Ireland or the U.K. Or from the G.M.C. or medical insurance societies for Murdock.

There was one case of maternal death, using Insulin and abdominal stabbing in Australia when Beth was there. But it was the other side of the country and her alibi checked out - it was the woman's husband who did it. But hospital records from thirty years ago are patchy, and most haven't been digitised, so we can't rule them out entirely yet. Keep digging."

He stared at their tired faces, feeling sorry for them. But they were getting closer to their killer, he could feel it. They couldn't relax just yet.

"Let's re-focus on what we have. Four deaths now, similar M.O. and we're looking for a tall, strong man with easy access to maternity and electrical knowledge. Let's tidy up the loose ends and dig deeper on Melissa Pullman. And we need to find that primary scene. I want you all to work on the Pullman case first. It's our best lead so far. If you find anything at all that fits, bring it directly to me please.

Go back over anyone who was in that Unit on Monday evening and dig into their pasts. Find out about any links between our suspect list and Melissa Pullman. Check how their family members died, and if anyone's female relative died in childbirth flag them up to me."

Craig was speaking so quickly that Nicky gave up trying to take notes, recording him instead.

"Find Melissa Pullman's husband. Where is he? I want to interview him. Liam had Randle in all weekend on possession of the knife, so don't waste any time on him. And I'm pretty convinced that our killer's not Iain Lewes. So just get their D.N.A.s, check Randle's knife and rule them out.

Equally, Tommy's cronies are weak propositions. We're looking at someone much more sophisticated as our killer. Get McAllister and Greenwoods' photos over to Melissa Pullman's family immediately, Liam. And Joe, can you make sure that all the protection officers are doing their jobs please."

"All fine as of an hour ago, sir. Should I tell them about Mr Murdock?"

Craig thought for a moment. The detail of Murdock's death needed to stay within the team, but the protection officers needed to know.

"Update the officers, but not their charges, Joe. And reinforce the message that no-one goes anywhere without protection. The killer could still go after Katy, Beth Walker and Laurie Johns. Especially Beth Walker. She needs to be protected."

'Katy'. Liam smiled and Craig avoided his eyes. They didn't have time for his banter right now.

"Couldn't Tommy still be Murdock's murderer, sir? He was free on Sunday night."

"If Murdock had been killed in a simple way like shooting or being beaten to death, then I'd have said maybe yes, Annette. But this isn't his style. He wouldn't know enough to mimic the incision, and John said that it was accurate. Although we'll hold him for a while longer on the stalking. We're still missing something obvious about our killer so we need to go back over all the evidence. Liam, can you chase-up the Cocaine and Carotid occlusion links."

"Carotid occlusion is a military or martial arts technique, boss. Unfortunately that only rules out the people we've already ruled out. Lewes was in the officer training corps at Uni and so was McAllister. Randle does Karate, and Greenwood's a weekend warrior."

"Greenwood does martial arts too, sir. I noticed a book about Taekwondo on his desk, when I went to collect the floor plans."

"Fine. Dig a bit more on Greenwood. Joe, give his territorial commanding officer a call and find out what he knows. And I want McAllister's background checked out further. Davy, can you do that please."

"W...we did that on everyone and I told Liam about McAllister's problems. Greenwood came up clean as a w...whistle."

Seeing Craig's wry look he added. "But I'll dig even deeper."

"I'll get warrants for searches if we can find grounds, boss."

"Right. Can everyone be back here at 8am please, Nicky, I'll be up with the D.C.S. if you need me. Liam, can you join me at the lab at five to see what John has on Murdock. There was less than ten days between Evie's and Murdock's deaths, so our killer's definitely escalating. We need to catch him quickly. Before we have any more victims."

"But surely, if its revenge for something personal and he's killed Mr Murdock now, won't that be the last of it, sir?"

"I'd like to say yes, Annette, but we can't be sure until we get him. He could be having a psychotic break, or have an agenda that none of us can guess at yet."

Chapter Twenty-Five

Tuesday. 5pm.

"Based on the fact that his Rigor had started to relax when we saw him at one o'clock, and allowing for the temperature in the shed, I'd put time of death no earlier than eighteen to nineteen hours ago. He died between ten and eleven last night, Marc. We're looking at a maximum of nineteen hours since death, and then face down for at least six hours for Lividity. None of his bones were broken, so he was definitely moved, stripped and laid flat *before* full Rigor set in at twelve hours."

Craig nodded. "It would have been much safer to move him in darkness. I checked sunrise time this morning and it was light at about six. So I'd say he was left at Queen's Quay no later than five this morning."

"That makes sense. OK. We know that he was definitely alive on Sunday night at eight, so the killer could have held him just over twenty-four hours, before killing him last night. There are no signs of sexual abuse or torture, just blunt assault. He may even have left him alone somewhere for those missing hours - it all depends how cool this bugger is."

"Very. I think he feels virtually nothing for his victims."

"He couldn't have any empathy, or he wouldn't be able to kill like this. A psychopath then. Although he did express regret at killing Evie."

"It didn't stop him." Craig paused, thinking for a moment.

"The roads would have been clear at five this morning, so

we might be lucky with the traffic cameras."

"Nicky's got Traffic pulling the tapes already, boss. The area around there is pretty deserted at that time, so I doubt there'll be any eye witnesses."

John nodded, continuing. "OK. Murdock was a big man, so this was someone very strong, or more than one person. Earliest findings indicate that he was bound with hemp-based rope. The pattern and thickness matches common household varieties, although obviously we'll be more accurate given time. But we're definitely not looking at handcuffs here. It was rope or thick string, and probably available anywhere. His clothes were cut off while he was alive. Just. There are superficial cuts consistent with that. Have you found the primary scene yet?"

"No, still looking, Doc. Queens Quay's a big area."

"It might not be there, Liam. You should be looking for a primary with a specific significance to the killer. I think the Trust is a better bet."

Craig closed his eyes. "You're right - hang on a second."

He made the call quickly. "Joe, can you get some men over to the M.P.E. Have them search it inside and out for any areas that have complete privacy. Somewhere near Maternity. There'll be signs of massive bleeding. Thanks."

John continued. "He was struck on the base of the skull very hard before death The fracture fits with a hammer, or something of similar size. And there are multiple bruises between one and two days old, all over him. That fits with our timeline, and it's consistent with him being man-handled or dropped from a height. There are also multiple lacerations." He pointed to a large cut on Murdock's elbow.

"The skin over the bone split on impact, probably from a fall. And the grazes on his face are consistent with common gravel. Des says that it's stone you could find anywhere. The white powder was definitely Cocaine, but it was just spread superficially. The nasal mucosa showed that Murdock had been a significant past, but not a recent user."

"Calming down in his old age, Doc."

"Maybe. Anyway the coke was sprinkled around, probably deliberately. Some sort of symbolism perhaps? It might be significant."

"Any sign of the Insulin/Pethidine mix?"

"We're just waiting for that now. Des put a rush on it. There were recent injection sites on both thighs. We've excised them to check, but I'm certain that he'll prove positive for both drugs. The final cause of death was shock from blood loss. There are no signs of the occlusion method that we found in Evie. I think her occlusion was a deliberately kinder method of killing. I'm beginning to think that Evie was just collateral damage to draw our attention, which makes her death even sadder."

"And Tommy's attention, John. They wanted him involved for some reason."

"Then she died because she was Tommy Hill's daughter."

"What a bloody waste."

John continued gravely. "Evie's Pethidine was definitely because they wanted us to know she'd been murdered, but it might only be with Murdock that we're getting to the real point of all this. The women's Insulin and Pethidine levels weren't high, and if the killer's consistent, then Murdock's will be the same. Sedative or symbolic, not lethal. But I think you should add Cocaine as relevant to the basis for the killings, Marc. It was very deliberate staging."

He lifted a scalpel, gesturing at the body.

"The Pfannenstiel incision is very interesting. It wasn't jagged and there were no hesitation marks at all. It was done in a single long sweep, like this." He drew the scalpel from left to right in the air, demonstrating.

"This was someone who'd practiced a lot. If they aren't clinical then they've been rehearsing this for a long time. And it was definitely made with a smooth blade. A scalpel or a razor-sharp knife, not a domestic or sports-knife. So again they had access to medicines and medical equipment. The deaths have all been very well planned, so even if our killer is escalating now I believe they'll still go after specific targets."

Just then, Des Marsham appeared.

"I thought you'd need Murdock's results, John. The gravel is common builder's grade and it's found pretty much everywhere. The Insulin and Pethidine levels are there, but definitely not lethal. The Cocaine was very pure – medicinal, not street quality. But there's none in the blood, so it was just scattered or dropped on him. But there was something new as well. There were very high levels of Ketamine present, enough to immobilise even a big man. There are trace amounts in his stomach, and much higher levels in his blood. So he swallowed it first and it was partially digested before death, then he was injected with more of it later. The wound excisions and analysis will tell us more. I've got the bloods on Beth Walker and Janey Holmes as well. Both were positive for Rohypnol. I haven't finished looking at Murdock's note yet."

"Thanks Des. That's a thought. Marc, did Davy find where the Pethidine's coming from yet?"

"No, he's been searching for days, but there's nothing yet. All the hospital and G.P. surgeries are accounted for, and there's been nothing missing from any retail pharmacies. Karl says there's some street Pethidine out there occasionally, but he's heard nothing lately."

"What note, Des?"

Craig startled at Liam's question. He hadn't even registered Des mentioning it. He was getting tired.

Des warmed to his subject. "There was a note folded up tightly and wedged in Mr Murdock's right hand. We only found it when he got back here, because of the Rigor. And I think the removal of his left hand is significant."

Craig nodded. "We've confirmed with Theatres that he operated left-handed. What did the note say?"

"It was a Latin quotation 'Primum non nocere.' It shows us the killer doesn't have medical or nursing training, but is someone generally well educated. Third level education. College at least, but probably University."

"Primum non nocere...First, Do No Harm."

John smiled. "You were awake in Baxter's Latin class then, Marc." Des kept talking.

"Anyway, It's a quote that people often think is from the Hippocratic Oath taken by doctors, but it's actually not. It's completely separate, linked with The Epidemics, or from Galen. The point is that any doctor would know the difference. Your killer isn't a doctor."

Liam gawped at Des as if he was speaking Swahili and John laughed, interjecting.

"Sorry Liam, for one awful moment there we sounded like barristers. The note basically implies that Murdock was a bad doctor who harmed someone. Someone associated you're your killer? If the killer isn't medical, that could rule out Dr Lewes, Marc. If you still liked him for it."

'Liked him'. Liam smiled at John's gangster terminology. The Doc had been watching too many crime movies again.

"I agree. I don't think Lewes is our man."

Craig updated them on Melissa Pullman's death and John nodded. "If Murdock did her harm and it was linked to operating, that would explain the amputation of his left hand. Her death could be your answer."

Des continued. "Anyway, the note itself will probably yield nothing, just like Evie's. But we'll run all the usual checks anyway."

An angry look crossed John's face. "I bet there were notes left with the first two women as well. If Davis destroyed them then he's an even worse bastard than we thought."

Craig nodded. "They've been trying to point us towards something for months. And so far we've missed it."

He paused and Liam interjected. "What's with the

Ketamine, Des?"

"It's a horse tranquilizer, but it's also used as a street drug, called Special K or Ket. It's a clear liquid that can be drunk or injected. Medium doses paralyse in ten minutes. A higher dose puts you in the 'K-Hole', where you can't do anything but lie still and stare at the ceiling. If it's ingested with Cocaine the combination is known as CK1 - a fashionable death."

"The shit people put in their bodies never ceases to amaze me."

"And we never drink at all. Ha ha."

"The Ketamine must have subdued Murdock enough to avoid a struggle, Des. Although the blow to the head will have helped I'm sure. That's excellent. Thanks, both of you."

Craig stood up, ready to go. "We're going to head back now. We can charge Tommy's men with the Rohypnol and attempted kidnapping. The people from Sarajevo have positively identified Ralph Coyle and Rory McCrae as the two men they chased. And we've got Gerard Bonner for tailing Dr Stevens. But the most we can get Tommy for is conspiracy. That's only if the others will give him up, and there's no sign of that happening any time soon. They're a loyal bunch of idiots, I'll give them that much."

"If stupidity was a crime, they'd be lifers, boss."

"How long can you hold Tommy, Marc?"

"Another few hours. Then we'll either have to charge him with something, or let him go."

Liam chipped in. "I'll try his crew again, and if they cough then I'll do him on conspiracy. But if they won't, it'll just have to be a stiff warning for Tommy this time."

Craig nodded. "A conspiracy charge would be insignificant to a hard-timer like Tommy anyway. And I don't think he managed to do anything to Murdock but follow him. We could toss his place, but if we turn up drugs, which we will, it'll blow Karl's operation on the Demesne. Check if he saw anything when he was tailing Murdock, and then let him go,

Liam. Everyone's covered by protection and he needs to mourn his daughter. But make it clear that he's not to touch Brian Murray, or we'll lock him up permanently."

"Right you are then."

"If I get anything else I'll call you immediately Marc."

As they reached the door John remembered something. He followed them out quickly.

"Sorry, but there were two other things. Although Alan Davis seemed to die of a heart attack that can easily be mimicked by drugs. So I'll have another look at him, just in case our man had something to do with it."

Craig raked his hand down his face, almost laughing with disbelief. "OK. And?"

"Murdock had a laceration on his right cheek, identical to Evie's. I didn't see it at the scene with all the mess."

Another part of the staging, but it was significant.

"Thanks John. We'll investigate Davis' death later. Until we get this killer I'm more concerned about future deaths than past ones. But we need to catch a break on this soon, before we all end up on your table from stress."

Chapter Twenty-Six

Wednesday. 3pm.

Laurie Johns was bored sitting at home. She'd weeded the garden, visited her mother, and shopped and lunched with friends three times this week already. She really needed to get back to work. So when Charles McAllister's phone call came, she was pleased to hear from him.

"Sister Johns, I wonder if you could assist me?"

"I'd be very happy to, Chief Executive. I'm going mad with boredom at home."

"Thank you. Look, the builders need to start over at St Marys on the 29th. So they need to finish Maternity by the 19th and move onto the rest of the M.P.E. And work in Maternity has rather ground to a halt." He added hastily. "Very understandably, of course. But, well, we really need to progress things now. Time is money."

His tone became persuasive, softening his strong accent. "We need someone clinical to advise us on the best positions for the Unit's new close-circuit cameras. Could you possibly help with that today?"

"Yes certainly, I'd love to. When do you need me? I can be there in an hour."

"That's brilliant, Sister. I thought I'd ask you before anyone else."

Who else *could* he have asked? Stupid man.

"Just go along to Maternity and someone will meet you there at four. It might be me, if I can get away. And thank you again Sister."

She loved the importance of her title, and he'd used it three times. So she decided she quite liked Charles McAllister. And she couldn't remember seeing a wife at his introductory drinks...

She took a good thirty minutes choosing her outfit. After all, it wasn't often she got to wear her normal clothes to work. Or anywhere else that Nigel might see her nowadays, she thought sadly. She was going to make the most of it. And if she didn't see Nigel, then a builder or Charles McAllister would be a nice diversion.

The linen trousers and top she chose suited her dark colouring perfectly, and she made herself up discretely. Not like the slutty make-up those young nurses trowelled on. She saw them leaving her Unit every evening dressed like tramps. If she had her way she'd scrub all their faces.

Grabbing her bag and phone, she glanced out of the window at the protection officers' car. No. She'd had quite enough of their supervision, thank you very much. It was all a lot of drama for nothing. No-one was after her. She'd done nothing wrong. They should go after Beth Walker if they wanted to kill someone - she deserved it.

She left through the back door, walking briskly to the car port. Then she gunned her yellow convertible, turning left outside the gate to avoid her over-protectors. Backtracking onto the Drumbeg Road and Upper Malone, she meandered through the quiet country lanes to the sound of Celine Dion. She loved telling people that she lived in 'Upper Malone'. It was shorthand for prosperity in Belfast. And it said so much about a person. It said a lot more about Laurie Johns than she could ever know.

The eight-mile drive to the M.P.E. took her down leafy roads and over quaint stone bridges. Past the flowers of Lady Dixon Park, and through suburban BT9. After twenty minutes she turned into Elmwood Avenue, towards the M.P.E.

It was a sunny day and still quiet after the Easter Holidays -
the area was much nicer without students or noisy school-
children. Laurie Johns had never been young.

She drove into the staff car-park, stopping at the mark she'd
drawn, six inches from her name. Then she slipped on her
sunglasses, fluffed-up her hair and climbed elegantly out of the
car. Heading briskly for Maternity.

***

Nicky popped her head around the door, just as people
filtered in for the four o'clock briefing. "Two things, sir.
Firstly, the court has phoned and the Warwick summations
have just finished. The Judge is instructing the jury. And
secondly, there's an urgent call for you. It's Joe Rice. Can I put
him through down here?"

Craig nodded and went out to the corridor to take the call.
"Yes Joe, what can I do for you? We're just about to start. Are
you caught in traffic?"

"No, sir. But I thought I should let you know, I think we've
found Murdock's primary scene."

"Where?"

"At the back of the M.P.E., by the builder's Portakabin. Just
behind the old Dunmore Medical Centre."

Craig visualised it. It was near the consultant's offices,
where Iain Lewes and Katy had been on the evening before
Evie's death.

"Good work Joe. Right, stay there and call the C.S.I.s. Give
John a bell too please. We'll be with you in fifteen minutes."

He went back into the room. "Sorry everyone, the briefing's
postponed. Liam, come with me - Joe thinks they've found
Murdock's scene. Annette, I need that information on Melissa
Pullman."

"I'm just waiting for something to come through, sir. I
should have it in thirty minutes."

"OK. Meet me there with it. And bring the D.N.A. results too please."

***

On first inspection the patch of blood looked quite small, only about twelve centimetres across. Not a big monument for Nigel Murdock's fifty year life. Then the C.S.I. pointed out that, judging by the probe she'd used, blood had seeped down through the gravel for at least thirty more. The 3-D image she created left no doubt that someone had bled considerably here.

"We won't know the exact blood volume until we do the seepage calculations, sir. But several litres I'd say. I'll get it to you ASAP."

The blood had been found by a piecework joiner, calling to collect his wages at the Portakabin. The scene was certainly private. Hidden between the Portakabin and the rear entrance of the M.P.E. It would have been easy to kill Nigel Murdock there unseen.

They pieced together Murdock's final movements. He'd gone to his first-floor office at about eight on Sunday evening, to do some dictation. Then he'd left the tape for his secretary, to type up the next day. That was always his approach with private patients.

As his P.A. pointed out dryly. "His ordinary patients wait six weeks for their stuff, even with me chasing him. But the quicker he completes his private letters, the quicker he gets paid." She said that his voice had sounded slurred towards the end of the tape, adding sarcastically that it 'wouldn't have been a first for him'.

The C.S.I.s struck lucky. The cleaners hadn't been in the office since Friday, so Murdock's cup was still lying on the floor. He'd been drinking coffee as he dictated. They sampled the fluid but Craig already knew what they'd find – Ketamine.

275

Someone had followed Nigel Murdock there on Sunday night, well prepared and intent on murder.

If this was the primary scene, then he'd been abducted from his office on Sunday night. Probably just after his drug-filled dictation. Craig stared up at the first floor – a fire escape gave easy access for the killer. A strong man could have dragged or pushed a drugged Murdock down the steps, completely unseen in the dark. It would fit with the bruises and lacerations John had found. Gravity would have helped, but the killer's strength must still have been formidable.

Just then John appeared through the street entrance, and walked straight over to the C.S.I. kneeling beside the patch of blood. "Georgia, can you get some of that over to Des for D.N.A., please. And bag some of that gravel as well. Thanks." He spotted Craig and loped over to him.

"Hi Marc, this makes perfect sense. This gravel is fine enough to match the scratches on Murdock's face. And that amount of blood around such a small circumference would fit with bleeding from the incision. It would have seeped down rather than spread outwards, because of the porous nature of the ground here. The lab will confirm that. The location would have given plenty of cover as well - three walls and a locked entrance gate. But he would have had to move the body before anyone came here on Monday morning. Two moves?"

Liam overheard the question. "Just one, Doc. The security guard says no-one would've been here from last Friday lunchtime until tomorrow. They had a few days off. Some people were heading up to St Marys today for a big meeting. Work's gearing-up to start over there on the 29th."

"Check who was at that meeting and what time it ended please, Liam."

"Already done. McAllister and various doctors, including Lewes, were there." He glanced at his watch. "It's scheduled to end about now. Greenwood gave the tradesmen the days off before he went to Dublin for his conference. He's a bit of a control freak on the money side apparently. Doesn't like them hanging around swinging the lead. They all knew about it last Friday, so anyone working on the project knew this place would be empty from Friday until tomorrow. Including Randle, McAllister and Greenwood."

Joe Rice re-joined them. "Make that, everyone except the piecework joiner, sir. He hadn't been needed for two weeks, so that's why he didn't know. He lives in Lisburn and was taking his wife into Belfast shopping today. He just dropped in on the off-chance, to collect his wages. He found the puddle of blood and called us immediately."

"The privacy would have given Murdock plenty of time here to bleed out, Marc."

Craig nodded, agreeing. "And as long as he'd been moved before tomorrow morning no-one would ever have seen him here." He turned towards the hospital. "Some of those windows are filthy, so I doubt the secretaries would have seen much through them, even if they had looked out. The Portakabin would have obscured their view as well. Whoever the killer is, he really knows this place." He paused, thinking for a moment.

"OK. If this is the primary scene and it holds a special significance for the killer, it makes sense that we're looking for someone whose female relative suffered in the M.P.E. At Murdock's hands. Probably Melissa Pullman. It also makes it likely the killer has been working here and knew that it would be closed. That backs up everything we know. Liam, get a rush on those D.N.A.s please and Davy's deep backgrounds. Joe, get your guys up to those rooms. I want to know who uses them and if they saw anything between Sunday night and today."

"Randle and McAllister insisted on D.N.A. warrants boss. Lewes didn't. We just got them an hour ago." Craig raised his eyes in exasperation, with the legal system, not his team.

"We've got Randle's and Lewes' blood now, but not Greenwood's or McAllister's yet - he was in the meeting all afternoon. Greenwood's still at his conference. Lewes' alibi is fine but McAllister's using the wife again, you'd think he'd have learned by now. Still, I suppose it might actually be true this time."

"I want to interview McAllister and Greenwood myself, Liam. Get them both into High Street for interview ASAP. If Greenwood's not back from Dublin, I want him back. Ask the Irish Police to find him."

"Will do."

Just at that moment Annette appeared with Martin trailing after her. She waved at them urgently and rushed across the gravel, hindered by her heels.

"Sir, we may have something interesting. It's taken me a while to get the details– the Trust was playing hard to get. But Melissa Pullman's death was the subject of a major investigation against the Trust and Mr Murdock. The medico-legal people and G.M.C. were both involved, and Murdock was close to losing his job and paying huge damages. The reason it didn't flag-up before, was because the action was thrown out at inquest. The Trust was in financial straits at the time, and they were applying for major funding. You need your image and books squeaky clean to get that, so the case could have totally wrecked their application."

She took a deep breath and Craig smiled at her. She was going to ace her Inspector exams in June, no question. She hurried on while Martin excitedly echoed each word she said.

"Anyway, the old Chief Exec Robert Moore, Dr Davis and Sister Johns all testified for Murdock *against* Melissa Pullman's family. So the case was thrown out, without the family getting a penny's compensation. Ms Pullman's parents are bringing up the baby now - they live over in Jersey."

"What happened to the baby's father?"

"I'm afraid we've hit a dead end on that one. They weren't

married. His name is Stephen Barron, and all traces of him have disappeared. And there's something else, sir. It may be nothing, but Melissa Pullman was a pharmacist. She had a small retail place in Bangor, and Barron jointly owned it. It's been closed-up since she died but we're chasing to see who's paying the rates."

"Excellent work, Annette." She beamed at Craig and Liam squinted at her competitively.

"Right, I want everyone back in the briefing room in thirty minutes. Sorry, more overtime. John, I'll give you a call later if that's OK? Annette, check out that pharmacy - the killer's getting his drugs from somewhere. The Cocaine was medical quality, and there's Pethidine, Insulin and Ketamine now, plus the scalpel and needles. They had to be ordered, prescribed or stolen from somewhere. And nothing has flagged up anywhere in Northern Ireland.

Liam, see if you can access anything on Stephen Barron. Description and age, scars, anything we can use. He must have a passport or driving licence."

John turned to leave. "Marc, I'll chase everything at our end and summarise it for you. It doesn't surprise me about Davis testifying for Murdock. He and Moore were part of Murdock's social circle in Cultra. They went to school together. 'Jobs for the boys'. That's our incestuous little province for you." He smiled wryly at Craig, the irony of their joint schooldays not missing either of them.

Craig's attention was drawn by something in his peripheral vision, and he walked quickly to the side door of the Portakabin. A small note had been taped to the door - Greenwood would be back tomorrow morning at eight. Too late, they needed to see him tonight. Then something occurred to him. Murdock and Davis were dead, and Laurie Johns, Beth and Katy were protected but...someone was missing.

"Hold on, Liam. I'll come back with you in the car. I need to speak to Robert Moore. Now."

***

Laurie Johns had swiped herself into the Maternity Unit at three-fifty and made a coffee. Then she'd wandered in and out of the empty rooms while she waited. It was four-twenty now and they were late. She'd have to tell them off. She was doing them a favour after all.

She wasn't sure who was coming, but she hoped it would be that handsome Polish builder who did the plasterwork. He was a bit young, but very impressed by her, and she could happily enjoy an hour flirting with *him*. Maybe she could drag it out to a coffee in the canteen. If McAllister didn't come himself then she'd pop up to see him at Knock later. He'd make the time to see her. After all, she was helping him out.

She gazed around her, smiling. It was very quiet without all those noisy babies. Much nicer. She liked order in her Unit.

The main door opened, and she half-turned, smiling and posing with a back straight. She'd been a girl ballerina and a sense of the dramatic never went amiss.

She'd expected to see a man, but was disappointed instead by the sight of Beth Walker. She looked her up and down disdainfully, taking in her over-sized denim jacket and scruffy leggings. Just what she'd have expected. Johns' pose dropped immediately - it was totally wasted on a woman.

"What do you think you're doing here, Nurse Walker? The Unit is closed, and you're on investigation leave. How did you get in?"

"Oh...Sister...the door was open. I'm sorry, I just came to collect some notes for my exams. I'm doing my management diploma on Friday and I really need them for studying."

"I'm certain I closed that door." Johns eyed her suspiciously then continued. "Well, never mind. Just hurry up and get them. And then leave immediately, before I report you."

She drew herself up pompously and Beth had a moment's horrible image of her and Murdock having sex. They'd both have to be on top. She shuddered as the Sister kept talking, self-importantly.

"I'm here for a vital meeting with the project team and the Chief Executive. They'll be here any minute."

"Sorry Sister. I'll be very quick."

Beth ran hurriedly into the staff room and opened her locker, gathering armfuls of notes and dropping some papers in her rush. She left the Unit quickly without looking back, passing a tall man approaching by the parallel glass corridor. He didn't seem to notice her, his face turned away, staring at the ground.

That must be Sister's meeting, poor bugger. She'll spend the whole time flirting with him. Beth gave a small shiver at the thought; not her problem. Then she ran quickly down the stairs to meet Janey outside.

***

He had to get there quickly. They would be searching for someone by now. They'd discovered the thing's body by the river, just as he'd wanted it found. The Visitor smiled to himself, thinking of Nigel Murdock's last moments. He'd cried and screamed for mercy, like the coward that he'd known him to be. He was skilled at being cruel to women, but he couldn't take it himself.

Now it was the bitch's turn. He didn't like to hurt women, but she wasn't really a woman, was she? Real women had warmth, compassion and heart. She was cold and unfeeling. He shook his head. This was no woman, this was a thing. Guilty.

***

Laurie Johns greeted him at the Unit door at four-thirty, instantly forgiving his tardiness with a smile. They shared a

281

long coffee in her office, laughing and chatting, before they started walking the floor. He followed her in and out of the rooms, while she talked incessantly and pointed out the best camera sites.

She was very pleased. She really liked men who asked for her advice. And he was handsome and well-mannered, her two absolute musts in a man. Of course, he was a little dreary, and his accent was quite strange, but he really did seem to hang on her every word...

The Visitor watched her preening arrogantly, bile rising in his throat. This thing was even more disgusting than the last, with its pathetic posturing and self-delusion. At least the other one had known it was revolting.

"I think we should have a camera there and there." She meandered ahead of him, displaying herself to what she thought was her best advantage.

His hand rubbed the blade's sharp edge, enclosing it completely in his pocket and pushing it down to cut through his skin. His own blood fed his pain and anger, but there was no heat with this one. The revulsion was almost too strong. How could a woman be as callous as she was? So loathing of her own sex, so cruel to other women, to Melissa?

Instead of the heat he'd felt with Murdock, The Visitor's pulse slowed, and his skin cooled until he shivered. Each movement was broken into a million frames, like time-lapse photography. Watching himself, watching her.

She pointed to the theatre door.

"What about putting a camera there, just above the theatre entrance?"

His free hand found the barrel of the first syringe. One to slow her down, the second to make it all fit perfectly. He flicked the cap off the small green needle, turning it from his own flesh, and reached behind it for the rope.

"Or maybe a camera inside the theatre? No, well, maybe not. Patients are quite litigious enough nowadays without giving them any encouragement. We don't want to give them ideas for suing people, do we now?" She laughed sarcastically, only amusing herself.

"No, indeed." His accented voice grew suddenly cold. "But then you could always lie about it. Couldn't you Sister?"

"I beg your pardon, what do you mean?"

She railed at the harsh tone of his voice, turning angrily. He grabbed her wrists hard, wrenching them up behind her. Then he tied them expertly with the rope and pushed her to the ground face–first, standing above her gazing down.

She struggled futilely against his strength as he drew the rope down to her ankles and bound them together, linking all four limbs in the midline. She'd been so busy showing off that she hadn't noticed his hands in his pockets the whole time.

Laurie Johns lay on the ground too shocked to speak. Then she signalled her intention to scream by taking a deep gasping breath. The man clasped a bloodied hand over her throat, obstructing her windpipe, so that no air escaped and none entered. Then he expertly withdrew the first syringe and pushed the needle into her neck, forcing the plunger down and emptying it rapidly. She slumped forward, unsupported, her face cracking hard against the sealed polymer floor.

He turned her over and swiftly injected the second syringe. It all had to fit, it had to be perfect. The kill had to have order to it. He tore open her waistband and stared into her widening eyes, enjoying her fear. *Now* he could feel the heat between his thighs. He wanted to roar as he had done with the other one, but that would bring them running.

He'd seen them downstairs looking for something. If they heard him they would come. And if they came then they would try to save the thing, and the work would be incomplete. That could never be allowed.

He'd always known this one must be silent, more secret to him. It saddened him a little, as if it robbed him of some joy. But he would roar next time. Next time he would rent the air and howl at the sky. Guilty.

He drew the blade from his pocket and tore it urgently across her dry freckled skin, skinny and shrivelled like her soul. He pressed down hard, cutting through the scarce fat and sinewy muscle, until she was open to the ward's neon light. He smiled into her dying eyes as he cut, watching as her fear mixed with confusion.

He had a special joy for this one. Another cut to the chest, then he plunged both hands in deep, tearing out the heart that made her live. Showing her what they had done to him, in her last few seconds of life. He watched her brown eyes screaming. Their light fading and flickering like a breaking bulb, until they finally fixed and dulled.

The Visitor rejoiced, careful to be silent, as he watched the useless life seep away. He rocked back and forth to some private melody, for minutes that seemed like hours. Pure joy. Finally he moved and placed the thing on its stomach, reluctant to leave his masterpiece.

Then he thought of the next one and walked off the Unit without a backward look, the door drifting half-closed behind him. There was no need to move this one. They wouldn't visit the closed ward until tomorrow, giving him plenty of time for his next target. He mustn't be discovered yet. There were still tasks to perform.

Laurie Johns took her final breath on the Unit that she'd managed for five years. Her final pulse just strong enough to pump out her remaining blood. All over her nice clean 'NHS Green' floor.

***

Beth turned over her last page of notes, watching as Janey surfed the TV channels, finally settling on the five o'clock news. There was nothing else for it. She'd just have to ask.

Her exam was in three days' time and she needed more

books from the M.P.E., so she put on her best wheedling smile.

"Janeeeey...I know you're going to give me a hard time, but I got so flustered bumping into Johns that I've left some of my stuff on the Unit. I really need it to study, so...would you drive me down again. Pleeeease?

Janey stared over at her, feigning exasperation. Beth spotted the act and continued hopefully. "Honestly, it'll only take ten minutes. And she should be well gone by now."

"All right. But you can buy me a takeaway on the way back. And with your own money this time. The police guys might fancy one as well."

"It's a deal."

"And when this is all over, I'm teaching you how to drive..."

***

Craig reconvened the briefing at five-twenty. The only new outcome was the assignment of a protection detail to Robert Moore's home in Cultra. Craig had spoken to him and explained why. Until they caught the killer he had to be protected. He got no argument from Moore.

"Any word on the D.N.A. match yet? And what about Melissa Pullman's partner?"

"Bad news, boss. Des called through and there's no match with Randle or Lewes. That only leaves McAllister and Greenwood. Melissa Pullman's partner, Stephen Barron, is in the wind. The grandparents say that he took her death very badly and threatened everyone at the inquest. No-one's seen him since, and that was five years ago. He was an engineer, did his degree somewhere in England. But checks show that he hasn't been practicing as one. There's been no activity on his bank account or passport since 2008 and their house was repossessed."

"His passport's come through, sir, but it expired fifteen

years ago. The photo was taken when he was eighteen! So all we know now is that he's forty-three, Caucasian and has blue eyes. But he could be wearing coloured lenses. He had no distinguishing scars or marks back then, and it says that he's six-feet-two. About the same as Randle and Lewes."

"McAllister's about six- three and I think Greenwood's six-feet-one, which is near enough as well, boss. And in those days height was self-reported. People often got it wrong or exaggerated upwards. So Barron might be a shorter than the six-two it says on his passport."

"Or taller, Liam. He was eighteen when it was issued, so he may have grown after that. I did."

Craig was tapping the desk repeatedly with his pen and Liam recognised his tension. He decided to risk a joke to relieve it. "Aye, you're right, boss. So did I. Even though my parents didn't feed me."

Everyone laughed at the ridiculousness of it, and the humour relaxed the room for a minute. Liam restarted in a relaxed drawl, deliberately slowing the meeting's pace before Craig blew a gasket.

"So… Barron's disappeared off the map. We're getting the grandparents to dig out any recent photos and get them over to us stat. And I've got the States of Jersey Police on it."

Without realising why, Craig slowed his speech slightly as well.

"Right…thanks Liam. OK, McAllister's and Greenwood's photos are already over with the grandparents, but keep on them. Annette - send that passport photo over to Des for aging, please. Let's see what Barron would look like now. The deaths all mimic Melissa Pullman's, except she wasn't diabetic."

"Actually, sir - she was. We've got her full notes now. They show that she was a newly diagnosed diabetic in pregnancy, and that it was very badly handled. It seems Murdock left her in the care of a doctor who'd only qualified four weeks before."

'The Killing Fields'. It was what John called the weeks after new doctors started. Craig didn't want to think about the ones caring for his father.

"He botched up her insulin dosage and they had to do an emergency Caesarean. Murdock was bleeped but he took ages to answer. Apparently he'd gone sailing near Cushendall while he was on-call."

"Isn't that against the rules, Cutty?"

"It certainly is. Anyway, eventually Murdock ran into theatre, the worse for wear. But the junior had started the operation and Melissa Pullman died from the bleeding. There were rumours of Murdock being under the influence when he arrived. Either Cocaine or alcohol. It was a mess from beginning to end." Annette's voice tailed off sadly and Martin jumped in, covering her.

"It seemed certain disaster for the Trust, sir. Until the junior suddenly got a job at St Arthurs in London with one of Murdock's friends, and developed amnesia! He's still working over there. Annette checked and he has a definite alibi for the past ten days. There's no record of him flying back here, and no-one's been bothering him."

"*Yet*, son. No-one's bothered him yet."

Craig smiled wryly at Liam's comment and Annette continued reporting. "It sounds like Melissa Pullman's inquest was a complete whitewash, sir. The junior and all the others testified that there was no negligence by Murdock. It seems that the only person who told the truth was Beth Walker. But everyone ignored her. Murdock even tried to use her sexuality to discredit her as a witness. I've confirmed everything with her. Apparently the case was a big part of why he hated her."

Liam whistled loudly. "What a shower of shits! If we tried to get away with that we'd be up in court!"

Nobody disagreed.

"Is there anything in her notes about a facial laceration, Annette?"

Everyone held their breath while Annette flicked through

Melissa Pullman's medical notes, scanning each page with what seemed like deathly slowness. Eventually she turned to Craig, her face a mixture of triumph and anger. She said nothing, just pointed to a line on the operation sheet. 'Scalpel slipped and cut patient's right cheek'.

There was only one explanation for the scalpel being anywhere near a patient's face during a Caesarean. Murdock must have been waving it around, drunk. He was left handed, so her right cheek got cut.

Craig felt like someone had kicked him in the stomach. The extent of Murdock's negligence was breath-taking. It was no wonder it had caused such extreme retribution. If anyone hurt his father like that he would hunt them down too.

"The baby's Dad had a complete breakdown. He ended up in St Marys' psychiatric unit. The grandparents took the baby, Lucy. Barron's never even seen her, and they have no idea where he is now. I've had uniform checking-out the pharmacy in Bangor. It's closed and boarded-up. But Martin called the main medical suppliers and they're still receiving orders from it. The last one was a week ago."

She nodded Martin to continue and he jumped in again eagerly. "They've been delivering parcels by appointment, sir. A man always signs for them. He fits Barron's description exactly. Tall, white and middle-aged."

Craig and Liam smiled at each other wryly. He'd just described both of them. "The delivery people said he had an English accent of some description, sir. Mr McAllister has an English accent."

"Aye. And Ted Greenwood lived in England for a while too, boss. You can hear a definite twang." Craig smiled and wondered what they made of his Belfast/Italian/London tones.

"OK. Annette, get down to the suppliers and get a copy of that signature. It might match the passport, or someone from our suspect list. And get the delivery staff to look at some photos. Now, please." Annette left the room swiftly, with

Martin trailing behind. "Liam, what about McAllister?"

"We lifted him ten minutes ago at the M.P.E. He was on the cross-corridor near Maternity when uniform found him. He's in High Street now and moaning like hell about it."

"OK, we'll get to him later. Let him cool his heels. What's happening with Greenwood?"

"Irish police say there's no sign of him yet."

"Ask them to keep trying. I'm going back to the M.P.E. to take another look around." Craig moved to leave the room, and then turned back quickly.

"Did you say Barron was an Engineer?"

"Yes, sir."

"So was Charles McAllister, and Ted Greenwood's an Architect so he might have some engineering knowledge. Did anyone check if Greenwoods' degree was really Architecture? If not, do it now please. Either way they would both know enough to knock out the CCTV and they both had unlimited access."

Just then Nicky rushed into the room. Craig could tell from her face that it wasn't good news. "Sir. Sister John's protection detail has called through. She gave them the slip and left the house sometime this afternoon. She wouldn't allow them inside the house, so they didn't even know she'd gone. The officer says she must have driven down the back roads. I've tried her mobile but it's ringing out. And I called her mother's house, but she hasn't seen her all day."

Damn.

"Tell them not to beat themselves up Nicky. She'd probably have slipped them anyway. She's the type. There's only one place she'll have gone to. The M.P.E. Liam, there are some uniforms still over there, get them to start looking for her and I'll meet them there. Nicky, check that the protection officers have secured everyone else. The junior is safe in London for the moment, but ask The Met to keep an eye on him just in case. Everyone else, please keep going this evening for as long

289

as you can. We're close to catching this bastard."

He left the room running and John phoned just as he reached the car.

"Marc, something's not right here. The primary scene should have significance to the killer - not just to Murdock." Craig drove quickly through town as they talked. Belfast's rush-hour traffic slowed his progress, so he finally gave up playing the civilian and blue-lighted his way towards Elmwood Avenue.

"Melissa Pullman died in the M.P.E. Murdock was responsible and we think the killer works in the Trust. Isn't that the link?"

"Yes, but it's not just the M.P.E., it's *where* in the M.P.E. On the building site."

"Thanks John, but that makes sense for all our remaining suspects. I'm heading there now. Laurie Johns has slipped her protection detail."

"Stupid woman." He didn't get an argument from Craig.

"Uniform are looking for Greenwood and we have McAllister in custody."

"OK. But watch yourself. This man's a complete psycho."

Chapter Twenty-Seven

5.40pm.

Charles McAllister was stuck in High Street, not best pleased to be 'helping with their enquiries'. Tough. Jack Harris watched him through the cell-door, taking in his tense posture and drumming fingers. He was a man in a hurry to be somewhere else.

It was cool in the cells, but McAllister was sweating hard. And there was blood on the table where his tapping must have split the skin. A guilty man if Jack had ever seen one. But guilty of what?

***

There was still no sign of Laurie Johns, and when Craig finally arrived at Maternity the door was lying open. He edged in cautiously with his hand on his service weapon and walked slowly in and out of the empty rooms. Suddenly he heard something move, and the sound of a radio crackling. He followed the noise down the internal corridor, to be greeted by the sight of a stunned P.C., staring down at Beth Walker.

She was kneeling over a body lying face-down on the floor, cradling it awkwardly in her arms. Her mouth was open to scream, but no sound emerged. Hot tears flowed unchecked down her face. Craig moved in closer and recognised a ring on the body's limp hand as one worn by Laurie Johns. His heart sank. He was too late.

Beth cradled the Sister's head on her lap, her leggings dark red with blood. Johns was trussed the same way Nigel Murdock had been, and her blood was everywhere. Sticky and red and smelling of copper. Craig leaned over Beth gently, feeling for the futility of Laurie Johns' pulse. Then he too was struck silent. Her injuries were even worse than Nigel Murdock's! Their killer was spiraling.

He unlocked Beth from her hopeless protection of the dead, and helped her to the ward office, leaving the P.C. to call the crime team. John's blood covered Beth completely. Her clothes were soaked with the liquid and streaks of it flashed bright red across her cheeks, where she'd futilely tried to give Johns the kiss of life. Craig soaked a cloth and dabbed gently at her face and hands, ignoring forensic protocol.

He coaxed her to speak, and succeeded just enough to confirm that the Sister had been alive at four-twenty. And that just as Beth had been leaving the ward she'd seen a tall man walking towards it. But she hadn't seen his face. Four-twenty, almost an hour before they'd brought Charles McAllister to High Street. Craig left Beth in the constable's care, and sped to High Street to interview McAllister.

***

The squad phone rang loudly, completely ignored by Davy and Liam. Davy was sitting at his horseshoe of computer screens, working remotely with Des on the aging programme. He had Stephen Barron's eighteen-year-old photo to his right, and the aging version on the screen in front of him. It was shaping up, but it was slow going. The photo had reached twenty-five-years-old now, but it still didn't look like anyone they knew.

Liam yawned loudly and listened to the 'hold' music provided by The Met, ignoring the ringing phone. The tune wasn't much better than the 'Greensleeves' they used.

Someone should buy both forces a copy of 'Hits 2012'. Finally the music stopped and a woman's voice came on the line. She had a London accent and greeted Liam brightly.

"Hello, can I help you?"

"Aye, hello. Can I speak to someone covering the St Arthurs Hospital area?"

"That'll be Battersea Division. Hold on."

He sat back again, swinging his legs onto the desk, and resigned himself to a long wait. The phone on Nicky's desk started ringing again and he turned to see where she was. Her chair was empty. Then he remembered she'd gone home to take Jonny to her Mum's and he covered his receiver with a hand, hissing at Davy to answer the other line.

Davy missed the hint and clicked repeatedly on the image in front of him, adding another few years.

When Liam's voice came again it was like thunder.

"Answer that sodding phone, Davy. It's doing my head in."

Davy startled and jumped off his chair, grabbing the receiver. "Hello. Nicky's desk."

He stood silently for a moment, his mouth opening wider as he listened. Then he dropped the phone abruptly and loped over to Liam's desk, cutting off his call.

Liam's mouth flew open to yell but Davy stopped him mid-flow.

"That was Jersey. They've been calling us for ten minutes. Melissa Pullman's parents have recognised one of our photos."

***

Liam reached Craig just as he entered High Street and Craig knew from 'hello' that it was urgent. "We've got an I.D. from the grandparents, boss. They weren't sure at first 'cos he's changed so much, but it's Ted Greenwood - he's Stephen Barron! And you were right; his degree was engineering not architecture. It all fits. McAllister's not our killer. He's still on the loose."

Craig spoke quickly. "Step up the search for him, Liam. Laurie Johns is dead. Beth found her in Maternity. She's up there now with uniform."

"Shit."

Shit indeed. And there was no doubt who Ted Greenwood's next target was.

"Get Greenwood's photo to Moore's protection detail. He's heading out to Cultra."

Craig radioed Robert Moore's detail. Greenwood couldn't outrun a radio. Unless he was already there...

Liam contacted C District and put an all point's bulletin on Greenwood's car, while Craig raced up the A2 like Sebastian Vettel. He called Tactical Support and Armed Response to meet them at Moore's house. It was always going to come to this.

***

Ted Greenwood followed his sat-nav hungrily, searching for the oversized display of wealth that was Robert Moore's home. When he saw it he was unsurprised by its vulgarity. How many lives to pay for this I wonder? Blood money. Everything here echoes the life you've led and the friends you have. The sense of entitlement your inner circle reinforces in you every day.

His bile rose, heightened by the sight of a trailer in the driveway, the expensive boat perched on it barely touched by the sea. The house's electronic gates were closed and Greenwood pulled swiftly off the road into a copse, considering his next steps.

It was simple. The gates would be no barrier, he'd come well prepared. He pointed the universal remote at them and pressed it softly. Adjusting its frequency until the invisible trigger yawned the gates open onto the road.

He held them there suspended, waiting for what would come next. All the time edging his car forward slowly. Waiting...waiting...until his patience was finally rewarded.

A slim man walked warily towards the gate. A single policeman, with his radio to his mouth and his gun pointed down. He glanced this way and that. Then at the gates' opening device - the keypad against the wall. Then he made a single mistake, just one, but the one that Greenwood had been waiting for. He turned his back.

Greenwood drove fast and hard towards the man. Before he could turn, his feet were knocked away by the high-fronted bar of the SUV, forcing him cruelly under its wheels. His radio fell to one side, his gun to the other. Greenwood reversed quickly and climbed out, collecting them both and kicking the fallen man with his foot. Not dead.

Good, he was innocent. That would have been unfortunate. His death wouldn't have been right. But he would be dead, if it was necessary. The work must be completed at all costs.

He dragged him into the garden, placing him under the hedge and injecting him quickly for security. Then he drove in smoothly, closing the gates behind him and changing the opening code for delay. Just then the radio crackled into life.

"Officer Whitely to base. Officer Whitely, come in."

"Whitely here." He mimicked the Ulster accent of his youth.

"The killer is Ted Greenwood. Consider him highly dangerous." They named and described him, saying that a picture would follow.

They knew him! But how could they know him? Then realisation dawned. They'd found the woman. They knew him, and now they were coming. Two miles away. There was no time. But the work had to be completed ...for Melissa.

He looked down at his dark clothes and had an idea. He parked by the large brick house and ran to its front door, activating the radio and strengthening his accent. "Mr Moore, its Officer Whitely. Please come to the front door, sir."

It crackled once and then silence. *Damn.* Was it broken? He bit hard on his lip, tasting his own blood. Then he tried again urgently, rewarded by broken static in response. A few seconds later Robert Moore spoke. "I'm coming."

Yes.

Robert Moore entered his hall, approaching the stained-glass front door. All he saw was the expected outline of a man in black, holding a gun. He opened the door just a crack, but wide enough and long enough, before his mistake registered on him. And gave plenty of time for access.

Greenwood pushed Moore to the ground, ripping the radio from his hand and crushing it furiously with his heel. A television was on somewhere and its normality enraged him even more. He kicked the man at his feet hard enough to draw blood, his own lips bleeding freely in response. Then he pressed the cold gun-barrel against Moore's neck, until his veins blued and throbbed, and forced Moore to crawl down the narrow hall, into a large bright room at the end.

This would suit well. It would be his stage, for when they came. They would come soon, but they would come too late. They were two miles away, the gates were locked, and he had time. And if he couldn't leave, then at least neither could this thing, and this theatre would suit the final act very well.

Chapter Twenty-Eight

"I'll be there in five minutes, Liam. The others are already in position. They've covered the perimeter and the road's being cordoned-off now. Where are you?"

"On the Bangor Road, boss. Just behind you." Craig glanced in the mirror and saw Liam's grey Ford. Blue light flashing and keeping pace with his 100mph.

Robert Moore's house was off the Clanbrassil Road in Cultra. It nestled in acres of ground and fronted the road with high electronic gates. The look-out reported that a black SUV matching Greenwood's was already in the grounds. He'd used his electrical skills to gain entry and re-lock the gates. But after a ten minute struggle the police technician got them open, breaking the complex code.

They'd arrived without sirens and Craig radioed everyone to park out of sight. They would approach on foot. Cars and armoured vehicles were abandoned three hundred metres from the gate and the men spread out, covering every access point. Some lay in the fields behind the house, the rest concealed at all points of the compass. An ambulance stood ready around the corner.

The spring evening was quiet and still, the road's other occupants too far away or other-worldly to interfere. The cul-de-sac meant that no-one would turn in looking for a shortcut to the A2. It helped the situation as well as anything could. The story would've been very different on the Demesne. Craig welcomed the silence. The last thing they needed was Greenwood being warned.

From his vantage point Craig could hear the sea's waves hitting the shore. The early evening sky was shot with greys and oranges, like a Monet sunset. Its beauty was almost surreal set against the incongruity of their task.

Greenwood's SUV was parked in the drive, its driver's door lying open. The garden gate behind it lay ajar. Everything said that Greenwood was already inside the house. He could have killed Moore already. Or be holding him hostage, and somehow Craig didn't think hostages were part of the plan. They couldn't delay any longer. Liam's radio crackled quietly, breaking the eerie silence.

"Officer down, front garden. Under the right hand hedge."

The protection officer. Greenwood must have caught him unawares. Craig craned his neck and could just see a body on the ground. "Is he breathing?"

"Yes. He's out, but he doesn't look too bad, sir. His weapon's gone."

The words validated his call for armed back-up.

"Get him to safety. Liam, line up Armed Response but keep them out of sight. And send their Commander up to me."

Time to move.

***

Ted Greenwood pushed the barrel deep into Robert Moore's neck, tempted for one brief moment to end it all quickly and leave. But a bullet wasn't enough. Moore had to feel everything. He had to suffer and beg and bleed. Then die.

He threw the gun away, hard against the wall, removing the temptation. It was too weak, too easy. There would be no pleasure with a gun. No blood to touch and hold, and no release.

He slipped his hand into one pocket, removing the needles and rope. From the other he withdrew the blade and paper. It all had to be there. It had to fit.

He subdued Moore with the first needle, and he slumped on the carpet, the rope soon trussing him like the others. The note sat to the right, the blade alongside, while Robert Moore lay face-down on the floor, immobile.

Greenwood gazed down at him, feeling distant, as if he was outside his own body. No longer just watching them die, but watching himself, watching them.

This was almost the last of Melissa's killers, the ones who had ended his life with hers. There was only one left in England, and he would be next. And when they were dead he would do this for other victims, other voiceless pawns. He would avenge them too. For Melissa.

**

Two black-suited officers entered the garden under cover of the SUV, and circled the back of the house. Craig nodded the Commander to radio them.

"Is there any movement inside?"

"This is Johnson at Back Right. There's someone in the downstairs back room. I'm moving in for a closer look."

"If you spot him, hold back. Don't go in. Repeat, do not go in. Just update your status."

The dark officer moved swiftly, hidden from the house's interior by a fortunately placed garden wall. He ran quickly and silently across the stone patio, reaching the brick column of the bay window unseen. Once there he stretched slightly and Ted Greenwood came into view.

He was standing in the centre of the room with every light glaring, throwing a spotlight on the scene. His eyes burned as he stared wildly towards something at his feet. Johnson stretched another inch and Robert Moore came into sight. He was lying on his stomach, wrists and ankles bound behind him, his four limbs roped together.

With one swift movement Greenwood dropped to a kneeling position, falling hard onto Moore's back. A sequence of loud cracks made the bile rise in the Johnson's throat. It was the sound of a spine being snapped. Greenwood lifted the second syringe, holding it just above Moore. Then his arm froze and he drove his knee in deeper. No, no Pethidine yet. This thing should feel the pain for longer.

Johnson saw something shine on the carpet and a single sheet of paper lying beside it. He signalled and another man moved in to replace him, then backed off to radio Craig. His replacement scanned the scene and hid behind the column, lining-up his rifle, ready to take the shot.

"He's got Moore trussed like a turkey, sir, and I think he's broken his spine. He's kneeling on his back with what looks like a syringe in his hand."

"Did you see the gun or a knife?"

"The gun's there but it's ten feet away, he wouldn't reach it before we got him. There was something shining on the floor but I couldn't see what it was. It might have been a knife. There was a sheet of paper in the way."

The note and the knife. The gun wouldn't have fulfilled his ritual.

The Commander looked at Craig and they nodded in silent agreement. There was no time to negotiate - that was a blade shining on the floor. They had to give the order.

"Give the warning and if he doesn't surrender, shoot to stop."

They would aim for the torso to stop him but they all knew it might end in death. Craig had no other choice. Greenwood's next step would be to slice Moore open. He had to complete his ritual. It was a compulsion.

Ted Greenwood gazed at the thing at his feet and pushed the syringe hard against its neck. He could feel the heat building between his thighs, and the urge to kill growing stronger. He needed to touch its blood, and maybe this time...dare he taste it? Would that be too much reward?

He would. This time he would drink the thing's blood.

His tongue swelled in anticipation and his saliva flowed freely, wetting his lips. His pulse raced and his eyes focussed more sharply, every sense heightened by desire. His heartbeat drowned out every sound. He urged the needle deep into Moore's neck, releasing the Pethidine deep into his blood. Moore's body relaxed instantly, inviting the next step.

The officer at the window put a finger to his neck, signalling Greenwood's action. With a heavy heart Craig nodded to give the warning.

The black-suited officer shouted loudly through the window. "Armed police, Mr Greenwood. Step away from Mr Moore, now. We don't want to shoot you, but we will. Step away."

Ted Greenwood heard a voice, and he paused, listening. It wasn't his voice, it wasn't the thing's filthy lies, and it wasn't Melissa's sweet tones. He turned slowly to find the source. A black suited gun-man came into view and then into focus... asking him to stop.

But he couldn't stop, he wouldn't. It would be wrong to stop. Surely they must know that? A sudden joy filled him and he smiled broadly at the gun aiming at his chest. Now he understood. It must be this way. The work needed an audience, deserved an audience. They would all see the truth at last.

The officer stared at Ted Greenwood and then shook his head, gesturing that he was ignoring the warning. Craig nodded. Greenwood was beyond reason now. Insane. He'd known it as soon as he'd seen Murdock's body. Only someone unhinged could have done that.

Greenwood's eyes focussed far in the distance, where they were all irrelevant. He saw her smiling at him, with their baby in her arms, and he smiled softly in reply. He listened carefully, as if he heard her gentle voice, mouthing a silent answer. Yes, Melissa....I'm coming.

Then he reached across urgently, flipping Robert Moore over as easily as a child, and lunged towards the floor. His right hand shone and ripped down violently, as deep as it could go. Payment for what they had done. Leaning across Moore's face he cut again, the silence torn by Moore's gut-wrenching screams.

The bullet exploded the window inwards, large shards of glass hitting the carpeted floor. Needle-fine splinters caught Greenwood's face, peppering his cheek with red dots. The round sped on for its destination, scything through his arm and making the blade fall from his grasp, into Moore's gaping abdominal wound. It skewered through Greenwood's torso, his flesh, muscle and bone no barrier as it travelled deep into his chest. Finally finding his heart and ending his work forever.

Ted Greenwood's body fell on top of Robert Moore, their blood seeping and mingling, the room completely silent except for the echoing aftershock. The silence was broken abruptly, by shouts of "get the ambulance." And officers rushed in, pushing the body off Moore and checking for his pulse. It was weak but it was there.

Ted Greenwood lay on his side staring up at them, with wide open eyes and a faint smile fixed on his pale dead face. Finally at peace, believing that he'd succeeded. Craig stared at Robert Moore, trying to hide his shock and failing. Greenwood had cut off his lips. *Liar.*

Moore's pulse slowed and cooled as the ambulance arrived, to siren him to surgery in the Trust he'd once run so badly. The Trust where they'd killed Melissa Pullman and God knows how many others. Now they'd killed her partner, Stephen Barron. Or had he really died five years before? Replaced by the need for revenge.

The atmosphere in the room became subdued, as if all of the adrenaline they'd been running on had seeped out with the single bullet. Leaving them empty. John arrived just as the C.S.I.s were finishing-up, and he stared open-mouthed at the mess around him. Craig and Liam were sitting on a low windowsill and they nodded him over.

"God, Marc, what happened here?"

"I'll give you the details later, but basically Moore's alive and Ted Greenwood's dead. He was our killer. His real name was Stephen Barron." He outlined the day's events and John added what more he knew.

"He left the same note in Laurie Johns' hand as in Murdock's. The C.S.I.s have just found another one on Moore's floor. We'll find the same drugs in all of them, I'm sure."

"What was this all about, boss? Was it all revenge for Melissa Pullman?"

Craig nodded slowly. "For her death and maybe for the life they would have had together. Or, maybe for the lack of justice his daughter received from the Trust?"

"But why kill all those innocent women? Why not just go straight for Murdock and leave it at that? He had to be mad."

"Even mad people have their reasons, Liam. Maybe he felt the whole Trust had betrayed her. Remember, they allowed Murdock to get away with negligence. He couldn't have kept working without their permission. Perhaps he hoped that by killing other women the same way Melissa died, it would have drawn attention to her case. Then Murdock would've been struck off and the Trust would've gone under. But each time he killed someone it was just covered up again.

The only relative that really kicked-up was Tommy. Everyone else was too polite. He killed Evie knowing that Tommy was her father. I think he believed Tommy would make a hell of a noise and bring things out in the open. Maybe even kill Murdock and save him the job. But when we got involved he must have known he was running out of time. So he started killing whoever he held responsible for Melissa's death."

"Or maybe he intended to kill them all from the start, Marc? I think we'll find that Alan Davis was a victim as well. But I agree he wanted to bring the whole Trust down. I don't doubt his D.N.A. will match the patch on Evie's forehead. That's how confused this all is. He killed the women to show up negligence, but he was sorry he had to kill them. They were just collateral damage."

Craig nodded sadly. What a bloody waste.

John pulled up a chair and sat down. He took off his glasses and rubbed his eyes tiredly.

"He amputated Murdock's left hand because it was the hand that killed Melissa. And the coke left at his scene was because he'd been using it on the day Melissa died. He cut off Moore's lips because he lied at the inquest." He paused for a moment, looking thoughtful. "And he cut out Laurie John's heart."

Liam gasped, shocked by the information. "Why?"

Annette arrived, joining them. "Because she was heartless, Liam. She worked with vulnerable people all day and she didn't care about any of them. Maybe he thought that a woman should have cared more?"

"And maybe because his heart was broken, he broke hers."

They fell silent for a moment. Then John spoke again, angrily.

"I'm certain Alan Davis pressured the families to cremate the women, to stop further enquiries. If he did, and he destroyed their notes, then he thought they'd been murdered by Murdock and yet he still covered up for him. Evil bastard."

"I wonder if the territorials taught Greenwood Carotid occlusion. Maybe that's why he joined."

Liam shook his head. "They don't teach that stuff, boss. But he was really interested in assassination techniques. The lads searching his house say there are tons of 'Kill' websites on his computer."

"I agree with Liam, Marc. I think he just joined-up to keep fit. But I bet the original project manager's accident was caused by Greenwood, to free up the job for him. That's how long he'd been planning this whole thing. This was a mission."

"The press will live off this for weeks."

Craig allowed himself a small smile. "Harrison's part of the Assistant Chief's recruitment board. The coverage on this will ruin his week."

"Boss, do you really think Greenwood chose Evie because of Tommy's past?"

"I'm certain he did, Liam, but we can't even hint at that to Tommy. Much as I think he's a thug, it would kill him if he thought her death was his fault."

"Greenwood was an almost perfect fit for your profile, Doc."

"As are half the men here, Liam. I don't think you should beat yourselves up on that. You can't go around arresting people without sufficient reason."

"More's the pity."

"Agreed. But more realistically, if we'd had his D.N.A. on file to compare the kiss against, we could have saved at least two lives. Think about it, a world D.N.A. database." A D.N.A. bank was John's latest hobby-horse.

"How many homicidal maniacs would that catch, Marc? There was an episode of C.S.I. New York where they..."

Craig interrupted his fantasy, smiling. "And the civil liberties lobby would arrest us for even thinking about it. Mind you, maybe we'd catch a few barristers and hacks up to no good."

They all laughed.

"Look. Warwick has summed up. The verdict won't be back till next week, but I'm going to hold some drinks on Friday anyway. Everyone's been working really hard. Will you and Des come along, John?"

"I'll see you there and I'll see if Des and Annie can get a

babysitter. We all need a lift after this."

"Liam, could you and Annette go back to town, stand McAllister down and check that Beth's OK? I'm going to tell Tommy that Evie's killer is dead. He deserves to hear it personally. Then I'm heading for Templepatrick."

Chapter Twenty-Nine

By Friday lunchtime the reports had been written, only waiting for forensics to tie a bow on them. The press had been given the facts and they would write their lurid columns all weekend. Stephen Barron would finally have his story told.

The Maternity Unit would re-open the following week, and Craig had just heard that Beth might be in line for the Sister's role. She certainly deserved it.

Melissa Pullman and three other mothers were dead, so were Nigel Murdock, Laurie Johns and Alan Davis. Robert Moore was alive, just. And he would soon wish that he wasn't. He and the junior doctor were the only survivors of the group that had lied at Melissa Pullman's inquest. They would both be carrying whatever penalty there was for that.

Pressure was growing to re-open the earlier deaths. Charles McAllister had promised a full investigation, and that the Trust would look at compensation for the families concerned. It wouldn't bring back the lost mothers, but it might help their daughters' lives.

Tommy Hill had walked free, but to what? A life without the daughter he'd loved and had just got to know. Craig really hoped that the Kerrs would help him, and that he'd manage to stay out of prison. At least for long enough to know his granddaughter, better than he'd ever known Evie. As for his crew; they would get a spell in Maghaberry to cool off, and probably to make new contacts for their rackets. The Drug Squad would sort them all out eventually. Not his problem, mate.

It was seven o'clock and Craig was mellow. He'd spent the afternoon bringing his father home from St Marys and settling him back in his armchair, ready to be fussed over and coddled for weeks by his mum. She was agreeing with everything he said at the moment and allowing Discovery Science to be on 24/7. That would last until he annoyed her again, and then their usual lively banter would re-start and life would get back to normal.

Craig had been propping up the bar at The James for the best part of two hours, and now it was returning the favour. Liam and Annette had their better halves there. Davy, Martin, uniform and John's team had arrived, and Karl was in a corner, chatting up one of Lucia's mates. Even some of the press, normally his mortal enemies, had sneaked in with Maggie. But he was feeling sufficiently benevolent even to talk to them today. Amanda Graham had joined them too, and just as long as no defence barristers appeared then he'd be very happy.

The Warwick jury had been deliberating for two days. There was no verdict yet, but at least they could relax a bit tonight. Even Teflon had popped in for a quick one, beaming bonhomie and smoothing back his Brylcreem. He hadn't stayed long. Off to press someone's flesh. But he'd stayed long enough to tell Craig that the Chief Constable had noticed how many serial killers Craig's team had investigated. And to suggest the C.C.U. murder squad as the force's lead team on serial or unusual murders in the future. Craig couldn't deny the logic behind it, but it was something for him to think about tomorrow.

Lucia had landed in thirty minutes earlier with five of her friends. They'd been at the funfair and met some sailors from the Abercorn Basin Marina, so they had them in tow. Word had got to High Street that the girls were there, and a crowd of off-duty Tactical Support lads had turned up with Jack and

Sandi. Craig wondered vaguely who was manning the place, but decided that it wasn't his business. He just stuck more money behind the bar and watched a black-kitted officer defeat a sailor in his bid to chat up his sister. A police win. He shot him a drunken smile, knowing that he wouldn't get anywhere. Lucia's boyfriend Richard returned from tour tomorrow.

By eight o'clock the party was in full flow, and the paved expanse of Barrow Square was filling with street entertainers. Craig went out to watch the fire-eater, leaning against the wall of the Rotterdam and gazing down Pilot Street's smooth tarmac. He was in a daydream when he saw Nicky teeter towards him in black stiletto boots and a mini-skirt, waving an A4 envelope.

"I went home to change and popped back to the office before I came over. This was on my desk - they sent it across from the court. It's stamped five pm and marked urgent, so I thought that you'd better see it, sir."

Craig smiled at her, too drunk to get really excited. "You should have a drink, Nicky." His distant look gave away his alcohol level, and she laughed her loud navvy's laugh.

"I'll get one later, thanks. It looks like you've had enough for both of us! Gary's coming after work, so I'll be drinking all evening, trust me." She held the envelope out towards him.

"You open it for me, Nick."

He wasn't that drunk. It was just that if it was bad news he'd know soon enough, and if it was good, it would be nice for her to tell him. She smiled and gave in, ripping the envelope open expertly, with a long red fingernail.

"How do you type with those nails?" He dragged the 's' out, slurring it slightly.

"Very quickly, that's how." She read the envelope's contents and grinned.

"It's guilty, sir. They've found Ewing guilty of murder. Sentencing is in two weeks and they want your report."

Craig stood so still that at first she thought he hadn't heard her. Then he grinned broadly and punched the air. "Brilliant. Bloody brilliant." *Now* he wished that Roger Doyle would turn up!

"Come with me." He dragged her inside the bar. "Everyone, Nicky's got some good news"

"You're not pregnant again are you, Nicky?"

John's secretary Marcie raised her orange juice in sympathy, and Nicky shook her head furiously.

"God no, he's just winding you up. It's you guys who have the good news. Ewing was found guilty of murder. We've just got the verdict through."

The bar erupted in whoops and air punches, giving the party fresh energy. Craig got Nicky a drink and put even more money behind the bar. This was excellent news.

The bright spring evening made the party stretch on, until the funfair's fireworks started at nine. Everyone moved to the water's edge, to watch the noisy rainbow. John stood beside Craig quietly, leaning on a cast-iron bollard.

"It makes me feel young when you wear your jeans, Marc. I don't feel half as stupid in my silver shoes." He stared at his feet. "They seemed so normal in the lab."

"Anything seems normal in your lab." They sipped their beers in a communicative silence built over thirty years.

"I'm going to look at the Marina tomorrow, John. Lucia said it's great. You should come with me. I'm taking up sailing again. I could teach you."

Before John had a chance to reply he felt a sudden tap on his shoulder. He turned to see a petite, dark-haired woman smiling up at him. "Hello, John."

For a moment confusion flicked across his face, like when you see someone familiar in an unexpected place. Then he smiled down at her tenderly. "Hello, Natalie. How have you been?"

She gazed up at him, unblinking. "I've missed you, John.

I...I can't stand this being apart."

Bright tears filled her eyes and he reached down to hug her, whispering softly. "Neither can I. We need to talk."

Craig moved away discretely, leaving them alone. As he walked back towards the bar he pulled out his mobile to make a call. He was just pressing 'dial' when he recognised a familiar perfume. Its warmth enveloped him, the soft scent of jasmine reminding him of nights spent in the Mediterranean. And Julia.

He wheeled round, to see her standing there, her long ruby curls shining in the fading light.

"But...how? I thought you were working this weekend?"

She reached forward and kissed him deeply, ignoring the curious looks of the crowd outside the bar. He smiled at her, unembarrassed, the question still in his eyes. She pointed towards The James and he turned, to see Lucia raise a glass towards them.

"Lucia called me and told me about your week, so I swopped my shift. I...I hope you don't mind?"

Her uncertainty touched him and he stroked her cheek gently. "Mind? I couldn't be happier. It means we can start looking for somewhere to live first thing tomorrow."

"Not with the hangover that we'll both have."

As they walked towards the bar laughing, no one but Natalie saw Katy Stevens turn on her heel and walk away.

THE END

Fantastic Books
Great Authors

Meet our authors and discover our exciting range:

- Gripping Thrillers
- Cosy Mysteries
- Romantic Chick-Lit
- Fascinating Historicals
- Exciting Fantasy
- Young Adult and Children's Adventures

Visit us at:
www.crookedcatbooks.com

Join us on facebook:
www.facebook.com/crookedcatpublishing

Made in the USA
Middletown, DE
10 January 2015